Where the Pieces Lie

JD Kirk is the author of the multi-million bestselling DCI Logan series, set in the Highlands of Scotland. He also does not exist. Instead, JD is the pen name of former children's author and screenwriter, Barry Hutchison, who was born and raised in Fort William. He still lives in the Highlands with his wife and children. He has no idea what the JD stands for.

Also by JD Kirk

DCI Logan Crime Thrillers

A Litter of Bones
Thicker than Water
The Killing Code
Blood and Treachery
The Last Bloody Straw
A Whisper of Sorrows
The Big Man Upstairs
A Death Most Monumental
A Snowball's Chance in Hell
Ahead of the Game
An Isolated Incident
Colder than the Grave
Come Hell or High Water
City of Scars
Here Lie the Dead
One For the Ages
In Service of Death
A Dead Man Walking
Where the Pieces Lie
A Killer of Influence
A Rock and a Hard Place

JD KIRK

WHERE THE PIECES LIE

CANELO CRIME

First published in the United Kingdom in 2024 by Zertex Crime

This edition published in the United Kingdom in 2025 by

Canelo, an imprint of
Canelo Digital Publishing Limited,
20 Vauxhall Bridge Road,
London SW1V 2SA
United Kingdom

A Penguin Random House Company
The authorised representative in the EEA is Dorling Kindersley Verlag GmbH. Arnulfstr. 124, 80636 Munich, Germany

A CIP catalogue record for this book is available from the British Library.

Paperback ISBN 978 1 80436 835 0

Printed and bound in Great Britain by Clays Ltd, Elcograf S.p.A.

Look for more great books at
www.canelo.co | www.dk.com

For John Morrison

Chapter One

It was, Seamus reckoned, one of the finest knobs he'd ever seen, and he'd seen more than his fair share. Certainly, this one won out in terms of sheer scale. It was shaped perfectly, yes, but it was the size—easily ten feet long from tip to balls—that really marked it as something out of the ordinary.

Even Sandra agreed, and Sandra wasn't usually agreeable to anything. Quite the opposite, in fact. She enjoyed nothing more than butting heads with people, both metaphorically and literally. But, mostly literally. That was how she'd ended up as the other half of Seamus's two-person Community Payback clean-up crew.

She was so short and stocky that she looked like one of the squarer of the Mr Men. Mr Strong, Seamus reckoned, though he didn't dare say that out loud for fear of his nose being plastered across his face by a well-aimed forehead.

Her hair was short, masculine, and upright, like Brigitte Nielsen's in *Rocky IV*. Or Dolph Lundgren's in *Rocky IV.*

Someone from *Rocky IV*, anyway.

Sandra had been in the year below him in school but had been kicked out halfway through fourth year after a tête-à-tête with the headmaster that had left him with two black eyes, eight stitches and a four-month sick line for PTSD.

Despite her reputation as a violent nutter—well-earned and entirely accurate as that description was—Seamus liked her. She didn't say much, but the few things she did say were often worth waiting for.

'I like the balls,' she remarked, nodding the head that had launched a dozen rhinoplasties. 'The jaggy wee pubes on them are weirdly cute looking.'

Seamus couldn't argue with that. The gonads were works of art in and of themselves, as were the detailed veins on the shaft, and the three flying blobs of spunk, each one smaller than the one before, but otherwise perfectly identical.

Whoever had painted this wasn't just your average, run-of-the-mill vandal, they were a bona fide artist.

Seamus gestured around at the road, which was flanked on two sides by pine trees that towered thirty feet tall and creaked as they swayed on the breeze.

'A work of this importance doesn't belong scrawled on a scabby wee junction off the A9,' Seamus declared. 'It should be in a museum or art gallery somewhere.'

'That big one in France,' Sandra agreed. 'They love all that, the French. Cocks and that. Don't they?'

A voice from behind them made Seamus jump and caused Sandra's head to give an instinctive and involuntary forward jerk.

'Oh, aye. I can just see the Louvre shifting the *Mona Lisa* through the back so they can hang a big cock and balls on the wall.'

Jonathan Milburn stood over them, his hands buried in the pockets of his bright red waterproof jacket, the hood so tightly fastened that Seamus and Sandra had to peer at his face along a narrow tunnel of Gore-Tex.

The Community Payback supervisor was tall and angular, even under the bulk of the jacket. Physically, there was an insect-like sharpness about him—all elongated limbs with pointy knees and elbows.

There was a sharpness to his personality, too. He rarely got angry, but instead maintained a general air of waspishness that suggested he was mildly irritated by everyone and everything at all times. Even when he was offering words of encouragement and support—which, in fairness, happened regularly—it felt like he should be accompanying them with a slow, sarcastic clap.

'You know it's pretty much stopped raining, aye?' Sandra asked. 'It's barely spitting.'

Jonathan made no move to unzip his hood, and Seamus wondered if maybe it wasn't meant to shield him from the rain at all, but to cushion any surprise flying headbutts that Sandra might attempt to launch in his direction.

'You're not here to admire the daubings,' the supervisor reminded them, ignoring the girl's remark. 'You're here to scrub them off.'

'If we clean off a work of art like that, though, does that not make us the vandals?' Sandra asked.

Jonathan stared at her along his waterproof tunnel. 'No,' he said. 'It doesn't.' He snapped his fingers and pointed in Seamus's direction. 'Seamus, you're with me. Sandra, I want this penis gone within the hour.'

'What about the balls?'

Jonathan tutted. 'And the balls. Of course, the balls. Why would I want you to leave the balls?'

'You can't be expecting me to do it all on my own?' Sandra protested.

'Aye. That's exactly what I'm expecting,' Jonathan confirmed. 'Unless you want to switch with Seamus and go on rubbish pick-up?'

'Fuck, no. I'll scrub the knob,' Sandra said, snatching up one of the hard-bristled brushes and a bottle of detergent they'd been supplied for that very purpose. 'But it's a travesty, and we all know it.'

Pausing only to snap off a quick photo of the giant genitalia on her phone, she set to work, leaving Seamus to trudge forlornly along behind the supervisor as he picked his way along the side of the road.

'I'm not really on rubbish pick-up again, am I, Johnny?'

In reply, Jonathan handed the younger man a claw-ended litter picker and a roll of thick black bags. 'It's Mr Milburn. And get a grip, Seamus. It's not exactly hard work in the grand scheme of things, is it?'

'Picking up coffee cups and shitty nappies folk have chucked out their car windows? It's not exactly a great time, either,' Seamus countered. 'Especially with trucks hurtling past you at eighty miles an hour.'

Jonathan waited for a car to pass before replying. 'You're not here to have a great time. In fact, that's the opposite of why you're here, when you think about it. You're here because you did bad things, and you're paying the price. You're rebalancing the scales. If you can't do the time, don't do the crime, Seamus. Isn't that how the saying goes?'

'Aye, but—'

'You ever been on a submarine?'

Seamus frowned. 'Eh?'

'It's not a trick question. A submarine, Seamus. Have you ever been on one?'

The younger man shook his head, not entirely sure where this was going. 'No…'

'My grandfather was. In a wee skirmish called Double-U Double-U Two. Maybe you've heard of it? He'd be down there for months at a time, trapped in an airtight tube with forty other men. All farting away. Deep below the surface. Couldn't stand fully upright without hitting your head. Couldn't lie down properly in your bunk without bashing your feet. And the heat… Absolutely roasting, so it was. Even if you could lie down, it was too hot and noisy to sleep.'

He rocked back on his heels, like some point had been proven. Seamus could only frown in confusion. 'What's that got to do with anything?'

'I'm saying, it could be a lot worse.' The supervisor unzipped and lowered his hood, giving further weight to Seamus's head-butt shield theory. 'Aye, you're picking up rubbish other folk have tossed away. Aye, it's raining. Aye, there's a slim-to-middling chance that you'll be dragged into the slipstream of a passing juggernaut and crushed beneath its wheels—'

'Jesus,' Seamus muttered.

'But are you sweating in an airtight submarine with forty burly sailors? Is Hitler in power in Germany, and is his Nazi regime carrying out atrocities just a few hundred miles away from your current location?'

Seamus blew out his cheeks and shook his head. 'You've got me there, right enough.'

'Well, then. It could be worse. It could *always* be worse. That's my point. If you really don't want to pick up litter, you can always go collect dog shit with Malcolm outside Tesco. Do you want that, Seamus? Is that what you want? You remember how Malcolm picks up dog shit, don't you?'

Seamus winced. 'With his hands.'

'With his hands. Exactly. The dirty bastard. But, listen, hey, if that's what you want, it can be arranged. I can have you down there in a flash.'

The supervisor crossed his arms. The movement made the neck of his zipped jacket creep up so it almost throttled him, but he held fast, pretending it wasn't a problem.

'So,' he asked, the pressure on his throat straining his voice a little higher. 'What's it to be?'

-

Seamus kicked his way through the wet grass, the claw of his litter picker snapping in half-hearted anticipation. Jonathan had picked the area for Seamus to work on, and had even told him he could work further back beyond the line of trees at the side of the road, rather than at the roadside itself.

It could've been done out of kindness, but more likely it was the thought of the paperwork that would have to be filled in if Seamus had been bounced off the bonnet of a speeding Renault Clio.

The downside of this was that there wasn't a lot of litter this far back from the road, and Seamus was under strict instructions to fill two bags before showing his face again. He was also up against the clock. If he wasn't back with his bounty in half an hour, it was shit-picking with Malcolm for the rest of the week.

There was a big pile of McDonald's wrappers a few feet ahead. They spilled out of a sodden wet brown paper bag that he just knew was going to disintegrate as soon as the claw made contact. Still, it would be a good haul. It'd take up maybe a third of one bag, if he arranged it properly. Another few scores like that, and he'd be done in no time.

He didn't head straight for it, and instead continued to kick through the grass for a while.

'Nice,' he announced, when he spotted a partially crushed Red Bull can amongst the tangle of greenery. A quick snatch and grab with the claw, and the bag in his hand was no longer empty.

Still mostly empty, obviously, but at least it was a start.

His sweep found nothing else, so he headed for the discarded McDonald's debris and spent a couple of minutes picking up each individual piece before carefully placing them in the bin bag. He didn't want to risk crushing the cups, since that would make the bag look less full. Efficiency was the key in this situation—much better to fill a bag with twenty intact paper cups than with a hundred crushed-up ones. That was just science.

A couple of minutes later, deeper still into the woods, he struck gold. Someone had been camping here. Several someones, he guessed. They'd abandoned a couple of disposable barbecues, twenty-odd beer cans, and a few litre bottles of supermarket brand spirits.

Most of the cans had been crushed, which was a bit annoying, but the barbecues really helped fill up the bag, and after trapping some air inside to help pad the whole thing out, Seamus pulled the drawstrings tight and tied them in a double knot.

'One down, one to go,' he said.

And then, he saw it.

It lay maybe thirty feet away from the scorch marks the barbecues had left on the ground, partially blending in with the grass around it.

A bag.

It was not unlike the ones he was carrying, but it was thicker and shinier, and coloured in a deep forest green.

At first, he thought that all his prayers had been answered. If this was a sack of rubbish, he could decant it into his own bag, then sit twiddling his thumbs for the rest of the half-hour before emerging triumphantly from the woods.

As he got closer, though, he realised that whatever was in the bag looked more solid than an assortment of litter. Rain had pooled on top of the bag, the weight of which would have squashed anything soft contained inside. The contents held firm, though, and a quick prod from the litter picker confirmed that whatever was in there didn't have a lot of give to it.

It was a rubble sack, he thought, though the contents weren't hard enough to be rocks. Firm, yes, but not solid. Not really.

He took a step back, some soft, nagging voice telling him to turn around and walk away. Telling him not to look any closer.

Begging him not to.

He should backtrack to the camping spot. Head to the right this time, maybe find a few more cans or empty bottles. A discarded sleeping bag, even. That would fill his quota in one fell swoop.

'You all right?'

For the second time that day, Jonathan's voice almost made him jump out of his skin.

'Fuck!' Seamus hissed. He looked back over his shoulder to find the supervisor standing a dozen feet away, Sandra picking her way through the trees behind him.

'Sandra managed to get that penis off,' Jonathan explained.

'It was all in the wrist,' Sandra added, then she smiled, evidently proud of her own joke.

Jonathan ignored the remark. 'Something wrong?' he asked Seamus.

'Eh, no. Just...' Seamus gestured to the bag in the grass. 'Found that.'

Jonathan's gaze swept across the grass for a few moments until it settled on the green rubble sack. 'What is it?'

'I don't know.'

Jonathan tutted. 'Then what's the problem? If it's litter, bag it up.'

'I don't know if it is litter, though.'

'Is it a bush?' Jonathan asked.

'What?'

'Is it a tree? Is it a type of big mushroom?' He beckoned Sandra closer. 'Gather in, both of you, this is a lesson for you both.' He spoke slowly, like he was spelling it out to a child. 'If it's not meant to be there, then it's litter. If something's in a place that it doesn't belong, then it doesn't matter what it is, it's litter.'

'What if it was a sword?' Sandra asked.

Jonathan turned to her. 'What?'

'What if it was a sword lying in a supermarket?'

'What are you talking about?'

'Is that litter?' Sandra pressed.

'Yes. Yes, that's technically litter. I mean, it's weird, but—'

'What if it's two swords in a library?'

Jonathan blinked several times in rapid succession. 'What's that got to...? Is there an exhibition on?'

It was Sandra's turn to look confused. 'Eh?'

'Libraries sometimes have exhibitions on, maybe the swords are there for...' He tutted and shook his head. 'It doesn't matter. I don't care. The point is, *that*'—he pointed to the dark green bag—'is very clearly litter. So, what do we do with it? We...'

There was a pause. Jonathan held his breath, then let it out in a big sigh.

'You two were supposed to chime in there. We pick it up. That's why we're here. Community clean-up. That's what we're doing. So, come on, chop-chop. Get it shifted.'

Sandra and Seamus exchanged looks, then shuffled closer to the bulging sack.

'Jesus,' Sandra muttered, drawing back. 'It stinks.'

'Does it stink as bad as a handful of fresh dog shit?' Jonathan asked. 'No? Then get cracking.'

'I'm worried it might be puppies or something,' Seamus muttered, eyeing the opening of the bag. This close, he could see that it was actually two bags, one upside-down inside the other, so the contents were cocooned inside.

'Why would it be puppies?' Jonathan wondered, though he gave the bag a cautious side-eye as he said it.

'You hear about that, don't you?' Sandra ventured. 'People putting puppies in bags and drowning them.'

'It's a forest,' Jonathan pointed out, gesturing around them. 'You can't drown something on dry land.'

'You can if you try hard enough,' Sandra said ominously.

'Just get it open,' Jonathan barked. 'It's going to start pissing down again soon.'

Slowly, carefully, Seamus brought the claw of the litter picker closer to the gaping opening of the bag. It looked like a mouth with the arse end of the other bag sticking out of its throat, choking it.

He snapped the claw shut and stepped back. 'I can't. I can't do it.'

Jonathan rolled his eyes and scowled like a pantomime villain, then marched over to the bulging bag. 'God Almighty. Fine. I'll open it,' he said, squatting down next to it.

His throat constricted and his nostrils narrowed as he tried not to let on how unpleasant he was finding the smell. He took out the small pair of scissors he used for cutting up soft plastics that might get wrapped around the necks of curious birds, and poked a hole in the innermost bag.

'Then you two can pick it all up, and we can move on to the next area before it's time to call it a...'

He stopped talking.

Stopped moving.

Stopped breathing.

And then, like an electrical charge had been passed through his long, spindly legs, he launched himself backwards onto the wet grass.

'Is it puppies?' Seamus cried. 'Aw, fuck, is it puppies?'

He risked a step closer. The smell caught him from below like an uppercut. Down in the grass, Jonathan sprawled onto one side and vomited.

'Oh, God,' Seamus whispered. 'Oh, God.'

'What is that?!' Jonathan managed between heaves. 'What the hell is that?'

It was a strange question, given the circumstances. There was no great mystery. The contents of the bag were plain for all to see.

There, visible through the freshly cut hole, were the five red-painted toes and grisly ankle stump of a woman's severed foot.

Chapter Two

'Body's over there, boss. Well, some of it, anyway.'

DCI Jack Logan ran a hand down his face, sweeping the rainwater out of the crags. He could see an evidence tent through the gaps in the trees, and a few Scene of Crime officers in white paper suits shuffling around searching the area immediately surrounding it.

He gripped the back of his neck and gave it a stretch. The drive to Aviemore had taken less than forty minutes, but it had further compounded the effects of a few sleepless nights on the trot.

'Some of it?' he asked, raising his eyebrows.

Detective Constable Tyler Neish nodded, sluicing rain from the folds of his hood onto the wet tarmac between them. 'Aye, boss. It's in bits. The body, I mean. And I'm pretty sure it can't be the full thing. Unless it's a dwarf, I suppose,' Tyler reasoned. 'Big feet for a dwarf, mind you, so it probably isn't.'

'Hang on, hang on, stop wittering shite for a second, son,' Logan said, waving the DC into silence. 'So the body's been dismembered? Is that what you're telling me?'

'Aye, boss. Very much so by the looks of it. Shona's in poking about at the bits and bobs now.'

Logan scowled. 'She'll be carrying out an initial medical check of the remains, you mean. She's not "poking about" at anything.'

Tyler nodded. 'Oh. Aye. Sorry. That's what I meant, boss. She'll be doing that.'

Logan grunted and turned his eyes to the guys in the white paper suits. 'What about Palmer? Is he here?'

'Afraid so, boss,' Tyler chirped. 'He was sniffing about the tent last time I checked. Think Shona gave him short shrift and told him to do one until she was finished.'

The DCI nodded approvingly. A year ago, Shona would have been willing to give Geoff Palmer the benefit of the doubt. In recent months, though, she'd started to see the Scene of Crime head honcho for the snidey, weasel-faced, grubby wee bastard that he was.

It was fair to say that Logan wasn't the man's biggest fan, either.

Unlike Shona, who tried to see the good in people—especially the dead ones—he'd had the measure of Geoff from the start. Though he knew that it was neither big nor clever, Jack relished the memory of Palmer's face when, during a particularly nasty bout of flu, the DCI had projectile-vomited all down the front of the Scene of Crime man's pristine white PPE.

He took a moment to enjoy the thought of it once again, then nodded along the road to where a cordon tape was keeping traffic at bay. 'Get that pushed further back,' he instructed. 'Same on the other side. They're too close. I can see the whites of their bloody eyes, so you can bet video of all this'll be all over Twitter already.'

'X, boss.'

Logan's eyes narrowed. 'What?'

'It's not called Twitter any more. It's called X.'

The DCI regarded him in silence for a while, then shook his head. 'Well, that's the stupidest bloody thing I've ever heard. And considering some of the conversations I've had with you, that's saying something. Whatever it's called, I don't want the drivers of those cars live-streaming this whole bloody circus. Turn them around, tell them to fuck off, then get that cordon moved back. And you!'

A uniformed constable who was standing minding his own business nearby suddenly jumped to attention. 'Me, sir?'

'Aye. You look like you're doing bugger all. Get me a coffee.'

The constable glanced around like he was expecting to see a barista hovering nearby. 'A coffee, sir? From where?'

'That's not my problem, son. Just get it. Black, four sugars. Chop-chop.'

While the constable scurried away, DC Neish risked giving Logan a quick look up and down. 'Everything all right, boss?' he ventured. 'You seem a bit, you know, stressed. I mean, I know you're always stressed. I know that's like your default, but you seem more stressed than usual.'

Logan scratched at his salt-and-pepper stubble like he was considering his answer, then huffed out a sigh. 'Them cordons haven't shifted yet, Detective Constable. Finger out your arse and get it done.'

He ran a hand through his hair and grimaced as rainwater trickled down the back of his neck and spoke to nobody in particular.

'Right then, I suppose I'd better go and see if I can find that useless bastard'—he turned and came face to face with a pudgy red face in a white paper hood—'Palmer.'

-

Detective Sergeant Hamza Khaled stood at the back of an ambulance, the rain flattening his hair against the top of his head. Inside, a young man in a hi-vis 'Community Payback' vest wheezed into an oxygen mask, his eyes ringed red with tears.

'Take your time, Mr…'

'Seamus.'

Hamza took his pad from his jacket pocket, quickly concluded that it had no chance of surviving the current precipitation, and slipped it back in.

'Mr Seamus.'

The lad in the ambulance shook his head. 'Seamus Starkey.' He drew in a shaky breath. 'But just call me Seamus.'

Hamza smiled thinly. 'Seamus. Right. Thank you. I'm Detective Sergeant Hamza Khaled. Hamza's fine. You've had a rough morning, I hear.'

Seamus coughed into the mask. 'Aye, you can say that again.'

A gust of wind gave the falling rain a bit of welly. Hamza shuffled closer to the ambulance, teasing some shelter from the vehicle's back doors.

'You mind telling me what happened?'

The younger man rasped into the mask a few times before responding. His eyes blurred, but he fought hard to force back the tears.

'There was a bag. On the ground,' he explained. 'There was a foot in it. Probably other bits, too.'

'You didn't see anything else?'

'We didn't look. The foot was enough. I mean… It was a foot. A human foot. A woman's foot just sticking out of the bag. Cut off at the ankle.'

'How do you know it was a woman's foot?' Hamza asked.

Seamus inhaled deeply, then shrugged. 'It might not be, I suppose. But it had nail polish on, and it just…' He glazed over, his eyes taking on a distant, haunted look. 'I just think it's a woman's,' he finally muttered.

'Right. I see. And was it you who opened the bag?'

Seamus shook his head. 'No. No, I didn't… That wasn't me. I was just the one that found it.'

He looked past the detective sergeant to where a Community Payback van was parked up with two wheels on the road, and two on the grassy verge.

'It was Johnny who opened it up.'

–

Detective Constable Sinead Bell had the right idea. She sat in the front passenger seat of the Community Payback van, enjoying the warmth from the blowers and the protection of the roof above her head. The windscreen wipers were off, and the glass was a rippled wash of moving water, blocking the view of the world beyond.

The man in the driver's seat was the local Community Payback supervisor. Sinead pegged him to be in his mid-thirties, though his hairstyle skewed slightly older. He sat straight-backed and rigid, his hands gripping the steering wheel like he was easing the van along a precarious mountain road in a snowstorm.

'I've never seen anything like that before,' Jonathan said, his voice a croaky whisper. 'I mean, I deal with what some people would think of as'—he made air quotes—'undesirables,' but they're decent kids, by and large. They're a bit wild, maybe. A bit off the rails, but they're not… You know. They're not…'

He gesticulated towards the front windscreen a few times, searching for the right word, before finally settling on, 'Feet!'

'No,' Sinead said. 'No, I'd imagine it must've been a shock, right enough.'

'I was sick. I was actually sick,' Jonathan said, his head whipping around to look at the detective constable, his face offering up some sort of desperate apology. 'Can you believe that?'

'I can. It happens,' Sinead assured him.

'But *sick* sick. Proper sick. I wasn't just queasy, I actually threw up!'

'You'd had a shock. It's understandable. It could've happened to anyone.'

Jonathan made a low, noncommittal humming sound between his pursed lips, then faced forward again. He flexed his fingers, adjusted his grip, and watched the rolling waves of rainwater on the outside of the glass.

'Poor Seamus looked shaken. Proper broken up. He didn't spew, though. I'll give him that.' Jonathan inhaled slowly. The air trembled all the way down into his lungs. 'We both froze. Freaked out. You always think you'll be cool in situations like that, don't you? But we weren't. Neither of us was. If it hadn't been for Sandra, we'd probably still be standing there just staring.'

Sinead glanced down at her notepad. 'Sandra? She's the one who made the 999 call?'

'She's the only one who had the presence of mind, yes. Although, to be fair, she's called a few ambulances in her time. Not that it was the ambulance we rang, of course. I mean, what would be the point in that?' Jonathan asked, his voice creeping higher and higher with every word. 'I don't care how good a first aider you are, there's not a lot you can do for a bag of feet.'

'She did the right thing,' Sinead assured him. 'But what makes you think it's a bag of feet?'

Jonathan turned and fixed her with a stare of blank confusion. 'Well, I mean, I just assumed because…' His face paled. Or, more accurately, it *greened*. 'Wait. You mean there could be other bits in there? Not just feet? There could be a head, or… Oh, Christ.'

The wind and the rain rushed in as he opened his door and leaned out. Vomit cascaded onto the grass, and Sinead turned away to afford the man some dignity.

And, more importantly, to avoid the smell.

'Tell me what you need me to do. I'll do it. Anything,' Jonathan wheezed, when he had fully emptied his guts. He pulled the door closed, and the roaring of the wind dropped to a background rumble. 'Because whoever did that—whoever could do that to another human being—they need locking up, and they need locking up now.'

–

'You're looking tired, Jack,' Palmer announced. There was a smirk on the Scene of Crime man's face that spread up his cheeks like a rash. 'What's the matter? Not been sleeping well? Has herself been keeping you up for some late-night—'

'Stop talking, Geoff,' Logan instructed. He held up a hand that was larger than the other man's head, silencing him.

Palmer gazed expectantly up at the DCI, then glanced around like he was waiting for some sort of cue. 'Why?' he finally asked.

Logan shrugged. 'No real reason. I just don't like the sound of your voice. And you were skirting dangerously close to saying something that could get you fired.' He considered this for a moment. 'Actually, what was I thinking? Just you carry on with whatever it was you were about to say.'

Palmer shifted his weight uncertainly from foot to foot. His smile was still fixed in place, but it was a hollow plastic replica of the real thing.

'Doesn't matter,' the Scene of Crime man said. He glanced back through the trees to where the white evidence tent was being buffeted by the wind. 'Your other half is—'

'Dr Maguire,' Logan corrected.

The smile faltered further. 'Sorry?'

'She's not my other half. She's Dr Maguire.'

Palmer's expression veered dangerously into 'demented glee' territory. 'She's not your other half? So you two have…?'

'No!' Logan barked. 'I mean, we're meant to be bloody professionals here, Geoff. On the job, she's Dr Maguire. Her relationship status is irrelevant.'

'God, you're a barrel of bloody laughs today, aren't you?' Palmer replied. His smile returned. 'Here, speaking of which, did you hear me on the radio the other day?'

'Thankfully not.'

'I won a comedy contest. You know how I've been doing stand-up for a while now?'

Logan's eyebrows rose in surprise. 'What? No. You've never said a thing about it.'

'What? Aye, I have. I've mentioned it loads of times.'

The DCI sighed. 'It was a joke, Geoff. You might want to give one of them a try sometime.'

'Well, ironic that you should say that, given I just won myself an HMV voucher for telling the best joke on Northsound Radio. Fifty quid. That's two and a half Blu-rays. Or, like, four CDs.' He raised his eyebrows as if to stress that neither of these numbers were to be sniffed at, before saying the words that Logan had known were inevitable. 'Do you want to hear the joke I told?'

'No.'

'It's a bit blue, so brace yourself,' Palmer warned, choosing to completely ignore the detective's response. 'Here we go. Why don't boxers have sex on the night before a fight?'

Logan said nothing. He just stared down at the man in the crinkly white hood, a drip of rainwater dangling precariously from the end of his nose.

'They just don't really like each other,' Palmer concluded, then he clapped his hands together, made a little *tadish* sound, and grinned triumphantly.

Logan drew in a deep breath and blew the hanging raindrop off the tip of his nose. 'That's actually not bad by your usual standards,' he begrudgingly admitted, though his face remained totally impassive. He nodded into the woods. 'But how about we take some time out from the gags, and maybe focus on trying to solve this murder, eh?'

Chapter Three

After a few false starts while she tried to find the door, Dr Shona Maguire emerged from the white and yellow evidence tent with an unusually sombre demeanour. She practically rolled her eyes at the sight of Geoff Palmer waddling through the woods towards her in his protective gear, looking like some sort of white supremacist Teletubby.

Even when she spotted Logan, she was barely able to raise a smile. She pulled her rubber gloves off in a hurry, like she was in a rush to rid herself of them, then rolled them up together and stuffed them in the disposal bag in her pocket.

She looked straight up then, eyes closed, the rain falling like a baptism across her face.

'All right?' Logan asked, once he and Geoff eventually reached her.

'No.' Shona shook her head and wiped some of the rainwater off her face. The usual lightness in her voice was missing, her Irish accent sounding dull and flat. 'Definitely dead.'

'Eh, no. You, I meant,' the DCI pressed. 'Are you all right?'

'Me? Fine,' Shona replied, though the shortness of it said otherwise. 'Where's Taggart?'

'Up the road with Ben. Thought it a bit cruel to drive him all the way down here to a big forest and then not let him out of the car.'

Shona nodded. 'Right,' she said. 'Fair enough.'

Logan sensed Palmer's grin even before it spread across the bastard's face. 'Oh-ho! What's this? Trouble in paradise? This is becoming a habit!'

'Shut up, Geoff,' they both said, though Logan's had more venom behind it.

Palmer held up his gloved hands. 'I'm just saying, if either of you need to talk, I'm here, all right.'

He eyed them both with a sincerity that could've reduced a Hallmark card to tears at fifty paces.

'I mean it. Come vent. Anytime. I'm here. I'm a good listener. Ask anyone. Here.'

He looked around, then pointed to a passing Scene of Crime officer and clicked his fingers. The gloves completely deadened the sound, so he resorted to shouting instead.

'Here. You. Bev. Am I a good listener?'

The woman who stopped looked completely confused by the question. 'Well, I mean, I can't say that—'

'See?' Palmer said, turning back to the detective and the pathologist.

Bev fell silent, shrugged, then shuffled off again.

'Look, guys. Like it or not, we're a team. We're like the Three Musketeers. The Three Amigos.' He ran his tongue across his lips. 'What's another one?'

'Three Stooges?' Shona suggested.

'Don't encourage him, for fuck's sake,' Logan muttered.

'Yes! Hilarious! Them!' Geoff cheered. He put a hand on their arms, gripping Logan's and lightly rubbing Shona's. 'And just like them, we support each other.'

'I don't think that's what the Three Stooges did,' Logan pointed out. 'Were they not usually leathering shit out of one another?'

Geoff smiled. The sincerity was still there. Patronisingly so. 'Hey, I'm just saying, whatever it is that's bothering you, don't keep it in here'—he pointed to his heart—'let it out here'—he pointed to his mouth—'and I'll take it all in here.'

He finished by pointing to both of his ears. They were hidden under the unflattering elasticated hood, but the point he was trying to make was clear enough.

Propping his foot on one of the big plastic equipment cases his team had brought, he rested an elbow on his knee and leaned forward.

'So, come on. Spill. Tell Uncle Geoff what's going on.'

'No,' Logan intoned.

Shona shook her head in agreement.

Palmer sighed and took his foot off the case. 'Fine. Suit your fucking self, then.'

With that, he turned and marched off, bellowing at Bev for an update.

'The hell was all that about?' Shona wondered.

Logan puffed out his cheeks. 'The usual Palmer being an arsehole. He's just trying a new approach to it.'

'Keeps it fresh, I suppose,' Shona said. She shot him a cagey sort of smile. 'You all right?'

The question reminded Logan of how tired he was, and he was forced to stifle a yawn before replying. 'Aye. More or less. Bloody exhausted, though.'

'I'll talk to her when I get back,' Shona promised. 'That was out of order, staying out that late. I think she's just testing boundaries. David, her care worker, he said that would happen. And, I mean, we both know Olivia enough that it's not exactly a surprise.'

Logan almost pointed out that this had been one of his issues with the idea of fostering Olivia Maximuke right from the start. They both knew the girl was troubled, even before her useless bastard of a mother had upped and died on her.

And they both knew who her father was, and while Shona didn't know *all* the terrible things that Bosco Maximuke had done over the years, Logan had a pretty good idea of most of them.

For a few years now, he'd harboured the suspicion that, when it came to Bosco's daughter, the apple hadn't fallen far from the tree.

And now, she was living under his roof.

He decided just to nod. Nodding would avoid an argument, or at least postpone one for a few hours. Indicating the tent beside them, he steered the conversation onto safer ground.

'What have we got?'

Shona glanced at the tent, and Logan thought he saw her give the slightest shudder of revulsion. That wasn't like her. She'd seen enough of this stuff to be hardened to it, any sense of horror long ago replaced by enthusiastic fascination.

Now, though, she took a moment to compose herself before replying.

'Not a lot. We've got parts of a torso—upper and lower, no midsection—a section of scalp, and a pair of feet.'

'Jesus,' Logan mumbled. 'No head?'

'No head, no arms, no legs, no stomach,' Shona said. 'Torso pieces are just chest and pelvis.'

Palmer popped up as if he'd been waiting in the wings for his cue. 'You might say that she's all tits and arse!'

His smile evaporated quickly as even he realised that this may have come across as a little insensitive.

'Sorry,' he muttered, then he hurried off again before Logan or Shona could shout at him.

'You think it's all the same victim?' Logan asked.

Shona scratched at a forearm, dragging the nails up and down, leaving white marks on her skin. 'Can't say yet for all of it, but the torso parts, yes, so probably the rest, too. Adult female. Age…?' She shrugged. 'Twenties? Thirties. Long hair. Blonde. Recently bleached, though, by the looks of it, so most likely darker.'

'Right. Any ideas on anything else yet? Rough time of death, or…?'

'I'd be guessing. Days ago, though. At least three. And the cuts were made afterwards. Saw of some sort. Messy. Probably not someone who's done anything like it before.'

'That's something, at least,' Logan remarked. He wasn't sure *why* it was something, or what that something was, but he felt reassured by it all the same.

'Yeah. Let's just hope they don't start making a habit of it.' She tapped the area at the top of her stomach. 'Looks like there's a stab wound right at the bottom of the upper torso. Here. The edge of one, anyway. The cut goes right through it.'

'Cause of death, you think?'

It was Shona's turn to stifle a yawn. The last few nights really had been rough, and based on how the day was shaping up so far, tonight wasn't likely to be any more restful.

'No idea,' she admitted. 'Not a clue. I'll need to get it all back for testing and we'll see where we're at. I'll head up the road and start prepping.'

'Eh, aye. Aye, good,' Logan said. He wanted to say more, to check how she was doing—how she was *really* doing—but there were too many people within earshot for him to risk it. 'Well, just, you know. Keep me posted.'

Shona smiled thinly at him. 'Will do. Oh! There was one thing that might be useful. She's got a tattoo on her shoulder. Quite distinctive. I took a picture. I'll send it over. Might help you find out who she is.'

She looked back at the tent again, her gaze lingering on the seam of the entrance. The falling rain played a rattling rhythm on the canvas roof.

'Poor cow,' she whispered. 'It's no way to end up, is it? It's not really fair.'

'No,' Logan agreed. He joined her in looking at the tent, thinking of the human wreckage that lay within, and the horrors the person it had once been must've gone through to get here. 'It really is not.'

Chapter Four

Aviemore Police Station was a low, long building standing right by the side of the main road. It was bigger than some of the stations Logan and his team had made use of around the Highlands, but it still lacked all but the most basic facilities.

Still, it had a roof, it had a semi-functional heating system, and it had a kettle. Given that the constable had failed to turn up with Logan's coffee, that last one was particularly welcome.

'Aye, this'll do,' the DCI said, glancing around the briefing room while he sipped from his steaming hot mug of tea.

The room wasn't much bigger than the living room of Logan's house, and flakes of paint were peeling from the walls. They lay scattered around the edges of the room like bits of yellowing dandruff, suggesting it had been a while since anyone had treated the place to a hoovering.

'We'll set up here for now, but we're close enough to Inverness to make that our main base. No point in complicating things.'

'Makes sense, sir,' Hamza agreed. 'They've got a couple of interview rooms, too, in case we want to question the witnesses again. Might get more out of them when they've calmed down a bit.'

'We've still to talk to'—Sinead checked her notepad—'Sandra Hogg. She made the 999 call, but left before anyone turned up.'

Sinead's husband, DC Neish, gave one of the briefing room chairs an experimental pat, like he was concerned it might collapse. 'She probably bottled it,' he said. He risked sitting down, but held himself ready to leap to his feet again at the first sign of danger. 'Must've been pretty scary, finding that stuff.'

'Not according to Jonathan Milburn, the supervisor,' Sinead countered. 'She seemed pretty fine with it, he reckoned. She was the only one who held it together while they were freaking out.'

'Some people hide their emotions well, though, don't they?' Tyler said. 'Like you, boss.'

'I don't have emotions, son,' Logan replied. He slurped at his tea. 'Wait, is contempt an emotion?'

'Pretty sure it is, boss, aye,' Tyler confirmed.

'OK. I take it back, then. I have one emotion,' Logan said. 'Now, what the hell are you sitting down for? I want you talking to the local Uniforms. See if anyone's missing. We're looking for a woman in her twenties or thirties, long blonde hair, though it's been bleached, so not sure yet of her natural colour.'

Tyler got to his feet again. The chair squeaked like it was glad to be shot of him. 'Eh, OK.' Tyler sounded hesitant, like he was suddenly concerned by something. 'No bother, boss. Anything else I should tell them? Any like, eh, distinguishing features, or that? Tattoos, maybe, or...?'

'Aye, actually,' Logan said. 'Hang on.'

The DCI took his phone from his coat pocket and tapped into the messages, finding the one he'd received from Shona back at the roadside.

'One tattoo that we could see. Quite distinctive. Here.'

He held up the phone, the screen angled so DC Neish could see the image.

Tyler's face paled. He swallowed, but his Adam's apple caught somewhere in his throat, almost choking him.

'You all right, son?' Logan asked. 'You look like you just saw a bloody ghost.'

'Oh, God,' Sinead muttered. 'Don't get him started on that again. I've only just heard the end of what happened at Halloween.'

Tyler wasn't listening. He just stared for a while at the photo on the screen. It showed much-loved Scottish comic book icon, Oor Wullie, sitting on his bucket while smoking the world's biggest spliff.

'Eh, boss,' he croaked, finally finding his voice again. 'Mind if you and me have a quick word in private?'

-

Logan had ushered Hamza and Sinead from the room, dumping the task he'd assigned to Tyler on them so he could keep the DC back.

Tyler had hummed and hawed for a few moments, until Logan, sensing something major was about to come out, had ordered him to, 'Hurry the fuck up and spit it out.'

Then, the DCI had stood with his mug of tea halfway to his open mouth, listening in growing disbelief at the babble of words that came tumbling out of the detective constable.

So much disbelief, in fact, that he had no choice but to endure it all again.

'Just so I can be sure I'm getting this straight, son,' he said, his grip on the mug handle tightening until his knuckles turned white, 'run through that one more time.'

Tyler winced. Voicing it all the first time had taken a lot out of him, and the way the DCI was looking at him was further sapping his resolve.

Still, he'd come this far. There was nowhere to go but onwards.

'The, eh, the body, boss. I think I know who it is.'

'Right,' Logan intoned.

'Because of the tattoo. I mean, I had suspicions before then. Or, you know, not suspicions. Just, like, thoughts. I just wondered if it might be her, you know? And then, with the tattoo, and everything. I mean, that basically proved it.'

'You know who the victim is,' Logan said. It wasn't a question, but Tyler answered like it was.

'Yes, boss.'

Logan's mug *clunked* as he sat it down on the table he was currently resting his not-inconsiderable weight on.

'Right. And—this is the bit I'm having some difficultly with, Tyler—you know this because…?'

Tyler gulped back his fear. Logan's face had darkened when the DC had said this next part the first time around. This time, the boss was ready for it, which somehow made saying it out loud even scarier.

Especially now that both Logan's hands were free, and Tyler was easily within lunging distance.

The DC cleared his throat.

Then, he cleared it again.

He opened his mouth, closed it, raised a finger like he was about to make a very interesting and valid point about something, then let it drop back to his side like all his strength had left him.

'Hoon, boss.'

'Hoon.' Logan said the name like it was dirty and he wanted it out of his mouth as quickly as possible. 'You know this because… *Hoon*?'

'Aye, boss.'

Logan stood up. For a man of his size, this was quite a long and involved process, and by the time he'd reached his full height, his shadow cast DC Neish into near-total darkness.

'There seems to be a lot of detail missing in that sentence, son,' the detective chief inspector pointed out. 'There's a gap in the middle I'm going to need you to fill in for me. And, if I was in your shoes—and I count my lucky bloody stars that I'm not—I'd fill it in quickly.'

Tyler took a shuffled step backwards, so he didn't have to crane his neck quite so much to look up at Logan. Although, given the current expression on the boss's face, looking at him might not have been the wisest move.

'Well, uh, you know he's, like, set himself up doing private investigation stuff? Hoon, I mean.'

'I'd heard something. Didn't pay much attention,' Logan replied. 'Don't care, if it keeps him out of my hair. What about it?'

Tyler slipped a finger between the collar of his shirt and his throat, like the room was suddenly stiflingly hot. Given the ancient, barely functional heating system, though, it definitely wasn't.

'Well, eh, like, he sort of asked… A while back, I mean, he sort of… We had this…' Tyler took a deep breath and spat it out. 'I've sort of been working with him.'

The words hung there between them like a particularly pungent fart.

When Logan finally spoke, his voice was like the rumbling of long-dormant tectonic plates shifting deep below the earth's crust.

'You've "sort of been working with him"? In what sense have you "sort of been working with him", Tyler?'

'Not much! Hardly anything, boss!' the DC insisted. 'Like, I've just been sort of looking stuff up.'

The lines of Logan's face etched themselves deeper. Darker. 'What, in polis records?'

'What? No, boss! No, nothing like that. I swear. Just on Google, really. He doesn't seem to know how to use it. He calls it "Googly" half the time. He'll be like'—Tyler adopted a gruff, no-nonsense tone—'"Boyband. I need you to fucking Googly me something", and I'll have to just type it in, or whatever, and then send him a screenshot. It's not even anything that important, it's usually like bus times, or taxi numbers, or whatever. I had to find him a scone recipe last month.'

'A scone recipe?'

'Aye, boss. Plain or fruit, he didn't care, but he said if I sent one with cheese in it, he'd shove his thumbs in my eyes so hard that they'd come out through my arse.' Tyler shuffled his weight from one foot to the other, as if imagining what this might feel like. 'I don't know if he meant my eyes or his thumbs. Either way, I wasn't keen on the idea, so I just sent him a recipe from some baking site, and he never mentioned it again.'

Logan crossed his arms and lowered his weight onto the corner of the desk again. 'What the hell have scones got to do with anything?'

'Eh? Oh, nothing, boss. That was just an example. But, eh, day before yesterday, he asked me to look up tattoo artists. He was trying to find someone who'd done any just like the one you showed me. Oor Wullie smoking a joint. Said it was to do with a case he'd just been asked to look into. A lassie that had gone missing.'

'That's a police matter,' Logan pointed out.

'Well, aye, true, boss,' Tyler agreed. 'But the parents weren't happy with how the local crew was handling it. She's been missing for days, apparently. They wanted outside help, so they found Hoon. Not sure how, he doesn't seem to advertise anywhere, as far as I can tell. He took it on, though. He's been looking into her disappearance.'

'Since when?'

'Eh, just since the day before yesterday, I think. Not sure if he's done much on it, or anything, actually. All he mentioned to me was the tattoo.'

Logan ran a hand down his face and let out a groan of such exasperation that it echoed at the corners of the room.

'Jesus Christ, Tyler. This is serious. Do you have any idea how serious this is?' he demanded. 'You're a serving detective constable. You get a part-time job, you need to report that. You need to ask permission from the bastards upstairs. And what do you think they're going to say to you providing information to a man they fired? To a man they almost brought corruption charges against? Hmm? Do you think they're going to look positively on that sort of thing? You think they're going to rubber-stamp that and say, "Aye, go ahead. Fire on. See if we care"?'

'Eh, no. Doubt they'd say that, boss.' Tyler saw a potential way out of what was sure to be his upcoming bollocking, and grasped for it. 'But I don't technically work for him, boss. It's not really a job. He's not exactly paying me.'

Logan's eyes narrowed. 'He's not *exactly* paying you? What does that mean?'

Tyler tugged on his collar again, then loosened his tie. 'It's more, sort of, a favour. He and Berta don't charge us for babysitting. He helps out with, like, a couple of other things now and again. And I help him Googly stuff.' Tyler gave a quick shake of his head. 'Google stuff, I mean.'

Logan stared down at the squirming detective constable. Even half-seated on the desk, he was still half a head taller than the younger man.

'He's never paid you? Money's never changed hands?'

'No, boss,' Tyler said truthfully. 'Though, I should say, he has helped cover the cost of—'

Logan silenced him with a raised hand. 'Has he ever paid you directly? Has he put money in your hand, or in your bank account, or given you a cheque?'

'No, boss.'

'And all you've done is search for stuff for him on the internet?'

'Yes, boss,' Tyler said, then doubt flitted across his face. 'Well, I helped him hang a telly on the wall a few weeks back, but then he said I was just getting in the way, called me a useless bastard, and told me to fuck off. So I don't know if that counts.'

Logan sighed. 'Christ Almighty. So, why the big secret? Why not tell me about this before now?'

Tyler shifted awkwardly. 'Um, I wanted to, boss, but Hoon told me not to.'

'Jesus Christ, Tyler. And if Hoon told you to jump in a loch, would you do it?'

Tyler thought about this, but not for long. 'Probably, boss, aye. You know what he can be like.'

Logan rose to his feet again, then brought up an index finger and held it just inches from the detective constable's nose. 'To be continued, Tyler. This isn't done.'

'Right you are, boss. And sorry. I shouldn't have listened to him. I should have said something before.'

'Aye. You bloody well should've,' Logan agreed. He picked up his mug, knocked back the tea in one gulp, then slammed it back down on the desk. 'Now, am I going to have to phone the boggle-eyed mad bastard myself, or can you at least tell me the lassie's name?'

Chapter Five

Logan guided his BMW up the incline of an unsurfaced driveway towards a grey stone farmhouse a few miles north of Aviemore town centre. Lambs gambolled in a field to the left, the slit-eyed stares of a few anxious mother sheep watching carefully as the car rumbled to a halt.

Over on the right, the rain rattled against the roof of a metal barn like falling ball bearings.

'Did you know?' Logan asked. He turned to DC Bell, who sat in the passenger seat alongside him. 'About Tyler doing work for Hoon?'

'I didn't know it was work, sir, no. I knew they were in contact more these days, but I thought maybe they were just, like, getting friendlier.'

'Friendlier? Tyler and *Bob Hoon*?'

Sinead conceded with a smile. 'Fair point, sir. As far as I know, though, he was just helping him out with odd jobs, or whatever. Finding train times. Getting the number for the council tax office. Think he tried helping him design a business card a while back, but Hoon ripped it up and said it was shite.'

Logan raised an eyebrow. 'Was it?'

'Oh, awful, sir. Tyler's not got an artistic bone in his body. Looked like it had been done by a three-year-old. But he's never been paid. Not for any of it. Not as far as he's told me, anyway, and he knows better than to keep secrets from me these days.'

Logan let out a sound which, under closer examination, could've been the start of a chuckle. 'Aye. I can imagine. I'm still not happy about it, but we'll worry about that later.'

He straightened his tie, adjusted his collar, then fixed his gaze on the farmhouse door just a few dozen yards ahead.

He hated this bit. They all did. What kind of monsters would they be if they didn't?

'Right. Let's get this out of the way,' he said, opening his door and stepping right in a muddy, limestone-grey puddle.

A sharp laugh and a cry of, 'Nicely done, ya fanny!' made his heart sink and his hackles rise.

The man himself, Bob Hoon, stepped out from the pool of shadow that filled the recessed barn doorway, grinning from ear to ear.

'No,' Logan snapped at him. 'No. You're not here. You can't be here.'

'Here, that's no' a very friendly fucking attitude!' Hoon barked back. 'I'm here in a professional fucking capacity, I'll have you know.' He jabbed a thumb in the direction of the house. 'This is my case. You arseholes wanted fuck all to do with it.'

He set off marching towards the car. Logan met him halfway, his coat billowing on the wind, the rain battering at both of them.

'No, Bob. It was never your case. You're not in the polis.'

'I'm still a fucking consultant,' Hoon reminded him.

'But no one's consulting you on this.'

'The lassie's old man is. He's hired me to look into his wee lassie going missing.'

'Fair enough. But she's no longer missing,' Logan pointed out.

'Bits of her still are, from what I've been hearing,' Hoon shot back.

Logan's jaw clenched so hard that his teeth creaked in their sockets. 'Tyler?'

'What? No. Fuck's sake. What do you think I am, Jack? You think I'm having Boyband feed me polis info? He's a glorified Ask Jeeves without the fucking private education and etiquette lessons. But I've still got ways and fucking means, Jack. I've still got ways and fucking means.'

Logan continued to stare at him until, eventually, Hoon gave a tut.

'There's a lassie blabbing about it all over town. Heard her talking to some dozy lad picking up dog shit outside Tesco with his bare fucking hands. Can you believe that? Clarty bastard.' He put his clenched fists on his hips and shook his head. 'I tell you, this town's fucking weird. And I once lived in fucking Dingwall.'

'Right. Fine. Well, whatever. You're done here,' Logan told him. 'This is in our hands now. We're going to talk to the parents and we'll take it from there. In the highly unlikely event that we need to talk to you about anything, we know where to find you.'

Before Hoon could respond with his full, uncensored thoughts on that idea, the front door of the farmhouse swung inwards. A man in his fifties, all grey tweed and green wellies, stood in the doorway with two steaming mugs in his hand.

'Tea's ready, Mr Hoon,' he announced.

His gaze fell on Logan and Sinead. It lingered there just long enough for him to work out who they were, and what that meant.

'I'll refill the kettle,' he said, then he retreated inside, leaving the door open.

'Looks like the old boy wants me in there with him,' Hoon said. He gave Logan an encouraging pat on the back. 'Lead the way, Jack. And don't you worry, I'll be right fucking here behind you.'

–

The tweed-clad farmer introduced himself as Roman Howard as he stood in his ancient but impressive-looking kitchen, waiting for the blackened kettle to come to the boil on top of an old Aga cooker.

Despite Logan's reasoned arguments against the idea, he insisted he wanted Hoon present for the conversation that followed—a conversation he had no interest in starting until he had led them all through to what appeared, based on the number of doors, to be one of several sitting rooms in the farmhouse.

This one was reasonably small, with room for just a couple of mismatched antique leather chairs, a tatty wicker couch, and a hospital bed with a shrunken old woman asleep on top of it.

It wasn't clear what was wrong with her, exactly, but Logan knew immediately that she was dying. In a sense, they all were, of course, but the colour of her skin and the shallowness of her breathing made it clear that she was racing ahead towards the finish line.

'My wife. Isobel,' Roman explained, gesturing for the detectives to take a seat on the couch. 'She doesn't get out much these days.'

'Aye. I can see that, right enough,' Logan said.

'But she's still listening,' Roman said, though Logan wasn't sure if that was true, or just wishful thinking. 'Oh, she's bloody listening, right enough! Isn't that right, Isobel?'

Isobel did nothing to either confirm or deny the claim. The only movement from her was the slow, shallow rise and fall of her chest.

Undeterred, her husband pressed one. 'So, whatever it is that you've come here to say, I'd like you to say it here for both of us.'

'All three of us,' Hoon said, helping himself to the larger of the two leather chairs. He met Logan's glare, and batted it back to him along with some waggling eyebrows of defiance.

Sensing the growing tension in the room, Sinead did her best to calm things down.

'Thank you, Mr Howard. We completely understand. I'm Detective Constable Sinead Bell, this is Detective Chief Inspector Logan.'

'You can call him Jack,' Hoon said. 'That's all right, isn't it, Jack?'

Logan chewed on his bottom lip. 'Fine. Of course.'

'Keeps it friendlier,' Hoon said. 'We're all friends here, right? Jack and I go way back, actually. He might look like a sack of room temperature shite, but he's actually a surprisingly decent—'

'She's dead, isn't she?'

Roman's voice cut through the chatter. He was knocking on in years—seventies, Logan guessed—but he looked fitter and sturdier than a lot of men half his age, and his voice resonated with a natural authority.

'We, uh, we don't know,' Sinead told him. 'There has been a discovery, though.'

'A body?' Roman asked, lowering himself into the only remaining chair.

'Remains, yes,' Sinead said, after a moment's pause. 'Not too far from here. I'm sorry to have to tell you that there are some signs that indicate that it may be your daughter.'

'Eleanor. Call her by her name,' Roman barked, like a strict old teacher correcting an unruly pupil while lamenting the outlawing of corporal punishment. 'She might not have liked it, but that was the one we chose for her. That was who she was.'

Sinead stole a sideways glance at Logan. He was masking it well, but she could tell he was as intrigued by that remark as she was. Something to come back to later.

'Eleanor. Yes. Sorry. I'm afraid we have reason to believe that the remains may be Eleanor's.'

Roman looked across to his sleeping wife and combed at his short grey beard with the tips of his calloused fingers. 'And, what? I need to come with you to identify her, do I?'

He asked the question like it was all a big inconvenience to him. Like he had better things to be doing with his time than confirming the identity of a dead loved one.

The bluntness of the question took Sinead aback, making her stumble over her response.

Fortunately, Logan was ready to step into the breach.

'Not at the moment, Mr Howard. Let's not worry about that for now. We're led to believe that Eleanor had a tattoo, though. Were you aware of that?'

'God. Yes. Painfully aware. That bloody thing. The arguments that caused. She thought it was funny.' His lips drew back in distaste, revealing some impressively well-maintained teeth for a man of his years. 'She and I had a very different understanding of humour. Isobel put it down to the age gap—I was pushing fifty when Eleanor inflicted herself upon us—but I personally just think it was because much of what amused her was crude, crass and juvenile.'

'Right. OK. I see.'

Even Logan seemed to be caught off guard now by the man's attitude. Hoon, however, hadn't batted an eyelid. Clearly, he'd heard this before.

'So, this tattoo, then…?' prompted the DCI.

Roman rolled his eyes and shook his head, making his feelings on the matter very much clear, even though he'd been doing a pretty admirable job of that already.

'Are you familiar with Oor Wullie, Detective Chief Inspector? The DC Thomson comic strip character. Spiky hair. Dungarees. Sits on an upturned bucket and likes playing with his wee pals. Loved and admired by generations of children and adults alike, myself included.'

'I'm aware of him, aye,' Logan confirmed.

'Good,' Roman said, and he seemed genuinely quite pleased by this. His face soon fell again, though. 'And you'll be familiar with drugs, I'd imagine, given your profession? Cannabis. Wacky baccy. *Marijuana*.'

He spoke the last word like a British holidaymaker addressing a waiter in a non-English speaking country, all slow enunciation and big, wide-open mouth movements.

'Pretty up to speed with that, aye,' Logan confirmed.

'Tell me, then, the thought of Oor Wullie'—he stabbed an emphatic finger in Logan's direction—'your Wullie, *a'body's Wullie*, smoking a big marijuana cigarette, Detective Chief Inspector—a child, remember. An innocent, fun-loving wee laddie. Mischievous, aye, but with a heart of gold. High as a kite, smoking drugs. Is that funny? Him, sitting there on his wee upturned bucket in his dungarees, eyes rolling back in his skull from the effects of the poison in his system. Is that funny?'

It wasn't. Of course, it wasn't. Everything about this whole situation was about as far away from funny as it was possible to be.

And yet, in that moment, Logan knew that he daren't look Bob Hoon in the eye.

'No. I don't find that funny at all,' he said, keeping his gaze fixed firmly on Roman.

'No! Exactly. Thank you!' Roman said, sitting back in his chair. 'Dudley D. Watkins would be absolutely bloody furious.'

'Sorry, who?' Sinead asked, flipping to a clean page of her notepad.

Roman's sigh was a long, drawn-out thing that whistled faintly through his hooked nose. 'Dudley D. Watkins, dear. The original illustrator of *Oor Wullie* and his sister publication, *The Broons*.' He held up a finger. 'Not the creator, mind. The artist. A lot of people make that mistake, but...'

He choked on the rest of the sentence. His head lowered quickly, hiding his sorrow and his shame.

'It's her, isn't it?' he whispered, and all his authority vanished like so much cartoon cannabis smoke into thin air. 'It's our Ellie.'

'Like we said, Mr Howard—' Sinead began, before Logan butted in.

'Yes. We think so. I'm sorry.'

There was a sniff from the older man that had a whiff of a whimper about it.

'Murdered?'

Logan hesitated, but only for a moment. 'At this stage, it would appear so, yes.'

Roman nodded. Or maybe his lowered head was just trembling as he fought to stifle his grief. Either way, he cleared his throat, thumbed at his eyes, then thanked the DCI for the directness of his answer.

He straightened up then, and the stern mask of indifference was fixed in place on his face once again.

'And what are you going to do about it?' he asked, staring Logan right in the eye. 'And please, no big gestures or empty promises, Detective Chief Inspector. They won't do you any credit. We're all adults here. My wife and I can handle the truth. We demand nothing less, in fact.'

Logan considered his next words carefully. 'We're going to investigate,' he said. 'We've already started. We're going to find out what happened to your daughter.'

'Eleanor.'

'To Eleanor,' Logan said. 'You didn't want empty promises, and I get that. But I can promise you one thing—we're going to do our damnedest to find out what happened to Eleanor, and to find whoever is responsible. We'll leave no stone unturned. We won't stop until they're brought to justice. I give you my word on that.'

'That was a fucking marvellous speech,' Hoon said, wiping an imaginary tear from his eye.

Logan didn't look at his former superintendent, but pointed a finger in his direction.

'He's going to have to keep out of it. He's going to get in our way. He'll slow us down.'

'The fuck?' Hoon protested. 'After everything I've done to help you before? That's fucking charming!'

'Were you in the military, Jack?' Roman asked, and Logan immediately saw how the rest of this conversation was going to play out.

'No,' he admitted.

'I was. Twenty-seven years. First Battalion, Royal Highland Fusiliers.' He snapped off a salute to nobody in particular. 'Mr Hoon here, he's an army man. I could tell the moment I met him. I trust army men, Detective Chief Inspector. You learn to. You have to. That's what keeps you alive.'

He stood up and tugged on the bottom of his tweed waistcoat, snapping out any creases that might have started to form while he was sitting.

'So, Mr Hoon is going to represent Isobel and I in this matter. I ask that you give him access to any and all information pertaining to Eleanor's death.'

Logan stood up, too, so he faced the other man across the coffee table. 'I'm afraid I can't do that. It's a live investigation. There are details that we aren't able to share with anyone, not even you.'

Roman gave an irritated shake of his head and checked his watch. Logan got the impression that the farmer was back to viewing this whole thing as an unfortunate inconvenience.

'Fine. But, I have matters to attend to. I've already this morning given Mr Hoon my thoughts on who could be responsible for Eleanor's disappearance.' His wiry white eyebrows dipped for a moment, before he added, 'Death. Who could be responsible for Eleanor's *death*.'

He looked over at his wife, still lying almost motionless on the bed, then gestured with the flat of one hand to the sitting room door.

'I'm sure, if one of you asks him very nicely, he'll be happy to pass that information on.'

–

'Here, what the fuck was all that about?' Hoon demanded when the front door of the farmhouse was closed behind them. 'I was trying to fucking big you up in there.'

Logan turned sharply, his face a dark map of shadows and crags. 'I don't need you bigging me up, Bob. I need you to stay out of our way. I know you're playing at being back in the polis, and fine. I don't give a shite. But if you interfere in our investigation, I'll arrest you myself. Is that clear?'

Hoon's forehead creased in confusion. He leaned past the looming DCI until he caught Sinead's eye.

'The fuck's up with this crabbit bastard? He finally realised that his big brown coat makes him look like a 1980s sex pest? High fucking time.'

For the second time that day, Sinead inserted herself into an argument between two men before it could escalate any further.

'Mr Howard said he'd told you who he thought might be involved,' she prompted.

Hoon shot Logan a sideways look, taking in the knotted brow and the scowling mouth.

'Aye,' he said, stepping out of the DCI's shadow. 'Mentioned it on the phone yesterday, then told me again this morning when I came and met him.'

'Tyler said you'd been on this for days,' Logan pointed out. 'You had him looking up tattoo places day before yesterday.'

Hoon sniffed. 'Aye. Well. That was the day your man in there got in touch. I poked about a bit from home, and said I'd come and see him in a day or two.' He looked off in the direction of the town, but the mist of drizzle hid it from view. 'Maybe didn't take it as seriously as I fucking should have. Maybe if I had done…'

Logan gritted his teeth, fighting back the next few words for as long as he could.

'She's been dead for days. She was dead before he phoned you.'

'Oh. Well, that's…' Hoon nodded slowly, then shrugged. 'I don't fucking know what it is. Oh, and fuck knows what's up with the wife, by the way. She's no' batted a fucking eyelid the whole time I was here. When I walked in, I thought she was fucking deid, but didn't have the heart to tell him.'

'Bob!' Logan hissed.

'Fuck's sake, all right! I'm getting to it!' Hoon spat back. 'It's someone at her old work. That's all he knows. He reckoned she was getting hassle from someone. Some guy, he reckons.'

'Hassle in what way?' Sinead asked.

'Dunno.' Hoon shrugged. 'By the sounds of it, she didn't tell him much. They didn't really speak. She spoke to the mother, apparently, but she's no' exactly being fucking forthcoming with the information. He reckoned the guy was a bit overly keen, though. Like, kept trying his hand, even when she told him she wasn't interested.'

'And where did she work?' Sinead asked.

'Family fucking Fun Factory. Fun House of Family fucking… I don't know. Some combination of words like that. Fun Family… Fuck knows. It's in town, apparently. Crazy golf. Bowling. All that sort of shite. It's got a giant fucking clown head for a front door, he tells me, so we'll struggle to fucking miss it.'

Logan shook his head. 'No. *We* won't, Bob. You're not coming.'

'Here, fucking come on, Jack. You heard what your man said. I'm his fucking representative.'

'Aye, maybe, but since when did we bring family members along to question suspects? I know you've been off the force a few years now, Bob, but things haven't changed that much.'

'This is my fucking case, too,' Hoon insisted.

'No. It isn't,' Logan told him. 'You're not a part of it, Bob. You're basically Roman's personal secretary.'

He reached into his pocket and thumbed the button of his car keys. Behind him, the BMW chirped as its headlights illuminated.

'Don't worry, though. If we decide there's any information that should be passed on to the family, you'll be the first to know.'

'Fuck's sake,' Hoon muttered. He gestured to the car. 'You can at least give me a lift into town, though, eh? I took the fucking bus down here 'cos Berta needed the car.' He pointed to Sinead. 'To look after your fucking weans, I should add.'

Logan turned and looked over his shoulder at the BMW.

He turned back to face Hoon again.

'Nah,' he said.

And then, with a spring in his step for the first time in days, he turned and walked off through the rain.

Chapter Six

'Aye, aye. What's all this?'

Constable Dave Davidson brought his wheelchair to a halt next to the desk of Detective Inspector Ben Forde. Under the desk, down by Ben's feet, Logan and Shona's dog, Taggart, opened one eye, checked there was nothing happening that required his immediate attention, then promptly fell back asleep.

Ben chewed hurriedly, carefully palmed the uneaten half of his Tunnock's caramel wafer so the constable wouldn't see it, and then tapped a finger on the holiday brochure spread on the desk in front of him.

'It's a cruise,' he said, swallowing down a mouthful of soggy, delicious, biscuity mush.

'Aye, I guessed that from all them pictures of big boats,' Dave said. 'You thinking of going on one?'

Ben wrinkled his nose like he wasn't keen on the idea, but then nodded. 'Moira's got it into her head that it'd be a fun adventure for us. A week cruising around Europe. Five countries in seven days. Or seven countries in five days, maybe? I forget. Either way, it sounds like a lot of bloody hassle to me.'

Dave wheeled himself over to his own desk. 'Didn't think she'd be into that sort of thing,' he said. 'You know, because there's other people there. When I've met her, she's never struck me as a fan of, like, human beings in general.'

'Oh, no, you're wrong there. Well, I mean, aye, individually she doesn't like them, but she loves big groups like you get on stuff like this,' Ben said, having a quick nibble of his chocolate-covered wafer while the constable's back was turned. 'She actively enjoys annoying people, see? It's one of the few things she takes real pleasure in. And this would give her a chance to wind a lot of them up all at the same time. She says that's the main reason she wants to go—not to see the places, but to "shite in some stranger's cereal". I'm assuming metaphorically,' he concluded, though he didn't seem wholly certain.

Dave reached his desk, paused to give this some thought, then shrugged. 'Fair play to her. She clearly knows what she likes.'

Ben chuckled. 'Aye. She'll be up at the crack of dawn to put towels on all the sun loungers round the pool. Because they've got pools. Actual swimming pools, can you believe that? On the boat. More than one on some of them. There's a big twisty slide thing you can go down on a few of them, too, that shoots you straight into the pool. Whoosh!'

'Aye?'

'Aye.' Ben winced and shook his head. 'Course, knowing my luck, the ship'd swing a hard left when I was halfway down, and I'd suddenly find myself suspended in mid-air above the Atlantic bloody Ocean.'

'If that happens, I reckon falling in the sea'll be the least of your worries. You'll have completely broken the laws of physics,' Dave pointed out. 'We'll all be in trouble.'

'Ha!' Ben put his hand over his mouth and chuckled. It was all a cunning ruse so he could slyly scoff the last bit of biscuit. 'Fair point.' He gave the brochure a nudge, like he was fending it off. 'But I don't think it's for me. It's all bingo and karaoke. And silent discos. Have you ever heard of that? A silent disco.'

Dave confirmed that he had.

'What is it, exactly? Just a load of folk dancing around in silence? How the hell does that work?' Ben crossed his arms and sat back in his seat. 'In my day, if we saw someone dancing when there was no music, we didn't call it a silent disco, we called it a mental breakdown.'

Dave cupped his hands over his ears. 'Aye, they've got headphones on, like. They're listening to music on them, they're not just dancing away to nothing.'

'Oh.' Ben stared blankly out of the window for a moment, watching the rain battering against the glass. 'That makes a lot more sense, right enough.'

He drummed his fingers on the desk, then turned back to Dave.

'There's some folk retire on them, would you believe? On cruise ships, I mean. Just spend the rest of their days on board, roaming around the ocean, doing bloody quizzes and… and… *jazz aerobics* all day long.' He shook his head firmly. 'No. That's no' for me, that.'

'Decent buffets on them, though, I hear,' Dave said.

'Aye?' Ben reached over and pulled the brochure closer. 'I didn't see that bit.'

'Can't see you retiring to one of them, though. Can't see you ever retiring at all!'

Ben didn't look up. His only reply was a short, soft, 'Ha!' which didn't really say much of anything.

He still had his head down, searching the contents page for details of the on-ship catering, when the door to the Incident Room opened and Detective Superintendent Mitchell came striding in.

Once again, Taggart woke up just enough to assess the situation. Once again, he concluded that it didn't warrant him getting involved.

There was something different about the Detective Superintendent today, Ben noted. Usually, she was pristinely turned out, her white shirt glowing, not a hair out of place. She was short for a police officer, but what she lacked in height she made up for in presence. Whenever Mitchell was in the room, it was clear to everyone just who was in charge.

Today, though, her hair had a little more frizz to it, and her shirt was lined by almost three full creases.

By her usual standards, she'd really let herself go. The way she clutched her enormous mug of coffee with both hands added to the effect, and Ben couldn't help but comment.

'Rough night, ma'am?' he asked.

Mitchell's expression darkened, and for a moment it looked like Ben might regret, if not the question, then at least the tone in which he'd asked it.

But then, the detective superintendent shrugged and shook her head. 'Rough morning. Three meetings so far, two more to go.'

'Rather you than me,' Ben told her. 'That's why I settled at this level. I don't have to have meetings with the *High Heid Yins*, and no bugger expects me to chase anyone. It's pretty much ideal.'

'Can't interest you in a swap, then?' Mitchell asked.

'Not on your nelly,' Ben told her. 'But I'm sure, between the three of us, we can find a way to get you out of your other meetings.'

'Nosebleed,' Dave suggested. 'That's what I do. Gets you out of anything.'

Ben gestured over to the constable to suggest he was onto something, then frowned. 'Hang on. That was the excuse you gave for not coming to Moira's surprise birthday lunch last month.'

Dave looked at him for a few seconds, saying nothing, then he tilted his head back, pinched the bridge of his nose, and tutted. 'There's another one started.'

'Aye, ya bloody chancer,' Ben said. He chuckled, then rotated his chair until the detective superintendent had his full attention. 'What can we do for you, ma'am? I'm assuming it's not a social call?'

'Oh, to have the time,' Mitchell said. 'I've heard from Jack. He thinks he has an ID on the victim. He wants to set up base here, and travel up and down to Aviemore as needs be. Seems like a lot of unnecessary mileage to me.'

'He'll have his reasons, I'm sure,' Ben said, leaping to his friend's defence.

'Hmm,' Mitchell mused. 'And would that reason have anything to do with the daughter of a certain Russian gangster?'

'I wouldn't know a thing about that, ma'am.'

'How's it all going, anyway? How's it working out?'

'I wouldn't know a thing about that, ma'am,' Ben repeated.

Mitchell's face remained almost completely impassive, aside from the slight upwards tug at one corner of her mouth.

'Very well, Detective Inspector. We'll leave it there.' She raised her mug like she was toasting him, then headed for the door. 'Oh, and when it comes to cruises, Transatlantic is the only way to go.'

Ben glanced down at the brochure, then looked back up in time to see the door swinging closed at the Detective Superintendent's back.

'Right, then,' he declared, folding over the glossy magazine. 'We should probably make a start on the Big Board.'

'I'll check the inbox and start printing off what we've got,' Dave said, firing up his ancient computer with a prod of a finger.

'Good lad,' Ben replied.

His watch gave a bleep, and his face lit up when he saw the time. Under the desk, Taggart scrambled to his feet, his stumpy tail wagging enthusiastically.

'But first, I think a wee spot of lunch is in order!'

Chapter Seven

'You reckon this is the place, boss?'

Tyler leaned down by Logan's car, peering in through the narrow gap the DCI had opened at the top of the driver's side window.

Behind him, a neon 'Family Fun Factory!' sign flashed in the gaping mouth of a giant fibreglass clown's head.

'I'd say there's a pretty good chance this is it, son, aye,' Logan confirmed.

Tyler grinned and raised both thumbs, apparently missing the sarcasm.

Logan rolled the window back up, leaving Tyler alone in the rain, then turned his attention to DC Bell in the passenger seat beside him.

'Right. I'll take Blunderboy in with me and see what we can find out. You go get yourself back up the road.'

'Are you sure, though, sir? You might need me here.'

'You know what Ben's like with the Big Board,' Logan replied. 'I mean, he's no Tammi-Jo, thank Christ—it won't all be love hearts, smiley faces and cartoon frogs—but he'll make an arse of it. We both know it. So, I want you there until it's up and running.'

'OK, then. No bother, sir,' Sinead said. 'And it's just a coincidence that I'll be nearer the twins, aye?'

'Just a stroke of good luck. Nothing more to it than that,' Logan confirmed, but a smile passed between them.

'Thank you, sir.'

'Better get a shifty on before your other half catches his death out there.'

Sinead's smile widened. 'Good enough for him,' she said.

But with that, she pulled up her hood, got out of the car, and ran around the front until she met up with her husband. Logan stayed where he was, watching the windows start to steam up, and giving them a moment to say whatever they needed to say.

Eventually, Tyler handed his wife the car keys. As Sinead set off for the other vehicle, Logan threw open his door, muttered darkly when his foot found another puddle, and pulled the collar of his coat tighter against the back of his neck.

'Right, then,' he said, regarding the garish frontage of the building before them with clear distaste. 'Let's go see what we can find out.'

–

A lad in his late teens, with a face full of make-up, sat on a tall stool behind the front counter, swivelling slowly back and forth as his thumb swiped idly upwards on his phone.

He wore his hair in a tall quiff that looked like it had been sculpted out of tar, and the flicks of dark liner at the corners of his eyes gave him a vaguely Egyptian sort of look. Although, this was offset slightly by the green and orange striped T-shirt he wore with a laughing clown logo roughly above where his left nipple would be.

A plastic name badge introduced him as 'Phoenix', and Logan immediately concluded that he must've picked that one out for himself. Either that, or his parents had hated him from day one.

Though he had to have heard the door blowing closed, and couldn't possibly have missed the clumping of the detectives' approaching footsteps, Phoenix didn't look up from his phone screen. Instead, he just stared vacantly at the videos scrolling past as he dabbed a glossy lip balm onto his bottom lip with the tip of a straightened pinkie.

It was only when Logan slammed the flat of a hand down on the counter that the young man acknowledged them. Even then, there was no real urgency to it.

'Welcome to The Family Fun Factory,' he said in a bored drawl. His gaze flitted from Logan to Tyler, sizing them up. 'Are you here for bowling or golf?'

'Eh, neither,' Tyler said.

'Go-karting's off. It's too wet,' the staff member said. 'If you just want the restaurant, it's through that way, but we're out of hot dogs. Toilets are for customers only.'

He gestured across the cluttered main foyer of the building, with its cardboard cut-out clowns promoting a rolling series of current and upcoming special offers. 'Fun' circus music trumpeted from ceiling-mounted speakers, and an assortment of flickering signs helped turn the whole place into a sort of external migraine that did nothing to lift Logan's already downbeat mood.

'We're looking for the manager,' the DCI intoned.

Phoenix slipped his phone into his pocket. He blew a bubble of gum that he'd been chewing away on, then burst it with his tongue.

'Why?'

'That's none of your business, son,' Logan told him.

The DCI had arranged his face into one of his more intimidating expressions, but Phoenix either hadn't noticed this or wasn't remotely bothered by it.

'It is my business if you're going to complain about me,' he countered. 'What am I meant to have done? Is it because I was on my phone? My mum's in hospital. She might message. It's important.'

'You were looking at videos.'

Phoenix tutted. 'Well, I mean, duh. I'm not just going to stare at the message app waiting for her to text me, am I? I'm not a psycho.'

Logan's hand was still pressed flat on the countertop. The wood gave an audible creak as his fingers gripped it like a claw.

Beside him, Tyler hurriedly produced his warrant card and held it up for the employee to see. 'It's not about you. It's a police matter. We really need to speak to the manager.' He returned the ID to his pocket. 'Is he around?'

'*She*,' Phoenix corrected, shooting the DC a look that said he was disappointed by this blatant misogyny. 'Is *she* around? And yes. She is.'

Logan's fist thumped the counter. 'Can you get your finger out your arse and go get her, then?'

Phoenix stopped chewing his bubble gum just long enough to mumble a 'sake', then he invited them to take a seat between two cardboard clowns while he set off to find the person in charge.

Tyler took one of the offered seats and pulled his wet jacket to the side so it wasn't encroaching onto the chair beside him. Logan didn't sit down, however, and instead just paced back and forth, leaving a criss-crossed trail of rain droplets on the vinyl floor behind him.

'You all right, boss?' Tyler ventured.

'Fine.'

'Right. Good.' The detective constable shifted on the hard plastic seat. 'It's just, I thought you were going to rip that kid's head off.'

Logan just grunted and continued to pace from side to side. The cardboard clowns that flanked the seats seemed to be dressed like golfers. Although, to be fair, there was a big crossover in the fashion sense of both groups.

Somewhere further back in the building, a giggling recorded voice announced a 'Ho-ho-hole in one!' and some young children erupted into cheers.

'I know you'd probably rather talk to Ben, or Hamza, or Sinead, or… Well, pretty much anyone, boss,' Tyler continued. 'But, if there's anything I can help with…'

Logan reached one end of the route he'd been carving out for himself, turned as if to head back the other way, then sighed.

The whole row of chairs shook as he sat down next to Tyler. 'Harris,' he said.

The DC's eyes widened. 'Shite. What is it? What's he done?'

'What? No.' Logan shook his head and scowled, like he was regretting this already. He ran a hand through his hair before continuing. 'He was already a teenager when you all moved in together, wasn't he?'

'Eh, not quite, but not far off, boss. How come?'

Logan exhaled slowly and stared straight ahead. Another cardboard clown informed him of a Buy One Get One Free deal on bowling.

'Was it hard? You know, that relationship? You coming in like that? Did he push back?'

'Is this about you and Olivia Maximuke?' Tyler asked. When Logan failed to reply, he shrugged. 'Wasn't particularly hard, boss, I have to say. A bit, maybe. Think he was just sort of sussing me out, really, seeing how far he could push his luck. It had mostly just been him and Sinead for a few years, so it was all new. Sinead generally sorted him out, though. And I'd known him for a wee while by that point, so it wasn't like we were going in cold.'

Logan clicked his tongue against the back of his teeth and nodded. That made sense. He'd known Olivia for a few years, too, though during that time he'd used her as a pawn to entrap and arrest her father, which didn't exactly feel like a great foundation on which to build a relationship.

'I suppose it was a bit strained for a while,' Tyler continued. 'And he wasn't dealing with half the stuff Olivia's gone through.'

Logan turned to look at him for the first time since the conversation started. 'His parents were killed in a car accident and he was held at knifepoint by a murderer. Two different murderers on two different occasions, in fact.'

'God, aye. So he was,' Tyler muttered. He bit down on his bottom lip, then suddenly smiled, brightening. 'Well, in that case, if it worked out all right with us, it'll work out with you and Olivia, too, boss. You just need to give it time, and maybe, you know, be a bit less'—he flapped a hand up and down, indicating the whole of the DCI—'this.'

'What the hell's that meant to mean? Less what?'

'Just, like, less angry. Less like you want to rip someone's spine out with your bare hands. Maybe just start by not scowling as much.'

The look on Logan's face turned Tyler's smile into an anxious shadow of its former self.

'Or keep it up. Scowl more. Whatever you think yourself, boss.'

'Officers?'

'Oh, thank God,' Tyler whispered, springing to his feet as a woman in her fifties shuffled across the foyer to meet them.

He had never seen such a contrast between the brightness of someone's clothing and the drabness of their demeanour. He offered out a hand, and the woman audibly sighed before shaking it.

'Phoenix said you wanted to talk to me,' she said. 'I have eight minutes until my shift's over. If you can put up with the smell in my office, then I'm prepared to give you four of them.'

-

She wasn't joking about the office. Tyler gasped as they entered the room and a smell like week-old rotten fish assaulted them from all directions.

'Bloody hell, what is that?' he asked.

'We don't know,' the manager replied. 'People have looked into it, but nobody's any the wiser. It comes and goes, though. You should try being in here in August. Your eyes'll be bleeding.'

She indicated a teetering pile of confectionery and crisp boxes that lined one wall of the compact, eight-by-six-foot room.

'I'd open the window, but I don't know where it is. I'm not even sure there's one there. I mean, they told me there's one behind all that stuff, but God knows.'

'Maybe we should leave that open, boss?' Tyler wheezed. He grimaced when Logan finished closing the door, cutting off the airflow and trapping them in there with the smell. 'Or not.'

'That's a minute up,' the manager announced, checking her watch. 'What do you need?'

Logan didn't particularly appreciate being rushed, but he respected the woman's clear contempt for authority, so he pressed on.

'Eleanor Howard,' he began.

'Oh, surprise, surprise. What's she done? Punched a traffic warden?'

'No.'

'Shagged a traffic warden?'

'I don't think that's a criminal offence,' Tyler remarked.

The manager shuddered. 'If you've seen the ones round here, it should be. But, anyway, she doesn't work here any more. She's not my problem. Thankfully.'

'When did she leave?' Logan asked.

'Months ago. Right after the big bust-up.'

Out of the corner of his eye, Logan saw Tyler take out his notebook.

'Bust-up?' the DCI pressed.

'Aye. Her and Sandra laid into each other on the crazy golf course. Completely fucked the wee windmill. It hasn't rotated since.'

'Sandra?' said Tyler. 'Sandra Hogg?'

'Aye. That's her. Another bloody liability I'm well shot of. One minute left, by the way.'

'What were they fighting about?' Logan asked.

'God knows. I didn't ask. I just told them they were both fired and sent them packing. I tell you, though, Eleanor got off lightly. That Sandra's a bloody head case. Ellie's lucky she lived to tell the tale.'

The detectives exchanged a look before Logan continued. 'Was there anyone else giving Eleanor any trouble? Or anyone she was particularly close with?'

The manager sighed. 'God. I don't know. Most of the teenagers in town have worked here at some point. I mean, I do care about these kids, but fuck me, they make it hard sometimes. I can't be expected to keep track of all their comings and goings. I'm not their mother.'

She checked her watch again. Rather than tell them time was up, though, she appeared to soften a little.

'Look, Ellie's a good kid underneath it all, just troubled, I think. The stuff with her mum… It must be rough. But she was into all sorts. Underage drinking—they all are, mind you—but drugs, too, I think, in recent years. There was a guy who used to hang around waiting for her after her shift some nights. Older. Dirty looking. Thirties, maybe.'

'You got a name?'

'Not a clue, no. Ellie never mentioned him, and I never asked.' She put her hands on her hips. 'What is it she's done, anyway? Is she in trouble?'

'Not as such, no,' Logan said. 'Is there someone who can get us a list of everyone Ellie worked with?'

The manager looked at both detectives in turn. Logan could practically see the cogs whirring as she ran through the various scenarios that could have brought them to her door before finally settling on one that made her jaw tighten and her lips draw together.

'Uh, yes,' she said, and all thoughts of her shift ending appeared to have been forgotten. 'I'm sure that can be arranged.'

Chapter Eight

Hamza was on the phone when they made it back to Aviemore Police Station, Tyler having already texted ahead with the update on Sandra Hogg. He gave a thumbs up when the DC and the DCI entered, thanked the person on the other end of the line, then returned the handset to the cradle.

'They're bringing her in,' he announced.

He tried to spin in his chair to face them, before remembering it was a solid wooden seat, and not his usual one from the office. Half-standing, he lifted the chair a few inches off the floor, then waddled around with it until he was looking their way.

'Uniform's already picked her up. She was mooching around outside Tesco, apparently.'

'They know her?' Logan asked.

'Aye, sounds like it. She's been pulled in a few times for assault, drunk and disorderlies, and generally making an arse of herself. Hence her being on community service.'

'Where she just happened to be the one to find Ellie's body in the woods,' Tyler pointed out.

'Did you get the list of names?' Hamza asked.

'Not yet. She's emailing it through,' Tyler told him. 'Shouldn't be long, though. She's staying back to do it. How she copes in that office, though, I don't know. It stinks. I thought I was going to throw up. Did you not, boss?'

'Eh?' Logan had become distracted by his phone. He tore his eyes from it and looked up at the DC. 'Oh. No, because I've no' got the constitution of a child.'

'What does it smell like?' Hamza asked.

'I don't know. How would you describe it, boss?'

Logan was back looking at his phone and didn't appear to be listening.

'Sort of, fish, I suppose,' Tyler explained. 'Like, rotten and fishy. But quite meaty at the same time, and a bit shitty, like a walrus waltzed in and did a big dirty protest in the corner.'

Hamza raised his eyebrows. 'That's quite a vivid image,' he remarked. 'Thanks for that. Sorry I missed it. Sounds like a fun time.'

Logan returned his phone to his pocket and shut down the discussion. 'You two all right handling Sandra Hogg?'

Hamza nodded. 'Aye, sir. No bother.'

'What's up, boss?'

'Shona's going to be finishing up with the PM soon. Easier for me to head up the road and see what's what than do it over the phone.'

'Fair enough, boss. Don't you worry about us,' Tyler assured him. 'She's one wee lassie.'

He flopped down into a seat. The solid wooden chair had absolutely no give to it whatsoever, and pain jolted all the way up the length of his spine until it arrived as a grimace and a grunted, 'Ooyahbastard.'

The detective constable took a moment to readjust himself, and to erase the expression of pain from his face.

'I'm sure she's nothing that me and Ham can't handle.'

–

'This is a bloody nightmare,' Tyler whispered, as he and Hamza huddled together outside the interview room. 'She's running rings around us in there!'

'She's running rings around you, you mean,' Hamza corrected.

'She keeps twisting everything I'm saying.'

'Aye, I noticed. She nearly had you crying at one point.'

'What?! Did she nothing!' Tyler protested. 'That was me getting annoyed.'

'Oh, aye. I forgot that your eyes well up and your voice goes all shaky when you get annoyed, right enough.'

'Aye, exactly. You know that! We've talked about that!'

'Sorry,' Hamza said, fighting back a smirk. He tilted his head to the door beside them. 'You ready to go again?'

Tyler groaned. 'God. Aye. Fine. OK. But if she starts asking me what one of the Muppets it is I remind her of again, I'm going to lose my shit.'

Hamza nodded in understanding. 'What, and start crying?'

Tyler gave the DS a thump on the arm. 'No! Shut it, you.' He straightened his tie and pushed back his shoulders. 'Come on, then. Let's go and get this over with.'

He opened the door and led the way inside, then closed it again behind DS Khaled.

Sitting across the interview table, Sandra Hogg uncrossed her arms just long enough to point in the DC's direction.

'Beaker! That's who it is. That's who you remind me of!'

'What? No way. No way I'm Beaker!' Tyler objected. 'With the big nose and the…?' He tutted and pulled out one of the chairs across from her. 'I'm not getting into it.'

Sandra grinned, showing a row of yellow teeth and one gold one. '*Mee-mee-mee-mee-mee-me-me-me.*'

'What's that meant to be?' Tyler demanded.

'I think that's meant to be Beaker,' Hamza said, taking the seat beside him.

Tyler frowned. 'Beaker doesn't talk like that, does he?'

'He does, aye,' Sandra confirmed. 'He talks exactly like that.'

Tyler looked between his fellow detective and the suspect sitting on the other side of the table. 'What one am I thinking of, then?' he demanded. Then, annoyed with himself for being drawn into the conversation again, he said, 'Doesn't matter. This isn't funny, Sandra. We're not laughing here. You could be in big trouble.'

'Ooh, scary,' Sandra replied, pretending to nibble on her fingernails. 'I'm shaking.'

'You should be, actually,' Tyler insisted. 'You should be worried.'

'I'm trembling in my boots! Or, I would be, if I still had them on.'

She grinned proudly as she lifted a leg up onto the table, revealing a dirty grey sock with a big toe sticking out of it. The heel left a shiny damp streak on the tabletop, like the silvery trail of a slug. She gave the toe a waggle, flashing them a glimpse of a thick, yellow, fungal-infected toenail.

'Jesus. Your foot's bloody horrible,' Tyler told her.

Sandra's smile faltered. 'What?'

'It's like a troll's hoof or something.'

'Fuck off!' The foot was slid back out of sight under the table. 'It is not.'

'It is! It's like Shrek's been wearing the wrong-size shoes. Proper stinks in here now, too,' the DC announced, wafting the smell away from in front of his face with a flapping hand. 'When did you last shower?'

Sandra's pug-like features became even more of a grimace. 'He can't fucking talk to me like that,' she told Hamza.

'Eh, I can, actually,' Tyler said, jumping in before the DS had a chance. 'And are you sure there's nothing you want us to get you? Glass of water? Bucket of swill? Toothbrush, maybe?'

Across from him, Sandra leaned forwards and gripped the table, like she was getting ready to rip it right out of its fixing and flip it into the air.

Instead, the smile crept back across her face. 'Nice one, Beaker,' she said, tipping her head towards him in a gesture of respect. 'You're actually all right. I quite like you.'

'Aye?' Tyler asked, his pitch rising in surprise. He lowered it again, then nodded back to her. 'I mean, aye. Good. Maybe we can get on with this now.'

Sandra ran her hands across the surface of the table like she was polishing it, then sat back. 'Fire on.'

Hamza opened the folder on the desk in front of him. 'Right. Well, like we already said, Sandra, you're not here because you're in any trouble. We just wanted to ask you a few questions about the discovery you made today in the woods just off the A9.'

'I didn't discover nothing,' she said.

'I thought you phoned it in?'

'Aye, but I didn't find it. Seamus found it. Are we talking about the bag of feet, aye?'

'What else would we be talking about?' Tyler asked, but Hamza quietened him with a nudge of his foot below the table.

'That's right,' the DS said. 'We saw the transcript of the 999 call. You said, "We just found a bag of feet." *We*. Just to be clear, you're saying now that you weren't involved?'

Sandra sighed. 'Fuck's sake. It's not difficult. Seamus found the bag. Jonathan cut it open. We all saw what was inside. I called the cops. I didn't find it, but I was involved in the finding of it.' Her square-ish head tick-tocked between them. 'That clear enough for you, lads?'

'Fine,' Hamza said. 'What can you tell us about it?'

Sandra shrugged. 'Bag of feet. Or, I don't know, maybe other bits. Just saw the one foot. It'd been cut off at the top. At the ankle bit.'

'According to the Community Payback supervisor, you didn't seem disturbed by it.'

'It's a foot. Just a foot. Not exactly scary, is it? I've seen feet before.'

'Aye, we noticed,' Tyler said, glancing at the sweat streak on the table. 'With feet like them, no wonder this one didn't bother you.'

Hamza spoke over the end of the sentence, heading off any further back and forth between the detective constable and the witness.

'They're usually attached to a leg, though. This one wasn't, was it?'

'No,' Sandra admitted.

'And it still didn't bother you?'

She shook her head. 'No. The sight of blood or that doesn't put me up or down.'

Hamza drummed his fingers on the top sheet of the open folder, and Sandra's eyes were drawn down to her arrest record.

'Aye, so we noticed,' the DS said. 'You've been involved in quite a few altercations over the years, Sandra. Why's that, do you think?'

'Because some people just need headbutting,' she replied.

Hamza smiled. 'Aye. Maybe some of them do, right enough.' He clasped his hands. 'What about Eleanor Howard? You had a run-in with her a few months back. What did she do that warranted headbutting?'

Sandra's unkempt eyebrows shot up her forehead, like they were trying to make their break from the rest of the face below.

'Fuuuuuck!' she gasped, drawing the word out. 'Ellie? Was it Ellie? Was Ellie the feet?!'

'The remains haven't yet been identified,' Hamza said, but the woman across the table paid him no heed.

'Fuuuuuuck! That's mental. Holy shit! I bet that is her foot! She used to piss about with nail polish!' She gripped her head like failure to do so would cause it to explode. 'Fuuuuuck! No way!'

Hamza cleared his throat. 'Like we say, we haven't officially identified—'

'Hang on,' Sandra snapped, leaning sharply forwards again. 'You're not trying to pin this shit on me, are you? You don't think I killed her and cut her up?'

'Oh, look! Now she's worried!' Tyler declared, elbowing Hamza. 'Look at her. Now she's panicking.'

'Fuck off, Beaker! No, I'm not!' Sandra crossed her arms and slouched back, shrugging with a practised indifference. 'I didn't do it, so you've got fuck all on me.'

'Ignore my colleague, Sandra,' Hamza said, shooting Tyler a warning look. 'We don't think you did anything. We're just following up on some information we were given so we can tick it off our To Do list. That's all.'

Sandra eyed them with suspicion. 'And what? After that, I can just go?'

'As long as we've got it ticked off our list, sure. No bother,' Hamza assured her. 'So, you had a fight? You and Eleanor?'

Sandra ground her teeth together, picked at a corner of the wood veneer table, then nodded.

'What was the fight about?'

A shrug. A grunt.

'You don't know?' Hamza asked. 'From what we were told, it was a pretty full-on scrap.'

'You broke a wee windmill,' Tyler added, in a reproachful tone that suggested this was perhaps the worst crime of all.

'But you say you've no idea how it started?' DS Khaled concluded.

'She called me a dyke.' Sandra's eyes flitted up to theirs, just for a split second. 'Aye, like a lesbian, I mean. She said I was a lesbian.'

Hamza nodded. 'And that made you angry? Her questioning your sexuality?'

'What? No. I am a dyke,' Sandra said. 'It was her using it like it was a fucking insult that bothered me. Like it was something I should be ashamed of. Like it was dirty. That's what riled me up.'

'So you hit her?' Tyler asked.

'No. I more sort of threw her,' Sandra replied. She smiled fondly at the memory. 'By the hair. Sort of swung her around. She threw a golf ball at me and then tried to hit me with one of the metal flags, so I shoved her, and she fell into the windmill.'

'And what then?' Hamza prompted.

'Nothing. That was it. Manager called us into her office and gave us both our marching orders. Paid us for the week up until then, though, which was decent. Mind you, she tried to take it back when she realised the windmill was fucked.'

'And what happened with you and Eleanor after that? Did you continue fighting?'

Sandra shook her head. 'We went to the pub. In the hotel. Right next to the Fun Factory. We got smashed and had a laugh about it.'

'Are there any witnesses to that?' Tyler asked.

Sandra's eyes narrowed again. 'Aye. Loads. I didn't kill her. Ellie was all right. Total fucking psycho, but all right.'

Hamza jumped on the remark. 'What makes you say that? What makes you call her a psycho?'

'Well, OK, no. Maybe not a psycho. But she was wild,' Sandra said, and the detectives saw a glimmer of admiration go fluttering across her face. 'Drinking in school. Giving teachers shit all the time. One day, she sucked off a sixth year in the French corridor. Everyone watching. Just knelt down and sucked him off. She didn't give a fuck. Think that's why she got kicked out.'

'That'd do it, right enough,' Tyler said.

'She had some boyfriend guy, actually,' Sandra said. Her chair squeaked as she sat back. 'Older guy. Much older, like twice her age. Saw him waiting for her a few times after work, too.'

Tyler clicked the top of his pen and scribbled a note in his pad.

'Any idea who he was?' Hamza asked.

'No. Don't think she mentioned his name. People just call him "Moomin".'

'Why's that?'

Sandra shrugged. 'Because he looks like one of the Moomins.'

'What?' Tyler looked up from his notes. 'How? Are they not, like, space hippos or something?'

'Dunno.'

'How does a human being look like a Moomin? Was he in an accident?' the DC demanded. 'Or is there something wrong with your eyes, maybe? Is that the problem? Between Moomins and Muppets… Are you sure you don't need glasses?'

'Tyler,' Hamza said, before turning his attention back to Sandra. 'Anything else you can tell us about him?'

'Not really. Though…' She grimaced like she was passing a kidney stone. 'Actually, he might've been Matt? Aye, his name, I mean, not his finish. Maybe, Matt? Could've been Matt.'

'Matt.' Hamza wrote the name on his pad.

'Or Paul. Might have been Paul, actually.'

Hamza wrote the word 'Paul' underneath the word 'Matt'.

'They're quite different names,' he pointed out.

'You sure you're not taking the piss?' Tyler asked.

'No. It's one of them. I think. I don't know, though,' Sandra said, suddenly doubting herself. 'Like I said, most people just call him Moomin because—'

'Don't say he looked like a Moomin,' Tyler warned. 'He couldn't have. Look.'

He stood up, took his phone from his pocket, and opened the search app.

After a moment, he thrust the phone out for the woman across the table to see.

'See? That's a Moomin.'

'I know,' Sandra said. 'That's what he looks like!'

'How?! They're doughy wee hippos!' Tyler cried. 'Has he got elephantiasis of the chin? No one alive looks like that.'

'Matt does. Or Paul. Or whatever his name is. David, maybe? Dunno.' She clicked her fingers. 'Hang on. Seamus'll know.'

Tyler returned his phone to his pocket and sat down again, still smarting about the Moomin thing.

'Seamus?' Hamza said. 'As in Seamus Starkey, who was with you when you found the remains?'

'Aye. He was totally in love with Ellie. All through school. He was the only one that didn't watch when she sucked off that guy. He just ran away greeting.' She winced. 'He's going to be gutted when he finds out it was her in the bag.'

Hamza nodded slowly. 'He still had a thing for her, then?'

'God, aye. He was right into her. He used to sit there in Old Kenzie's history class, giving Moomin the evil eye when he was waiting out in the car park for her. Don't think Moomin ever noticed, though. Or maybe he did but didn't care, since Seamus was a scrawny wee fourth year, and he was a man in his early thirties. I bet he knows his name, though. He'll have found it out. Think he followed him around for a while, trying to scare him away from Ellie. But, again, scrawny wee fucker, thirty-year-old man.' She sniffed. 'Want me to phone him?'

'Eh, no. No,' Hamza said. He clicked the top of his pen to retract the nib. 'Maybe best if we have a chat with him ourselves.'

–

It was Hamza who saw Sandra to the door of the station, mostly out of fear that she and Tyler might come to blows.

When he returned to the briefing room, he was immediately confronted by an A4 sheet of paper, still slightly warm from the printer.

'What's this?' Hamza asked, glancing at the page.

'It's that list the boss asked for. At the Fun Factory place. The list of people who worked with Eleanor.'

'Oh, aye?' Hamza said.

Before he could start to read it, Tyler whipped it back out of his hands and pointed emphatically at a name halfway down the page.

'Aye. And it turns out that one of the people she worked with is Seamus Starkey!'

Chapter Nine

Logan looked down at the hand that was shaking his, then followed the line of the arm all the way to where a young man with movie star looks was smiling up at him.

'Detective Chief Inspector Logan. Wow. In the flesh. I can't believe it. Dr Maguire's told me so much about you. I feel like I'm meeting royalty.'

'Well, just as long as it's no' Prince Andrew,' Logan replied. He thought for a moment. 'Or any of the rest of them, actually. I'm guessing you're Neville?'

'That's me!' Neville's smile widened, and Logan got the feeling that, had he been an impressionable lassie in her late teens or early twenties, it would've been nigh-on a religious experience.

The man wasn't just attractive, he was *magnificent.*

Logan hated him immediately. Although, to be fair, he hadn't been a fan of him before that moment, given how often Shona had remarked on her new assistant's remarkable good looks.

Having only just glimpsed him briefly in the background of a video call before, Logan had written Shona's glowing testimony off as a wind-up. But, now that he was face to face with the bastard, he realised that she'd been playing it down.

The DCI tensed his grip, lightly crushing the other man's hand, before letting it go.

'Shona around?' he asked.

Neville's smile didn't falter, even as he gave his fingers a quick flex to pop all the knuckles back into alignment.

'She's through in the mortuary,' he replied, indicating the double swing doors at the back of the office with a tilt of a head that might well have been sculpted from marble. 'I'm sure she won't mind you going straight through, though.'

He stepped aside and held out an arm, inviting Logan to pass.

'It really was a pleasure to meet you at last,' Neville said, practically bowing as Logan headed for the door.

'Eh, right. Aye. Fair enough.'

'Oh! Jack! Sorry, can I call you Jack? Do you mind?'

Logan did mind, actually, but he couldn't exactly make a big song and dance about it without looking like a right arsehole. 'It's fine. What is it?'

'I'm finishing up in a few minutes, so can you let Dr Maguire know that her sandwich is in the fridge, as usual?'

'Her sandwich?'

Neville's smile became so dazzling that Logan was all but forced back a step. 'Yes. And tell her it's her favourite.'

Logan's eyes darted to the fridge in the corner of the office. 'Tuna?' he said.

One of Neville's glorious eyebrows lowered, while the other raised. 'Eh, no. Chicken, bacon, and banana.' He winked, still giving it both barrels with his smile. 'We'll get her weaned off those Pot Noodles yet, eh?' He gave a little wave, chirped, 'Ciao!' and then pulled on a coat that immediately made him look like a male model.

'Aye,' Logan muttered, then he waited for Neville to leave before quietly adding, 'Good fucking riddance,' and heading on through to the mortuary.

The post-mortem slab looked different today. There was no carefully covered body filling it from one end to the other, with the toes sticking out at the bottom.

Instead, a plastic sheet about the size of a bath towel had been draped over the various pieces that made up what was left of Eleanor Howard. Or what they'd found of her, at least.

'Oh, you just missed Neville!' Shona said when Logan entered. 'He was just here a second ago.'

'No, I saw him.'

'Ah!' The pathologist grinned and gave her eyebrows a suggestive waggle. 'See? Didn't I tell you he was fecking gorgeous?'

'You may have mentioned it once or twice,' Logan said. He shrugged. 'Can't say I see it myself.'

'Bollocks you don't. Sure, ye'd have to be blind, so ye would,' Shona insisted.

'He said to say your sandwich is in the fridge. He made you your favourite, apparently.'

'Ah, great. He's a good lad. I tell you, I don't know what I was worried about. Don't know what I'd do without him now.'

'That's good,' Logan said. He wiped at the sleeve of his coat like there was a speck of dust there that only he could see. 'I thought tuna was your favourite?'

'It is! Well, I mean, it was. I mean, I like it. I like it a lot, but I had it so often I just got a bit, you know, like sick of it?'

'Oh. Right.' Logan gave his sleeve another wipe, then shrugged. 'You should've just said. I could've done chicken, bacon, and… whatever.'

'Banana,' Shona said. A smirk played across her face. 'Hang on, are you jealous of another man making me sandwiches?'

'No! Jealous? Of him? No!' Logan insisted. 'Although, I mean, it is a bit weird, isn't it?'

'No, it's not weird. He's just being nice.'

'Aye, but is he, though?' Logan asked. 'Or is he up to something?' He prodded himself in the chest with a thumb. 'I know what men are like. You might think it's just a sandwich, but that's not what's going through his head. He's thinking—'

'He's gay,' Shona said.

Logan exhaled. 'Oh, well, why didn't you say so? Thank Christ for that!'

'I think so, anyway. I mean, have you seen his hair?' Shona laughed and held up her gloved hands. 'Kidding. He's definitely gay. He told me. If he's going to make a move on either of us, it'll be you, so if anyone should be worried, it's me. Because he is an inexplicably attractive man, is he not?'

Logan let out a single-syllable chuckle. 'I felt like I was being hypnotised,' he admitted.

'Right?! I mean, how does that happen?! I've never been religious, but after seeing him, I'm having second thoughts about the whole thing. A face like that doesn't happen by accident, I don't care what Charles Darwin has to say.'

They both smiled at that, and some of the tension from earlier in the day melted away. As soon as they got onto the subject of Olivia and their new living arrangements, of course, it would all come back.

But for now, Logan was happy to at least skirt close to the edges of normality again.

'So,' he began, pulling a pair of blue latex gloves from the box on the wall. 'What have you got for me?'

–

She'd been dead for four or five days, but hadn't been chopped up until at least a day or two later. Turning the upper torso over had revealed a jagged downward knife wound between the shoulder blades that had punctured the rear wall of the heart.

Blowflies had started to colonise that wound, but hadn't yet moved in on the various cut surfaces, which was the big indicator of the gap between the times of death and dismemberment.

Whoever had killed her had waited until her back was turned, but some shallower incisions on her front, just below her breasts, revealed that the attack had continued after that.

Or maybe those other few stabs had been first, and when she'd tried to run, the killer had struck from behind.

Either way, she hadn't had a good time of it.

'Like I said earlier, the cuts are messy, but the placement's not bad if you want to avoid hacking through too much bone,' Shona said. 'They used a saw. Fine toothed, but quite long, I think, based on the stroke pattern. Manual, obviously.'

'Obviously,' Logan agreed, though he had absolutely no idea why that should be the case.

'They hurried through it, or at least didn't take any real care over it. It was like they were cutting up wood for the fire.' The pathologist sucked in her bottom lip. 'Though, you'd probably use an axe for that, I suppose, so not that. But there was no beating about the bush, anyway.'

'What do you make of it?' Logan asked. 'Of the way she's been cut up, I mean?'

'Oh, God, don't ask me about the "why" of it all,' Shona said. 'Why does anyone do anything? But it's interesting that the stomach is missing. Maybe there was a clue there. Something she'd eaten, or ingested. Something that could've told us something about who did this to her.'

Logan conceded it was possible, but it felt like a bit of a stretch. If you wanted to hide the stomach, there were easier ways to do it. Hiding the whole body in its entirety, for example, would have saved a lot of unpleasant cutting work.

The feet, the torso parts, the hair… It had all been left for a reason. He wasn't sure what it was about those particular pieces, exactly, but he was sure there was some meaning behind them.

Someone was sending a message, he was certain of it.

He just wished that he knew what it was.

Chapter Ten

Hamza pulled his car up outside the address that Seamus had given them earlier that day. It was a small, dated-looking terraced house with a front garden that was eighty per cent stone chips, and twenty per cent weeds.

Beside him, Tyler let out a whispered, 'Aw, shit!' then tried to squeeze himself into the passenger footwell, out of sight of the man strolling along the pavement towards them.

His attempt at hiding didn't work. Sharp knuckles rapped on the glass.

'Oi! Boyband? The fuck you doing?'

'I think he's seen you, mate,' Hamza said.

In a desperate, and ultimately futile attempt to save face, Tyler mustered up a look of confusion. 'Who? I was just tying my shoe.' He reacted in surprise when he saw Hoon glowering at him from the other side of the window. 'Oh! Bob! It's you!'

'No, it's Mr fucking Hoon,' Hoon corrected.

'Mr Hoon!' Tyler said. 'Didn't see you there.'

The door was opened from the outside, and Tyler practically tumbled out onto the pavement.

'What are you doing here?' Hamza asked, stepping out of the driver's side. 'The DCI won't like you being here.'

'Well, he doesn't have to fucking know, does he?' Hoon reasoned. 'And I reckon I'm here for the same reason you are. To talk to the fucking stalker in there.'

He turned to the house and bounced from one foot to the other, like a footballer limbering up.

'How do you want to do this? Kick the fucking door in and see what's what?'

'Eh, don't know if that's a good idea,' Tyler muttered.

'Course it fucking is!'

Hamza shook his head. 'It really isn't. And DCI Logan made it very clear that you weren't to be in any way involved in any of this. If you try, we're meant to arrest you.'

Hoon's eyes widened in surprise, even as his eyebrows dropped into a frown. The resulting crash made him look like he was having a seizure.

'Arrest me? Fucking arrest *me*? No fucking way Jack said that.'

'He, eh, he did,' Tyler confirmed. He grimaced. 'Sorry. He was pretty adamant about it.'

'He was very clear,' Hamza agreed.

Hoon tutted. 'You don't have to listen to that fucking bandy-legged horse molester, though. He's no' the boss of you!'

Tyler shot Hamza an anxious look before replying. 'He is, though. He literally is the boss of us. I even call him "boss". Because that's what he is.'

'Jesus fuck. You're really no' letting me come in?'

Hamza shook his head. 'No. We can't.'

Hoon threw his hands into the air, then let them fall sulkily to his side. 'I did a lot of fucking digging to find where this arsehole lived. I had to talk to a guy with shite on his hands. And now you're saying I can't...'

He raised a finger and pointed angrily at them both in turn. When he spoke, the words were a hiss through his tightly clenched teeth.

'I'll fucking remember this moment. You two bumblefucks can mark my fucking words! I'll no' forget!'

He turned and marched off, then changed his mind and headed back the way he'd come, glowering at them as he passed.

They watched him until he had rounded the corner at the end of the street and vanished out of sight. Hamza's gaze flitted to Tyler, then down at the footwell of the car beside them, where Tyler had been attempting to hide.

He decided, on balance, that it was better not to know.

'Right, then,' he announced, opening the gate to Seamus's garden. 'Let's go see if our man's home.'

After a couple of rounds of knocking on the front door, it was opened by a woman wearing yellow Marigolds and a look of weary resentment.

'What?!' she snapped, scratching her nose with the dry back of one glove. The soapy bubbles on the palms told them she'd been busy doing the dishes, and the expression on her face said she wasn't happy about the interruption.

She was in her mid-forties, though she dressed a bit younger in tight, ripped jeans and a sparkly top that billowed out around her hips, then drew tight again halfway down her thighs. She wore bright yellow slipper socks instead of shoes. They were the same colour as the rubber gloves, so at first glance, it looked like she'd been using her feet to help get the dishes done in half the time.

'Hello. I'm DS Khaled. This is DC Neish,' Hamza said, and both men held up their warrant cards for her to see. She barely paid them any attention.

'Right. And?'

'We were hoping to have a word with Seamus. He told us he lives here.'

'When he feels like it,' the woman said. 'I don't know if he's in. I'm only his mother. What do I know about his comings and goings?'

Before either detective could comment, she turned towards the stairs, drew in a deep breath, then bellowed her son's name at the top of her voice.

Somewhere else in the house, a dog barked. A big bugger, too, by the sounds of it. Tyler instinctively scanned the area for emergency exits, in case he had to do a runner.

'Wolfram! Shut up!' Seamus's mum screeched, and the dog fell silent again. 'Pain in the arse,' she muttered. 'Aye, it and Seamus.'

There was movement at the top of the stairs. Some footsteps. A yawn. A voice that sounded barely awake.

'What? What you shouting for?'

'Come here. Come down here.'

'What for?'

'Just hurry up and get your arse down them stairs!'

A low, petulant, 'Fuck's sake,' was whispered, then heavy footsteps thudded sullenly down the steps.

The detectives recognised Seamus from earlier, though he'd showered since then and his hair was just drying into a fuzz. He'd changed into a bright blue tracksuit and yellow trainers that once again echoed the colour of the Marigolds.

He stopped at the bottom step, and a range of emotions crossed his face when he spotted Hamza and Tyler standing outside. None of them suggested he was happy to see them.

'These two policemen want a word with you,' his mum said. 'I've not said they can come in, though, so that's up to—'

He shot off like a firework whose fuse had just burned down, turning away from the front door and making a bolt for the kitchen at the back of the house. He charged through the door. A crash of pots and pans rang out. Somewhere, Wolfram started barking again.

'Suspect fleeing. Entering the premises in pursuit!' Hamza declared, mostly for Seamus's mother's benefit.

Running had been a bad decision by the lad. If he'd stayed put, he could've just refused to let them enter. Just ignored their requests to talk to him until they'd managed to secure a warrant.

Turning on his heel and running away, though? That meant they could chase him, even through his own house.

The woman in the Marigolds clearly hadn't read up on the legislation, though, and protested with a shouted, 'Oi! You can't fucking come in here!' as Hamza and Tyler raced past her, heading for the kitchen.

Barrelling through, they dodged and hopped over cookware that lay scattered on the floor like landmines, and almost crashed into each other as they both tried to exit the back door at exactly the same time.

'Go, go,' Hamza urged, shoving Tyler ahead of him. The DC was younger. Faster. If either of them was going to shut down the suspect's head start, it was him.

There was just one problem.

'Where the hell is he?' Tyler cried, spinning on the spot and searching the garden.

It was walled in at the back, fenced high on both sides. There was no obvious gate or other exit, and nowhere to hide except in a big jaggy bush that hadn't yet grown enough of its spring foliage to conceal anything.

'Up and over,' Hamza said, pointing to a stack of bricks scattered by the back wall.

With a bit of imagination, they could've been laid out like steps, though if Seamus had used them, he'd been sure to kick them over on his way up.

'Get after him,' the DS urged.

'How? The wall's seven feet high!' Tyler pointed out. 'I've not got springs for legs!'

Hamza tutted, interlocked his fingers, and held his hands down low next to the wall. 'Here. I'll boost you up.'

Tyler groaned, but then placed a foot in Hamza's joined hands. 'I don't like heights!' he reminded the sarge, then he launched himself towards the top of the wall, with DS Khaled providing a springboard assist.

'Shit, wait!' Tyler hissed, but it was too late, his momentum and Hamza's pushing powered him head-first over the top of the wall.

There was a strangled cry of fright.

There was a thump.

Then, there was silence.

'Tyler?' Hamza said, bringing his ear closer to the aged brickwork. 'Tyler, you all right?'

A grunt.

A moan.

'It's higher on this side,' the DC wheezed. 'I think I broke my arse.'

'Do you see him?' Hamza asked.

Tyler used the wall to pull himself back to his feet, one hand leaning on the bricks, the other rubbing at the base of his spine. A long, wide strip of grass ran along the backs of the houses, eventually meeting a row of trees fifty yards further down an incline.

If Seamus had made it to the woods, he was long gone.

'No,' Tyler admitted. 'No sign. Although… hang on.'

He squatted, grimacing at the pain it sent stabbing up his coccyx. There was a footprint in the muddy grass. He was no tracker, but it was fresh, he thought. It headed off along the length of the wall, not towards the treeline.

There were maybe a dozen houses, and then the wall ended in what might have been the opening to an alleyway.

Worth a try.

'I'm going to look around. I'm heading left.'

'Your left or my left?' Hamza asked.

Tyler hesitated. 'I don't know what way you're facing.'

He heard the DS tut. 'I'm facing the wall, Tyler. What other way would I be facing?'

'OK, right. Well…' Another hesitation as a calculation was made. 'Your right, then.'

'I'll meet you out there,' Hamza said, his voice fading as he retreated towards the house.

Tyler set off at a limping jog, complaining through clenched teeth every second step. The ground was soft and slippery, and while that had no doubt saved him from injuring himself more seriously in the fall, it made running more of a challenge.

And that was before you factored in the falling rain, and the pain radiating from the top of his buttocks.

Sure enough, though, as he drew closer to the end of the row of houses, he spotted a gap in the wall. An opening between this block and the next.

There were shuffled footsteps, too, he was sure of it. He could hear movement. A person. Someone hiding there, trying to stay out of sight.

Gotcha, he thought.

Then, he launched himself around the corner, barked, 'Police! Stay where you are!' and was immediately caught in a headlock.

'Fuck's sake!' his attacker grunted. 'Boyband?'

The headlock was released. Tyler stumbled back to find Bob Hoon glowering at him.

'The fuck are you doing sneaking about like a fucking pervert in a boarding school? I could've fucking broken your neck there.'

'I wasn't sneaking about,' Tyler pointed out. The hand that wasn't currently rubbing his backside took to rubbing his throat, instead. 'I literally shouted at the top of my voice.'

He looked along the narrow alleyway behind the former detective superintendent. It showed a slit of residential street, and the front door of a house across the road.

What it didn't show was Seamus Starkey.

'Did you see him? Did he come past you?'

'See who?' Hoon asked, then the penny dropped. 'Wait a minute, fuck's sake, did you let him go? Did you let the bongo-eyed wee fuck get away?'

The look on Tyler's face was the only answer Hoon needed.

'Aw, well that's fucking marvellous, Boyband. Top fucking notch polis work there. They should really give you a fucking medal,' he raged. 'Aye, with, "My name is DC Tyler Neish, and I am a clueless fucking jebend" printed on it in massive gold letters.

'It'd be too fucking big for a medal, in fact. You'd have to carry it about like a fucking shield. You'd be like Captain

America, but instead of a fucking magic potion being injected into you to make you a superhero, it'd be hot liquid shit and fucking'—he ran out of steam a bit then, and gestured angrily while he tried to find an appropriate conclusion to the rant—'Pop Tarts!'

He winced, clearly not happy with how he'd stuck the landing, but what was done was done.

'I take it that's a no to having seen him, then?' Tyler asked, even though he was risking getting himself stuck in another violent headlock.

A sudden movement at the other end of the alleyway caught his eye, but it was only Hamza arriving on the scene. Tyler shook his head, and the sergeant's disappointment was clear from the drooping of his shoulders.

'I could've questioned him. I could've had that wee fucker's balls in the palm of my hand right now, making him spill every dirty wee fucking secret he ever had,' Hoon spat. 'But, oh no, you two jolly wee bumblefucks have to wade in and put the kibosh on that plan. Well, I hope you're fucking happy with yourselves. If we don't get our fucking hands on him soon, that's on you.'

He spun away from the detective constable, then sighed, turned back, and took out his mobile phone.

'Here. Look. Berta sent me this,' he said. 'Check it out.'

Tyler watched as a video of his infant son, Cal, appeared on-screen. The baby was snuggled up fast asleep, pudgy hands resting on the mattress either side of his head.

'Wait for it,' Hoon urged.

Suddenly, there was the *parp* of a fart. Eyes still closed, Cal let out a little giggle, then settled back down to sleep again.

'Is that no' the most adorable fucking thing you've ever seen in your life?' Hoon demanded, in the same angry bark he'd been using through the rest of the conversation.

'Aye. It is,' Tyler confirmed. 'Can you send me that?'

A vein bulged at the side of Hoon's forehead. 'Can I…?' He tutted. 'Fucksake.'

Tyler stood watching while the other man went through the process of sending the video across to him. Hoon's thumbs moved slowly, like he wasn't quite sure what he was doing, but there was no way on God's green earth that he was going to ask the detective constable for help.

Eventually, Hoon's phone gave a *whoosh*.

Tyler's buzzed in his pocket.

'Cheers for that,' the DC said.

Hoon stabbed a finger at Tyler, stopping just inches from the end of his nose. 'You're still a useless bastard,' he reminded him.

Then, pocketing his phone, he turned and marched off towards the road, only detouring to mutter something uncomplimentary to DS Khaled along the way.

Tyler rubbed at his bum-bone and shook his head. 'That is one weirdly complicated man,' he mumbled, then he set off limping along the alleyway to join his sergeant.

Chapter Eleven

Despite her earlier protests, Seamus's mother seemed happy enough to let the detectives back in the house, though she didn't invite them any further than the front hall.

That suited Tyler fine, given that he could hear the dog snuffling away on the other side of a door on his left.

Seamus's mum'd had 'more than enough of his shit', she told them, and if he was going to keep bringing the police to her door, then he'd have to deal with the consequences.

While talking to her, it quickly became clear that Seamus hadn't told her about the discovery in the woods earlier that day, so the detectives skirted around the edges of it to avoid complicating matters.

She seemed to be on their side for now, but that was a fine balancing act, and her son potentially being traumatised after finding a bag of body parts—or worse, being a murderer—might tip things too far in the other direction.

He could be at his dad's, she reckoned. He sometimes went there, though they didn't exactly have a great relationship. She wrote down the address and Tyler folded it between the pages of his notebook.

'Anywhere else he might have gone?' Hamza enquired.

'Pub, maybe? Spends half his bloody time there. The Winky.'

'The what?' Tyler asked.

'The Winky. The Winking Owl. That's where he usually goes, but he's skint, so probably his dad's. Or one of his workshy mates. Tam, Ross, and… I don't know. Don't have addresses, either. Don't really know them.'

Tyler jotted the names down, just in case, before Hamza pushed their luck.

'Any chance we can get a quick scope around in his room?' asked the sergeant.

The woman in the Marigolds groaned. 'What is it he's actually done this time? What are you after him for?'

'We just want to talk to him,' Hamza assured her, fixing on his friendliest smile. 'We're just trying to clear a few things up. I'm sure it's all just a misunderstanding.'

He glanced upwards towards the top of the stairs, then met her eye again.

'And I reckon we could get it all squared away much quicker if we could get a wee look in his room.'

-

Seamus's bedroom was cloaked in a reddish shade of darkness, thick crimson curtains drawn fully across the single square window. Hamza flicked the light switch by the door, but the bulb in the fitting refused to illuminate.

It was perhaps for the best. The room looked bad enough under its blanket of red gloom. Dirty clothes were strewn across the floor, along with a few crushed cans of Tennent's lager, a couple of dirty dinner plates, and a half-eaten bowl of cereal that had congealed into a semi-solid ball of mush.

The place was pungent with the aroma of sweat, stale smoke and Lynx body spray. The leather and cookies scented one, unless Tyler was very much mistaken.

Next to the unmade bed, an ashtray sat atop an upturned cardboard box, overflowing to the point that several smaller satellite ashtrays had been called into play. These were fashioned from bottle lids, crisp packets and the foil container from a Mr Kipling's Cherry Bakewell, half of which was still in the packaging, coated in ash and nestled between some stubbed-out fag ends.

There were half a dozen posters on the wall that were mostly just women with breasts large enough to spell back problems a few years down the road, plus one of a red Ferrari with a horse running alongside it like they were racing.

The Ferrari was winning, although it didn't really seem like a particularly fair contest.

'This place is a shithole,' Tyler remarked. 'And coming from me, that's saying something. I thought I lived like a pig before me and Sinead moved in together, but compared to this, my place was spotless.' He pointed to something half-hidden under a pair of skid-marked boxers. 'Is that a dead rat?'

Hamza looked down at the hairy grey ball, then nudged it with his foot. It fell apart, revealing its dried-up mouldy innards.

'I think it was an orange,' he said.

'Jesus Christ. I want to arrest the guy just for all this,' Tyler said. 'No wonder his mum didn't mind us coming up. She's probably hoping we take it all away as evidence, and she can finally see the carpet again.'

Hamza's gaze flitted from surface to surface, searching for… What? He didn't really know. Between the shit-stained pants and nicotine-yellowed walls, there were plenty of things to catch the eye, but none of them jumped out as obviously helpful.

'What is it we're looking for?' Tyler asked, reading the sergeant's mind. 'He's not going to have stashed a head and a load of body parts here, is he?' He looked around at the floor. 'Although, he probably could, if he put his mind to it.'

'I don't know,' Hamza admitted. 'Just look around and see if anything jumps out.'

He squatted and shone his phone torch into the gap below the bed. There were a couple of other discarded dinner plates under there, a half-empty vodka bottle, and a small pile of socks that would probably crackle if anyone was daft enough to pick them up.

Tyler picked his way across to what was either a desk or a dressing table—the layer of litter on top and the discarded clothing draping over the sides making it difficult to tell which. There were a few more homemade ashtrays here, and a quick sniff of a half-smoked roll-up confirmed the contents weren't Golden Virginia.

'We could get him on possession if we really pushed it,' Tyler said, returning the roll-up to the ash-filled CD case it had been resting in. 'There's not much, but if we had to hold him for something, I mean.'

They poked around for a few more minutes, searching under the mattress and inside the pillows, feeling below the furniture, checking around the non-functional ceiling light.

Tyler pulled open the curtains, but the light from the grey, overcast sky did little to lift the gloom.

'There's something missing here,' Hamza announced.

Tyler turned to find the DS standing over by the opposite wall, scanning a corkboard that hung from a single pin stuck into the plasterboard. There were a couple of ticket stubs from a concert by a band that neither detective had heard of, some photos of Seamus drinking in the sun with various groups of topless, tattooed young men, and then an empty space where something had clearly been removed.

'You can see the colour's different,' Hamza pointed out. 'There's a rectangle that's not as yellow. Something was there.'

'Probably another photo,' Tyler said. 'It looks about the same size as the others. Might be worth asking his mum. See if she knows.'

Hamza nodded. Something about the notice board was bothering him, though. Something he couldn't quite put his finger on yet.

'Does something look off to you?' he asked.

Tyler glanced around the room. 'Everything looks off to me. Smells it, too.'

'About this notice board, I mean?'

Tyler leaned back a little. 'What, besides it being squint? Not really.'

Hamza's eyebrows crept upwards. It was squint, but that wasn't it. It was *recently* squint. There was a triangle of lighter-coloured wallpaper down one side, where the board had been saving the wall from the yellowing effect of Seamus's smoking habit.

He reached to unhook the board from the wall, then some nagging wee voice in his head told him to pull on a pair of protective gloves first.

Once he'd snapped the gloves into place, he lightly took hold of the board at both sides, and lifted it off the pin, revealing a near-perfect rectangle of comparatively pristine wallpaper beneath it.

Hamza flipped the board over, and both detectives found themselves looking down at a square purple envelope with the words 'FOR YOU' written on the front in silver ink, the lettering evenly spaced, the line-work careful and neat.

'Well, now,' Hamza said, locking eyes with the detective constable. 'What do we have here?'

Chapter Twelve

Logan had just stepped out of the lift at Burnett Road station when his phone rang.

'Hamza, two seconds,' he said, pushing through the double swing doors into the Incident Room, and nodding a greeting to DI Forde.

He squatted to pat the explosion of fur and excitement that raced out from under Ben's desk to greet him, acknowledged Dave and Sinead with a wave of a hand, then turned his attention back to the voice on the other end of the line.

'Sorry. Popped into the office. What's up?'

He stalked over to his chair, Taggart trotting along beside him, and listened as Hamza laid out what had happened since he'd left.

The DS told him about the interview with Sandra, about the Seamus revelations, and the encounters with Hoon. He used very particular language when he spoke of Seamus's escape, like he was taking care not to shift the blame onto anyone.

Probably Tyler's fault, then, Logan guessed, but he respected the sergeant's tact.

'It's this next bit that's really weird, though, sir,' Hamza said. His voice went a little distorted and distant. 'Hang on.'

Logan took his seat, then shook his head and mouthed a, 'Thanks,' when Sinead mimed holding a cup of tea.

'Just sent a photo to the inbox,' Hamza said, his voice becoming clearer again.

Logan's computer was off, so he rolled his chair across to Ben's desk until both men were sitting shoulder to shoulder.

'Inbox,' he said, nodding to the screen of the DI's computer.

'Hello, Jack. How you doing, Jack? Don't you worry yourself about invading anyone's personal space, Jack,' Ben said.

'Aye, aye. Quit your whinging,' Logan said. 'Inbox. Chop-chop.'

Ben gave an exaggerated but good-natured tut, then put a hand on his mouse and stared at the icons on the screen like he'd never seen them before in his life.

'Right. Inbox. Inbox.' He puffed out his cheeks. 'What one's the inbox again…?'

'I've got it up here,' Dave said. He angled his screen towards Logan, who immediately rose from his seat, leaving Ben searching the computer desktop for clues as to the whereabouts of the shared email account.

'It's an envelope,' Logan said, bending to look at the picture on the screen.

'Aye,' Hamza and Dave both simultaneously confirmed.

'So what? What about it?' Logan asked. He tapped the speaker icon on his phone so the others could hear the detective sergeant's reply.

'We found it in Seamus Starkey's room, sir. Hidden on the back of a notice board. He clearly didn't want it found,' Hamza explained. 'Have you got the other pictures there?'

Dave tapped one of the arrow keys on his keyboard and the photo of the envelope was replaced with a picture of what looked like a party invitation. Unlike the handwritten envelope, the text had been professionally printed on a postcard that was the same shade of purple.

'"New player has entered the game",' Logan read. He straightened up. 'The hell does that mean?'

'Don't know, sir,' Hamza said. 'Bit weird, though. And if you look at the third picture…'

Dave moved to the next image on cue.

'…there's an address written on the back. Same block handwriting as on the envelope. Not a match for Seamus's, so it looks like someone gave it to him. We asked his mum about it, but she didn't have a clue.'

By this time, Sinead had come over to join him. She stood with her arms folded, watching as Dave flicked back through the images again.

'What game?' she wondered aloud.

It was Tyler's voice that replied, Hamza clearly having switched over to speakerphone, too.

'Dunno. He's not got an XBox or anything. His mum says he's never really been interested. She reckons he might play round at his mates' houses sometimes, but he's not a gamer.'

'You looked into the address?' Logan asked.

'We're just doing it now, boss,' Tyler said.

Dave gestured to his screen and raised his eyebrows in a silent question. Logan gave him the nod of approval, and the constable switched over to Google Maps.

A few seconds of typing later and a red marker appeared against an otherwise uniform block of green.

'It's in the middle of nowhere,' Tyler said.

'Aye, so I see,' Logan confirmed.

There was a moment of wary silence from the other end of the line.

'How?' Tyler asked. 'Are you watching us, boss? Can you see me?'

Logan closed his eyes for a moment and exhaled through his nose. 'No, son. We're looking it up at our end.'

'Ah. Right. Thank God for that. You had me worried there.'

Logan frowned. 'Why? What are you doing that you don't want me to see?'

'Nothing, boss,' Tyler replied. 'I just mean, if you were watching me now, and I didn't know it, when else might you have been watching me?'

'What, like I'm a bloody peeping tom, you mean?' Logan asked.

'Eh? No. Just… Maybe forget I said anything, boss,' Tyler said.

His voice faded as he retreated from the phone, letting Hamza take over again.

'It's a couple of miles off the A9,' the DS said.

'Looks to be about halfway between here and there,' Logan said, as Dave zoomed out to reveal the area around the location marker.

'Want us to go check it out? Uniform's on the lookout for Seamus, so we've got time to go scope the place out and see what's what.'

Logan scratched at his chin, his fingernails rasping across his stubble. He gestured towards the screen and Dave, somehow correctly interpreting the signal, flicked back to the photos.

New Player Has Entered The Game.

What the hell did that mean?

'Take a couple of Uniforms with you,' the DCI eventually said.

'Don't think they can spare any, sir,' Hamza replied.

'Then we'll get them radioed in from here. You don't go in there without support. That clear?'

'Clear, sir,' Hamza confirmed. It had been a few years since he'd been attacked while investigating a remote house on his own, and he was in no rush to repeat it. 'We'll wait for backup.'

'Right. Good.' Logan checked his watch. 'I'll swing by on the way back. Should be there in about forty minutes. Keep me posted.'

'Will do, sir,' Hamza said, and Logan prodded the big red button that ended the call.

At his desk across the room, Ben let out a little cry of triumph. 'Inbox! Finally! I knew the bloody thing was there somewhere. Think you can hide from me, you bastard?' He double-clicked the icon and turned to the others. 'Now, then, what is it I'm meant to be looking for again?'

Chapter Thirteen

The turnoff was not where Tyler expected it to be. He could see the road leading to the spot marked on his phone's map, but it was running perpendicular to the one they were currently driving on, and thirty feet below it.

'We're meant to be down there,' he announced, leaning over to point across Hamza and draw his attention to the road beneath the raised viaduct. 'You're going the wrong way.'

'How am I going the wrong way?' Hamza asked.

'Because you're driving.'

'Aye, but you're meant to be navigating! You told me you'd direct me.'

'I am directing you! It's that way!'

Hamza shot him a dirty look. 'Oh, aye, Tyler, hang on and I'll just crash us through this railing. I'm sure that'll be fine.'

'It's not my fault. The map makes it look like you just turn right here,' Tyler protested. He held his phone in front of the sergeant's face. 'See?'

'No, I can't see, Tyler, which is a problem, given that I'm trying to drive!' Hamza said, shifting his head around to see past the DC's screen. He pointed to a sign up ahead, then clicked on his indicator. 'There's a turnoff coming up on the left. Maybe we can double back that way.'

Tyler looked at the sign, then down at his phone, then back towards the road they'd just crossed above.

'Aye. Take a left up ahead,' he said, with an air of authority that was entirely unearned. 'We can follow the road round and double back.'

'Right,' Hamza muttered, checking his mirrors and pulling onto the slip road. 'What would I do without you?'

Ten minutes and two minor arguments later, they pulled up outside an old stone cottage set back just a few feet from the road. It had been painted white once, but time and the elements had worn away the lustre, turning the exterior into a blotchy patchwork of blacks and greys.

There was a large pond or maybe a very small loch behind the house, which hadn't shown up on the maps, so they both checked and double-checked their phones to make sure they were in the right place.

'I reckon this is it,' Hamza declared. 'It's where Google thinks it is, anyway.'

'It's definitely it,' Tyler said. He pointed to a faded sign beside the decaying wooden doorway. 'The Hollows. That was the name on the card.'

Hamza nodded and returned his phone to his pocket. The rain had eased off during the drive, but seemed to gather momentum again the moment they got out of the car.

'No sign of Uniform,' Tyler said, looking up and down the narrow, single-track road. He pulled the zip of his jacket as high as it would go. 'We should probably go sit in the car, eh? Don't really want to stand around in this.'

'Looks empty,' Hamza said, sizing the place up.

Two of the downstairs windows were boarded up, and the others were caked with grime, but the place was giving off definite vibes of having long-since been deserted.

'Door's barely hanging on,' the DS pointed out. 'We could just go in.'

'What, in there? Are you mental? We're meant to wait for backup.'

Hamza looked up and down the road, indicating the lack of traffic, then turned back to Tyler.

The detective constable groaned.

'Ugh. Right. Fine,' he relented. 'But if we get murdered, either by someone in there or by the boss when he finds out, I'm holding you personally responsible.'

–

Inside, the house was as grotty as Seamus Starkey's bedroom, albeit in an entirely different way. Where Seamus's room had been filled with clutter, this place was pretty much empty, aside from a lot of mouse droppings and the occasional pile of plaster dust lying beneath cracks in the blackened ceiling.

Every floorboard groaned in a different note as the detectives made their way across the empty front room, tunelessly underscoring their growing tension.

The place may have been empty, but there was something about it that neither man liked. Not the mould, or the damp, or the wind howling down through the fireplace. Something intangible that, if pushed, they wouldn't be able to put a name to.

Whatever it was, it was giving them both the willies.

'Maybe we should've waited for the boss, after all,' Tyler whispered. 'This place is a bit...'

He left the rest of the sentence hanging, unable to voice exactly what he was feeling.

At Halloween, he'd been convinced the big castle they were stuck in had been haunted. This place didn't feel like that, though. It felt worse. Not haunted, but possessed.

'Can you hear something?' Hamza asked.

'Don't, Ham! Don't be a dick and wind me up!' Tyler warned. 'I mean it, it's not funny.'

'No. Shh. Shut up. Listen,' the DS said, holding a hand up for silence.

He nodded ahead to an ornate archway leading off from the space they were in. Darkness lay beyond the opening. Presumably, the room ahead was one of the ones with the boarded-up windows.

Tyler held his breath and willed his heart to stop crashing in his chest long enough for him to listen. He tilted his head, straining in his ears.

There was *something*, he thought. A low droning sort of sound, like an old radio that hadn't been tuned to quite the right frequency.

'Aye,' he was forced to admit. 'I hear it.'

They proceeded together, Hamza a step or two ahead. He'd brought the big torch from his car, and the beam burrowed a tunnel through the darkness, painting a circle on a patch of peeling paint, then on a rotting kitchen cabinet sagging against the wall…

And then, on the rusted front of an ancient freestanding freezer that took pride of place in the centre of the room.

The sound changed a little as they passed under the archway, becoming an electrical hum.

A cable ran from the back of the freezer to a grubby extension, which snaked across the floor until it vanished into the shadows at the corner of the room.

Somehow, despite its condition, the place still had power.

And it was powering one specific kitchen appliance.

'Well, this is creepy as fuck,' Tyler whispered. He nodded to the freezer. 'You should check that.'

'Why should I check it?' Hamza asked. Clearly, he was finding the thought of opening the door and having a snoop inside roughly as appealing as Tyler was.

'You're the senior officer,' Tyler reminded him.

'Aye, but that means I get to boss you around!' Hamza shot back, but then he sighed. 'It's fine. I'll do it.'

'You sure?' Tyler asked.

'No. Why, do you want to do it, like?'

Tyler held his hands up in surrender and backed up a step. 'Fire on, Sarge. You've got this.'

Hamza ran a hand down his face, then pulled on a pair of gloves. He examined the freezer from a variety of angles, like he was a snooker player lining up a difficult black into the centre pocket.

He paced all the way around it.

He shone his torch at the floor in front and on either side.

It was a freezer, that was all. Just a freezer.

A manky old freezer in an abandoned house miles from anywhere, with a possible connection to a killer who'd dismembered his victim.

He thought back to all the body parts that had been found. All the worst ones—the head, for example—were still out there somewhere, waiting to be discovered.

'Bugger it,' he muttered.

Then, keeping as much distance from it as he could, he stretched over, pulled on the handle, and opened the freezer door.

Tyler rocked from side to side below the archway, squeaking out a rhythm on the uneven floorboards. He chewed his lip and waited while Hamza shone his torch into the iced-up insides of the freestanding appliance.

'Anything?' he asked, when the sergeant straightened and closed the door.

Hamza's breath formed a fog in the chilled air as he whispered a reply.

'Fingers.'

The floor beneath Tyler stopped squeaking. 'What?'

'Fingers,' Hamza said again. 'It's a load of fingers.'

Tyler looked from the DS to the freezer, then back again. 'I'm really hoping you just forgot to put the words "Birds Eye Frozen Fish" in that sentence somewhere.'

Hamza shook his head. He swallowed. 'Sadly not, no.'

'Bloody hell,' Tyler whispered. 'That's not good.'

'Not great for whoever they belong to, no.'

Before either of them could say anything more, a floorboard fanfare rang out, a tuneless crescendo of creaks and groans racing up at Tyler's back. A shadow fell across him. He spun around, panic rolling up his throat and bursting from his lips as a high-pitched yelp.

'I thought I told you to wait for backup?' boomed the towering figure that came marching across the room towards him.

'Jesus Christ, boss! Are you trying to do me in? I thought I was a goner there!' Tyler cried. He put a hand on his chest, settling his heart, then pulled himself together. 'The door was open. Well, mostly missing, actually. We thought it wouldn't do any harm to have a quick look around in here while we were waiting.'

Logan stopped beside him, his head almost touching the peak of the arched doorway. 'Oh, aye?' He looked at the freezer, and at the expression on Hamza's face. 'And how's that working out for you?'

–

Thirty minutes after Hamza had found the fingers in the freezer, the outside of the house was a hive of activity. Three marked police vehicles had come out to secure the area and block the road, though since no traffic had passed in the whole time that Hamza and Tyler had been there, the constables on cordon duty were left twiddling their thumbs.

'Palmer's lot will be on their way shortly, sir,' Hamza said, shoving his mobile phone back into his inside jacket pocket. 'Just waiting for a couple of the team to arrive.'

Logan stood with his hands in the pockets of his overcoat, the rain pattering against his broad shoulders as he studied the outside of the crumbling cottage.

'Shona's already left,' he said. 'Not that there's exactly a whole lot for her to look at, mind you, from what you've told me.'

'Doubt she'll feel the need to check for a pulse, sir, no,' Hamza agreed. He shuddered at the memory of the fingers laid out on a metal tray, like sausages waiting to be slung in the oven.

Ten of them, all lined up in a row, the ends all ragged stumps of bone, skin and gristle.

'You all right?' Logan asked.

'Fine, boss. Aye. Bit of a shock, but I've seen worse. We all have.'

'Unfortunately, aye,' Logan said. 'But, you know...'

He sort of rolled his head around a bit in a gesture that, despite its opaqueness, Hamza took to be supportive.

'Thanks, sir,' he said. 'I appreciate that.'

Logan nodded, and they both went back to looking at the house.

It was a bungalow, but a grubby window in the roof peered down into some sort of attic space. A quick scope of the inside of the building hadn't turned up any obvious hatches or ladders leading up there, though. In fact, aside from the fridge, a few knackered old kitchen cabinets, and a scattering of animal droppings, the whole place had been empty.

'Why tell him to come here?' Logan wondered aloud, thinking back to the card that Hamza and Tyler had found in Seamus Starkey's bedroom. 'If that's what that message even was. Why tell him to come all the way out here to this place?'

'No idea, sir. But it's looking like Seamus is definitely mixed up in all this somehow.'

'Aye. Seems like it,' Logan agreed. A thought struck him, and he looked around at the bored-looking Uniforms. 'Where's Tyler, by the way?'

Hamza blinked. 'Eh, dunno.' He glanced around. 'I thought he must have been with you, sir. I haven't seen him in a few minutes.'

'Christ Almighty. Where's the daft bugger wandered off to now?' Logan muttered. 'Maybe you'd better go and get the diving team on standby, in case he's fallen in the bloody water.'

'Ah, you're all right. No need, sir,' Hamza said. He pointed to where Tyler was just emerging from the other side of the house, his hands on his hips, a frown of absolute bewilderment on his face.

Although, to be fair, that wasn't an unusual look for him.

'What's the matter?' Logan called over to him. 'If you're looking for a way in, it's that big rectangular hole in the front.'

'Eh?' Tyler turned to see who had spoken, then headed quickly in their direction. 'Oh, no. It's not that, boss,' he said, once again proving immune to the DCI's sarcasm.

'What the hell are you doing traipsing around outside the place before Scene of Crime's had a chance to go over it, anyway?' Logan demanded. 'Last thing we need is you compromising the scene.'

'Sorry, boss. I was careful. I just had to check something, though,' Tyler said. He gave a backwards tilt of his head, drawing their attention back to the house. 'There's something a bit weird about this place.'

'What, besides the freezer full of human fingers, you mean?' Logan asked.

Tyler stopped beside them and looked back in the direction of the bungalow. He stood there in silence for a moment, scratching at the top of his head. His sculpted hair remained completely stationary.

'Eh, aye, maybe,' he said. 'Could actually be weirder than that.'

Logan and Hamza exchanged a look of confusion. 'Well, you'd better hurry up and fill us in then, son,' the DCI told him. 'You've got us intrigued.'

'Right, well, you know how we went in the house earlier? We found the freezer, and then you turned up and made us shite ourselves, and then we checked out the other rooms?'

'It was half an hour ago, Tyler. We don't need a recap,' Logan assured him. 'What about it?'

'Right, well, there was nothing else in the rooms, boss, right? There was the freezer and some kitchen stuff, but otherwise it was empty.'

Logan and Hamza both agreed that this was correct. They also agreed that Tyler should hurry up and get to the bloody point.

'I'm getting there,' the DC assured them. 'So. Right. We were looking in the rooms. We needed the torch in the kitchen, but that was it. Didn't need it in the other rooms, did we?'

'No,' Hamza confirmed. 'Just the kitchen. The window was boarded up.'

'Exactly. That's just it,' Tyler said. He gave the house another quick look over, had another scratch of his head, then turned to face his two senior officers. 'If that was the only room that was in darkness, then how come there are two boarded-up windows on the outside?'

Chapter Fourteen

Sinead pinned a handwritten index card to the timeline she was building on the Big Board, then stepped back to check out her handiwork.

It was only then that it occurred to her.

'Hang on. Do we have a photo?' she asked, leafing through a small pile of printouts on the desk beside her.

Ben, who had been scrolling through the initial post-mortem report, looked up from his computer. 'Of what?'

'Of the victim. Of Eleanor,' Sinead said. 'I can't see one here.'

DI Forde's eyes crept back to his screen. There had been pictures in Shona's report, though none that he'd really want printed off and pinned to the board.

'Eh, I've not seen one, no.'

Sinead put her hands on her hips. 'Bugger. We didn't get one.'

'Did you no' ask the parents?'

'No. Should've done, but forgot. We were a bit distracted with Hoon being there.'

Ben nodded in understanding. 'Aye, he'll put you off your stride, right enough.'

Dave drummed two fingers on the edge of his desk, then looked back over his shoulder. 'Want me to see if there's any online? Social media, or whatever?'

'Please. If you could.'

The constable cracked his knuckles. 'I've been playing Minesweeper for the last twenty minutes, so I'm sure I can squeeze it into my schedule.'

He set to work. Sinead glanced at her watch, then double-checked it against the clock on the wall.

'No word from them yet?' she asked Ben.

'Not yet, no. Jack should be there soon, though, if he's not already,' the DI reckoned. 'I'm sure we'll hear shortly.'

Below the table, Taggart let out a little whine. Ben rolled his chair back far enough that he could look down at the dog. He was standing, and his tail gave a few quick, urgent wags when his and Ben's eyes met.

'Right you are, then,' Ben announced.

With a grunt of effort, he pushed himself up out of his chair, stretched his lower back, then plodded towards the door. Taggart followed cautiously, only allowing himself to get excited once Ben had unhooked the dog's lead from its hanger on the wall.

He barked excitedly, danced two full circles around the DI's feet, then sat down while the lead was clipped to his collar.

'Taking the dug to stretch his legs,' he said. 'I can go by the place across the road if anyone's wanting any grub. A late lunch, or early dinner, or whatever you want to call it.'

Dave looked up from his screen. 'One roll and square sausage, one roll and bacon and one with a fried egg and a tattie scone,' he said, fishing in his pocket for his wallet. 'And do they still do them brownies? If so, one of them. If not, just any cake.'

'Jesus Christ, son,' Ben cried, looking the constable up and down. 'Congratulations!'

Dave's wide brow creased in confusion. 'On what?'

'On the baby. I'm assuming you must be expecting? I'm guessing that's why you're eating for two?'

The constable grinned and patted his stomach. 'I'm a growing lad.' He handed the DI a twenty pound note. 'Oh, and brown sauce on the Lorne. And a can of Irn Bru. One of the sugar-free ones.'

Ben took the money. 'I think the damage is already well and truly done on the calorie front, son, but I'll see what I can do.'

He turned to DC Bell, who was condensing the information on one of the printouts onto a handwritten index card. 'Sinead? Grub?'

Sinead looked up in surprise. Clearly, she'd been too caught up in her task to have paid attention to the previous conversation.

'Eh… aye. What are you two having?'

'Well, this bugger's having one of everything,' Ben said. 'I'm thinking maybe a red pudding supper.' Beside him, Taggart danced impatiently, so it sounded like he was stamping his feet on the vinyl floor tiles. 'Aye, aye, we're going. Hold your horses.'

'Fish and chips, then, sir, if that's all right?' Sinead said. She looked around for her jacket. 'Hang on, I'll get you cash.'

'You can sort me out when I get back,' Ben told her. 'Otherwise one of us is going to be cleaning up after this dug, and I'm telling you now, it's no' going to be me.'

He turned to the door, and Taggart almost pulled his arm from its socket in his rush to leave.

Once they'd gone, Sinead finished filling out the card, pinned it to the Big Board, then called across the room to Dave. 'Getting anywhere?'

'Think so, aye. She's got Facebook. It's pretty locked down, but I can see a couple of her profile pictures.' He leaned to one side, giving the detective constable a clear view of his monitor. 'That her, do you reckon?'

On-screen, a girl with a bob of bright red hair was grimacing and giving the middle finger. She'd gone heavy on a dark purple eyeshadow, and her black-painted lips stood out like a bruise against her porcelain white skin.

Sinead wrinkled her nose. 'Not sure. How old is that?'

Dave checked the date below the picture. 'Posted eleven months ago. I'm pretty sure it's her profile—Ellie Howard, lives in Aviemore, last job listed is The Family Fun Factory.'

'Sounds like her, then.'

'I'm just not sure if this is her in the photo. There are a few others with different people in them. Don't want us sticking some other lassie's face up on the board.'

Sinead nodded, then considered the picture again.

'Could've grown her hair out,' she said, thinking back to the patch of scalp with its attached blonde locks. 'The hair we found had been bleached, so that could fit. Can you email me that over, and I'll get in touch with her father for a description?'

'No bother,' Dave said.

'Actually, hang on. You could always try—'

The thought struck the constable at the very same moment. 'Reverse image search. Aye, worth a go. Give me a sec.'

Sinead busied herself back at the Big Board while Dave clicked, typed, copied and pasted.

'No, that's not her. That's not her. That's a cartoon character. That's a lamp.' He looked back over his shoulder again. 'God. Reverse image search is a load of shite, isn't it?'

'Sometimes,' Sinead agreed. 'Still, worth a try. Just send it over.'

'Hold on.'

Dave leaned in closer to his screen. His mouse wheel clicked as he slowly rotated it, scrolling the half-visible next line of image results fully into view.

There was the same picture he'd used in the search.

The same face.

The same girl.

He shifted his gaze to the website address below the photo.

'Oh,' he remarked. He released his grip on the mouse like he was worried about compromising crucial evidence. 'I think you're going to want to see this.'

Chapter Fifteen

Tyler was right. An entire room of the cottage was completely missing. Two windows outside were boarded up, but only one could be seen from inside the house.

The three detectives stood in the sitting room, the broken front door hanging open behind them as they stared at a blank, featureless wall that had no business being there.

'It's got to be behind that,' Logan declared. 'That's got to be where the window is.'

Hamza shone his torch across the wall. The plasterboard didn't look as old as in some of the other rooms, but it was far from fresh. It had been there for years, not months. Decades, maybe.

'Can't see any obvious secret door, or anything,' the DS said. 'You?'

Logan shook his head. 'No. Though, if it was obvious, it wouldn't be very secret.'

'True,' Hamza conceded. He swept the torch beam into the corners, then up the seams where the plasterboard had been screwed to the wooden frame of the wall. 'You'd think there'd be something, though.'

Behind them, Tyler looked back in the direction of the door. 'We should probably wait for forensics to come and do their bit, boss. We should probably let them try and figure it out.'

'Aye. We probably should, right enough,' Logan concurred.

But instead of retreating, he took a step closer to the wall. The uneven floorboards droned ominously beneath his shifting weight.

He traced his gloved fingertips across a join in the plasterboard. If he really tried, he could probably force his fingernails into the seam, but they wouldn't have the leverage to prise the board away, and the gap was too narrow to fit anything else in there.

'Doesn't make sense,' he muttered. 'It's completely blocked up.'

'Maybe they just remodelled, boss,' Tyler suggested, clutching at straws. 'It looks like it's been like that for ages. Doubt there's anything behind there. We should probably just leave it for Palmer and his lot.'

'You were the one who was so bloody intrigued by this a few minutes ago,' Logan reminded him.

Tyler shifted his weight on the balls of his feet and winced. 'Aye, but that was when we were outside, boss. I was quite happy when we were outside.'

Ignoring the DC's protests, Logan rapped his knuckles in a straight line along the wall, and listened to the sounds they made. The vertical wooden struts were positioned around two feet apart, and the gaps between them rang with a dull, hollow echo.

'Definitely an empty space back there,' Logan concluded.

'Aye, well, glad we figured that out, boss,' Tyler said. He jabbed a thumb back over his shoulder. 'Should we maybe…?'

'Actually, he might have a point, sir,' Hamza said. 'We might have more luck outside. We could see if the board over the window's loose. Try and get a look in that way.'

'Or we could just leave it,' Tyler said, but nobody paid him any attention.

Logan considered the wall for a few more moments. They'd checked the only other room with a wall that might adjoin the hidden space. It was a small bathroom with a rotting floor and a bath and toilet both caked in black mould.

The wall that would back onto the secret room was tiled, though several of them had fallen off and smashed into the blackened bathtub below. Dark lines of water damage ran down over the crumbling old mortar, but the wall seemed otherwise solid. No signs of a hidden doorway, anyway.

Logan nodded and stepped back. 'Aye, let's do that.'

'Go outside and wait for Scene of Crime, you mean, boss?'

The DCI turned towards the exit. 'Go outside and check the window.'

Tyler winced as he backed towards the door, still trying to argue his point. 'I'm just saying, I know it's interesting, but maybe we should be patient here? We don't know what might be back there. We don't want to go rushing in and—'

His heel caught on a raised wooden board. Panic painted itself across his face. His arms flailed in matching concentric circles.

And then, with a thud, he landed heavily on the floor.

'Ow! Jesus. My arse keeps getting it today,' he moaned, then he accepted the hand offered by Logan, and was easily hoisted back up onto his feet.

'Eh, you guys seeing this?' Hamza asked.

Tyler dusted the seat of his trousers with a hand, then turned to see what the detective sergeant was looking at.

The raised board Tyler's heel had caught on stuck up almost an inch from those surrounding it. As Hamza shone his torch on the spot, the beam revealed three other ridges, the four of them making up a near-perfect square on the floor.

'Is it just me,' the DS began, 'or does that look like a hatch?'

Logan knelt beside it, but it was already apparent that the hatch—if, indeed, that was what it was—was far too small for him to fit through.

'We should leave it,' Tyler insisted. He'd already worked out the size issue, and realised he had a fifty-fifty chance of being the one sent down to explore whatever might be down there. 'Let Palmer's lot check it. We could be messing with evidence here, boss. I can't believe I'm being the sensible one here!'

Logan felt around the edges of the hatch. It wasn't easy with the gloves on, but his fingers found purchase near the corners.

He gave it an experimental tug, and felt it lift half an inch from the floor.

'It's definitely something,' he said. 'I can shift it.'

'Just because you can do something, though, boss, does that mean you should?' Tyler posited.

Logan looked up at him, then over at the blank wall. He stared at that for a few moments, like he was hoping he might suddenly develop X-ray vision, and be able to see straight through.

'Palmer'll be ages yet,' Logan reasoned. He shrugged. 'And anyway, I only really joined the polis because I'm a right nosy bastard.'

With a grunt, he heaved on the hatch. It rose a little, resisted for a moment, then pulled free.

Warm, stagnant air rose from the darkness below, like the breath of some slumbering monster.

'Aw, God,' Tyler muttered, but he shuffled closer as Hamza shone his torch down into the hole, and leaned over to get a better look.

The first thing they saw was a muddy puddle around six feet below the hatchway, and their own faces reflected in the dark, murky water.

Then, they saw the steps. Eight of them, crudely built from lengths of rough, unsanded wood. They looked newer than anything else in the house, and were clearly a recent addition.

'Give me that,' Logan said, holding his hand out for Hamza's torch.

Once he had it, he lay down on the floor so he was partly hanging over the hole, then he leaned his head and one arm through, and shone the light around.

A low, narrow passageway walled in by stone blocks ran from the foot of the stairs in the direction of the hidden room. There, at the far end, the beam of the torch picked out a second set of steps, rising from the cottage's wet and filthy foundations.

The entrance to the hidden room was just a few feet away. The answer to the mystery of what lay behind the wall was easily within reach.

Just not for him. There was no way he could squeeze himself through the hatch, let alone along the passage itself.

'See anything, sir?' Hamza asked.

'Aye,' Logan replied, his voice echoing around in the space beneath the floor.

It was so close.

Just a few feet away.

And he really was a nosy bastard.

He pushed himself up onto his knees and looked at the other two detectives, first Hamza, then Tyler. They were smaller. Either one of them could fit.

He sighed and got to his feet. With a click, he turned off the torch, then handed it back to DS Khaled.

'But no point in us taking any chances,' he told them. 'We'd better go outside and wait.'

Tyler didn't need to be told twice. He raised a grateful thumb as he hurried for the door.

'You know, boss,' he called back to the DCI, 'that's my favourite thing you've said since you got here.'

–

They had just returned outside when Logan's phone rang. It was a special ring that he'd had Hamza set up for him, and it shrieked like an alarm warning him of danger.

'Christ,' he groaned, reaching into his pocket. 'Hoon.'

Muttering below his breath, he tapped the button to answer, then brought the phone to his ear.

'What do you want? I'm in the middle of something here.'

'Aye, well, you're no' the fucking only one, Jack,' Hoon replied. 'That lad we're looking for. The one them two club-footed fanny pads let escape. I've found him.'

Logan pinched the bridge of his nose. The rain rattled a rhythm on his coat. 'You shouldn't have found him, Bob. You shouldn't have been bloody looking for him. That's not your job.'

'Tough shit, because I've found him. He's just gone into some… I don't know. A barn or a big fucking shed, or something. It's just off the railway line, about a hundred feet from where I'm standing.'

The urgency of Logan's shout made Tyler and Hamza both jump in fright. 'Do *not* go in there! Don't try any of your shite, Bob. I mean it, if you even wave at the bastard, I'm going to arrest you myself. Is that clear?'

'Eh?' Hoon's voice was distant, then returned to its normal volume. 'Sorry, wasn't listening, I was texting you the address. Better get a fucking shifty on, Jack. Fifteen minutes, or I'm tackling the bastard solo.'

'Bob, don't you bloody dare—'

The line went dead. Logan gritted his teeth and squeezed his phone so tightly that the colours on the screen became briefly inverted.

The message Hoon had sent arrived with a ping. Logan glowered at it like it was the man himself, then huffed out a sigh of frustration.

'You two all right here until Shona and Palmer turn up?'

'Long as we can sit in the car, boss, aye,' Tyler said, his hands held above his head to shield his hair from the falling rain.

'You sure you don't need one of us with you as backup, sir?' Hamza asked. 'You know what Hoon's like.'

Logan shook his head as he headed for his car. 'No, I'll go on my own. If anyone else comes along, they'll only try and talk me out of murdering him.'

Chapter Sixteen

Ben needed a seat. He gestured vaguely back towards his own, like he could summon it from his desk using sheer willpower alone. As luck would have it, Sinead spotted this and quickly wheeled it over to him before his legs could give out from under him.

Taggart, thinking this was the start of some fun new game, chased the chair across the floor, then quickly lost interest again when it stopped moving.

He lay down on the floor at Ben's feet, and watched events with interest, though mostly in the hope that some biscuits might make an appearance at some point.

'Jesus Christ, son, a bit of bloody warning next time!' the DI told Dave. 'My ticker's not built for a shock like that these days.'

He removed his glasses and polished them on the end of his tie, not able to bring himself to look back at the screen quite yet. Taggart watched him with interest.

'Christ on a bike,' he muttered to himself, then he held the spectacles up to the light to make sure they were clean, placed them back on the bridge of his nose, then put his hands on his knees to brace himself. 'Right. Roll VT.'

He watched the screen, jaw clenched, as the naked lassie with the dyed red hair selected an object from the wide range of those available on the bedspread beside her.

'Oh, Jesus,' Ben mumbled. 'That's a hell of a big bottle, is it not?' He crossed his arms, his initial shock giving way to a sort of morbid fascination. 'What size is that? Is that a magnum?'

He tilted his head so he could read the bottle's label. 'Can't see the name. Looks French. That'd no' be cheap. Unless she went over on one of them booze cruises. Apparently, you can pick up some real bargains if you…'

A movement on-screen made the rest of the sentence fall away. He adjusted his glasses and leaned in a little closer, his head twisting to one side again.

'Hang on. Is that a tub of Dairylea Light? What in the name of the wee man is she going to do with…? Oh. Oh, no. No, no, no!' He sat up straighter, his hands gripping his knees again, like a man locked in a long-running battle with chronic constipation. 'What are you…? Jesus Christ, lass, don't stick it up…'

He relaxed his shoulders as he tried to convince himself that all would be well.

'That's never going to fit. She's never going to manage to get that…' His eyebrows rose an inch straight up from their starting position. He stroked at his chin thoughtfully, like a chess player whose opponent had just moved his bishop in new and interesting ways. 'Hang on, she's putting it *there*? Good grief. That's a bloody twist. I didn't see that coming.'

'I think we get the idea,' Sinead said, shooting Dave a look that made him stop the video. 'And she linked to that from her Facebook?'

'Not directly,' Dave said. 'Don't think they'd allow that. Link goes to a sort of blog page, and then links on that take you through to some sketchy-looking site with a Russian domain. The reverse image search I tried brings up the same site.'

He hit the back button on the browser and scrolled through a seemingly endless parade of thumbnail images, each more graphic than the one before.

'Most of the videos are behind a paywall. That one is free. According to the description, that's one of the tame ones.'

'One of the tame ones?!' Ben yelped. 'Sticking a range of big bloody implements up her you know where? Good God

Almighty. What does she do in the other ones, wank off RoboCop?'

Dave grinned. 'I'd buy that for a dollar!' he declared. Then, when this drew blank looks, he added, 'It's a RoboCop quote. From the film. And, eh, not that I've seen, no.' Turning his attention back to the computer, he continued, 'But there's a lot to look through, so your guess is as good as mine.'

Ben slumped back into his chair and rubbed his eyes with a finger and thumb, like he was battling exhaustion.

'I tell you, I'll no' be able to look a Dairylea Triangle in the face again, that's for bloody sure.'

Dave scrolled back to the top of the screen and clicked another link. 'The video's not even the really interesting bit,' he announced.

'You're kidding me on!' Ben replied. 'I mean, it's no' my cup of tea, and I'm horrified on a number of levels, but say what you like, you can't tell me it wasn't interesting.'

'Aye, but this is going to blow all that away,' Dave said. 'Check this out.'

The original video appeared. Ben braced himself again, but then Dave scrolled down to the caption below it. It was written in dark grey text against a black background, but when the constable dragged his cursor across it, the writing appeared in a stark white highlight.

It was still far too small for Ben to read, however, no matter how much he squinted. Fortunately, Sinead was on hand to help.

'"Model, El Ho",' she read, with a tut and a roll of her eyes.

'Keep going,' Dave urged. He turned the screen a little further so it was directly facing her.

'"Photography and Videography by—"'

Sinead stopped suddenly, her eyes going wide.

Dave leaned back in his chair, looking really quite pleased with himself.

'See? What did I tell you?' he asked. 'Interesting, eh?'

'Bloody hell,' Sinead muttered.

'What?' Ben demanded, looking between them both. 'What is it? What's going on?'

'The person who made the video, sir. It gives their name,' Sinead explained.

'Right. And?!'

'Moomin,' Sinead replied. 'It says the videographer's name is Moomin.'

Chapter Seventeen

'About fucking time,' Hoon said, when Logan got out of his BMW beside him. 'What did you do, stop for a three-course meal and a leisurely shite?'

Logan ignored the remark, and instead followed Hoon's gaze, which was locked on a wooden building about the size of a double garage set back a little from the side of the railway track running south of Aviemore.

'That where Seamus is?'

Hoon nodded, still not taking his eye off the door of the building. 'Aye. Asked around at a couple of his mates' houses. A few of them hang out here sometimes. Drink. Smoke weed. Or whatever the fuck it is that young people get up to these days. Maybe just watching Japanese cartoons and Tweeting about their fucking gender, as if anyone gives a flying fuck. I don't know what they do.'

'But you're positive he's in there?'

'Aye. Spotted him buying a sausage roll on the way here and followed him the rest of the way. The stalky wee fucker's in there, all right.'

'Unless he's gone out the back,' Logan reasoned.

Hoon tore his eyes from the shed long enough to shoot the detective a disparaging sideways look. 'Come on. Who the fuck do you take me for, Jack? I know your days are spent surrounded by banjo-arsed fuckwits, but I'm no' one of them. I've scoped it all out. That door's the only way in and out. The panty-sniffing bellend's well and truly shafted himself.'

'OK. Good. Then, you can go,' Logan said. 'I'll go get him myself.'

'Fuck off!' Hoon ejected. He prodded himself in the chest. 'I'm the one who found him! I should be there to bring the fucker in.'

Logan shook his head. 'That's not how it works, Bob. You're a member of the public who has provided the polis with information. That's all.'

'I'm a paid fucking consultant! I'm allowed to tag along on stuff like this.'

'If I ask for your help, aye,' Logan said. 'Which I'm not.'

Hoon tutted. 'Don't be an arsehole!'

He glanced down at his feet for a moment. When he spoke, his tone had softened. Not by much—barely enough for the human ear to detect—but huge by his standards.

'I fucked up, Jack,' he admitted. 'The guy, her old man, he got in touch five days ago. I didn't do fuck all about it until the day before yesterday. No real reason, even, just plain and fucking simple couldn't be arsed.' He gripped the back of his neck and squeezed, massaging at a knot of tension there. 'Maybe if I'd shifted myself, that lassie'd still be alive. Or, at least no' just a pair of tits and an arse in a fucking plastic bag.'

He looked over at the shed again, and Logan got the feeling that his old boss couldn't quite bring himself to hold his eye.

'Look, I won't get in your way,' Hoon promised. 'You're in charge. I'll hang back and do as I'm told.'

'Christ. That'd be a refreshing change,' Logan remarked.

Hoon turned back to him, and the anger that usually burned behind his boggle-eyed stare had been dampened by sorrow and guilt. 'I just want to fucking help on this one, all right? I owe the poor lassie that much.'

Logan blew out his cheeks. The rain was easing off, but rivulets still ran down the faces of both men.

At last, the DCI shrugged his broad shoulders. 'Right. OK. Fine,' he conceded. 'Could be handy having you with me in case he tries to make a run for it, I suppose.'

'Yes!' Hoon punched a fist into the opposite palm, then stabbed a finger in the direction of the shed. 'Let's go drag the fucker out of there by his ball hairs!'

Logan buried his hands in his pockets and peered down his nose at the other man. 'Don't make me regret this already, Bob,' he intoned.

And then, with puddles splashing beneath their boots, both men set off along the tracks.

'Sorry to hear about your old man, by the way,' Hoon said after just a few seconds of silence had passed. 'That's shite craic.'

Logan shrugged. 'Aye. Not ideal.'

They trudged on, neither man saying anything.

'Didn't really know him, though.' Logan frowned, as if surprised the words had come out of his mouth. 'Not really.'

'Still a pretty fucking rough time, I'd have thought?'

'Aye. Ended up getting lumped with the funeral arrangements. Maddie helped with that, though. My daughter.'

Hoon grunted. 'I know who Maddie is. I do take a passing fucking interest in the lives of people I know.'

'Do you?' Logan raised his eyebrows. 'Christ, you've surprised me there, Bob.'

Hoon let out another grunt, though this one had a note of amusement to it. 'I just fucking hide it well.'

They walked on, slow and steady, getting closer and closer to the building. It had no windows, as far as Logan could tell. That was good, as it meant that anyone inside would be completely oblivious to anything happening outside, including the approach of two big, surly bastards.

'The minister asked me if I'd do a speech. At the funeral, I mean. Eulogy sort of thing.'

'Did you?'

'Did I hell,' Logan replied. 'What was I going to say? "His hobbies included knocking my mother about, and he once took a shit on the kitchen floor?"'

'Aw, come on, that would've been fucking epic, Jack. Would've raised a few fucking eyebrows, anyway.'

Logan shook his head. 'Nah. There was hardly any bugger there. Anyone that did come was with me. Maddie brought flowers. Told her not to waste her money on the old bastard, but she insisted. Nice big wreath,' he said, and he looked up at the blanket of grey cloud overhead. 'It was the only one he got, and even that was probably one too many, but... Aye. It was a nice one.'

He shook his head as if in answer to some question that only he had heard, then motioned to the wooden building that stood just a few more seconds' walk ahead.

'Right. Wide awake. Here we go.'

They slowed and picked their way more carefully for the last few steps, so as not to alert Seamus and anyone else who might be inside.

A couple of faded signs marked the shed as the property of ScotRail, and warned that any and all trespassers would be prosecuted.

No need for a warrant, then. If Seamus was in there, regardless of what he was up to, they were catching him in the act of committing a crime. That would make the paperwork easier.

The DCI didn't bother to knock. The door was slightly ajar anyway, the only apparent latch mechanism fixed to the outside. The neglected hinges screamed as he pulled the door open the rest of the way, which meant stealth and secrecy were no longer an option.

'Seamus?' Logan bellowed into the dark, cluttered interior.

Rusted metal racks lined the back wall. A filthy old couch, presumably retrieved from a skip somewhere, slouched in the shadows beside it. An ashtray sat on each of the couch's arms. Empty beer cans and vodka bottles lay strewn around. The place looked like a dodgy student flat the morning after a party. Smelled like it, too.

In the middle of the floor, in a space cleared amongst the litter, a tall wooden barstool lay on its side.

'Seamus, I'm with the police,' Logan announced, his eyes gradually adjusting to the gloom. 'We know you're in here, son. You're not in any trouble, we just want to... *fuck*!'

'What? Hold on there, Jack. Speak for your fucking self,' Hoon objected, but Logan didn't hear him.

The DCI was already lunging, running, grabbing at the feet that swung a metre and a half off the floor, toes pointed downwards, legs hanging limp.

'Aw, shite!' Hoon hissed, diving in after him, righting the stool as Logan hoisted the swinging body upwards a few inches, taking the pressure off the rope that had been strung around its throat.

The smell of piss was sharp and acrid, even amidst the fetid stench of damp, and rot, and decay.

Hoon clambered onto the stool and teetered there, his fingers hurriedly working at the noose, pulling on the knot, loosening the whole thing.

'You got him?'

'Aye,' Logan grunted. 'Hurry up!'

Hoon pulled the rope free and Seamus folded forward at the middle, slumping over Logan's shoulder. The DCI set him down, quickly but gently, on the floor just as Hoon jumped down from the stool.

The lad's face was a pallid grey mask, with a bloom of black and purple discolouration stretching from his neck to his jaw. His swollen eyelids were half-open and red, bloodshot eyes gazed upwards at the swinging rope, and into the invisible void beyond.

'Don't just stand there, Bob!' Logan barked. He placed the heel of a hand in the centre of Seamus's chest and pressed his other hand down on top, fingers interlocked. 'Call a bloody ambulance!'

Chapter Eighteen

'Right! We're here!' Shona Maguire declared with the sort of enthusiasm usually reserved for primary school teachers leading a class trip. And even then, only the newly qualified ones who hadn't yet been broken by the experience. 'It shouldn't take too long, by the sounds of it!'

Her smile was dazzling, but the girl in the passenger seat remained completely unaffected by it.

'Great,' Olivia muttered, not looking up from her phone.

'I know we're meant to be watching a film tonight, and we still can,' Shona told her.

She looked ahead through the rain-streaked windscreen, to where DS Khaled and DC Neish were waiting for her just along the track from a run-down cottage.

'I just need to quickly check in on this, then we can go. We can maybe pick up a Blu-ray. Watch the special features. Do it properly.'

Olivia smiled, and Shona felt a little surge of excitement. Movies had always been their thing. It was how they'd always connected, right from when Olivia had first been dumped in the pathologist's lap.

'I knew you'd like that idea!'

The girl frowned and looked up from her screen. 'What? Did you say something? I was reading a text. Shelly wants me to go to hers after dinner. Her mum says it's all right.'

'Oh.' Shona tried to hold on to the smile that was rapidly sliding down her face. 'I thought we were going to watch a film?'

'Yeah, well, so did I.' Olivia shrugged and gestured at the wilderness around them. 'But here we are. So, will I tell her about an hour? It's not going to be longer than that, is it?'

Shona hesitated, thought of all the things she wanted to say, then said none of them.

'Yeah. That should be fine.' She opened the door, and the wind whipped some old receipts and chocolate bar wrappers out of the plastic door pocket and carried them off towards the brooding grey sky. 'I'll be as quick as I can.'

Olivia was already typing out a text, both thumbs dancing across the screen like Michael Flatley having a seizure.

Shona paused out there in the rain for a moment, then closed the door, pulled up the hood of her jacket, and hurried over to meet the detectives.

'All right?' Tyler said, raising a hand in a friendly wave. He squinted past her to the car. 'Is that…?'

'Olivia, yeah,' Shona confirmed, burying her hands down deep in her jacket pockets. 'School's over, and I didn't want her just left roaming on her own with neither of us there. We're meant to be providing a stable home environment. I'd have done air quotes around that, but my hands are fecking freezing.'

'So you brought her to an active crime scene?' Hamza asked.

'Yes!' Shona sounded a little defensive. 'But she's going to stay in the car. At least this way I can keep an eye on her. Or, you know'—she looked from one detective to the other—'someone can, while I'm doing my thing.'

Tyler shrugged. 'I'll do it. I don't mind. If it means I get to sit in a dry car for twenty minutes, I'm up for it.'

'Oh, you don't have to do that. I just meant, you know, keep an eye from here, make sure she doesn't—'

'It's fine,' Tyler said. He rocked back on his heels. 'The boss was sort of hinting about me having a chat with her earlier, anyway.'

Shona looked visibly taken aback by this. 'Was he?'

'I can't see that, mate,' Hamza reasoned.

'Well, you weren't there, so...'

'I mean, from here's fine,' Shona stressed. 'Honestly, just glance over every so often to make sure she hasn't wandered off, or anything. That'll do.'

Tyler tapped her lightly on the arm and winked. 'It's OK. I've got this,' he assured her.

'Um. OK,' Shona said. She swapped looks with Hamza, then gave Tyler a double thumbs up, and a, 'Good luck!' that made him second-guess his decision a little, before the lure of the warm vehicle proved too much for the detective constable to resist.

Squinching his face against the falling rain, he set off at a jog towards the car, while Hamza led Shona down the track towards the house.

The pathologist glanced back over her shoulder and winced a little. 'God help... one of them. I'm not sure which,' she remarked, before turning her attention to the job at hand. 'Geoff and his team not here yet?'

'No sign yet, no,' the DS told her. 'But I can show you the freezer. Not a lot in there to go on, though. Basically, we're looking at ten fingers all laid out on a tray.'

'Ten fingers or ten digits?'

Hamza turned to the pathologist as they walked. 'What?'

'Thumbs aren't fingers,' she explained, flexing her own like she was working the controller of a games console. 'They're digits. Ten fingers means we're looking at more than one person. Ten digits could be eight fingers and two thumbs, which would point to one victim.'

'Oh. Right. Eh...' Hamza ran a hand down his face, scooping away some of the water. 'Digits, then. Eight fingers, two thumbs.' He held both hands in front of him, fingers splayed wide. 'Laid out like that.'

'Ooh. Interesting,' Shona said, but before she could say any more, a shout from behind made her turn.

'She's locked me out!' Tyler called after her. He knocked on the side window, then shrugged. 'She won't let me in.'

Shona reached into her pocket, found the key fob, and pressed the button that unlocked the car. Tyler pounced as soon as the lights flashed, pulling open the driver's door before Olivia had a chance to lock it again from the inside.

'Cheers!' he cried, then he slid into the car and pulled the door closed behind him.

'Right, then,' Shona said, her face coming alive with excitement as she turned back to the house. She rubbed her hands gleefully, then wriggled all her fingers at once. 'Let's go get a look at these digits!'

Ben managed to end the call on his ridiculous desk phone on the third or fourth attempt.

Back in the day, you could've just hung up the receiver and that would be that. Now, though, putting the handset back in the cradle just switched you to speakerphone. To end a call, you had to first find and then press a wee button. And, of course, because people who made things these days liked to overcomplicate everything, they'd hidden the bloody thing away, burying it amongst a dozen other buttons that all did things Ben chose not to worry about.

Although, calling it a button wasn't quite right. He didn't mind buttons too much. Proper buttons. *Actual* buttons. Those, he was used to. It was all this touchscreen stuff, where all the buttons were just different blobs of colour on a display, and all needed two or three hard presses to even acknowledge his existence.

Those were the ones that got right on his tits.

The DI watched, breath held, until the screen blinked back into standby mode, confirming that he'd finally succeeded in ending the call.

He took a moment to curse the phone's existence, then called over to Sinead who was still writing up info on the Big Board.

'None of the local bobbies in Aviemore knows a "Moomin".'

'Damn,' Sinead said. 'Worth a try.'

'Aye, well, I'm no' finished. So, I called through to the station in Kingussie.'

Dave wheeled himself back a few inches from his desk. 'Had they heard of him?'

Ben shook his head. 'No.'

'Oh,' Dave said.

'Turns out the station's been shut for about ten years.'

'Ah,' Dave said.

'I probably should've known about that,' Ben conceded.

'So we got nowhere?' Sinead asked.

'Patience. I'm still no' finished. So, anyway, then I put a call through to Fort William. Got Moira. There's nothing in the records about him, but I knew that, if anyone would've heard of him, it would be her.'

'And had she?' Sinead asked.

'No,' Ben said, shaking his head again.

Sinead and Dave both resisted the urge to jump in this time.

A moment later, their patience paid off.

'But *then* she asked a couple of the local boys down there if they'd heard of him, and one of them thinks he might have.'

Sinead picked up an index card and removed her pen from where she'd tucked it behind her ear. 'Got a name?'

'Richard Mathers, or possibly Matheson.'

Sinead frowned. 'That's not one of the names Tyler and Hamza were given,' she pointed out.

Ben shrugged. 'I'm just saying what they told me. Richard Mathers, or Richard Matheson, but he's eighty-three per cent sure it's Mathers.'

Dave, who had been typing at his keyboard, looked up. 'Eighty-three? That's weirdly specific.'

DI Forde raised his hands, fending off any and all questions or criticism. 'Again, just passing on the message. Personally, I'd have rounded up, but I'm just passing on what I was told.'

'Found him,' Dave announced, whipping his fingers away from his keyboard as if the speed of his search had turned the keys red hot. 'Richard Mathers. Thirty-six. Address is down as care of his parents in Kingussie.'

'Bloody hell, that was quick work,' Ben remarked. 'You sure it's him?'

Dave shrugged. 'Well, he was cautioned two months ago for shooting a naked couple in a field, so I reckon it's him.'

'Cautioned? For shooting two people?!' Ben asked in disbelief. 'How the hell did he get away with that?'

'Eh, no. Sorry. He was shooting them video-wise, I mean. They were filming a porno,' Dave explained. 'Probably could've phrased that better. The couple themselves legged it, and it doesn't look like it went any further than a slap on the wrist.'

'Sounds like that's our guy, right enough,' Sinead said. She wrote his name on a card and stuck it to the board. 'I'm assuming we're going to talk to him?'

'Too bloody right we are,' Ben confirmed, then a buzzing from his pocket derailed his train of thought. 'Hang on, it's Jack,' he said, checking the screen. 'Hello, Jack. Good timing. We've got some news that we…'

Sinead heard the squawk of the DCI's voice from halfway across the Incident Room. She watched as the smile on Ben's face first straightened, then continued curving downwards.

'Oh. Right. I see. Aye,' Ben said, his voice lifeless. Flat. Monotone. 'Aye, will do, Jack. I'll get that on right away, and ask Mitchell to put a bit of weight behind it. I'm going nowhere tonight. Just call when you're done.'

He stared blankly at the screen for a few moments, then poked at a virtual button.

'Everything all right?' Dave asked.

'Eh… No. No, not really,' Ben said. He pointed to the Big Board. 'That card you've done for that Seamus lad. You're going to need to change it.'

Sinead looked from the detective inspector to the card and back again. 'How come?' she asked.

'Because Jack's just found him,' Ben told her.

'Is he going to bring him in?'

Ben shook his head. 'No. Not much point in that,' he said. 'He's dead.'

Sinead almost dropped her pen. 'Dead?'

'Hung himself, Jack reckons. Tried CPR, but he was already a goner.'

'Oh, God. That's horrible,' Sinead said. She looked at the board, then down at her stack of cards. 'What does that mean, though? For the investigation, I mean?'

Ben puffed out his cheeks. Taggart, sensing the distress in the DI's voice, nuzzled a wet nose against the back of his leg.

'No idea,' Ben admitted. 'But if the cause of death was a guilty conscience, then it's possible we're going to get this one all wrapped up in record time.'

–

Tyler tapped his fingers on the steering wheel, his mind a dark, empty void.

Usually, he had no problems when it came to starting a conversation. He had plenty of things to talk about. Too many, DCI Logan had often said.

Today, though, this power had failed him. All six of his initial attempts to initiate conversation with Olivia Maximuke had been immediately shut down by the girl. He'd tried a few different approaches, but none of them had earned more than an impatient sigh, a frustrated tut, or—in one instance—a strained, aggressive-sounding, 'What the fuck do you want now?!'

She was proving to be a tough nut to crack.

He wasn't going to give up that easily, though. This was partly because he was determined to break through her defences, but mostly because it was still raining, and he didn't fancy getting out of the car.

'It's wet out, eh?' he ventured. 'Easing off a bit now, but it was proper pouring a wee while ago.'

There was no reaction from the girl. Of course there wasn't. Talking about the weather—were things really that bad?

He tried again.

'You into K-pop?'

She snorted, gave a little disbelieving shake of her head, then carried on typing on her phone.

It wasn't the reaction he'd been hoping for, but Tyler was secretly quite relieved. He knew absolutely nothing about K-pop, and if she'd taken him up on the conversation, he'd have eventually been left with no choice but to throw himself out of the car and make a run for it.

Better to focus on something he did have some knowledge and experience of. That didn't leave him many options, though, he realised. They didn't exactly have much in common, either—his father wasn't a murderous Russian gangster, and she'd almost certainly never come close to being flattened by a speeding train.

Actually, maybe that would intrigue her.

'I came close to being hit by the train from Harry Potter once,' he told her.

'Not close enough.'

Tyler blinked at that. 'Bit harsh,' he murmured, but the girl's attention was focused fully on her phone again.

He tapped his fingers on the wheel again. This was getting him nowhere. She had him beat.

Unless…

He turned to face her again, suddenly remembering that there *was* one thing they had in common.

'How's it going living with DCI Logan?' he asked. 'Is he hard going? I bet he is. I bet he's on your case all the time.'

Olivia's thumbs hammered away at her on-screen keyboard.

'Bet he's a nightmare. Isn't he? He's always giving me grief for stuff,' Tyler continued. He adopted a voice that was finely balanced between gruff and whiney. '"Watch what you're bloody doing, Tyler!" "Do you ever listen, Tyler?" "Don't stick your fingers in that, Tyler, or you'll blow yourself up!"' He crossed his arms and shook his head. 'It's never-ending. Can't imagine what it'd be like living with him. Is he like that with you?'

Olivia finished typing out one text, then moved on to another. Between the two, though, she gave a shrug. It was the most positive interaction Tyler had managed to tease out of the girl so far, and it gave him a much-needed confidence boost.

'Him saying all that stuff, it used to drive me up the wall. I mean, it still does a bit, but not as much as it used to,' he told her. 'It was Sinead, my wife, who told me that he only does it because he cares. I know he hides that well, and sometimes you think he hates you and wants to, like, punch you through a plate-glass window or something because you've really wound him up somehow, even though you didn't mean to, and you were genuinely just trying to work out what one of the *X-Men* you'd most like to be.'

He stopped suddenly, like he'd lost the thread of what he was trying to say and couldn't quite grasp it again no matter how hard he tried.

'But, I think that's just how he shows he cares about people,' the DC reasoned. 'By whinging at them.'

It wasn't quite where his previous sentence had been headed—he felt like he'd been building towards some really clever, well-made point for a moment back there, which was now eluding him—but it was close enough.

'So, you know, if he's giving you grief, or moaning at you, or keeps asking if you've suffered a recent head injury, you might *think* that's just him being an arsehole, but that's him being nice. In his own way.' He shrugged, and a smile broke out across his face. 'That's what I keep reminding myself, anyway. It's either that, or I cry myself to sleep.'

Olivia's thumbs slowed, then stopped. She tore her eyes from the screen and turned to Tyler, finally looking at him for the first time since he'd come clambering into the car.

‘Sorry, what one are you again?’ she asked.

The detective constable’s smile dimmed a little. ‘Tyler,’ he said. ‘DC Neish. We’ve met before. Couple of years back.’

‘I don’t remember you,’ the girl replied, and there was a sharpness to it, like the words were intended to injure. ‘Like, at all.’

‘Really?!’ Tyler said, his surprise apparent. ‘Your dad’s guys kidnapped me and held me hostage? No? We interacted quite a bit, so I’m amazed that… Doesn’t matter. The point is, all that stuff I said a minute ago, it’s all true.’

Olivia exhaled heavily. ‘What stuff?’

‘The stuff I just said. Just a second ago. About the boss, and how he might come across like a miserable bugger, but it’s only because he cares.’

‘Right.’ Olivia pursed her lips, then turned back to her phone. ‘Sorry,’ she muttered, her thumbs setting to work again. ‘I clearly wasn’t listening.’

Chapter Nineteen

Like most people, Hamza wasn't really a fan of Geoff Palmer. He didn't carry the same deep-rooted grudge for the man that Logan did, but that was because the DCI had kept the rest of the team largely sheltered from him.

Today, though, there was no one else to take the brunt of him. Hamza was on his own.

'Where's that big bugger?' Palmer asked, snapping his elasticated hood into place as he marched over from his van. Behind him, the rest of the SOC team worked to unload their equipment. 'He off skiving somewhere, is he? Eating his pre-dinner dinner, I'll bet!'

'Geoff,' Hamza said, acknowledging the other man's presence with a nod and just the faintest of sighs. 'No, he's not here. DCI Logan's off dealing with another matter.'

Palmer pulled a face that made him look like a hungry cartoon bear, then patted at his pot belly with both hands, slapping out a rapid drumbeat. 'Aye, I bet he's off dealing with another matter! His stomach!'

'No. Actually, it's a suicide.'

Palmer slapped at his stomach just a few more times, each one slower and less enthusiastic than the last, until his hands eventually fell back to his sides.

'Oh. Right. I didn't know. I hadn't heard, or I wouldn't have said…' He rubbed at his chin through the paper hood. 'He *is* quite fat, though. So it was, you know, legitimate humour.'

Hamza frowned and shook his head. 'He's not, though.'

'Well… he's big,' Geoff said, going fully on the defensive. 'So, he probably eats a lot. So, again, the joke was fine. Perfectly valid. It's not my fault that someone'—he mimed slitting his wrists, then hanging himself, his tongue lolling out as he tightened an imaginary rope—'or whatever they did. What did they actually do?'

'They hanged themselves,' Hamza confirmed, and Palmer winced.

'Right. I hoped it wasn't that one. Probably shouldn't have done the…' He started to repeat the mime, then thought better of it, and instead pointed to the bungalow a little further down the lane. 'Is this the place?'

Hamza confirmed that it was, then took the opportunity to step back while Palmer barked orders at his team. They already seemed to know exactly what they were meant to be doing, and the only response to his bellowed commands was the occasional rolling of eyes or sarcastic sounding, 'Aye, right. Whatever you say, Geoff.'

He really was not a popular man.

'That's Shona's car,' the Scene of Crime man announced, once his power trip had petered out. 'I take it she's already here? Or is she off having pre-dinner dinner with…' The grin that had started to spread across his face spluttered and died. 'Oh, no. Suicide. Forgot.' He put his hands on his hips, his face taking on a pained expression. 'Shame. It was quite a funny bit.'

'Mm. Was it, though?'

Palmer bristled. 'Well, one of us is a professional comedian, and one of us deals with murders all day, so…'

'We both deal with murders all day,' Hamza pointed out.

This knocked the wind from Geoff's sails a little. 'Not *all* day,' he eventually countered, then he brightened considerably when the front door of the house swung outwards on its broken hinges and Dr Maguire emerged. 'Oho! There she is! Here she comes!'

Hamza watched from the corner of his eye as Palmer drew himself up to his full height, ran a gloved finger across his teeth, and smoothed down his unkempt eyebrows.

It was like watching someone polishing a dog turd. And, given the colour of his head-to-toe outfit, not just any dog turd, but one of the dried-up white ones that you rarely saw lying around these days.

'Hello!' Palmer called, once he'd finished making himself more presentable. Without Logan around to cramp his style, his chances with Shona could only be improved, and he was planning on making the most of the opportunity.

He'd never understood what she saw in the DCI, anyway. Besides his height, rugged good looks, and a certain air of authority that even Palmer had to admit he wielded well, just what did Jack Logan have that he didn't?

Was he funny?

Sometimes. Maybe. In his own way.

But was he *HMV voucher* funny? Could he call into Moray Firth Radio and take the station by storm?

Palmer smiled at the very thought of it.

Not a bloody chance!

'In your dreams, Jack Logan. In your dreams.'

It was only when Hamza asked him what the hell he was talking about that Geoff realised he'd spoken that last part out loud.

His face, which was already quite red in its natural state, reddened further.

'Nothing,' he muttered, then he hurried down the slope to intercept Shona, only to have to back up again when she strode straight past him and stopped beside Hamza instead.

'Right. So, we have a problem,' the pathologist announced.

'What do you mean? Besides a load of fingers in a freezer?' Hamza asked.

'The load of fingers is the problem,' Shona told him. 'You were right, ten digits. Eight fingers, two thumbs.'

Hamza nodded. 'Aye. Thought so. Why's that a problem?'

'What? No. That's not the problem.'

'Hello, Shona,' Palmer said, grinning and widening his eyes in a way that made him look utterly unhinged.

Shona shot him a quick look to acknowledge his existence, then turned back to DS Khaled. 'The problem is that all of them—all eight fingers, both thumbs'—she took a deep breath, like she had to prepare herself for what came next—'they're all from different people.'

Chapter Twenty

The doorbell had a shrill urgency to it that felt appropriate, given the circumstances.

It kicked off the barking of a big, angry-sounding dog, and Logan heard the female constable he'd dragged along with him take a shuffled step backwards.

'Wolfram, fucking shut up!'

The shout from the other side of the door silenced the animal immediately. Logan took his hands from his pockets as the door was unlocked, his warrant card held ready in one.

The woman who opened the door had a cigarette hanging from a corner of her mouth, and a tartan tea towel slung over one shoulder. She gave the detective and the constable a quick, up-and-down once-over, then sighed, like she'd been expecting to see him.

'You not found him, then? Well, no point coming round here. Don't ask me where he is. That boy's a law unto his bloody self.'

'Mrs Starkey?' Logan ventured.

'God, no. That's his useless bastard of a father's name,' she said, the cigarette dancing up and down with the movements of her mouth. 'Morna Fraser.' Her gaze flitted over the DCI again, a little more appraisingly this time. 'Miss,' she added.

'Miss Fraser. I'm Detective Chief Inspector Jack Logan.' He showed her his ID and then nodded past her into the hallway beyond. 'You mind if we come in?'

Morna took a long, thoughtful draw on her cigarette, then pincered it between two fingers and leaned the other hand against the door frame, blocking their way.

'I do mind, actually,' she told him. 'I let that other two in, and they went poking around in Shay's bedroom. He'll be raging about that when he gets home. So, no. Sorry. You want to ask him questions, you want to look at his stuff, then you need to ask him.'

'I understand, Miss Fraser, but I'm afraid it's not about that,' Logan told her.

She sucked on the end of her cigarette again. The tip flared orange-red.

'What's it about then?' she asked, exhaling a lungful of smoke. 'You'd better not be accusing me of having done anything. Chance'd be a fine thing. Like I've got time to be getting up to antics.'

'I think it would be best if we came inside, Miss Fraser. We can sit down and have a chat.'

She didn't say anything, but something about her face shifted. Logan wouldn't have been able to describe precisely what had changed, just that something had. Some suspicion had been aroused. Some conclusion had been drawn.

'What do you want? What's happened?'

'I really think it would be better if—'

'Where's Seamus? What's happened?' Morna demanded, cutting him off. 'Where's my son?'

Logan returned his warrant card to his pocket, then briefly wondered what to do with his hands. He'd been in this situation more times than he cared to count, broken the worst possible news to a string of faces, most of which he could barely even remember.

Like everyone in this job, he'd tried for a long time to find the best way of breaking bad news. Like everyone, he'd assumed there had to be one. He'd assumed that, if only he could find the perfect combination of words and the correct body language, it would all be easier. He could spare a lot of people a considerable amount of pain, if he could only figure out the right way to go about it.

He'd eventually concluded that the whole thing was an exercise in futility—there was no right way. Nothing he could say would save the affected loved ones from one iota of grief. There were no perfect words. The angle of his eyebrows or the tilt of his head made no difference to anyone. It was just a part of the job like any other, and you did it to the best of your abilities.

But he'd still never quite worked out what to do with his hands.

'Well? Don't just stand there. Tell me!' Morna spat. 'Where is he? Have you locked him up?' Her eyes blurred. Her bottom jaw shook. 'You've locked him up. That's it, isn't it? You've locked him up. Tell me you've locked him up.'

Logan interlocked his fingers, clamping his hands together in front of him. It didn't feel right.

But then, none of this ever did.

'I'm sorry, Miss Fraser. I'm afraid there was an incident earlier. I'm sorry to have to inform you that Seamus passed away before the ambulance could reach him.'

Her eyes bulged. Her mouth moved wordlessly. A shaking hand brought the cigarette to her mouth, but it slipped from between her fingers before it could get there, and landed butt-first on the welcome mat.

'What do you mean? What are you saying?' She glared past him to where the uniformed constable was trying her best to turn invisible. 'What's he saying? Why's he saying that? He shouldn't be saying that!'

'I think we should go sit down and talk, Miss Fraser. The constable here will make us a cup of tea and we can—'

He didn't flinch when she hit him. She'd telegraphed it with a wild lunge, and it hadn't been the first time a mother, recently robbed of a child, had lashed out at him in grief. He'd been ready for it. He could take it. Part of him even welcomed it.

'I understand how you must be feeling, Miss Fraser,' he told her. 'And we're going to get to the bottom of it all. But first, I want to make sure you're OK.'

'OK?! *OK?!* Of course I'm not fucking OK!' Morna screeched, and the piercing sound of her cry set the dog off again in the back room. Hot tears of rage burned tracks down her cheeks. 'It's not true. You're lying. You're a fucking liar!'

'I wish I was. I really do,' Logan told her. 'But I'm afraid it's the truth, horrible and unfair as that is. Do you have any family locally who could—'

'Oh, *fuck you*!' Morna shrieked.

She hit him again, a flurry of clenched-fist hammer strikes to his chest. Despite her anger and her pain, the blows were limp, with very little power behind them. He let her get it out of her system.

'You did this to him,' she croaked, her arms dropping and shoulders sagging, like all her strength had suddenly left her. 'You lot. You were after him. You chased him. You chased my boy away!' The next sentence almost got stuck in her throat. She forced it free with a strangled sob of anguish. 'You killed him.'

'I understand you're—'

Logan didn't get a chance to finish. The door was slammed, the lock fastened. He heard the woman go running along the hallway, her sorrow escaping as a warbling, high-pitched wail that followed her into the house until the frenzied barking of the dog drowned it out.

Behind the DCI, the young constable let out a breath she'd apparently been holding in for quite some time.

'Oof. That was hard going,' she said. 'Are, eh, are you OK, sir?'

'Fine,' Logan said, turning away from the door. 'It happens. We'll get a liaison officer over. They'll hopefully have more luck.'

'She seemed really upset,' the constable said. She shook her head. 'Obviously, I mean. Obviously she's upset. Of course she is.'

'Aye. Understandable,' Logan said. He looked up into the darkening sky, feeling the rain on his face. 'But if you think she's upset now, just wait until we rock up tomorrow morning with a warrant to search the house and impound her car.'

The uniformed officer flinched. 'Ooyah. That's rough, sir.'

'That's the job, Constable,' he told her. 'Sometimes it's shite.'

And with that, he pulled his collar up, and set off into the worsening weather.

He was back in his car when he saw the text message from Shona, and took a moment to dry his face on his sleeve before reading it.

The words she'd written were clear enough, but for a moment they didn't make sense.

For one brief and blissful moment, things were not as fucked as they were about to be.

10 different fingers, the text read. *10 different victims.*

Logan locked eyes with the shocked-face emoji that concluded the message, and knew exactly how it felt.

'Oh,' he groaned, firing up the engine. 'Bollocks.'

–

Beverley really wasn't up for this. This wasn't what she'd signed up for. She was a scientist, not a…whatever the name was for people who crawled through narrow passageways under creepy old stone cottages in the middle of nowhere.

She had never harboured nor expressed any desire to be one of those.

And yet, here she was, inching along a darkened tunnel with her head down, and her boss calling to her from a few feet behind.

'Get a shifty on, then,' Geoff Palmer urged.

The sudden loudness of it in the confined space made her jump and bump her head on the wooden boards above.

'Shit!' she hissed.

Palmer didn't seem to notice her distress, or the way she rubbed at her head through the hood of her paper suit.

'I'm dying to know what's in there,' he told her.

'You can't be that dying,' Bev pointed out, 'or you'd have gone yourself.'

'I'm coordinating things from here,' Geoff shot back, sounding mortally offended by the remark. 'I suppose you'd like to swap places, would you?!'

'Yes!' Bev hissed. 'Of course I would. You go check out the creepy trapdoor and I'll swan about back there doing bugger all!'

'Swan about doing…? I am *not* doing bugger all, Beverley. I'm talking to you. I'm keeping your spirits up. And I'll tell you something, you're not making that easy. I feel like I'm tap dancing on the deck of the bloody *Titanic* here. Oh!'

Bev stopped and looked back towards the hatch at the top of the rickety staircase. Geoff's head had been poking through it, but he'd now vanished out of sight.

'What is it?' the Scene of Crime officer asked. She glanced anxiously around the narrow passageway. 'What's wrong?'

There was no reply. No sound but her own breathing and the slow, steady *creak-creak-creak* of feet on floorboards somewhere up above.

'Geoff?' she whispered. 'Geoff, what's happening?'

Palmer's head appeared suddenly in the hatch, making her jump again.

'Jesus!' Bev hissed, clutching at her aching skull. 'Stop doing that! Where did you go?'

'Nowhere. I was just writing down "tap dancing on the deck of the *Titanic*". Might use it in a routine,' her boss explained. He nodded past her to where the second set of steps rose up towards the hatch in the floor. 'Now, come on. Chop-chop. Let's see what's up there.'

Bev knew that there was no point in trying to argue. She was halfway along the passage now. There was no backing out.

She resumed her slow, steady shuffle, the light from her head torch sending shadows scrabbling across the rough stone blocks on either side as she closed in on the inexpertly cut wooden steps.

They'd tried the window first, prising up the corner of the wood that covered the frame. It had revealed a second board on the inside. Whoever had barricaded the window had been very keen to stop people having a nosy.

They'd deployed the thermal cameras then, but had picked up no heat signatures from the room, and nothing else had indicated that anyone was in there.

It was perfectly safe, Geoff had insisted. He'd have done it himself, but his back wasn't what it used to be, he suffered from mild claustrophobia, and he just didn't want to.

Besides, Bev was the perfect height for getting through the passage. Unlike everyone else on the team, she'd barely have to duck her head.

And so, she'd given in. She'd taken the head torch and the fibre optic camera, and had lowered herself down into the underground chamber.

She'd barely been down there a minute, but the surface world already felt like a lifetime ago.

And she still had no idea what the room she was about to peer into might hold, although she was quietly confident that it wasn't going to be anything good.

It was only when she reached the staircase that Bev saw the blood.

It wasn't much—just a few drops on a couple of the steps—but they were enough to make her take a step back, her heart thudding against her ribcage like it wanted to get the hell out of there as quickly as possible.

She fully sympathised.

'There's blood spatter here,' she announced. 'Dried in, but doesn't look old.'

'Oof,' Palmer said, and she heard him wincing from a dozen feet away. 'That doesn't bode well.'

'You don't have to tell me it doesn't bode well!' Bev snapped. 'I'm the one stuck down here dealing with it.'

'Just put the thing through!' Palmer urged. 'It's not like I'm asking you to climb up there yourself!'

Muttering, Bev uncoiled the fibre optic camera, switched on the broadcast unit, then placed a hand on the underside of the hatch.

'OK. Here goes,' she whispered, and her voice formed a faint cloud in the chill of the underground air.

The hatch lifted without any trouble. She snaked the camera wire through the half-inch gap she'd created, and slowly panned it from left to right.

'See anything?' She spoke in a whisper, but the words seemed recklessly loud in the narrow space.

'Left a bit,' Palmer urged. He had vanished again, presumably to get a better look at the footage being broadcast to the remote screen. 'Bit more. Bit more. Bit more. Little bit more.'

Bev adjusted her position, twisting herself so one foot was on the bottom step. 'That any better?'

Palmer's head lowered back down through the hole. 'Can't see a thing. You'll need to climb up there yourself.'

Bev almost snapped her neck while glaring back at him. 'You just said you weren't going to ask me to climb up there myself, Geoff! You just said those words!'

Palmer sniffed. 'Aye, well. I'm not asking you, am I? I'm telling you.' He formed a hoop with a finger and thumb of one hand, then poked the opposite forefinger up through the hole like he was inserting a suppository. 'Get up there and see what's what.'

'Oh right. Just go up? And what if an axe swings down and decapitates me, or something?'

'Well, then you duck!' Palmer sighed and shook his head. 'Jesus Christ, do I have to think of everything? It's not rocket science.'

'God!' Bev groaned, though it was barely loud enough for even her to hear. 'I'm not doing this again,' she announced, more forcefully, then she summoned her courage, gritted her teeth, and climbed upwards into the dark.

Geoff Palmer waited, halfway through the hatchway, his neck craned so he could see the other ladder as Bev's feet plodded up it.

'What do you see?' he asked.

There was no response from the other end of the passageway.

'What is it? What's up there?' he called, raising his voice.

When there was no answer, he pulled himself up and checked the camera feed on the screen beside him, then almost screamed when he saw the washed-out features of the face staring back at him.

'God Almighty, Bev! Maybe turn the camera away from your coupon? That angle and that lighting's not doing you any favours!' he shouted, aiming the words at the blank expanse of wall that now separated them both.

The footage became a grainy smear as the camera was quickly moved. When it stopped, it had settled on Bev. Palmer instantly realised his mistake.

'Wait. Was that not your face?' he shouted.

'Was it…? What do you mean? Of course it wasn't my face! It doesn't have any eyes!' came the barked response from beyond the false wall. 'Is Dr Maguire still here?' Bev demanded. 'If she's not, then get her back. Because she's *really* going to want to see all this.'

Chapter Twenty-One

Roman Howard didn't look particularly happy to see Logan on his doorstep but, unlike the occupant of the last house, at least he didn't resort to physical violence. Instead, he finished drying his hands on the towel he was carrying, and invited the DCI inside with a jerk of his head and a warning that he couldn't talk for long or he'd 'burn the arse' out of his dinner.

Logan followed him through to the same room as before, and waited while Roman informed his still-unconscious wife that they had a guest.

'Eh, aye. Sorry to drop in unannounced,' Logan said. 'I just had a couple of quick questions for you, if you don't mind?'

'Is it going to help find out who killed our daughter?' Roman asked.

'That's the hope, aye.'

'Then go on. Quick, quick. I don't want this pastry ruined.'

Despite the circumstances, Logan's mouth watered. Pastry suggested a pie, and the rich aroma drifting in from the kitchen heavily implied some sort of beef-based dish. Combined, that meant there was a very good chance that a homemade steak pie was baking in an oven just a few feet away from where he stood.

And it had been such a long time since he'd eaten anything.

Ignoring the rumbling of his stomach, Logan pushed the thought away, and started with the basics.

He asked if the 'stalker' that Roman had mentioned had been Seamus Starkey, but the farmer had just shrugged and said he didn't know. He thought he'd maybe heard the name mentioned before, but couldn't say if Seamus was the one who'd been hassling Eleanor.

The enquiring glance he'd fired in his wife's direction had gone unanswered, and so he'd finally shrugged, apologised for not being more help, and waved a hand to hurry the rest of the conversation along.

Logan had suggested that Roman take a seat for the next part, but the older man had dismissed the notion with an impatient scowl.

'Whatever it is, spit it out,' he said. 'I don't have time to pussyfoot around.'

'Right. OK.' Logan drew in a breath, but Roman beat him to the big reveal.

'Was it the pornography? Is that where this is going?'

The DCI exhaled again. 'You knew about that?'

Despite his protest from just a moment before, Roman sat down heavily on the leather chair that Hoon had claimed earlier.

'Of course we knew. Everyone knew. She plastered it everywhere. She didn't even bother to hide it,' he said. 'Not after all those bloody threats, anyway.'

'Threats?' The fine hairs on the back of Logan's neck bristled like a draught had just passed over them. 'What threats would they be?'

'This pie's going to be bloody ruined,' Roman complained, but he made no move to get up from the chair. 'Someone sent her a… postcard, I suppose. A few months back. There was a letter with it, saying that whoever it was had found out what she was up to. The videos she was making. Said that they were going to tell everyone. Us. Her friends. Her employer. Threatened to share the worst of it to all of us.'

'Were they looking for money?'

'I don't know. No. I don't think so. She didn't say what it was that they wanted. Maybe money, but… I don't know. She just sat me down and told us what had happened, and then sent us links to all her videos. All of them. Told us we were free to watch them if we wanted.' He shuddered and leaned back in the seat, like he was trying to put distance between himself and the very suggestion. 'We didn't, of course. Look at them, I mean. Of course we didn't. But it didn't matter. What mattered was she hadn't backed down. They had no power over her.'

'And what happened then?' Logan pressed. 'Did she hear back from the blackmailer?'

'I don't know,' Roman admitted. He looked down at his hands. His fingers were knotted together, the swollen, arthritic knuckles interlocked. 'We, uh, we stopped talking after that. I, um, I found it difficult. To accept it. What she'd been doing. Flaunting herself like that. Degrading herself for a few bloody pounds at a time, or whatever it was she was making.'

He slapped his hands on his thighs and rubbed them, his fingers gripping his trousers, raking at his leg muscles through the thick fabric.

'I should've talked to her. I know that. I should have said something. Because that wasn't her. *Whoring* herself like that. That wasn't the Ellie we knew,' the old man said. 'Isobel would've. She'd have known what to do. What to say to her. But, not me. I didn't. I blanked her. I told her she wasn't welcome here. My own daughter, and I cast her out.'

The cooking smells had become burning ones. The chirping of a smoke alarm shook Roman free of his guilt, and he sprang to his feet with a surprising agility for a man of his years.

'My bloody pie!' He grimaced at Logan, like it was all his fault—like *everything* was his fault—then hurried past him.

Logan followed, eventually catching up with the old man in a farmhouse kitchen that could've come straight out of a period drama. Pots and pans hung from a rack-and-rope system up near the high ceiling. A soot-coated old Aga opposite the big double window spewed a stream of black smoke.

The alarm blared a chorus of ear-splitting chirps, each one like a knife to Logan's skull. While the old man retrieved his dinner from the oven, Logan stretched up, prodded the button with a finger, and silenced the screeching.

'Bugger it.' Roman sighed, dumping a baking tray on top of the oven. There was a chance the inside of the pie was still edible, but what should've been a flaky golden pastry was a shrunken tumour of dark browns and blacks. 'This is your doing. I told you I didn't have time for this!'

The old man gripped the worktop with both hands and leaned down so his head was almost touching the edge. He took a few deep breaths, like he was enduring some great pain, then tucked his chin to his chest.

'I should've talked to her. I wish I'd just talked to her.'

'I'm sorry for your loss, Mr Howard,' Logan told him. 'I've got a daughter myself. We don't always see eye to eye. It's difficult. We can only do what we think is right at the time. We might look back on it differently later, but there's no way we can know that at the time.'

Roman straightened up, but still didn't turn to look at the detective. Instead, he picked up a fork from the worktop and prodded disdainfully at the charred pastry.

'I suppose there's something in that, yes,' the farmer agreed. 'Now, if you don't mind, Mr Logan, I'd like to go and eat with my wife.'

'Of course.' Logan stepped aside. 'But, there's one last thing. Just quickly.'

The look on Roman's face made his displeasure clear. Ruined or not, he wanted to get on with his dinner.

'What is it?' he asked, fetching a plate from a cabinet and slamming it down on the counter beside the oven.

'You mentioned a postcard that came with the blackmail letter,' Logan reminded him. 'I don't suppose you happen to know where that is?'

Chapter Twenty-Two

An hour later, Logan placed an evidence bag on Hamza's desk, and motioned for both him and Tyler to take a look.

'Look familiar?' the DCI asked them.

'Aye, boss,' Tyler confirmed.

'It's the card from the back of Seamus's board,' Hamza replied.

'His mum let you in, then?' asked Ben, leaning back in his chair. 'I thought from your message that she'd given you the heave-ho.'

'She did,' Logan said. He picked up the clear plastic bag again and held it up like it was a prize to be admired. 'I didn't get this in Seamus's room. I got it from Roman Howard.'

They all looked from the DCI to the purple postcard.

'The victim's father?' asked Sinead.

'I don't get it, boss. Did he go round there? Was he kicking off?'

'No. I mean this isn't Seamus's card,' Logan explained. 'It's Eleanor's.'

Silence fell over the Incident Room, aside from the happy panting of Taggart, who was delighted that everyone had come back to see him.

'What do you mean?' Ben asked, then he shook his head. 'I mean, I get what you're saying, but…' He frowned. 'Eh?'

Logan handed him the evidence bag, then shrugged off his coat. 'She was sent a note. Someone tried to blackmail her about the porn stuff. Roman didn't see the letter itself, but she showed him the card.' He pointed to the bag Ben was now studying. 'That card.'

'The same one Seamus Starkey got,' Hamza said.

'She didn't give in to the blackmailer,' Logan continued. 'She decided to just go ahead and show everyone the videos instead. Her old man included.'

'Oof.' Hamza winced. 'That had to be a tough call.'

'She stole away their power. Robbed them of any control they had over her.' Sinead sat on the edge of a desk. 'Ballsy move. What were they after, do we know? Money?'

'We're not sure yet. Don't have the note, just the card, and Roman says she didn't tell him, just that she wasn't giving in to it.'

'Good for her!' Tyler cheered.

'Unless that's what got her killed, of course,' Dave chimed in from his desk. 'Then it probably wasn't the best call.'

Tyler stared into space for a moment. 'Aye, there is that, right enough.'

Ben passed the evidence bag to Sinead to look at, then scootched his chair closer to his desk. 'But, hang on. Wait. What are we saying?' he asked. 'That it was Seamus who was blackmailing her?'

Tyler pointed to the DI and raised his eyebrows. 'Could be that, boss. That could be it. That could be why he had that card at his place. Maybe he was going to send it to her.'

'Nah.' Hamza shook his head. 'The address on the back wasn't Seamus's handwriting. We compared samples.'

Tyler swung his finger in the detective sergeant's direction, and shot Ben quite a scathing sort of look.

'That's a point. Aye. Exactly. It couldn't have been him that sent the card to Eleanor.'

Sinead shrugged. 'Unless he was disguising his handwriting. Maybe using the other hand to write it.'

'Unless he was doing that,' Tyler agreed. 'In which case, maybe it was him.' He crossed his legs, rested an elbow on a knee, and stroked his chin. 'It's a tough one, right enough.'

There was a world, Logan thought, where it was all just that simple. A world where one bad man did a terrible thing, then took his own life. It was a neat wee world, that. Everything nicely squared away.

He hoped it was this one.

He had his doubts.

'We should know more tomorrow,' he said. 'Warrant came through. We're searching the place and seizing his laptop and phone tonight. They'll be here for us in the morning. We're taking in the mother's car, too.'

He looked at the Big Board. There were a few hanging questions, but with a bit of hope and a wee touch of imagination, he could almost see that neat and tidy conclusion to this whole thing spelled out up there.

If only he could force himself to believe it.

'Anything in the inbox from Shona or Palmer?' he asked.

Dave flicked over to the shared email folder and pulled up the correspondence that had arrived just a few minutes before the DCI had come marching in through the door.

'Palmer reckons there was a van coming and going at the house fairly recently. Maybe a four-by-four. Something heavy, anyway, with chunky tyres. He's got a scan of the tread, but there's no obvious markings on it.'

'Still, it's something,' Logan said. 'Anything else?'

'The remains that were found in the hidden room in the house have still to be brought in, but Shona reckons it's the other half of Eleanor Howard. All her fingers are there, though, interestingly.'

'So we're still looking for ten other victims,' Logan said.

'Looks like it, aye,' Dave confirmed. 'They're looking at the other stuff found in the room. Tools. Workbench. Some rope, cleaning chemicals, plastic bags, all that sort of stuff. Palmer's pretty confident she was dismembered there, though. They'll run blood work to see if it all matches Eleanor, or if it can help ID some of the other victims.'

'Sounds like they're in for a long night,' Ben reasoned.

'Aye, though Shona's not tackling the PM until tomorrow. Reckons the remains won't arrive until the early hours, anyway.'

'That settles it, then,' Logan announced, rising to his feet. 'Let's call it a night. We can't do a whole lot more until tomorrow, and I've a feeling it's going to be a busy one. Hopefully, by then we might at least have an ID on some of those fingers.'

'CID's going through missing persons, boss,' Tyler said. 'Going to check prints and DNA when the results come through. That'll be tomorrow, too, though.'

'Do we know who owns the house yet?' Hamza asked.

'Nothing in the land registry for it,' said Ben, picking up a sheet of paper from his desk. 'Last owner on record died in 1984. I've got Uniform trying to trace descendants, but no luck so far.'

The DS tutted. 'Bugger. What about the electricity? Someone must've been paying the bill.'

'We're waiting to hear something on that,' Ben replied. 'But Scottish Power seemed quite surprised to hear it was connected. I'm thinking it might take a wee while to hear back from them while they try and figure it out.'

He yawned and stretched, then wheeled his chair away from his desk and stood up, his joints creaking as he straightened his legs.

'So I'm all in favour of this going home idea. Be good to get an early night.'

Dave clapped his hands together. The sound they made was like the crack of a starting pistol. 'Or, hear me out…' He grinned up at the detectives as they all gathered up their coats. 'Pub. Get some grub in us. Few beers. Hit the town.'

Tyler flashed him an apologetic smile. 'Can't, mate. Sorry.'

'We need to go pick up the twins,' Sinead explained.

'Course. Aye. No bother,' Dave said. 'Anyone else?'

'Would love to, Dave, but I need to get back to the wee one, too,' Hamza said. 'Another night, though.'

'Aye, another night sounds good,' Ben agreed. 'But I'm dead on my feet, so I wouldn't be worth shite.'

'And I've got a bloody teenage tearaway to get back to,' said Logan. 'Don't want to leave Shona on her own with her.'

'No bother,' Dave said. His smile hadn't changed, and yet it was somehow completely different. 'Daft idea, anyway. Don't want us being hungover in the morning.'

'You want to come to ours for a bite to eat?' Tyler asked.

'God, no,' Dave spluttered. 'I mean, no offence, or anything,' he added quickly. 'Just, you know, babies. They freak me out. I don't mean just yours. All babies.'

Sinead paused with her jacket half on. 'Right…'

'But cheers for asking,' Dave said. 'I'll just get everything squared away here. You lot go, though. Enjoy your night.'

The feeling of guilt hung so heavily in the air that Logan could almost taste it. Dave had been through a lot in the past twelve months.

The DCI buttoned his coat. Shona was going to kill him for this.

Before he could open his mouth to say that, actually, a pub dinner sounded good, Ben swooped in to save the day.

'Thinking about it, if I go home now, I'll be out for the count in front of the telly by seven o'clock, which means I'll be up again at half-three in the morning,' the DI reasoned. He turned to Dave and nodded. 'A bit of grub and a couple of drinks'll no' do us any harm.'

He picked up one of the brochures from his desk, and the smile that had suddenly returned to Dave's face faded just a little.

'And anyway, we can put the time to good use, and you can help me look at a few more of these cruises!'

Chapter Twenty-Three

Hamza didn't recognise the flash-bastard sports car parked out front when he pulled up at the house. It was sitting there in his usual space, but since the on-street parking was all first come, first served, there wasn't a lot he could do but mutter below his breath and pull up near the kerb a few houses further along.

The rain had eased off, but the pavement was pockmarked with puddles, and he weaved to avoid them as he headed for home.

After some careful foot placement and quite an impressive wee jump, he arrived at his front door, wiped his shoes on the welcome mat, then headed inside.

A snippet of laughter rang out, then was cut off by the sound of the door closing.

'Hello! It's just me!' he called, taking off his jacket.

His wife, Amira, appeared from the kitchen. She wore a smile so big that Hamza almost missed the coat hook.

'You all right?' he asked.

'Fine. Yeah. Fine,' Amira told him. 'You're home early.'

Hamza checked his watch. It was almost seven. Not exactly early by normal job standards, but almost unheard of during an active murder investigation.

'Aye, the boss reckoned there wasn't much more we could do tonight, so we knocked off. Back early tomorrow, though.'

He headed along the hallway towards her, and something like panic flared in her eyes. He laughed, not understanding.

'What is it? What's up?' he asked, then his good humour left him. 'Wait, is it Kamila? Has something happened?'

He looked around, head jerking. Usually, at the sound of him coming home, his daughter would've come running to meet him. Today, though, there was no sign of her.

'Where is she? What's wrong?'

'Nothing! Nothing!' Amira insisted. Her gaze darted, just for a moment, into the kitchen. 'She's just playing out the back. Her and Hattie are jumping in puddles.'

Hamza exhaled with relief. 'Oh. Good. You had me worried there,' he said, heading for the kitchen again. 'We got anything in to eat, because I'm—'

There was a man sitting at his breakfast bar, nursing a cup of coffee.

Hamza had already noted all the usual details before realising he'd slipped right back into police mode.

Mid-forties; dark hair greying at the temples; well-dressed but in a casual way like he wasn't trying to flaunt it. His watch looked expensive. His teeth, too. There was no wedding ring on his finger, but a slight indent and colour difference suggested there had been until relatively recently.

'You know Thomas, don't you?' Amira said. She used both hands to present him to her husband, like Hamza had just won him in a raffle. 'He's Hattie's dad.'

'Oh. Of course, aye,' Hamza said, offering a hand to shake.

He had no recollection of ever seeing this man before in his life.

'Hello!' Thomas said. His grip was firm, but he didn't quite make eye contact. Not fully. Not all the way.

'Kamila wanted Hattie to come over for a play date,' Amira explained.

'Nice one!' Hamza said. From his side of it, his smile felt almost as unconvincing as his wife's had looked just a few moments before.

He crossed to the window and looked out into the back garden. Two girls in colourful jackets and boots stomped through the water on the grass.

'Looks like they're having fun.'

'Yeah, well, I guess I'll go be the bad guy again!' Thomas said, rising quickly from his seat.

Again.

He knocked back the rest of his coffee. Rather than awkwardly standing around trying to decide what to do with the empty mug, though, he ran it under the hot tap and set it upside-down on the draining board to dry.

Hamza noted how Thomas pointedly didn't look at either him or Amira as he headed for the back door. When he opened it, a gust of wind rattled the good mugs hanging from the branches of their little wooden tree. They were only ever used for guests, although Hamza couldn't help but notice that it was still full.

'Sorry, ladies. Time to go, Hattie.'

There was a collective *aww* from the girls playing out in the garden.

'Five more minutes!'

'Another one? That would be five more five more minutes,' Thomas said. He tapped his watch and beckoned the girls in with a jerk of his head. 'Come on, Hattie. We need to get you back to your mum's.'

Hamza looked over at Amira. She was rinsing her own mug under the tap now. Unlike the quick skoosh that Thomas had given his, she was really letting the water run over the cup, turning it this way and that in the stream of steaming water.

It was almost, he thought, like she didn't want to look at him.

'You're in the police, I hear?'

Hamza turned from his wife to where the man—the interloper—stood watching him.

'Aye.'

Thomas nodded, as if giving his approval. 'I'm in a similar field, actually.'

'Oh yeah? Security guard?' Hamza asked. There was a touch of spite to it. He didn't care.

The other man smiled. 'Not exactly. Cyber security. Got my own consultancy firm.'

'Ah. That explains the midlife crisis parked in my space, then.'

Thomas smiled. 'Ha! Yeah, bit excessive. Thought I'd treat myself.'

'Daddy!'

Hamza turned just in time to catch his soaking wet daughter as she ran at him, welly boots tracking muddy footprints in a straight line across the lino.

'Hey, sweetheart,' Hamza said, bending to catch the flying hug. Her jacket was dripping wet and immediately soaked his shirt, but he didn't care, and she laughed as he swung her around.

'Do you like my new wellies?' Kamila asked once he'd set her down again. She slapped a foot forwards to show him the bright yellow boot. 'They're big-size *two*.'

The way she said that last word, like she couldn't quite believe it herself, made him smile.

'They're lovely. Where did you get them?'

'Mummy and Tommy got us them after school!'

Amira shut off the tap and clonked the mug down on the drying board. 'They were determined they wanted to play in the puddles, and I wasn't sure where her old ones were.'

'Everyone except me and Hattie had wellies at school today. They were all jumping in the puddles.'

'Even Aiden,' Hattie said, elbowing her way into the conversation.

'Even Aiden!' Kamila gasped, like this was some shocking revelation. 'And he only ever wears shorts, even when it's *snowing*!'

Hattie's voice became an ultrasonic squeal of excitement. 'We'll be able to wear our wellies in the snow!'

Both girls gritted their teeth, clenched their fists, and trembled all over, like the thought of this was too exciting for their bodies to be able to contain.

'I wouldn't get your hopes up on it snowing anytime soon,' Thomas pointed out. He put a hand on his daughter's shoulder and angled her so she was facing the door. 'Now, come on, let's get you back to Mum's.'

'Bye, Kammie!' Hattie cried, waving as she was escorted out of the kitchen.

'Bye! See you at school tomorrow!' Kamila hollered back. 'Wear your wellies!'

They both giggled in anticipation of more puddle-jumping action.

'Thanks for the coffees,' Thomas said.

Coffees, Hamza noted. Plural.

'Eh, yes. Of course. No problem,' Amira said, drying her hands on a dish towel. 'I'll see you out.'

Thomas nodded, then flashed a smile at Hamza. 'Nice to see you.'

'Good night,' the DS replied. 'Bye, Hattie.'

'Bye!'

Everyone but Hamza left the kitchen then, even Kamila trotting along the hallway so she could spend another few seconds in the company of her friend.

Hamza filled the kettle, clicked it on, then loosened his tie.

He felt his pulse quicken as the front door was closed. For a moment, there was only silence, and he wondered if they'd all left together. Just got in Thomas's car and driven away, leaving him alone.

But then, Kamila came waddling past the kitchen door, still enjoying her welly boots. She grinned and gave him a wave, then continued along the hallway towards her bedroom.

'Jammies are in the bottom drawer,' Amira called after her.

Her voice came from just beyond the kitchen door, but it took a few more seconds for Amira herself to appear, like she'd been waiting out there in silence. Bracing herself, maybe.

She was all smiles and exaggerated exhaustion when she returned, huffing theatrically and letting her shoulders droop.

'Finally!' she declared, then she tucked the stool that Thomas had been sitting on back under the breakfast bar. 'How was your day?'

Hamza shrugged. 'A woman was chopped to bits. Found some fingers in a freezer. The usual, really.' The next question was a pointed one. 'You?'

'Eh...' Amira scratched at her head and frowned, like she couldn't remember a single event that had taken place that day. 'Fine. Yeah. Nothing exciting, really. You?' She flinched, but disguised it with a little laugh. 'Sorry, already asked that, didn't I?'

She turned away and snatched up Thomas's mug, giving it a cursory dry with the towel before shoving it way at the back of the mug cabinet like she wanted it hidden out of sight.

'Thomas seems nice,' Hamza said.

'You think?' Amira still hadn't turned. 'I suppose he's all right, yeah. Nice enough. Kamila and Hattie really get along.'

Hamza leaned on the back of the stool his wife had been sitting at just a few moments ago, his hands gripping the uppermost metal spar.

He didn't want to ask the question. He hated himself for even thinking it, and he was terrified of what the answer might be.

But he had to ask it. He had to know.

'Is it happening again?'

Amira stared straight ahead into the open cabinet. It took a moment for her anger to present itself, and Hamza got the impression that she'd been weighing up her options.

'What?! How dare you?!' she cried, slamming the cupboard door closed as she wheeled around to face him. 'What are you...? How could you even...?'

She grabbed for the closest object to hand, and hurled it to the floor. The effect was lessened somewhat by it being the dish towel she'd used to dry the mugs.

It struck Hamza as oddly performative, given that her own mug was still sitting on the drying rack.

'That is… I can't believe you could even…' Amira shook her head in disgust. 'He's Kamila's friend's father. He's a dad from school. That's all! And you're accusing me of what, exactly?'

'I'm not accusing you of anything.'

'Of… of *shagging* him?! Is that it? Is that what you think?'

Hamza felt his grip tightening on the stool, and suddenly it was twelve years ago, in a different kitchen in a different house, but with all the same feelings bubbling away below the surface.

Please, not again. Please, no.

'Are you?' he asked, looking his wife in the eyes, searching for something in them that would tell him he was wrong. That would tell him *he* was the one *in* the wrong here. That this time he'd be the one rushing to apologise, to beg for forgiveness, to promise that he'd never, *ever* do it again.

He searched.

But he found nothing.

'Daddy?'

His daughter's voice shook him back to the here and now. He plastered on a smile and turned to where Kamila stood in the kitchen doorway.

'I can't get my wellies off,' she said, holding up one foot. 'Can you come and help me?'

Hamza didn't look at his wife. He couldn't. Not yet.

'Course I can, sweetheart,' he said.

Her warm little hand slipped into his, and she led him in a welly-waddle along the hallway to her bedroom.

–

'She's taking the piss,' Logan said, for the fourth time that hour. He paced to the window, with Taggart trotting along behind him, peered out, then returned to the couch. 'She's absolutely taking the bloody piss.'

Shona couldn't exactly disagree. Olivia was supposed to have been back from Shelly's over two hours ago, and all attempts to contact her had failed. Calls had been ignored, messages had gone unread, and if it weren't for the fact that this same pattern had already played out several times before, Shona might even have been worried.

'She's playing up. Testing boundaries,' the pathologist explained.

'Aye, she's testing my bloody boundaries, all right,' Logan grunted. He plucked a nacho chip from the bowl on the table, considered it for a moment, then tossed it to the dog, who crunched it happily. 'I'm not even hungry! That's what she's doing to me. She's making me lose my bloody appetite!'

'God, that is serious,' Shona said. She put a hand on the DCI's belly. 'However will you survive?'

Logan was in no mood for jokes. He heaved himself back to his feet and checked the window again.

No sign.

'Do you think this is all right?' he asked, his anger at the missing girl homing in on the closest available target. 'Her staying out like this, not letting us know where she is, not answering messages? Do you think that's fair enough?'

'No. I don't,' Shona said. She joined him by the window. Taggart hung back at the nachos, and sat there patiently staring them down. 'I think it's completely out of order, and we'll talk to her. Again.'

'And do you actually think she'll listen this time?'

'No, probably not,' Shona said. 'She's a teenage girl. I didn't listen to anyone when I was her age, and I hadn't been through anything like the stuff she has. Although, to be fair, my dad was actively trying to encourage me to go outside and engage in conversation with people my own age, so it was sort of the opposite problem, really. But the point stands.'

'What was the point?' Logan asked.

Shona's mouth froze, half-open.

'I have no idea,' she eventually admitted. 'It's gone right out of my head.' She put a hand on Logan's arm and squeezed it. 'We knew this wasn't going to be easy. We knew she might push back, and that we'd have to be patient.'

'I have been patient. I've been a Zen bloody monk, all things considered!'

'You have. You really have,' Shona agreed. 'And it's going to pay off. It'll get better. We'll get through to her. We just need to give her time.'

The flaring of headlights on the street outside brought the conversation to a halt. A door opened. Voices mumbled in the rain, then the door was closed again, and the car drove off into the night.

Shona shot Logan an anxious look and gave his arm another squeeze as footsteps plodded their way up the path.

'Zen monk,' she whispered. 'Remember?'

Logan drew in a deep breath, held it, held it, held it, then finally nodded.

The front door opened and closed again. Taggart shifted from sitting to standing, but otherwise kept his attention trained on the bowl of cheese-coated tortilla chips.

Shona smiled warmly at the living room door.

The footsteps continued along the hallway, right past the living room, then thudded on up the stairs.

'Bugger this,' Logan announced. He charged out into the hallway, ignoring the whispered protests of Shona behind him. 'Here, where the hell do you think you're going?'

Olivia, who had just reached the top step, didn't bother to turn around. 'Upstairs. Where does it look like?'

She continued onto the upstairs landing and turned towards her room. Logan wasn't letting her off that easily, though. He powered up the steps, the bannister creaking under the force of his grip.

'You were meant to be home two hours ago,' he barked. 'We phoned and messaged you a dozen bloody times!'

The force and volume of Olivia's tut was almost enough to knock him back down the stairs. 'I didn't hear it.'

Logan reached the top step just as her door slammed closed.

'You didn't hear it?' he hollered. 'How's that even possible, given that your phone's never out of your bloody hand!'

'Jack!' Shona pleaded.

Logan was halfway across the landing, fully intending to barge straight into what was now Olivia's bedroom. Something about the tone of Shona's voice made him slow down, though, so by the time he reached the door, he had composed himself enough to knock.

It was a proper old-school police knock, but it was better than kicking the door down.

'*What*?' Olivia snapped.

The disdain in her voice made Logan's hackles rise. His hand went for the handle, but a shake of a head from Shona forced him to stop.

'Zen,' the pathologist whispered.

Logan gritted his teeth and mimed strangling the life out of someone. This seemed to help alleviate some of his rage, and he was able to bring the rest under control with a few slow, steady breaths.

Running a hand down his face, he turned back to the door.

'Can you come here a minute?' he asked.

There was no reply. He raised his voice and tried again.

'Olivia, can you come to the door, please?'

There was another tut. 'Why?'

'Because I fu—' Logan ran a hand down his face. 'Because we'd like to talk to you.'

'God's *sake*.'

Footsteps thumped across the room. Olivia pulled open the door, then crossed her arms, blocking the way.

Shona reacted before Logan could. 'Hold on. Is that a black eye?' she asked, barging the detective aside. 'What the hell happened? Did someone do that? Were you in a fight?'

'It doesn't matter,' Olivia said.

'It does so matter!' Shona tried to get a better look, but Olivia batted her away.

'I told you, it's fine. What do you want?'

Logan could sense the worry radiating off Shona in waves. She managed to keep a lid on it, though.

'I made nachos,' she said. 'Do you want some?'

Olivia glanced at the top of the stairs, then shook her head. 'I'm fine.'

'I could bring some up,' Shona suggested. 'You don't have to come down if you don't want to.'

The girl rolled her eyes and sighed, as if this was the most inconvenienced anyone had ever been in the entire history of the world. 'Fine, then. I'll have some, if it'll stop you going on about it.'

'Great!' Shona scurried for the stairs. 'I'll heat some up. Won't be a minute.'

Olivia watched her go, then slowly raised her gaze to where Logan was leaning against her doorframe. He'd angled his shoulder so that there was no way the girl could close the door until he'd moved.

'What?' she demanded. Her arms had already been folded, but she tightened the knot, putting a bit more emphasis into it. 'What are you staring at me like that for?'

Logan had been holding a breath for a while. He let it out with a long, low grunt, like a bear stirring from a long hibernation.

'What happened to your eye?'

'Nothing. I fell.'

'Did someone hit you?'

Olivia tutted. 'What? No. And if they did, they'd be in a worse state than me.'

Logan didn't doubt that. She concluded that she wasn't going to tell him what had happened, and part of him was almost relieved.

He ran a hand down his face like he was trying to rub away some of the stress and tension, then tried a different approach with the girl.

'I had doubts about you coming here,' he announced. 'Went back and forth on it. One day I was up for it, the next I thought it was a bloody terrible idea.'

'So?'

'Shona, though? She was adamant. There was no arguing with her. I think, had I put my foot down and said it wasn't happening, I'd have been given the elbow. I honestly think she'd have chosen you over me.'

Olivia didn't say anything for a moment, then she shrugged. 'You're not exactly a catch.'

'You want to know what convinced me in the end?' Logan asked, ignoring the jibe. 'It wasn't that. It wasn't the fear of being dumped. I went to see your dad. In prison. I went to ask his advice, would you believe?'

The barefaced mask of disdain slipped a little. Olivia blinked, and then her practised contempt returned. 'So?'

'I told him what I was thinking. We talked about it. About you. About the idea of you coming here to live with us.'

Olivia shrugged like she didn't care. Even as her shoulders were sinking back down, though, she asked, 'And?'

'And he was raging. Blew his top. Hated the idea. Warned me not to dare. Told me to stay away from you. But, you know, with a lot more swearing and a few threats thrown in for good measure,' Logan replied. 'And that's when I made my mind up. Before I'd even left the building. That's when I knew that I was going to let you come stay with us.'

'Right. Oh. OK,' Olivia said. She nodded quickly, her cheeks flushing red. Her arms unfolded and one hand gripped the edge of the door. 'Well, well done. Good job. You managed to get one over on him. Bet that was nice for you. Glad I could help you win a victory over him. Can you get out of my room, please?'

'What? No, that's not what—'

'Get out!'

'Ow! Jesus!'

Logan grimaced as she pushed the door over, trapping part of his arm between it and the frame, forcing him to step back and pull it free.

The door slammed in his face just as Shona arrived back at the top of the stairs with a plate of steaming hot nachos.

She looked at the closed door.

She looked at the detective standing outside it, rubbing at his arm.

'What happened?' she asked. 'What did you do?'

Logan sighed. 'Oh, damned if I know,' he remarked.

Then, he squeezed past the pathologist and, still rubbing at his arm, plodded sullenly down the stairs.

Chapter Twenty-Four

DI Ben Forde wished a good morning to a couple of Uniforms, entered the lift and pressed the button for the third floor, then sagged the moment the doors closed.

His head hurt—a dull pressure pushing down that occasionally gave way to a sharp stabbing sensation behind his right eye socket.

He couldn't quite describe how the rest of him felt. Dried out, maybe? Desiccated? Dehydrated like a strip of beef jerky?

Whichever it was, he wasn't enjoying it.

His throat felt like sandpaper. He was sure one of his eyes had shrunk. Someone had taken out his stomach and reinserted it upside-down.

Good God, Dave Davidson could drink.

'There he is!' Dave cried, when Ben shuffled into the Incident Room. The constable had packed away about twice as much alcohol as Ben had, but somehow looked as bright as a button.

The DI winced at the volume of Dave's voice, the harshness of the room's lighting, and just his own existence in general. He acknowledged the nods, waves and greetings of Hamza, Tyler and Sinead, then turned back to the man in the wheelchair.

'I'm no' even talking to you,' he rasped. 'You've broken me.'

'You do look a bit peaky, boss,' Tyler confirmed.

Dave's grin only broadened. 'Ah, come on! You loved it!'

'Well, I'll have to take your word for that, won't I?' Ben said, lowering himself slowly into his chair while keeping his head as level as possible. 'Because I don't remember about ninety per cent of it.'

'What bits do you remember?' Dave asked.

Ben grimaced. Rifling back through his disjointed memories of the night before took effort. Given that just staying alive this morning also took effort, he didn't have a whole lot more to give.

'That wee apple drink thing was the turning point,' he eventually replied. 'I remember before that. I remember you sitting that down in front of me, and thinking it tasted quite pleasant. And then things get a bit more vague.'

Dave nodded. 'Good. So, you don't remember the dancing on the tables or the strippers, then?'

'What?!' Ben jolted upright in his seat, then winced at the interesting new type of headache the movement triggered.

Sinead and Tyler both looked across their desks at him, their faces lighting up in delight.

'Oh-ho, boss! What's this?'

'Who was dancing on tables?!' Ben demanded.

Dave patted the arms of his wheelchair. 'Well, it'd be pretty impressive if it was me,' he announced, then he picked up his phone from his desk. 'Here, I took photos of you in action. You can see Channelle pissing herself in the corner. Aye, laughing, I mean, not literally.'

'Who the hell's Channelle?' Ben asked.

'One of the strippers we met,' Dave said. 'She told you she liked your moves.'

Ben grimaced. 'Christ. And what did I say?'

'You said you were old enough to be her grandfather,' Dave replied.

The DI relaxed a little. 'Well, thank God for that.'

'And then you offered to take her home and tuck her in, and read her a bedtime story.'

Ben's entire body clenched from the eyebrows down. 'I did not!'

Dave laughed. 'Nah, not really. You told them at length about how great Moira is, and offered to pay for them all to take taxis home.'

'Let's have a look at the photos, then,' Sinead said.

'Delete them!' Ben cried.

Dave held up his phone. 'But do you not want to—?'

'Delete all of them right now! That's a direct order! Nobody sees them!' Ben sagged back down in his chair, rubbed his hands up and down his face, then his hangover-hazed brain finally came to a realisation. 'How come Jack's no' here? I thought I'd be the last one in. Had to take the bloody bus, couldn't risk the car.'

Sinead glanced pointedly in the direction of the office at the back of the room. The door was closed and the blinds were pulled shut, making it impossible to see inside.

'Oh, bugger. He's no' in there, is he?' Ben groaned. 'I was planning on sneaking in for a kip later.'

'He went straight in when he arrived, sir,' Sinead revealed. 'Doesn't seem in the best of form this morning.'

'Aye, and he's not the only one!' Tyler said. He put a foot on the wheeled base of Hamza's chair and gave it a shake. 'This one got out of the wrong side of bed this morning, too. He's a right crabbit bastard.'

'I'm not,' Hamza assured them. Then he slapped at Tyler's leg and hissed, 'Fucking quit that!'

'See?' Tyler said.

He laughed, but a short, sharp look from Sinead shut him up. Both detective constables had arrived early, but Hamza had already been at his desk, and had just barely acknowledged their arrival.

He didn't look rough like Ben did, but something about his demeanour told Sinead he was suffering, all the same.

'What's that you're working on?' DI Forde asked, continuing to divert attention from the whole 'dancing on tables' conversation.

He had zero recollection of doing anything of the sort, although it would explain why his hips felt like someone had taken them out and used them as drum beaters.

'Seamus Starkey's laptop. Came in last night,' Hamza said, not looking up from the screen of a small, slightly battered-looking portable computer. 'It's been swabbed and checked. Thought I'd see if I can find anything out.'

'Right. Aye. Should you no' just bung it over to the tech squad?'

Hamza shrugged. There was something a bit absent-minded about it. 'Just thought I'd have a look first.'

'Is that no' a bit risky?' Ben asked.

'Not if I get peace and quiet to get on with it,' Hamza said, and there was a snap to his tone that took everyone else in the room aback.

Even Taggart, who had been sleeping soundly under one of the desks, opened an eye.

'Sorry, sir,' the DS said. 'Rough night.'

'Aye. Well, I know that feeling,' Ben said. He got shakily to his feet. 'I'd better go see himself. I'll be very disappointed if there isn't a cup of tea and a wee pile of chocolate digestives sitting here on my desk by the time I get back.'

Dave rolled himself back in his chair. 'I'll get it. I owe you that much.'

'Oh, if you think that's us square, you've another bloody thing coming,' Ben told him.

'Bacon roll?' Dave suggested.

Ben grimaced, like this was the worst idea he'd ever heard. His expression shifted, though, as he gradually reconsidered, and eventually he nodded. 'Aye. Fine. That'll do it,' he announced, then he shuffled gingerly towards the office at the back of the room, occasionally touching a desk or the back of a chair to stop himself falling over.

Once the DI and the constable had both left the room, Tyler glanced at his wife, then shot a meaningful look at the back of Hamza's head.

Sinead shrugged, pulled an *I don't know* face, then encouraged her husband to say something with a quick, urgent nod.

Tyler frowned and shook his head. He pointed to Sinead, then jabbed a thumb in Hamza's direction.

Sinead pointed to herself, looked outraged by the suggestion, then turned the finger on Tyler, deflecting responsibility back to him.

'What the hell are you doing?' Hamza asked, and both DCs hurriedly plastered on smiles when they realised the sergeant was watching them.

'Nothing,' Tyler said. Then, when it was clear that Hamza wasn't buying this, he added, 'Sinead just wanted to ask you something.'

The look Sinead gave him would've burned his eyelashes clean off had he not turned away just in the nick of time.

'Aye. No. Tyler was just wondering if you're all right?' she said, quite skilfully returning the responsibility to her husband. 'Weren't you, Tyler?'

Hamza's gaze was on him now. Tyler could only nod, both in agreement with the statement and in appreciation of the deflection. He'd been well and truly outplayed.

Or had he?

'Eh, aye. Just that you seem'—he saw a chance for victory, and went for it—'what's the word I'm looking for, Sinead?'

Sinead dead-eyed him. 'I don't know.'

'Aye, you do,' Tyler insisted. 'He seems a bit… What? He seems a bit something. What does he seem?'

'It's nothing,' Hamza said, tiring of the back and forth. He turned in his chair again to face Seamus's laptop. 'Get back to work.'

A few more looks bounced back and forth between the detective constables, then Tyler rolled his chair back over to his own desk, while Sinead returned to the Big Board.

'You, eh, getting anywhere with it?' she asked, as she leafed through a stack of printouts. Most of it was Geoff Palmer's report. The man used a lot of words to say very little.

'Yeah. I'm in. Just looking through his files,' Hamza said.

'Nice one! Find anything juicy?' Tyler asked.

Hamza shook his head. 'Not yet.'

'What sort of thing do you think you might—?'

Hamza tutted and raised his hands from the keyboard. 'I don't know, Tyler. All right? I don't know. Can I get on with it, do you think? Can you shut up for five minutes so I can do my job?'

Tyler blinked in surprise. He'd known the DS for a long time. They'd been through a lot of highs and lows over the years. He couldn't remember Hamza ever talking to him like that before.

'Eh, aye. Course. Sorry.'

A hush fell over the Incident Room, the only sound the clicking of Tyler's mouse buttons, and the rhythmic tap-tap-tap of Hamza's typing.

In the near silence, it was just possible to make out the sound of DCI Logan's voice from inside his office.

'On a table? You're lucky you didn't break a bloody hip.'

Sinead smiled as she skimmed through Palmer's report, searching for key points to add to the board.

There were no fingerprints on any of the tools or workbenches that had been found in the secret room at the cottage. Several different hair and fibre samples had been collected, but as of yet, they hadn't been identified.

The post-mortem was still to be carried out, but Shona had felt confident enough to say that the body parts found in the room were almost certainly those of Eleanor Howard.

The head, definitely.

She picked up her pen and began to summarise the report on a few index cards. She was two cards in when Tyler ejected a high-pitched, 'Holy shit!' of surprise.

'What is it?' Sinead asked.

Tyler pointed excitedly to his screen. 'The fingers! In the freezer! One of them, anyway. They've ID'd it!'

Hamza prodded a key on the laptop, then turned to the DC. 'What, they've found one of the victims?'

'No. I mean aye. I mean, sort of,' Tyler said. 'They ran the prints on all of them. Got a hit on one. A teacher from Aviemore.'

Sinead picked up a bundle of paperwork and leafed through it. 'A teacher? I don't remember a teacher being on the missing persons list.'

'That's it. That's what I'm saying! She isn't,' Tyler said. He pointed to the screen again, like all the information was right there, if only they'd bother their arses to look. 'She's not missing. She's alive. Uniform checked, and she's alive and well.' He shrugged. 'Well, I mean, she's a finger down, obviously, but other than that, she's fine.'

'Bloody hell!' Sinead muttered. 'Do we have an address?'

Tyler folded his arms triumphantly, despite the fact he'd done none of the actual legwork required to find out this new information. 'Yep! Got it right here.'

Movement at the corner of his eye caught Hamza's attention. He turned in his chair, then lunged for the laptop, his face contorting in panic. 'Shit! No, no, no, no!'

Lines of computer code scrolled upwards on the screen, moving far too quickly for anyone to read it. The only legible word was the first one, as it was the only one that appeared on every line.

'Deleting.'

'Shit, shit, shit!' Hamza stabbed his finger down on the laptop's power button. Whole minutes seemed to pass before the computer gave a *bleep* and the screen went dark.

Hamza's head fell forwards into his hands, his splayed fingers pressing hard against his forehead.

'OK,' he mumbled. 'So that might be a problem…'

–

A handful of minutes later, Ben and Logan both stood over Hamza's desk. The laptop remained switched off. The sergeant's hands lay clasped in his lap.

'Did I not say you should send it to the tech lot?' Ben reminded him. 'I told you to send it down to them.'

'You did, sir,' Hamza confirmed. 'Sorry, I just thought it would be quicker if I had a look myself.'

'And how's that working out?' Ben asked. He pointed to the screen. 'Is it going to keep deleting things when you turn it back on?'

Hamza shifted in his seat. 'I, uh, I don't know if it will turn back on,' he admitted. 'Depends on what's been deleted. If it's system files, then—'

Ben waved a hand to stop him. 'Right, right, don't confuse us all with your tech mumbo jumbo.'

Logan tutted. 'The word "files" isn't mumbo jumbo, Benjamin,' he said, then he turned back to Hamza. 'Look, it's not ideal, but mistakes happen. You're no' usually the one making them, though. What happened?'

Hamza's shoulders twitched in a suggestion of a shrug. 'Don't know, sir. I just… I got distracted. I wasn't paying enough attention. I'm sorry.'

'Did you get anything we can use? Anything at all?'

Hamza's face made the answer obvious.

'Bugger,' Logan muttered.

'I did find out his email uses IMAP,' Hamza said, offering up a sliver of a silver lining.

The others looked at him blankly.

'Internet Messaging Access Protocol,' he said.

Logan shook his head. 'Now *that's* mumbo jumbo,' he said. 'What are you on about?'

Hamza turned in his chair. There were dark rings below his eyes, and a hint of bloodshot in the whites. 'It means that his email probably syncs across his devices. So, anything that was on here should be on his phone.'

'Which you're going to send to the tech bods,' Ben told him. 'Isn't that right?'

Hamza gave a nod. 'Of course, sir. I'll get it sent over right away.'

At last, with a sigh, Logan turned to DCI Neish. Tyler had been bouncing excitedly on the spot throughout the entire conversation with the detective sergeant, a sheet of paper clutched in a sweaty hand.

'OK, Tyler. Go.'

'Good call on doing the bad news first, boss! That's the right way round. Get the bad stuff out of the way, then you get to perk yourself up with—'

'I don't need a blow-by-blow of my own decision-making process, son,' Logan nodded to the paper. 'What have we got?'

'Right! Aye!' The detective constable allowed himself a half-second pause for dramatic effect. 'We found a finger, boss!'

Logan and Ben both frowned. 'What? Another one?' the DCI asked.

'Oh, God. Is that us up to eleven?' This news did Ben's headache no favours whatsoever. He rubbed at his temples. 'That's all we bloody need.'

'Eh, no. Sorry. I mean we found the owner of one of the ones we already found. We got an ID. Fingerprint that was taken to exclude her after a break-in a couple of years back. It belongs to a teacher,' Tyler said. His face lit up as he reached the big finale. 'And get this—she's not dead.'

The confusion lines on the senior detectives' faces etched themselves deeper.

'She's what?' Logan asked.

'She's not dead!'

Ben leaned an elbow on his desk. 'You mean she's alive?'

Tyler shrugged. 'I mean, aye. That is another way of saying it, boss, but I thought "she's not dead" had pretty much covered it.'

'Then how the hell did her finger end up in that freezer?' Ben wondered aloud.

'Dunno, boss,' Tyler admitted. He held out the sheet of paper. 'But we've got her address, so we could always just go and ask.'

Chapter Twenty-Five

Charlotte Wilson lived on the downstairs floor of a small maisonette just off Aviemore's main street. Her car was a bright green Volkswagen Beetle from the 1970s with daisies and other flowers painted on the doors and bonnet. A set of large eyelashes had been attached above the lights, and this drew a low hiss from Logan when Tyler pointed out.

'Christ,' the DCI muttered, shutting off the engine of his BMW. 'She's one of them, is she? I bet that car's got a name. I bet it's bloody Estelle, or Suzanna, or something.'

The detectives both opened their doors, and almost immediately met Hamza and Sinead as they got out of the detective sergeant's car behind them.

'Want me to come in with you, boss?' Tyler asked.

'God, no. You wait out here in case she does a runner. Sinead, you're with me.'

'Right you are, sir.'

Logan looked along the short path to the front door of the maisonette. 'Give it a few minutes here. Then, assuming she doesn't try and bolt, you two head to the station. Take the dug. I want to talk to this Moomin character today. Find him, and get Uniform to bring him in.'

'Will do, boss,' Tyler replied.

'And the community service guy. The supervisor.'

'Jonathan Milburn,' Sinead said.

'Aye, him. Talk to him. I want to know how Seamus reacted when they found the bag. Talk to the lassie that was with them again, too. Same question. How did Seamus seem when they found that bag?'

Tyler's enthusiasm quickly waned at the prospect of having to interview Sandra again, but he nodded his understanding. 'Right you are, boss.'

Logan shifted his gaze to Hamza, but the DS didn't seem to have heard anything of what he'd just said.

'You with us, Detective Sergeant?' he barked, and the sharpness of his tone made Hamza snap to attention.

'Aye, sir. Sorry, sir. We'll get on that.'

Logan regarded him through narrowed eyes for a few moments, then he opened the gate and gestured for Sinead to lead the way.

Tyler studied Hamza for a moment, then crossed his arms and leaned against the driver's side door of Logan's car, watching as the DCI rang the doorbell of Charlotte Wilson's flat.

'So, what's up?' he asked.

Hamza's reply was instantaneous, like he'd had it loaded in the chamber, ready to fire. 'Nothing.'

'Nothing my arse. There's something up,' Tyler insisted. 'You can talk to me, mate.'

'Honestly, Tyler. It's nothing.'

'If it was nothing, you wouldn't have messed up that laptop earlier.'

'I didn't—OK. Well, maybe if you hadn't distracted me by talking, I would have spotted the problem.'

'That's just it, though,' Tyler said. 'I'm always talking, and it's never been a problem before. Hell, you used to do more complicated stuff with Tammi-Jo around, and she was like the Tasmanian Devil from them old cartoons, just burling around wittering shite. Never put you off your stride, though.' He shrugged. 'So, what is it? What's up?'

Hamza shoved his hands deep in his trouser pockets. Yesterday's rain had stopped during the night, but he still buried his head into his shoulders, like he was trying to stop water running down the back of his neck.

At the other end of the path, a woman in a pair of lemon yellow dungarees and big glasses stepped aside to let Logan and Sinead into her flat.

Charlotte, it seemed, was not the doing-a-runner type.

'It sounds stupid saying it out loud,' Hamza muttered. 'It's really nothing. I'm imagining things.'

'What sort of things?' Tyler pressed.

The detective sergeant let out a long, heavy sigh, whispered something that only he could hear, then spat it out.

'Amira had some guy round yesterday when I got home.'

Tyler straightened so he was no longer leaning on the car. 'How do you mean?'

'I mean there was a guy in my house when I went home. With Amira.'

Tyler's eyes widened. 'Shit. Like… *with* with her?'

'What? No! In the kitchen. They were having coffee.'

It took the detective constable a moment to process this. 'Coffee?' he eventually said. 'Is that it?'

'Aye. But it was weird.'

'The coffee was weird?'

'No, not the… The situation,' Hamza said. 'The whole thing. It felt… I don't know. It felt off. Gut feeling.'

'Bloody hell,' Tyler muttered.

It didn't sound like the most suspicious of situations to him, but he'd worked alongside Hamza for long enough to know the detective sergeant's instincts were usually good.

'What was he doing there?'

Hamza ran a finger along the top of Logan's car, like he was checking it for dust. Taggart watched him from the back seat, his tongue hanging out, his tail giving an occasional thump when he felt like a bit of eye contact might be on the cards.

'His daughter's friends with Kamila. She was round playing after school.'

'Right.' Tyler leaned on the car again. 'So there was a reason for him being there, then?'

'He could've dropped her off,' Hamza countered. 'Amira could've just picked them both up from school. But no, they went shopping together. The four of them. To buy *wellies*!'

He delivered that last word like it was the smoking gun in a murder case.

Tyler nodded slowly. He could sense he was on dangerous ground here, but it was his duty as a mate to offer a counterpoint.

'And did she need wellies, like?'

'Well, I mean, aye, but that's not the point!' Hamza shot back.

'What is the point?'

'He was having coffee!' Hamza cried, his hands held out at his sides like he was presenting some sort of damning but completely invisible evidence. 'He wasn't even using the nice mugs. And he washed up after himself.'

'What a bastard,' Tyler said. 'You think you can get him to pop round my place, too?'

The clenching of Hamza's jaw and the darkening of his eyes told the detective constable that he may have gone too far. He moved quickly to calm the situation.

'Look, mate, it's almost certainly nothing,' he said. 'You're overthinking it. Did you talk to Amira?'

'Aye. Of course.'

'And?'

Hamza shifted his weight from one foot to the other. 'She said it was nothing.'

'There you go, then!'

'Aye, but—' Hamza snapped his jaw shut, stopping himself just in time.

'But what?'

The DS shook his head. 'Nothing. You're right. I'm probably just overthinking it.' He smiled, but it was paper thin. 'Cheers, mate. Now, I don't think she's going to try and leg it, so I reckon we head to the station and do whatever it was the boss asked us to do.'

Tyler watched his friend as he walked back to his car and opened the door.

'And I hope you were listening to what he said,' the DS continued. 'Because I didn't catch a word of it.'

Chapter Twenty-Six

She had to be a primary teacher, Logan thought. There was no way that this thirty-something woman, with her bright yellow dungarees, fluffy pink socks and anxious, mousy wee movements would last two minutes in a secondary school. They'd eat her alive.

Possibly literally, depending on the catchment area.

She offered them tea, which they initially declined, until she insisted she was making one for herself, anyway, so it really wasn't a bother.

The drinks were brought through, one at a time, in colourful pottery containers that appeared to have been homemade, and most likely in something of a hurry. They were approximately mug-sized and, if you used your imagination, vaguely mug-shaped, too.

Each had been glazed a different shade of green, with white and yellow flowers painted inexpertly on the sides.

The handles looked like they'd been stuck on as something of an afterthought, and both detectives supported the mugs from below, assuming that the handles were almost certainly going to fail and fall off before their tea had been drunk.

'You've got a lovely flat,' Sinead said, as Charlotte took a seat on the chair across from the narrow couch.

The couch was built for two, but since Logan technically qualified as a one and a half, Sinead's space was limited, so she couldn't move much more than her head. She glanced around at the vibrant paint hues and the clumsily upcycled furniture.

'It's very... lively.'

Charlotte thanked her for the kind words, then shoved her thick-rimmed glasses up onto her head, using them like a headband to hold back her unkempt frizz of red hair. As she did, both detectives' eyes were drawn to the slightly grubby white bandage on her left hand.

They'd noticed it almost right away—it had been the reason she'd brought the mugs through one at a time—but she'd kept it out of sight as much as possible, like she was ashamed of it, or just afraid that they'd notice.

She saw how their eyes followed the hand now, and quickly lowered it to her side so it was tucked between her and the side of the chair.

'Uh, so... What is it I can do for you?' she asked.

'It's a bit of an odd one, Miss Wilson,' Logan said. She was definitely a 'miss', he thought, and her lack of reaction didn't say anything to the contrary. 'It's concerning a discovery that was made yesterday in a house a few miles from here.'

'A discovery?' Charlotte's gaze danced around the room, not settling on either detective. 'What kind of discovery?'

Logan took a sip of his tea, then instantly spat it back into the mug.

'Sorry, it's Earl Grey, is that all right?'

Of course it bloody wasn't. Earl Grey tea was an outrage at the best of times. Being subjected to it unexpectedly was, as far as Logan was concerned, up there with some of the more harrowing war crimes.

'That's fine,' he said, then he set the mug down on a coaster on the table, where it would remain untouched for the remainder of the interview.

'Is this about that young woman who was killed?' Charlotte asked. 'I heard you'd got someone for that.'

News travelled fast in small Highland towns, and gossip as juicy as a murder and a suicide must've ripped through the place like an inferno.

'We can't really comment on that at the moment,' he said. 'We're here because some remains were found at an abandoned cottage yesterday that we're trying to make sense of.'

'Remains?' Charlotte seemed to shrink down into herself. 'Human remains?'

'I'm afraid so. And one of them'—Logan stole a sideways glance at Sinead, not quite able to believe what he was about to say—'was yours.'

Charlotte stared back at him, puzzled. 'Mine? What do you...?' She looked down at her bandaged left hand and her missing middle finger. 'Wait. What are you saying?'

'There's no easy way of saying this, Miss Wilson. Your finger was found in a freezer,' Logan said.

'In a freezer? In whose freezer? What do you mean? How the... Jiminy Criminy did it get there?'

The 'Jiminy Criminy' threw Logan off his stride for a moment, but he quickly got back on track.

'That's what we're trying to find out,' he said. 'Do you mind me asking what happened?'

'Uh, bicycle accident,' the teacher replied. 'It got caught in the spokes.'

'Ouch,' Sinead said. 'That must've hurt.' Her brow furrowed in thought. 'How does that happen, exactly? Was someone else riding the bike, or...?'

'I fell off,' Charlotte explained. 'Hit a kerb too fast, front wheel twisted, stuck my hand behind me to try and break my fall and next thing I know, my finger's hanging off.'

'That must've been traumatic,' Sinead said. 'Where did it happen?'

'There's a gravel track from here to Kincraig. They've got a tearoom at the post office there. I was cycling along that. They do nice cake.'

'Alone?' Logan asked.

'Yes. Why?'

'Just building up a picture, Miss Wilson. Nothing to worry about,' Logan said. 'Can you tell us what happened after the accident?'

'Uh, someone came along and found me. Ten, fifteen minutes later, I think, although I was in a bit of shock, so it could've been less or more than that. They called an ambulance, then led me to the road to meet it. Older woman. Never got her name. Think she was just passing through.'

Sinead made a note. 'And what then?'

'I was taken to Raigmore up in Inverness. Into A&E, then whisked in for surgery. My, uh, my parents came and met me there. The finger was too mangled, though. The surgeon couldn't save it, so it had to come off.'

She held up her bandaged hand and cautiously waggled the four remaining digits.

'And that was the last I saw of it.'

'Do you know the surgeon's name, by any chance?' Sinead asked.

'No. He was'—she waved a hand in front of her face—'you know, Indian or something. Asian? Is that what you're meant to say? He sounded normal, though. I mean, not normal. Normal's not the right word. He sounded British. Scottish.'

Panic flashed in her eyes, like she was plunging headlong into some dark crevasse of unintentional racism and didn't know how to stop.

A memory rose up to save her.

'Wait! Singh! That was it. Dr Singh. He made a joke about singing through the operation, I remember. I mean, I think it was a joke, though he seemed very serious. Singh. That was him.'

Sinead wrote the name on her pad. 'Thanks. That's really helpful.'

'I'm sorry you had to go through such a traumatic experience, Miss Wilson,' Logan said. 'When did it happen, exactly?'

'It'll be two weeks ago tomorrow. I need to go back at the end of the week to get it all looked at.'

'Right. I see.' Logan smiled hopefully. 'This is probably a daft question, but I don't suppose you know how your finger could've ended up in a freezer fifteen miles from here?'

'Absolutely no idea. I'm... I'm a bit shocked by it. I mean, how does that even happen?' Charlotte asked. 'Aren't they meant to, I don't know, burn stuff like that, or something?'

'We're going to get to the bottom of it,' Logan assured her. 'The young woman who was found yesterday. Have you heard a name mentioned?'

'Um...' Charlotte looked from one detective to the other, like she was sensing this was some sort of test. 'I heard something about... Eleanor someone? I could've heard wrong, though. I'm not really one for gossip, it was just...'

'All over town?' Sinead guessed.

A smile alighted momentarily on the other woman's lips, then was gone again. 'Exactly. Sounds awful.'

'Did you know her?' Logan asked.

'No. Don't think so, anyway. Name doesn't ring a bell. I don't actually know all that many young people round here. I teach at Speyside Academy, and they all go to Kingussie High.'

This was the most shocking revelation of the interview so far.

'You're a high school teacher?' Logan asked.

'Yes.'

'You teach in a secondary school?'

'That's right. Why do you ask?'

Logan's gaze drifted from the yellow dungarees to the fluffy pink socks to where a 'Home is where the cat is' tapestry hung on a magenta-painted wall. 'No reason,' he said, then he immediately followed up with a question on what subject she taught. 'Is it art?' he asked, clutching at straws. 'Do you teach art?'

Charlotte shook her head. 'No, science.'

Logan had not seen that one coming. 'Science? Like, actual science?'

'What other kind is there? I do general science for the younger ones, biology from third year onwards.'

'Right. I see,' the DCI mumbled. He blinked several times like his brain was struggling to process the information.

Sinead stepped in to fill the conversational void.

'So, you can't think of any connection between you and Eleanor?'

'Connection? No. None. I keep myself to myself. I don't know a lot of people. I don't tend to go out much, just to work.'

'And cycling,' Logan prompted.

Charlotte glanced down at her lap. 'Yes. Cycling. And that.'

'Can I ask you something, Miss Wilson? Unrelated to any of this other stuff.'

'Uh, yes. Of course.'

'Where's your cat?'

The teacher looked at him like he'd spoken to her in some foreign language. 'Sorry, my...?'

'Your cat,' Logan said. He nodded to the tapestry. 'It says "home is where the cat is", but I don't see a cat anywhere.'

'Oh! That!' Charlotte self-consciously pinched and rubbed at one of her earlobes. 'I don't have one. I'd like one someday. But I don't have one yet. It's just sort of positive thinking, you know? You put it out there, tell the universe what you want, and it delivers. Noel Edmonds used to swear by it. It's how he ended up doing *Deal or No Deal*, before he went mental and moved to New Zealand.'

Logan studied the woman for a few moments.

'You know you can just get a cat? You don't need to will one into existence, there's loads of them.'

Charlotte at least had the decency to look embarrassed. 'Hopefully one day,' she said.

Logan reached for his mug, and took Sinead's from her. 'Aye, well. Fingers crossed,' he said, then he got to his feet. 'I'll just horse these through to the kitchen.'

'It's fine, I can get them,' Charlotte said.

'Not at all. You stay where you are,' Logan told her. 'And leave everything to us, Miss Wilson. As soon as we know more about how all this happened, you'll be the first to know.'

–

Sinead waited until they were back in the car to ask the question that had been bothering her for the past couple of minutes.

'OK, what was with you taking the mugs through?'

They pulled on their seatbelts and Logan started the engine. 'Just being a conscientious guest, Detective Constable.'

'Oh. Right. Well, maybe you'll start being a conscientious guest when you come to my house,' Sinead countered. 'Because I've made you loads of cups of tea, and you haven't taken them back to the kitchen once.'

Logan chuckled. She had him there.

'I just wanted a wee look.'

'At her kitchen?'

Logan shook his head. 'At her back garden.'

'Right. Any particular reason, or…?' Sinead's subconscious raced ahead of her, answering the question before she could even finish asking it. 'Oh. Wait. Shed?'

'Shed,' Logan confirmed.

'And? Did she have one?'

The DCI clicked on his indicator and pulled away from the pavement outside the teacher's house. 'No,' he said. 'She did not.'

'So, where does she keep her bike?'

'Just what I was wondering,' Logan said.

He checked the clock on the dash, then glanced at his fuel gauge, making sure he had both the time and the diesel to make another trip.

'Fancy a quick jaunt up to Raigmore? I think we should go and have a word with this Dr Singh.'

Chapter Twenty-Seven

They found Jonathan Milburn leaning against a railing outside the Aviemore branch of Tesco. He was watching a young lad who looked like some distant descendant of Shrek picking up dog shite off the pavement.

'Use the bag, Malcolm!' he cried, just as Tyler and Hamza came around the corner. 'Jesus Christ, how many times? Use the bag!'

Malcolm straightened up and looked back at the supervisor. He frowned. Since his face seemed to be about sixty per cent forehead, this took some time.

'I am using the bag,' he said, holding up a little black sack that bulged unpleasantly.

Jonathan pinched the bridge of his nose. 'You put the bag over your hand, then you pick up the shit. You don't pick up the shit with your bare hand and then put it in the bag. We've done this, Malcolm. We've gone over this.'

This was too much for the young lad to take in. He stood stock still, like his brain had fully seized up, then he eventually gave the little sack of shit another wee shake. 'I am using the bag,' he said again, and Jonathan just waved him away.

'Oh, do what you want. But you're not getting back in my van with shitty hands.'

'Mr Milburn?'

The Community Payback supervisor whipped around like he was about to be chibbed, then relaxed when he recognised the two men from the day before.

'Oh! Hi. Sorry. I'm on high alert,' Jonathan said. 'You're detectives, aren't you?'

'That's right,' Hamza said. 'Mind if we have a few minutes of your time?'

'Please do. Take as long as you need. There's a wee cafe across the road there,' Jonathan said.

He turned to Malcolm and addressed him in a stern voice, like he was chastising the dog responsible for all the mess in the first place.

'Get all this picked up. Watch where you put your feet. And for God's sake, Malcolm, do *not* eat any of it.'

–

It was possible to see the Tesco from one of the window seats in the cafe, but after placing an order for a tea, a latte and a Tunnock's Teacake milkshake that Tyler point-blank refused to pass up the chance of trying, the detectives followed Jonathan to a table at the very back of the room.

'I should be keeping an eye on him,' Jonathan admitted. 'But I can't be doing with watching him picking up fistfuls of shite, while I'm sat here trying to drink my coffee.'

'Looks like you've got your hands full with him,' Hamza said, pulling out a chair.

'Not as full as his, by the sounds of things,' Tyler remarked.

Jonathan chuckled. 'Ach, Malcolm's a good kid,' he said. '*Thick*, though. Jesus Christ, he's dense. There's more brains in a tin of baked beans. He was assessed for all sorts of learning difficulties over the years, the whole gamut, but nope.' He shook his head. 'Just thick. That's literally what's written on his medical records. 'Thick as mince.' So his mum tells me, anyway. But, aye, good kid, deep down.'

'What's he doing the community service for?' Tyler asked.

'He fucked up a lollipop man,' Jonathan said. 'Broke his nose with his own… What's it called? Lollipop? The big metal sign they hold.'

'Aye, he sounds a charmer, right enough,' Tyler said.

The men all leaned back to make room for a waitress to place their drinks on the table. Tyler's eyes almost doubled in size when the towering milkshake was sat down in front of him, complete with a full-sized teacake plonked on top.

'What?' he asked, when he caught the recriminating look from the detective sergeant. 'It's a teacake milkshake. How could I say no to that?'

He took out his phone, snapped a picture to show Ben, then started poking around in the shake with the straw.

'Anyway,' Hamza said, turning back to the man across the table. 'Thanks for taking the time to talk to us, Mr Milburn.'

'Jonathan's fine. And it's not a bother. Seriously. Nice to be inside for a while. Although, to be fair, I like being out and about. Beats sitting around in a pokey wee office all day listening to people's computer problems. I much prefer tackling real problems. You can't fix them by switching them off and back on again!'

He took a sip of his latte and peered at both detectives over the rim of the mug, his voice taking on a more serious note.

'I, uh, I heard about Seamus. I mean, I'm sure everyone in town has by this point, but… Yeah. Awful. Just awful. How's his mum doing?'

'We haven't spoken to her personally, but I wouldn't imagine great,' Hamza said.

A loud slurping came from his left. He turned and fixed Tyler with a flat, dead-eyed sort of look. The DC swallowed, and released the straw from between his lips.

'Sorry,' he mumbled. 'Carry on.'

Hamza exhaled through his nose, then directed his attention back to Jonathan. 'You were with Seamus when—'

'Christ!'

Tyler grimaced and clutched at his head.

'Brain freeze,' he whispered.

Without saying a word, Hamza picked up the milkshake and sat it down over on his right, well out of Tyler's reach.

'How did Seamus seem when you all found the body?' Hamza asked.

'Um… I don't know. Shocked, obviously. Freaked out,' Jonathan replied, looking off to his left as he thought back to the events of the day before. 'We all were, obviously. Well, us two. Thank God for Sandra keeping it together. You always think you'll keep your cool if things like that ever happen, then when they do, that all falls apart.'

'You'd say he seemed surprised, then?'

'Surprised? Oh, he was surprised, all right. He nearly shat himself. Not that I can talk, I threw up.' Jonathan wrapped his hands around his mug, drawing in its warmth. 'Poor bugger thought it was puppies to start with. When he found the bag, I mean. Didn't want to look.' He looked down into the frothy coffee. 'Maybe it'd have been better if we hadn't. Maybe he'd still… Christ. It's a mess, isn't it? All this, it's a right bloody mess.'

Hamza nodded. There was no arguing with that.

'What do you think made him take his own life?' he asked.

Jonathan blew out his cheeks and shrugged. 'God. Now you're asking. I don't know. The horror of it, maybe? He never struck me as the suicidal type.'

'Did you know him well, then?' asked Tyler, one eye still shut as he dealt with the repercussions of the icy-cold milkshake.

'Ish. I've had him on various squads over the last couple of years. Not for anything major. He liked to drink a bit too much. Tended to lose the heid a bit when he did.'

'Violent, then?' Hamza asked.

'Och, no. Not really. Just mouthy, and sometimes smashed stuff up that didn't belong to him.'

'Capable of murder, do you think?'

Jonathan snorted like it was a joke, then quickly realised that they were being serious. 'Seamus? No. Not a chance. No. No way. Not Seamus. And he certainly didn't kill whoever was in that bag, if that's what you're getting at. If you'd seen him at the time, you'd know that. That was real shock. And why would he lead us straight to it? He could've just left it hidden.'

He sat back, still clutching his mug, his head shaking in firm, emphatic denial.

'No. You're barking up the wrong tree there. That boy was shaken by what we found. He was broken by it. No way he had anything to do with that bag being in those woods. He didn't know what to do with himself.'

'But Sandra did?'

The other two men both turned to look at Tyler.

'Sorry?' Jonathan asked.

'Sandra. You said she was pretty calm. She handled it all. The 999 call, all that stuff.'

'Yes, she did, but...' This time, Jonathan hesitated a little before offering up his opinion. 'No. Not Sandra. She's, eh, a bit rough, aye, but she's not a killer.'

'You don't seem sure,' Tyler said.

Once again, there was a momentary pause before the Community Payback supervisor replied. 'I am. I'm sure. Sandra wouldn't hurt anyone. Well, not seriously hurt them, I mean.' He winced. 'Well, she wouldn't actually *kill* anyone.' He shook his head, and he sounded like he was trying to convince himself rather than the detectives. 'She wouldn't.'

'OK. Well, that's good to know,' Hamza said. He smiled, and folded closed the notepad he'd had open beside his tea. 'Thanks for your time, Jonathan. You've been a big help. We'll let you get back to it.'

'She wouldn't. Seriously. Neither of them would.' Jonathan got to his feet, and picked up his cup. 'I'll get them to give me this to go. But anything else I can do, please just let me know.'

'We will do.'

Jonathan started to leave, then had second thoughts. 'Oh, I forgot to mention, there was someone else asking quite similar questions earlier. I got the impression he was with the police, though I realise now that he didn't actually show any ID.'

'Can you describe him?' Hamza asked.

'Uh, fifties? Short greying hair. Stubble. Quite an aggressive air about him. Swore a lot. I mean *a lot*.'

Both detectives wrote the same four-letter name in their notebooks at the same time.

'Thanks. We'll look into it,' Hamza said.

The three men said their goodbyes, then the detectives watched Jonathan head for the counter to have his coffee decanted into a takeaway cup.

Only then did Tyler reach across the table and take back his milkshake.

'You're not really going to drink that, are you?' Hamza asked.

'It cost me four quid, and it's teacake flavour!' Tyler replied. 'Course I'm going to drink it.'

He took a big sip through the straw, swallowed, then immediately gritted his teeth and clutched at his head again. '*Ooyah-fucker*,' he groaned, then he pushed the glass into the centre of the table and glowered like he was challenging it to a fight. 'On second thoughts, maybe I'll leave it.'

–

Ben sat perched on the corner of his desk with an evidence bag in each hand, and half a mini Twix moving around and around inside his mouth.

The cards were identical. There was nothing to differentiate them, as far as the DI could tell. Both were printed on the same purple card. Both had the same text across the front in the same bold, black typeface: 'New Player Has Entered The Game.'

The back of the card that had been sent to Eleanor was blank, while the address of the abandoned cottage was written on the back of the one taken from Seamus's house. Otherwise, though, they could have been the same card.

'Bloody weird this,' he remarked, once he'd finished his Twix. He held both bags up for Dave to see, and the constable nodded his agreement.

'Aye, beats me. Glad it's not my job to figure it out.'

'You can feel free to have a go,' Ben said. 'Because, whatever it all means, I'm no' seeing it yet. What game? What does it mean? Snap, maybe? You could play that with them.'

'Be quite a quick game of snap with just the two cards, though,' Dave pointed out.

Ben brought the cards back over to Dave's desk and handed them over. The constable jotted two ticks in his logbook, then returned the bags to the box on the floor beside him.

'There was a film called *The Game* back in the day,' Dave said. 'Late Nineties, I think. Early two thousands, maybe? Dunno. Michael Douglas was in it. I think he paid some organisation or other to make his life hell for him.'

'Michael Douglas did?'

'Eh, no. The character he played.'

Ben tutted. 'That's what I meant. I didn't think the actor himself would do something like that.' He raised his bushy eyebrows. 'Mind you, you don't know with some of that lot, do you? They're into some right weird shite.'

Dave nodded gravely, like he was privy to some pretty disturbing tales of Hollywood debauchery. 'Aye. Anyway, the guy Michael Douglas played paid some group to basically torture him, break up his marriage, ruin his reputation, have people hunting him and stuff. But they wiped his mind so he couldn't remember arranging it. Or, I don't know, something like that.'

'Why the hell would you do that?' Ben wondered.

'What, pay someone to make your life a misery?'

'No. Star in that film, I mean. It sounds like a heap of shite. Give me *The Guns of Navarone* any day of the week.'

The ringing of a phone made his heart sink, before he realised it was his mobile and not his desk phone. At least he could work the mobile.

Most of the time.

'It's Hamza,' he announced, presumably for Dave's benefit, then he managed to swipe the answer button correctly after three attempts, and pressed it to his ear. 'Hello?' He looked at the screen. 'Is this bloody thing even on?'

A faint and tinny voice hissed out until Ben returned the phone to his ear.

'Hello! Hamza. Aye. Good. I can hear you now. How you getting on?'

He listened for a moment, using his tongue to sweep the last few bits of Twix from between his teeth and gums.

'Richard Mathers?' He glanced at the board. 'Oh, aye. The photo and video man. What was he…? Moomin. Aye. That's it. What about him?'

He listened again.

'Oh, he does, does he?'

Another few seconds passed.

'Oh, he is, is he?'

Hurrying back to his desk, he picked up his pen and opened a notebook.

'Give me the address, then, and I'll have a couple of big sweaty bastards scoot round there and bring him in right now!'

Chapter Twenty-Eight

'So, what do you reckon's up with Hamza?' Logan asked, as he and Sinead trundled up the A9 at the back of a queue of slow-moving traffic. The bends in the road meant they couldn't see what was at the head of the line, but Logan would put good money on it being a camper van.

The bastards.

Sinead interlocked her fingers in her lap. 'Not sure, sir.'

'He did seem off, though? I'm no' imagining things?'

'He did a bit, aye,' Sinead confirmed. 'I'm sure Tyler'll talk to him.'

Logan shot her a sideways glance. 'And you think that'll help, do you?'

Sinead smiled. 'Time'll tell, I suppose.'

They rode on in silence for a while, the only sound the rumbling of the engine, and the increasingly annoyed mutterings of the DCI.

'I've a good mind to turn on the siren and pull the bastard over, whoever he is,' Logan grumbled.

Sinead checked the speedometer and saw that they were doing just north of fifty miles an hour. Not too bad, considering, and not something you could really pull someone over for.

She chose not to mention that, though, and instead just nodded along.

But the DCI's growing irritation at the line of traffic did prompt a change of subject. It was risky, but she went for it.

'Speaking of people not being on great form, sir, I couldn't help but notice that you've been a bit tense these last couple of weeks. More tense than usual, I mean.'

'Tense?' Logan shook his head. 'Don't know what you're talking about. I'm not tense.'

'Oh, right. OK. Fair enough,' the detective constable replied. 'But, just so you know, I think you're actually bending the steering wheel.'

Logan frowned down at the shining white lumps that were his knuckles, then made a conscious effort to relax his grip.

'It's nothing,' he insisted.

They continued on for a few hundred yards.

'You're going to keep staring at me until I tell you, aren't you?'

Sinead nodded. 'That's the plan, sir, yeah.'

Logan sighed. 'Fine. It's Olivia.'

'Ah. Tyler did mention something.'

'I mean, it's not *her*. Well, it is her, I suppose. She's being a right wee arsehole. Staying out till all the hours, ignoring us when we try and call, practically blanking us in the house. Lying, giving us mouthfuls when we try and say anything. She's like a… Like a… I don't know what she's like!'

'A teenager?' Sinead guessed.

'No. It's not normal. They're not all like that. Maddie wasn't.'

'Wasn't she?'

Logan took one hand off the wheel long enough to rub at his chin. 'I mean, no. I don't think so. I wasn't around then maybe as much as I should've been. But, I don't…'

He left it there. Now that he thought about it, he remembered quite a few phone calls and angry conversations with his ex-wife during their daughter's teenage years, but he'd been too distracted or too damn drunk to listen.

'Have you tried talking to her?' Sinead asked.

'Maddie?'

'Olivia.'

'I've tried nothing but talking to her!' Logan cried. 'She slams the door in my face, or just stares at her phone until I shut up. She's a nightmare.'

He checked his mirrors, counting the cars queuing up behind.

'I tried to talk to her last night,' he said. 'Told her that I went to see her dad in prison before I agreed to take her in.'

'Bosco? How is he?'

'Alive and well.'

Sinead wrinkled up her nose. 'Shame.'

'So, I told her that I went to see him, and that he told me to stay away from her. And that's why I decided that Shona and I should take her in.'

Sinead shuffled up a little straighter in her seat. 'Right,' she said. 'But you didn't actually tell her that, did you?'

'Aye! And she practically slammed the door on me.'

'You said those actual words?' Sinead asked, her eyes widening.

'More or less, aye!' Logan shot her a worried look. 'Why? I was trying to be nice!'

'How's that nice? She probably thinks you did it just to spite him!'

It was Logan's turn to shimmy around in his seat. 'I mean, aye. That's pretty much what she said, right enough.'

'Of course it is! How else could she take it?'

'If she'd let me finish, I could've explained!' The DCI groaned. 'I mean, now you make me think about it, aye, I can see how it might've been taken that way. But I meant that I knew if that bastard was happy for her to be stuck in care, then he didn't give a shit about her. And if he didn't give a shit about her, then I should do the opposite of whatever he said, because…'

He swallowed the rest of the sentence back down.

'Because what?'

'Doesn't matter.'

'Because you do. Care about her.'

Logan grimaced, but didn't argue.

'Shona's right,' he said, after a while. 'Olivia… She might be difficult. She might be a full-blown bloody psychopath, in fact, but she needs someone who'll give a damn about what happens to her. Maybe then, she won't stay that way.'

'You're doing a good thing. You and Shona. And she'll come round,' Sinead promised. 'She'll be hurting right now. She's pushing back. Everyone who was supposed to care about her left her, one way or another, and they weren't exactly great when they were around. She won't trust that things'll work out. She's probably trying to push you both away before you can do the same to her.'

'Bloody hell. Did you sneak off and do a psychology degree or something?' Logan asked.

Sinead looked out through the side window at the passing trees. 'Nah. Just been there, done that,' she said. 'I could have a chat with her, if you like? Can't promise it'll do any good, but—'

'Yes.'

'I mean, like I say, there's no guarantee that she'll listen, but—'

'I don't care. Yes. Anything's worth a try at this point, and if I trust anyone to get through to her, it's you.' He smiled wryly. 'Well, you or Bob Hoon's sister, and let's no' go deploying the nuclear option quite yet.'

'Ha! No, probably best not. We'll try softly-softly first, then if that doesn't work, Berta can kick her teeth in.'

'Deal!'

Up ahead, the traffic started to pull away. Logan nudged down the accelerator pedal to keep up.

A few moments later, they passed a camper van sitting parked in a roadside lay-by, its left indicator ticking on and off.

'Well, would you look at that?' the DCI remarked, as they swept on past the stopped vehicle. 'Things might be starting to look up, after all.'

Shona nodded, even though Logan couldn't see her from the other end of the phone. The head movements were quick and sharp, like she was anxious about the question being asked.

'Sure. Yes. Ah, great. Yeah, I should have something for you by then,' she said, then her nodding stopped. 'Dr Singh? What, as in Manish Singh? The surgeon? The surgeon here? Yeah, I know him, why do you ask?'

Her brow furrowed as she listened to Logan's response. Across the office, over by the fridge, Neville saw her confusion and shot her a questioning look.

'No, random body parts shouldn't just turn up in the wild,' she said, answering both men at the same time.

Neville winced, then went back to rummaging in the fridge.

'He has an office upstairs somewhere, but I'm not sure where,' Shona continued. 'And he could be in surgery. The front desk should be able to point you in the right direction, though, and I'll see you'—she checked the clock on the wall, but it failed to predict the future—'whenever I see you, I suppose. See ya!'

She hung up the phone just as Neville presented her with a large, rustic-looking muffin. It had a carefully arranged butterfly of dried banana stuck to the top with a daud of golden caramel.

'Ta-daa!'

'Oh! What's this?' Shona asked, the echo of Logan's voice still hanging around in her ear. 'That's not for me, is it?'

'It is! I made it last night,' Neville replied, flashing a smile that could've launched a million toothpaste marketing campaigns. 'I mean, I didn't just make that one, obviously, it's quite hard to make just a single banana caramel muffin.'

'*Banana caramel*.' Shona whispered the words like they were imbued with some ancient and exotic mystical power.

'Do you want it?'

Shona practically ripped the muffin from his hand. 'Do I want it? What sort of question's that?'

Neville laughed and pushed back his hair. He was growing it out, and the curly locks slipped between the gaps in his fingers. For a moment, he was a model on a catwalk. A movie star on a red carpet. A god atop Mount Olympus.

And then he was talking.

Although, it suddenly occurred to Shona that he'd been doing this for a few moments now.

'Sorry, what?' she asked, snapping herself back to reality.

'I just asked if you wanted me to fill you up?'

Shona stared at him. Despite the coolness of the room, she suddenly felt uncomfortably hot. It spread up her neck as an advancing red army.

'Neville, I—'

Her assistant held up a near-empty mug with an inch of cold tea at the bottom. 'I've already got the kettle on. You want this filled?'

Oh, thank God.

'Yes! Tea! God Almighty, I love tea. More tea, please! Yes, great idea! I fully endorse the idea of—'

She took a bite of the muffin just to shut herself up. Then, still chewing, she announced that Jack was going to be coming in to talk about the PMs for the rest of Ellie Howard's remains, and the body of Seamus Starkey, the latter of which was still to be done.

'OK, cool,' Neville said as he washed Shona's mug in the sink.

He was properly washing it, too. Shona generally just gave it a quick rinse under the hot tap, until the build-up of brown stains eventually forced her to leave it sitting overnight filled with barely diluted bleach.

Neville, though, was getting right in about it, though, and the mug was sparkling when he sat it on the counter.

'I told him you were gay!' Shona blurted, then she hurriedly took another bite of the muffin.

God, it was delicious.

Neville's frown was one of amusement as he looked back over his shoulder at her. 'You did? Why?'

'Um-mmf…' Shona pointed to her mouth to signal she was chewing. She kept the finger raised and gave it a little twirl, indicating that she was working through it as quickly as she could.

Neville still wore a smile of confusion as he set the mug of steaming hot tea down in front of her.

'Thanks,' Shona managed, forcing down a swallow. 'I just… I think he thinks you're attractive.'

Her assistant raised his eyebrows. 'He thinks I'm attractive?'

'Yes.'

'So you told him that I'm gay?'

'What? No.' Shona shook her head. 'Not like… I think he thinks that I think you're attractive.' She laughed unconvincingly. 'Sure, I don't know what put that in his head!'

'Right.' Neville took a moment to work through the various levels of who thought who thought what. 'And do you?'

'No! What?! *Pfft!* No! I mean… No!' Shona shook her head, then suspected she might be over-egging the pudding a bit. 'I mean, you're fine. I'm not saying you're, like, hideous, or anything.'

'Thanks.'

'I mean, you're… You know.' She gestured at his whole body with a wave of a hand. 'And your…' She pointed to his face. 'I mean, it's not bad. The whole… But that's not… I just didn't want Jack thinking that I… Or that we might…'

In a panic, she crammed the rest of the muffin into her mouth, filling all the available space.

'Forget I said anything,' she mumbled, though the muffin rendered it mostly unintelligible.

Neville tapped a finger to his forehead in salute. He turned away, but faced her again a moment later. 'I'm not, by the way. Gay, I mean.'

Shona nodded and gave him a thumbs up.

'And I'm not in a relationship. I don't have a girlfriend.'

The pathologist managed to force down the smallest of swallows.

'Oh,' she said, through a tiny gap in the muffin-mush. 'I'm very sorry to hear that.'

Chapter Twenty-Nine

After a bit of back and forth, Sinead and Logan were finally directed to the right place. Dr Singh's office was one of the starkest, barest, and most personality-less rooms either detective had ever been in. And considering they'd both been in literal prison cells, that was really saying something.

Everything about the room felt bleak, from the faded olive green paintwork to the sticky grey carpet tiles. The only bright spot was a poster on the wall showing a cartoon dove, lifting a dumbbell against a rainbow background. A speech bubble proclaimed, 'You are so strong and will get through this!'

The face of the man who occupied the office didn't appear to agree with the sentiment.

He greeted the detectives with a sniff, and the rest of their conversation was punctuated by an endless number of them, as if his sinuses were a tap that had developed a slow, steady leak.

'Yes, I'm Dr Singh,' he confirmed, looking them up and down. Another sniff. 'How did you get up here, and what do you want?'

Logan and Sinead produced their warrant cards. Singh sniffed again. If he was worried by their presence, he had one hell of a poker face. The only movement he made was with his hands, as he passed an old tennis ball from one to the other, squeezing it between his fingers before returning it to the other hand.

'Can we have a quick word?' Logan asked.

The surgeon passed the ball to the other hand again, then stepped aside, inviting them in. He was in his late fifties, Logan guessed, and was short and slight enough that his school years had likely been a living hell. He would've been academic, too, going by his current role and all the certificates on the wall, which likely wouldn't have helped matters.

'I must warn you, I have to start prepping for surgery in fifteen minutes, so I can't give you very long.'

He placed the tennis ball on top of his filing cabinet, then took a seat at his desk. There was only one other chair in the room, and neither detective moved to take it.

'We'll keep it as brief as we can,' Logan said. 'We're looking to find out some information about a finger you removed.'

'A finger? That *I* removed? When?'

'A couple of weeks back,' Logan said.

Sinead started to rattle off the exact date, but the surgeon silenced her with a sniff and a jerk of his hand. 'The cyclist. I remember it. Nasty injury. She was lucky it was just the one.'

That very same thought had occurred to Logan, too. He could get falling off a bike and damaging a whole hand in the spokes. Maybe even a thumb. But the middle finger? He couldn't picture it.

'The damage was too severe for a neat repair, and blood flow had been restricted too long by the time she got here. I could've tried to reattach, but it wouldn't have been pretty, it wouldn't have been very functional, and there's every chance I'd be removing it a week later, anyway. So, I made the decision to amputate. This was all explained to her at the time.'

Logan nodded. 'Makes sense, but we're not here about the operation.'

'Oh?' The surgeon sniffed, and this time there was a note of something in his expression—if not concern, then confusion. 'Then why *are* you here?'

'We're here about what happened to the finger afterwards,' the DCI intoned.

'Afterwards? I don't follow.' Another sniff. A big one this time, with a suggestion of indignation. 'What do you mean?'

Logan looked around the room like he was getting the measure of the man who occupied it. His gaze lingered on the motivational poster for a while, his nostrils flaring a little in barely disguised contempt.

'What would usually happen to a body part like that after an operation?' he asked, turning his attention back to the doctor.

'It would be appropriately disposed of.'

'Burned?' Logan asked.

'Maybe. It depends on what it was, but often, yes.'

'Here?' The DCI pointed to the floor. 'At the hospital?'

'No. It's contracted out. A specialist company comes and takes it away. They cover all the Highland hospitals. Maybe all of Scotland, I don't know.' He sniffed. 'I just perform the operations. I really don't have time to concern myself with the logistics of cleaning up after them. For that, you'd want to contact someone in the administrative team. I'd imagine they'll be better equipped to help you.'

'Do you have the name of someone we could speak to?' Sinead asked.

'No, but you could talk to my secretary. She might be able to point you in the right direction,' Dr Singh replied. He shrugged and sniffed at the same time. The coordination was impeccable. 'From what I do know, though, it shouldn't be possible for waste to just "fall out" anywhere. If it has, there's a failing in the system somewhere. Where was it found, if you don't mind me asking?'

'At a suspected crime scene,' was all Logan was prepared to give away. 'Along with a few others.'

The surgeon looked confused. 'A few other what?'

'Fingers.'

'Oh! That's…' He stared into space for a moment, then a sniff broke the silence. 'I don't know what that is, but it doesn't sound good.'

'Did you do any similar procedures recently?' Sinead asked.

'I assume you mean fingers specifically? Not in a while, no. Last one would've been… I don't know. I want to say

July, August. Thereabouts. Again, my secretary will be able to advise.'

He made a big show of checking his watch, then picked up a monogrammed notepad with his right hand and scribbled a name and number with a slim silver pen he plucked from his shirt pocket.

'Here. This is her mobile number. Valerie. She's very capable. Much more so than I am. Call her anytime until seven in the evening, Monday to Friday. She'll be able to answer all your questions.'

He retracted the ballpoint then returned it to his shirt, stood up, and sniffed all at the same time, which almost felt like showing off.

'And if there's anything else you need from me, please don't hesitate to get in touch.' He glanced meaningfully at the monogrammed note clutched in Logan's hand. 'Again, with Valerie, I mean.' He smiled as he strode past them and opened the door. 'She really is *quite* exceptional.'

Logan decided to go easy on the guy and to take the hint. He passed Sinead the note with the secretary's details, then shoved his hands in the pockets of his overcoat. 'Thanks for your time, Dr Singh,' he said, leading Sinead out into the corridor. 'Minimal as it was. If there's anything you think of, just give us a ring.'

Sinead was primed with her business card. She passed it to the surgeon, but he barely gave it a look.

'Thank you. Though, as I said, I really can't…'

Both detectives saw the sudden change in the man as some half-forgotten memory made itself known to him.

'Oh. Hang on. There was something a bit strange about that procedure.'

'Aye?'

'Well, not the procedure itself, that was fine. Afterwards. Before and after, actually. Her father. The patient's father. He seemed quite domineering. Controlling. The poor woman was in her thirties, but he spoke to her like she was a child.'

Logan didn't really see how this was relevant, and was about to say so when Dr Singh continued.

'And he asked if they could keep it. The finger, I mean. He asked beforehand if they could take it home with them as a keepsake. I said no, of course, that sort of thing's not allowed, and dismissed it as a joke. It may have been—I hear that same comment about once every three procedures, so it's not exactly original—but, given what you've told me, I thought it might be worth mentioning.'

Logan let this new information bed in for a moment, but there was no obvious place in this jigsaw puzzle of a case for it to fit. Not yet, at least.

'Thanks. That could be useful,' he said, then he stared down at the much smaller man, his face slackening into an expression that bordered on the threatening. 'Or, it might not.'

He turned and walked off then, leaving the surgeon blinking and sniffing in surprise. Sinead offered a smile of apology, and gave the sheet of paper she was holding a little wave.

'We'll follow it all up,' she promised, then she shoved the note in her jacket pocket, and set off racing along the corridor after her boss.

She waited until they'd reached the lifts before voicing her concerns.

'That was a bit abrupt, sir. Something wrong?'

The door swished open. The detectives let a couple of surprised-looking nurses get out, then took their spots in the empty elevator.

'He's up to something,' the DCI announced, then he jabbed the button that would whisk the lift down to the ground floor.

'How do you know?'

'ACTOR,' Logan said.

Sinead didn't try and hide her confusion. 'You think he's acting?'

'It's a... what do you call it? An acronym. Awfully Convenient Timing of Revelations,' Logan explained. 'ACTOR.'

Sinead continued to look at him blankly in the mirrored elevator door.

'The whole, "Oh, I nearly forgot to mention!" shite,' Logan explained. 'I never buy it.'

'He probably sees a lot of patients, to be fair to him,' Sinead said. 'Must be hard to keep track of who said what.'

Logan grunted. 'And yet he suddenly, out of nowhere and with no prompting whatsoever, remembered that one joke that he said himself he's heard hundreds of times before? Nah, not buying it.'

'You think he's lying?'

A sharp chime from Logan's phone filled the inside of the lift.

'I don't know. Maybe not lying, but I get a feeling that he's not telling us everything. Message Tyler, tell him to go talk to the woman's parents, though, and see what they say,' he instructed. He checked the screen of his mobile and hissed a, 'Bollocks', just as the elevator doors parted to reveal a mother and two young children holding 'Get Well Soon!' balloons.

The detectives stepped out. Sinead smiled another apology at the mum, but she just scowled back and ushered her kids into the lift.

'Eh, is there a problem, sir?' Sinead asked, hurrying to catch up with the DCI.

She almost ran straight into his back when he stopped, held the phone at arm's length, and typed a reply on the tiny keyboard, squinting so he could better see the letters.

'No. But they've brought that Moomin fella in. The victim's ex. I want to be there to talk to the bastard.'

'I could go see Shona about the PM, if you like?'

Logan scratched at his chin and looked along the corridor that led, after several twists and turns, to the mortuary.

'I told Shona I was coming in myself,' he said.

'Ah well, she's a big girl, sir,' Sinead replied. 'While she'll no doubt be disappointed not to see your pretty face, I'm sure she'll somehow find the strength to get over it!'

'Aye, no doubt she'll find a way to soldier on,' Logan agreed. He started to head for the exit, then stopped. 'Oh, and do me a favour?'

'Course, sir.'

'Ask her what she thinks about Dr Singh. There's something about him that I can't quite put my finger on.'

–

'Oh, thank Christ!' Shona ejected, bending double and supporting herself with her hands on her knees. She exhaled heavily, then straightened up again. 'Oh, Sinead, I could bloody... In fact, I will. I'm going to hug you.'

True to her word, the pathologist wrapped her arms around the detective constable, sagged against her for a moment, then stepped back.

'Uh, thanks,' Sinead said. 'Is, um, everything OK?'

'It's great! I thought Jack was coming in, but now he's not!'

Sinead nodded slowly. 'Yeah. That's sort of what I was asking. I thought you'd be more pleased to see him. Or, you know, less delighted about not seeing him, anyway.'

'Oh, no, I do want to see him. Course I do!' Shona insisted. 'It's just...' She fired a sideways look at the double doors leading through to the mortuary.

Sinead followed her gaze.

'It's just what?' she asked, not getting it.

'It's just...' Shona lowered her voice into a whisper. 'I think he's worried I might be tempted by an'—she cupped hands around her mouth and the whisper dropped to just a breath above total silence—'unprofessional workplace relationship.'

She glanced at the doors again, then nodded meaningfully.

Sinead didn't quite know what to make of this. She stood almost motionless for a few moments, only the shape of her mouth changing as it tried out a few possible sentence starters that never went anywhere.

'What...' she eventually managed to mumble. 'With a body?'

'Jesus! No! What do you take me… Wait!' She grabbed the detective constable by the upper arms, and there was something manic in her eyes. 'You've never met him! You don't know!'

'Met who? Know what?' Sinead asked.

'Neville! Could you come here a moment?' the pathologist called, then she released her grip on Sinead and stepped back, watching the detective's face like a circling eagle watching for movement on the mountainside below.

The doors opened. A man emerged. At the sight of him, Sinead ejected a sharp, sudden, 'Fuck!' then clamped a hand over her mouth and turned away.

'Uh, everything OK?' Neville asked.

Shona smiled at him. 'Fine, Neville. Sorry, false alarm. You just carry on.'

She met Sinead's eye and held it until the door swung closed again, then raised both eyebrows and gave a single nod of her head.

'Now, tell me honestly, is that not the single most attractive man you've ever seen in your fecking life?' she asked.

It took Sinead a moment to compose herself. 'I mean, he beats a corpse any day of the week.'

'Actually, it would be great if he did. Beat a corpse, I mean. Then I could fire him.'

Sinead looked back at the door again, like she might be able to get another peek at the man. Sadly, it wasn't to be.

'Is he no good?'

'He's great! That's the problem. Knows what he's doing. Making my job a whole lot easier. Funny, too. And he brings me lunch. And he bakes! He made me a muffin. *Banana caramel!*' she exclaimed, like this was the most enticingly tempting muffin of them all.

Sinead whistled through her teeth. 'Bloody hell. And you're worried that DCI Logan thinks you two are…?'

'No! Of course I don't think that! I mean, I'd be daft to even— No, I do a bit, yes. I'm really quite worried that he thinks that,' she admitted, then she bit her bottom lip and winced. 'I told Jack he was gay. Is that bad?'

'Depends.'

'On what?'

'On if he's gay or not.'

'I should be so fecking lucky!' Shona said through gritted teeth. 'But, I mean, he's gay in the happy sense, so it technically wasn't really a lie, was it? It was just like a funny misunderstanding. There was no harm to it.'

She buried her face in her hands to muffle her cry of, 'Oh, God!' then dropped her arms to her sides again. 'Do you want him? He's a great assistant, like. He could be of huge benefit. Sure, he's probably got a degree in babysitting or something. Or, like, won awards for it. And he's very tidy. And he smells amazing.'

Sinead wrinkled her nose. 'Not sure Tyler would go for it. He's already third in the pecking order of "man of the house", after Harris and Cal. Doubt he'd be happy being knocked into fourth place.'

Shona tutted. 'What is it with men? They're so fecking insecure, the lot of them, thinking we're just ogling handsome young lads all the time.' She gestured towards the door. 'Now, come on in here and we'll see what's what. And for God's sake, I know it's not easy, but at least try and keep your tongue from hanging out of your mouth…'

Chapter Thirty

Logan removed his coat and dumped it at an empty desk just in time for Taggart to come racing towards him, all gangly legs, wagging tail, and floppy lugs.

'All right, I see you, ye daft wee bugger,' Logan said, giving the excited animal a pat.

Taggart immediately flopped onto his back, gleefully presenting his belly.

'Now you're just coming across as desperate,' Logan told him. 'It's no' a good look.'

He gave the dog's fur a quick *scritch*, then looked over to where Dave was working away at his computer.

'Ben already in with him?'

'Hm? Oh. Aye. Just a few minutes ago. He was watching out the window for your car pulling in,' Dave replied. 'It felt weirdly romantic, actually. Quite nice.' He pointed to his screen. 'You got a minute?'

Logan walked over to the constable's desk. 'What's up?'

'Eh, you know the porn stuff? The victim's account where she was posting all them videos?'

'What about it?'

'Well, I dug around a bit. Nothing pervy, or anything, all in a day's work, but I found more. Less extreme stuff. Still not family-friendly, unless your family's got a whole lot of problems I wouldn't want to delve too deeply into, but it's tamer. It's on OnlyFans. So, fairly accessible.'

'Right. And?'

'She's got quite a few followers on there. And a lot of people leaving comments.' Dave rolled his middle mouse wheel, scrolling down a page of semi-naked images until he reached the comments section. 'Like this one.'

Logan bent down so he could read the highlighted text on the screen.

'"Go and die, you dirty slut. The world would be better off without you in it."' He blew out his cheeks. 'Charming.'

'There's loads of these,' Dave said. 'Like that one, I mean. Pretty vicious stuff.'

Logan shrugged. 'I'd imagine that sort of thing gets posted a lot.'

'Not really,' Dave replied. 'The people commenting are generally paying subscribers. It's the only way they can see the content to say anything about it. Mostly it's just sort of saddo fanboy stuff.'

'How are you seeing it, then?' Logan asked. 'If it's just for subscribers?'

Dave tapped the side of his nose. 'Ways and means,' he said, then he shrugged. 'I subscribed with my card and DI Forde said I could take it out of petty cash. I don't think he quite understood what I was doing, to be fair to him.'

Logan groaned. 'Mitchell's going to love that. Paying for porn out of the polis budget. Tell me it was at least worthwhile.'

'I'd say so,' Dave replied. 'All the abusive stuff, it's coming from the same account. And I've got a name.'

'Christ, seriously?' Logan asked, suddenly excited at the new avenue of investigation that may have just opened up. 'What is it?'

Dave crossed his arms and sat back, looking quite pleased with himself.

'SpokeyDokey2023,' he declared.

Logan continued to stare at the constable, but the surge of fire in his eyes had already started to flicker out.

'SpokeyDokey2023?' he echoed. 'That's the name?'

'Well, I mean, I'm guessing it's not their real name,' Dave replied. 'But it's a start, right? We can request, you know, computer stuff from OnlyFans, and it might give us something more to go on. Probably.'

'Eh, aye. Aye,' Logan said, though his disappointment was clear. 'Well, good work, I suppose. Get on that, see if there's anything you can dig up. In the meantime'—he turned to the door—'I'm going to go fuck up a Moomin.'

-

'All right, ya wanks?'

Tyler and Hamza both groaned when Bob Hoon came bursting through the garden hedge beside them, leaves and bits of foliage clinging to his damp skin and clothing.

It was Hamza who asked the question on both detectives' lips.

'What the hell are you doing here?'

'Following you pair of monobrowed fudds,' Hoon told them, picking wee jaggy bits of bush off his jacket. 'You're shite at knowing when someone's tailing you, by the way. I could've been riding an elephant and bashing a big fucking brass gong and you wouldn't've batted a fucking eyelid.' He nodded at the end terrace house beside them. 'What's the score here, then? Whose place is this?'

Tyler instinctively opened his mouth to reply, then a warning glare from Hamza stopped him in his tracks. 'We can't tell you,' he said, then he added a quick, 'Sorry,' to try to keep Hoon onside.

'Suspect's house?' Hoon asked, squinting at the detective constable like he was auditioning for a stage production of Popeye.

'What?'

'It's nothing to do with the girl or her family, or I'd know about it. Witness? Is it a witness?' Hoon demanded.

Tyler shifted uncomfortably on the spot. 'I, uh, I can't say.'

Hoon shook his head, still eyeballing the DC. 'No, not that, then. It's another lead. Got to be. It's something new that's come up. Am I right? I'm fucking right, amn't I? The dead-eyed fucking looks on both your faces tells me I'm right. So what is it? What's the score?'

'We can't tell you,' Hamza reiterated.

'Aw, fucking come on! I'm trying to help here.'

The squeaking of a hinge made all three men turn and look up. An elderly man leaned out of an upstairs window of the house next door, peering at them in suspicion.

'What are you lot up to?' he called down to them. 'You shouldn't be hanging around there. Clear off, before I call the police.'

Hamza smiled. 'No need for that, sir.' He produced his ID. 'I'm Detective Sergeant Hamza Khaled, this is Detective Constable Tyler Neish.'

'How do I know?' the pensioner asked. 'You could be anyone.'

'We've got identification,' Hamza said, indicating the warrant card.

'Yes, but I can't exactly see that from here, can I? For all I know, that's just your library card.'

'You could come down,' Tyler suggested.

The old man laughed bitterly. 'Oh, aye. I could come down! And why's that, son? So you can rape me?'

'Jesus!' Tyler ejected. 'No! Just so you can read the card!'

'Oh, aye. A likely bloody story!'

Hoon elbowed his way to the front, then indicated the detectives with a jab of a thumb. 'Sorry about my colleagues there. Not to put too fine a point on it, but they're a pair of fannies.'

'They look it, right enough!' the old man agreed.

Hoon nodded to the house whose garden they were standing in. 'The owners at home, do you know?'

'No.'

'No you don't know, or no they're not home?'

'Second one,' came the reply. 'No idea where they are. They had some big fight a week or so back, then I haven't seen any sign of them since. Think they must be away on holiday, or something.'

'Lucky bastards, eh?' Hoon said. 'Had they mentioned going away?'

The old man gave a snort. 'Mentioned anything? To me? Have they hell. I'm just a neighbour, that's what they keep telling me. I'm just a nosy neighbour, I need to keep my nose out of their business. Well, fine. Here we are. I don't care where they are, or what they're up to, I'm just delighted they're not screaming at one another and throwing stuff like the other night.'

'Sounds like they had a proper barney,' Hoon said.

'Aye. Then one of them must've driven off in the huff. Engine roaring, tyres squealing. Middle of the bloody night, would you believe?'

'To hell with that. Make the most of your peace while you can, eh? Just one more question, then I'll let you go.' Hoon pointed to a grey Volkswagen Golf parked right outside the garden. 'Whose car's that?'

'Theirs,' the old man said. 'I didn't see them leaving on their holiday, or wherever they are, so I'm assuming they took a taxi to the station.'

'Right. Aye, makes sense,' Hoon said. 'Cheers for that.'

Hamza jumped in before the neighbour could retreat back inside. 'Eh, really quickly, sir, if you don't mind…?'

The old man's *harrumph* of displeasure said he very much minded, but he waited for the detective sergeant to continue. Despite outward appearances, Hamza suspected he was enjoying the attention.

'The night they argued. When you heard the car pulling away. Did you look outside and see if it was definitely theirs?'

'In the wee hours of the morning? You think I'm getting up for that? With my back? It takes me ten minutes to get to my feet, son. I'm not going to go through all that at the first sign of bloody road rage. Not at that time of the morning.'

'OK. Yes. Thanks for that.' The DS glanced across the fence to the man's front door. 'I don't suppose you've got a doorbell camera?'

'A *what*?' the neighbour asked, like Hamza had slipped into speaking some arcane ancient language.

'Doesn't matter,' Hoon said, nudging the detective sergeant aside. 'Thanks for your time.'

With some grumbling and groaning, the old man hauled himself inside and closed the window. He stood there, just beyond the glass, watching their movements with curiosity and suspicion.

'Aye, he is a nosy bastard, right enough,' Hoon declared, smiling and waving up at him to let him know they could see him.

The neighbour shuffled away, but Hoon and Hamza had no doubt that he was still standing up there, waiting to peek out again.

Tyler, though, had other things on his mind.

'Um, check this out.'

He indicated the edge of the door where the locking mechanism met the frame. The wood was splintered, like someone had jimmied the door open. Recently, too, going by the colour of the exposed grain.

'Bloody hell. Someone's been at that,' Hamza said. 'Looks like someone's tried to break in.'

Before he could say any more on the matter, though, Hoon stepped past him, pressed the tip of a finger against the door, and gave it a shove.

It creaked on its hinges as it inched inwards, offering a glimpse of a patterned carpet beyond.

'Looks like they've done more than fucking try,' Hoon remarked.

Hamza looked back at the parked car, then up at the window of the neighbour's house. There had been commotion. Fighting. Screaming. Then, the sound of a car speeding away.

What if it hadn't been a domestic? What if it had been something else?

'I don't know about you pair of fuckwits, but I'm going to look inside,' Hoon told them. 'If you two want to try and stop me, you'll have to fucking arrest me, and I'm warning you now, that's no' going to be a pleasant experience for any of us. I hope you've got a Taser, and that you've brought an extra fucking box of batteries, that's all I'm saying.'

He gave the door a slightly harder shove, and it opened all the way to reveal an empty and silent hallway.

'So?' Hoon asked, gesturing inside. 'Are you two coming in with me, or what?'

Chapter Thirty-One

Richard 'Moomin' Mathers was an oily bastard, both in terms of his physical appearance—shiny skin, greasy hair, and a general air of uncleanliness—and the way he had attempted to evade Logan and Ben's initial few questions.

They hadn't even been particularly probing—just some *getting-to-know-you* chit-chat that had been designed to put the suspect at ease, but had instead just made Logan increasingly annoyed.

Moomin was in his late thirties, looked about forty-five, and dressed like a homeless teenager with a grey hoodie under a black jacket, and jeans so tight they pre-emptively put Ben off the roll and sausage he had been planning on having after the interview.

He sniffed and rubbed at his nose a lot, like he had a sneeze brewing that just wouldn't quite come to the boil. Closer inspection of his wispy wee moustache would have revealed traces of white powder, Logan reckoned, but he couldn't bring himself to get close enough to him to look.

Despite the offer, Moomin had refused a lawyer, telling the detectives that he didn't trust them, and thought they should all be put to death.

It was, as far as Logan could tell, his one and only redeeming quality.

'I tell you what, Richard,' the DCI said, having decided against any formalities like 'sir', or 'mister', the moment he set eyes on the man. 'How about we just cut the shite and get right down to business? I'm sure you're a busy man with smut to make and high school girls to entice, so we won't keep you any longer than we have to.'

Moomin pulled an exaggerated frown at the first accusation, which deepened further at the second, as if both claims weren't just untrue, but utterly nonsensical.

'Well, I don't do them things, so…'

'Aye, you do,' Logan corrected. 'You've probably stuck too much shite up your nose to remember. Don't worry, though, DI Forde and I can keep you right. Can't we, DI Forde?'

'We can indeed,' Ben confirmed.

'You were done for shooting a porn video in a field, Richard. Remember? Wasn't that long ago, either,' Logan continued. 'And then you started making videos with Eleanor Howard, didn't you? You shoot all her stuff for her websites.'

'Did she tell you that?' Moomin asked, trying to laugh it off. 'If she did, then she's lying.'

Logan felt a twitch deep in his gut. He didn't know. The bastard didn't know.

'And why would she lie about something like that?'

Moomin shrugged. All his movements were quick and jerky, like he was a bad stop-motion animation. 'Because I chucked her. Told her I wasn't doing it any more. I wasn't filming her content, I didn't want anything to do with her.'

'Jesus Christ, son, that's a quick turnaround,' Logan pointed out. 'Five seconds ago, you said you didn't make the porn with her, now you're saying you did. Which is it?'

'It's not… It's not porn. I mean, it is, but it's more than that, is what I meant. I'm not like some seedy guy with a hard-on and a video camera.' He tutted. 'I mean, aye, I am that, too, but I'm also an artist. What we did wasn't "smut", like you said, it was art.'

'No' based on what I saw!' Ben interrupted. 'Art's an oil painting, or a nice sculpture, it's no' sticking a load of stuff up your hole!'

Logan made a subtle but significant hand gesture that Ben was quick to pick up on. With an incredulous shake of his head, the DI made a note in his pad. Logan waited for the scratching of the pen to stop before he continued.

'You're saying you ended your relationship?' Logan asked.

'*Relationships*,' Moomin corrected. 'Professional and sexual. They were two separate things. I'm a professional.'

'Oh, that's very clear. And what made you decide to do that? She getting too old for you, was she? The school uniform not fitting her like it used to?'

Moomin held up his hands. The fingers were scrawny and dirty, adding to the impression of a man who spent most nights sleeping rough. 'Look, nothing happened until she was old enough. She was sixteen when we started shagging.'

Ben adjusted his glasses and peered down his nose at his notes. 'Which would've made you... thirty-four? That sound about right?' He clicked the button of his pen and twiddled it between his fingers. 'I mean, obviously it doesn't sound *right*, it sounds pretty inappropriate to an old fart like me, but do my sums add up?'

Moomin nodded just once. 'About that.'

'But you first got together before then,' Logan said. It wasn't a question, he just wanted to hear the greasy fucker say it.

'Yeah. She was fifteen, but like I said, I didn't do anything to her then. I waited until she was legal!'

'And here they say that chivalry is dead, eh?' Logan muttered.

He tapped a finger on the tabletop, chewing on his bottom lip as he studied the younger man. He was maybe twenty pounds overweight, and had started to cultivate quite an impressive double chin. His hair was creeping backwards across his scalp, so about two-thirds of his face was now forehead.

None of this made him look anything like an actual Moomin, but Logan had to admit that there was *something* about the man that made him look not quite all the way human.

Quite what the hell a fifteen-year-old schoolgirl had ever seen in him was a mystery.

And, if the man was to be believed, he was the one who had eventually done the dumping. That, in itself, needed some delving into.

'So, what happened?' Logan asked. 'Why the breakup?'

Moomin tapped at a nostril with the back of a hand, then smoothed down his pube-like moustache. 'She told my mum, didn't she?'

Logan and Ben both stared at him, waiting for more.

'About?' the DCI prompted, boring of the dramatic pause.

'About the filming and stuff. The videos.'

'The porn, you mean?' Logan said.

Moomin looked like he might be about to argue the point, but then nodded. 'She said some guy was trying to out her, so she was going to tell her parents. Well, her dad, her mum's a vegetable, I think. Or, like, not all there, anyway.'

'And that bothered you? Her telling him?'

'I mean, not hugely. I was a bit worried her old man might try and hit me with his tractor or something, but I can handle myself,' Moomin replied. He gripped the edge of the table, like he was struggling to expel some painful memory. 'But she put it everywhere. On Insta, on Snap, everywhere. Tagged me in it where she could, too, and next thing I know I'm getting a phone call from my mum, and she's crying, saying I'm going to hell, wondering where she went wrong, all that stuff.'

'Where *did* she go wrong?' Logan asked.

'What?' The younger man seemed puzzled by the question. 'She didn't! What I'm doing is nothing to do with her. None of it's her fault.'

'So, it's your fault?'

'So what's my fault?' Moomin asked, even more confused.

'That you're a creepy bastard who preys on and exploits young lassies,' Logan clarified.

'She wanted to do it! It was all her idea!' Moomin cried. 'I think that's why she hooked up with me in the first place. I think she knew I did that sort of stuff. Ask her yourself, and she'll tell you. Unless she doesn't, then she's a fucking liar!' He gestured towards the door at the detectives' backs. 'Go on, go ask her.'

Ben's pen scratched across the page. Logan waited for it to stop, then changed tack.

'When did you last hear from Eleanor?'

Moomin shrugged. 'Dunno.'

'You don't know? You've got no idea?'

'Last week.'

'Whenabouts last week?'

Moomin shrugged. 'I don't know.'

'You must have some idea, son. Monday? Thursday? Saturday?'

'Thursday, maybe.'

'OK.' Logan nodded. 'Did you do it in person, over the phone, via text? How did you break the bad news to her?'

'Snapchat.'

Ben looked up from his pad. 'That's an app, isn't it?'

Moomin nodded, and the DI looked quite pleased with himself as he wrote another note.

'So you can show us, then? It'll be on your phone?' Logan said.

'Nah. Snapchat deletes messages automatically,' the other man replied, and Logan let out a little grunt of annoyance.

He had heard that same excuse before, and had assumed it was a load of old bollocks until Hamza had set him straight.

Stupid bloody system.

'We'll say Thursday, then,' Logan decided. 'So, six days ago. How did she take the news?'

'She was pissed off. But mostly about how I'd left her in the shit about getting new content done. Went on a rage about how all the self-shot stuff you see is shite—which it is, it looks really cheap—and how I wasn't getting any of the next payout. Which I'm legally due, by the way, so whatever she's saying about me, remind her of that, will you? We've got a contract. She needs to pay up. She's bringing in fifty grand a month. *A month!* And I'm entitled to my share of that.'

'Fifty grand a month?!' Ben spluttered. 'For flashing your bits and pieces to a load of strangers on the internet? Christ, we're in the wrong job.'

Logan stole a sideways glance at the detective inspector, but chose not to point out that the earning potential for an attractive lassie in her early twenties flashing her 'bits and pieces' on the internet was likely far higher than that of a man in his sixties with a potbelly and a heart condition.

Instead, he faced the man across from him again, and prepared to drop the bombshell.

'I wouldn't go counting on that hitting your bank anytime soon.'

Moomin sat forward suddenly and poked the table with a finger. 'I knew that's what this was! I'm due that money! That money's legally mine, and morally, so she can't just refuse to pay me what I'm—'

'She's dead, Richard.'

He didn't move.

He just sat there, frozen, the finger on the table slightly curved, his eyes staring emptily back at the DCI.

'Who's dead?' he asked, but then he worked it out himself, because he immediately followed up with, 'How's she dead? How can she be? How is she dead?'

'That's what we're all here to try to find out,' Logan told him. 'And, right now, our investigation has pointed us squarely in your direction, Richard.'

'Me? What? What do you mean? What are you talking about?'

Logan ignored the question. 'And, unfortunately for you, it's looking like she died around five days ago. Pretty much about the time you two were falling out.'

The enormity of what the detective was saying knocked Moomin backwards into his chair. He gripped the arms of it like it was about to blast off, and hurriedly shook his head.

'I didn't have anything to do with anything. Nothing like that! I didn't know. I didn't even know! I thought I was in trouble for something.'

'You may well be,' Logan countered.

'About the videos, I mean! Not about… I didn't… I didn't kill her! I wouldn't!' His voice cracked, and he buried his face in his hands. 'Oh, fuck! Fuck! Oh, fuck! I didn't hurt her! I didn't know! *I didn't know*, I swear to God, man. I swear to God!'

Logan thought back to those body parts left lying in a plastic bag like discarded pieces of meat.

He thought of the young woman, and the horrors she must have endured.

'I'm no' sure God's paying too much attention to this one, Richard,' he said, interlocking his fingers on the table between them. 'So, I suggest you stop concerning yourself with Him, and start worrying about me.'

Chapter Thirty-Two

Shona had very little news to report on the post-mortem front. Seamus Starkey's official cause of death was asphyxia due to hanging, and aside from some alcohol in his system, there wasn't much else to say.

The other body parts found in the cottage were all Eleanor's, with the exception of the fingers that had been discovered in the freezer. One of those was Charlotte Wilson's, but the rest remained unidentified.

Although, Shona had a theory about that.

'So, here's the funny thing,' she said, as she pulled off her gloves and led Sinead back through to the office. 'Remember Halloween last year? With the big storm, and everything?'

'Hard to forget it,' Sinead replied.

'Well, I was called to an RTA. Couple of people dead. Terrible business.'

'I remember.'

Shona led the way over to her desk and the dilapidated computer that sat on it. 'Well, one of them—the driver of the car responsible—I remembered that she was missing a finger. Ring finger of her right hand. I've done a DNA test.'

Sinead stood back as Shona clicked through a few files on her desktop, searching for one in particular.

'And? Is it a match?'

'Dunno yet. Waiting for the lab to get its finger out. Won't know for a few days, probably, and that's if Jack shouts at them. But!'

She clicked a few more times, tutted twice, then eventually found what she was after.

A picture of a severed finger appeared in a top-down view on-screen. It had been thawed out, revealing some blackening around the stump, and a general flatness from the centre knuckle down.

It was a woman's finger, Sinead thought, sporting a long nail that had been painted in a purple-leaning shade of red.

'Ring finger, right hand,' the pathologist said.

She clicked an arrow at the right of the screen and the photo of the finger was replaced by a picture of a forearm and hand that had been taken from a similar angle. The digits on the right hand lay splayed on the table. All four of them.

It took Sinead less than a second to spot the connection. 'The nail polish. It's the same colour.'

'Exactly the same colour, I'd say,' Shona confirmed. 'It's neater on the finger and a bit chipped on the hand, but if you ask me, that's a match.'

The detective constable stood there staring at the screen for a few moments as she let the significance of this new discovery bed in. What it meant, she didn't yet know, but it was important. She could feel it in her gut.

'Any idea what happened to it?'

'I checked her records at the time. It was some sort of power tool accident. Completely mangled the whole thing. They rushed her into surgery, but it was too far gone.'

'Surgery? I don't suppose you know who did the operation, do you?'

'Pretty sure it was Dr Singh, though you'd be better off talking to his secretary than him, because—and I mean this in the most professional way possible—he's an arsehole.'

Sinead nodded slowly. It wasn't easy, given how much her head felt like it was spinning.

'Well,' she mumbled. 'It's funny you should say that…'

Tyler, somehow, had been given the upstairs to search. That didn't feel right. He hadn't even really wanted to come inside in the first place, and now here he was tiptoeing across an upstairs landing, expecting something to come leaping out at him at any moment, or for a body to fall out of a cupboard, or for some other unwelcome catastrophe to strike.

Some people might dismiss these thoughts as paranoia, but Tyler knew better. The fact was, that sort of thing was pretty much how his life tended to pan out. He hadn't come across anything untoward in the house yet, but knowing his luck, when he opened this last door—the bathroom—there'd be a big hungry lion waiting in there to eat him.

On the one hand, he knew that was a ridiculous thought, but on the other hand, it felt like it would just be another day at the office for DC Tyler Neish.

He'd been hit by cars, bitten on the arse by angry dogs, and had to contend with an old lady's vibrator that he was convinced had a mind of its own.

And then there was the train, of course. He'd not been able to watch Harry Potter in the same way since. The sight of the *Hogwarts Express* on-screen lost much of its charm when you'd been chased a hundred yards along a viaduct by the fucking thing.

A big hungry lion in the bathroom would at least be something different, he supposed.

He took a breath outside the door, whispered a prayer to nobody in particular, then turned the handle.

No cats, big or otherwise, pounced on him. The bathroom, like the other upstairs rooms he'd checked, was empty.

It smelled a bit ripe, though. Not *rotting corpse* ripe, thankfully. It was more an acrid piss smell that caught at the back of the throat and made him want to gag.

He carefully lifted the lid of the toilet with the toe of a shoe, revealing a pan full of rust-coloured water. Whoever had last used it clearly hadn't bothered to flush.

The reasoning for this became clear a moment later, when he spotted a little laminated sign on the wall above the cistern that read: 'If it's yellow, let it mellow. If it's brown, flush it down.'

It didn't look like it was meant to be a funny sign. There was no flamboyant font or exclamation marks. The text was solid black on a white background, and it felt more like a government mandate than something that had been put there for a laugh.

Judging by the smell in the room, the yellow had been mellowing for quite a long time.

Tyler gasped with fright and clenched his fists when he caught sight of what he eventually realised was his own reflection in the mirrored door of the bathroom cabinet. Once his heart rate had slowed again, he opened the cabinet with gloved fingertips to reveal a selection of face creams and medicines.

There were two toothbrushes in a glass tumbler. Wherever the homeowners had gone, they'd left those behind.

Closing the door, he retreated out onto the upstairs landing in time for a shout to rise up from the bottom of the carpeted staircase.

'Oi! Boyband? You found anything up there?'

'Not really,' Tyler called back.

'Either you fucking have, or you haven't, son. Which is it?'

'Their bed's not made, and they've left their toothbrushes. And some piss in the toilet.'

'Dirty bastards!' came the reply. 'Right, get your arse down here, then.'

Tyler was more than happy to leave the upstairs. Even though he'd had a poke around inside the rooms and knew they were empty, a lingering sense of dread was still nagging at him.

The house didn't just feel empty, it felt abandoned. Even without the neighbour's description of the speeding car, Tyler would've guessed that whoever lived there had left in a hurry.

And that was before even mentioning the mess in the hall. A telephone table by the door had been knocked over, breaking one of its ornate spindly legs. The phone itself had broken, too. It lay in two pieces, its rechargeable batteries scattered across the floor.

Hamza joined Tyler and Hoon in the hall. He already had his mobile in his hand, his thumb tapping away at the screen.

'Nothing out back,' he announced. 'Door was locked. The gate, too. Whoever came in, they came in through the front.'

'Went out that way, too, by the fucking looks of it,' Hoon added. He sidled towards the door. 'Right, you two call it in and get Palmer to give the place a good going over. And if anyone asks if I was here—that big family-sized pack of fucks, Jack, especially—you deny all fucking knowledge of seeing me, all right?'

'No,' Hamza told him. 'We can't do that.'

Hoon glowered at him for a few long, tension-filled moments, then he shrugged. 'Suit yourself. Say what you like. I couldn't actually give two-thirds of a fuck.' He stabbed a finger at them, then raised it to the ceiling and spun it around like he was trying to create a miniature tornado in the air. 'But curiouser and fucking curiouser, eh?'

And with that, he was gone.

-

Dave Davidson whistled quietly as he wheeled himself over to DI Forde's ringing phone, and immediately pressed the correct button to answer it. Despite all Ben's protests, it wasn't exactly challenging, the button being a big green phone icon with the word 'Answer' written below it in white text.

'Detective Inspector Forde's desk. Constable David—'

'Dave. It's Hamza. Where's the DI?'

'Oh! All right, mate? How's it going? I was going to phone you and ask you something, so it's a good thing you called.

He's in with Logan interviewing that Moomin fella. What you after?'

'We've got a potential crime scene here,' Hamza explained. 'I need it locked down and looked over as soon as possible.'

'No bother. I can start the ball rolling from here. Where are you, and what exactly do you need?'

Dave stretched out of his chair to reach Ben's pot of half-chewed pens, then wrote down Hamza's instructions on the back of an empty envelope.

After double-checking the address, he promised to get the request kicked up the chain so that the house would be secured and at least a few key members of the SOC team would be dispatched to give the place a going over.

He almost hung up before asking the question that he'd been about to call the detective sergeant with.

'Eh, before you shoot off, I need your help with something. It's a computer thing.'

He heard Hamza wincing all the way along the line. 'Not so sure that's a good idea, after this morning.'

'Ach, forget that. These things happen. You weren't to know. You're still the computer geek round here.' Dave grinned. 'Genius, I meant. Computer genius.'

'No, you were right the first time!' Tyler's voice sounded tinny, but loud, like he was shouting from somewhere in the background.

'Right, fine,' Hamza said, though he didn't sound happy. 'What's the problem?'

Dave talked the detective sergeant through the comments he'd found on Eleanor's videos, and the username attached to them all. He'd already escalated it to the tech team, but there was no saying how long it would take to get anything back from them.

'I really just wanted to know if there's another way of doing it,' he said. 'Of finding out more about who's using that account, I mean. Like a shortcut, or something.'

'Not really,' Hamza said. 'Given their business, OnlyFans won't give that out without a fight. Could take weeks to get anything from them, if we even get it at all.'

'Bugger,' Dave muttered. 'Was hoping there might be some clever way of doing it.'

'No. Sorry.'

'Because, you know, if anyone could think of one, I reckoned it'd be you. Not to worry, though.'

Hamza didn't reply. Not right away. Dave glanced at the screen on the phone's base unit, but it still showed the numbers ticking up.

'You still there?'

'Aye. Sorry. Here,' Hamza confirmed. 'The username. What did you say it was again?'

'SpokeyDokey2023,' Dave replied.

Another silence, but shorter this time.

'OK, then. In that case, maybe there is *one* thing you could try...'

Chapter Thirty-Three

The Big Board was starting to fill up. Sinead stood in front of it, facing the rest of the team, a stack of index cards in one hand and a pen in the other. She'd already added some of the information they'd gathered over the past few hours, but it was still coming in thick and fast.

Unfortunately, all the different bits of data hadn't yet painted anything that resembled a clear picture. For all they'd learned, they didn't seem to have made a lot of tangible progress.

Perhaps as a result, the atmosphere in the room felt subdued. The frisson of excitement that buzzed in the air when a case was progressing quickly was notably absent. Even Taggart, who would usually have been trotting around the room to see if anyone had any treats going spare, was lying with his head on his paws under Logan's desk, awake but disinterested.

'That Moomin fella.' Logan took a gulp of his tea, then shook his head. 'It wasn't him.'

'How do you know? Has he got an alibi or something?' Sinead asked.

Logan shrugged. 'Not a clue. Haven't checked yet. We need to talk to him again, but it wasn't him. He was genuinely shocked to hear she was dead.'

'He could be lying,' Sinead suggested.

'Don't think so,' the DCI said. 'I mean, it's possible, I suppose. I'm just not feeling it. I've got a pretty good radar for these things, and I don't think that guy's switched on enough to beat it.'

DI Forde agreed. 'We'll dig deeper with him after this, but if he was acting, then he deserves a bloody Oscar.'

'Sorry, boss, I have to ask,' Tyler ventured. 'Does he actually look like a Moomin?'

'No,' Logan replied, with just a touch of weariness. 'No human being looks like a Moomin, Tyler. It's not physically possible.'

'See!' Tyler cried, giving Hamza a nudge. The detective sergeant, who was busily working away at his computer, tutted his annoyance. 'Because they're space hippos. As soon as we find Sandra, I'm going to tell her she's full of shite.'

Logan's expression darkened. 'What do you mean "as soon as you find her"? You were meant to have spoken to her.'

Tyler squirmed in his chair, then deferred to his sergeant with a panicky look. Hamza was so fixated on his screen that it took him a moment to pick up on the cue.

'Oh. Aye. We couldn't get hold of her, sir. She was last seen getting on the Perth train this morning. Her mum says she's off to visit some friend of hers who lives in Stirling. We got the address, and we've passed it to the local CID.'

'Did you try and get her intercepted getting off the train at Perth?' Ben asked.

Hamza shook his head. 'No, sir. It was too late by that point. She'd have already been there.'

'Bugger.'

'As soon as she's found, I want to know,' Logan instructed. 'From what you've told us, she's currently our most likely suspect.'

'But, eh, maybe it's just me being thick, boss,' Tyler said. He glanced around the room to see if anyone was going to agree on that. 'But, what about Seamus? He was apparently obsessed with her, and then he went and, you know? And the card. The address of that house. Where the body was found. That's a lot of evidence.'

'It is,' Logan agreed. He scratched at his chin. 'But evidence of what? That's the question. Your man, the supervisor…?'

'Jonathan Milburn,' Hamza muttered. He frowned at his screen and typed in a search query.

'He seemed to reckon that Seamus was shocked when they found the body, right?'

'Well, aye, boss,' Tyler confirmed. 'But then maybe he was just good at acting. And it's a big coincidence him finding the body in the first place, isn't it? Like, of all the places it could be, it's right there. And then he shouts everyone to come look.'

The detective constable looked around again, this time searching for someone to back him up.

'Some killers do that, don't they? They want an audience. They want to be there to see people's reactions to what they've done. Maybe that's what he was doing.'

Dave Davidson provided the moral support that Tyler had been hoping for. 'He could've been showing off. You're right, some of them do that.'

'They do, aye,' Tyler confirmed. 'They absolutely do.'

'What about the cards?' Logan asked, and all eyes went to the printouts pinned to the board showing the purple 'New Player' postcards that both Seamus and Eleanor had apparently received.

'What about them, boss?'

Logan rattled off his theory, although that was a generous way of describing what was still, at this stage, just a jumble of loosely connected thoughts.

'According to her old man, Eleanor was sent the card along with a blackmail note. We don't know what the note said, or what the blackmailer wanted, just that she went public with her… career choice, rather than give in to the demand.'

'You think Seamus was being blackmailed, too?' asked Sinead.

'It's possible, aye. We didn't find the note, but that doesn't mean it didn't exist.' Logan clicked his fingers. 'Oh. Anything back from his mother's car yet?'

'Not yet, sir,' Sinead replied.

'How would they have been blackmailing him, though, boss?' Tyler asked. 'I mean, like, what did they have on him?'

'No idea,' Logan admitted. 'There might've been something on his computer.'

Hamza winced. 'Sorry, sir. I should've put it straight to the tech team.'

'Forget it and move on, Sergeant,' Logan told him. 'There may well not have been anything there to find.'

'Or there was everything to find,' Ben countered, and Hamza shrunk a little behind his screen.

Sinead cut in, saving the DS from further embarrassment. 'If you think the blackmail angle is significant, sir, then there's something you need to know.'

Logan half-sat on the edge of his desk, then gestured with his mug for her to continue. 'Let's hear it, then.'

'You know I told you that Shona thinks she's identified another of the fingers? She thinks it belonged to a Nan Hilton, a driver killed in an RTA at Halloween.'

'Aye, you said that,' Logan confirmed, nodding to the card on the board.

'Well, I've done a bit more digging on the dead woman, sir,' Sinead continued. 'And her sister told Uniform just after the crash that Nan had mentioned someone trying to blackmail her. Nan didn't tell her much about it, but the sister reckoned she was scared, and hadn't really been herself.'

'Bloody hell,' Logan remarked. 'And was it followed up on?'

'Not in any depth, sir, no. Uniform spoke to the rest of the family, but nobody knew anything about it, and there was no physical evidence found that suggested she was being coerced into anything.' Sinead glanced back at the board. 'Given everything else, though, it feels relevant.'

Logan sat in silence, considering this new information.

Three people dead. Three of them potentially victims of blackmail.

If Moomin was to be believed, then Eleanor had the funds to pay up, but she didn't.

Seamus didn't have a pot to piss in, though, and no obvious means of raising any cash in a hurry, so why target him?

Unless the blackmailer wasn't looking for money...?

The DCI pointed to the board. 'We'll park it and come back to it. It might be something, or it could be nothing. Shona say anything else?'

'Not really, sir. The PM of Eleanor's remains didn't give much more away. The cuts were well placed, but amateurish, even given the tools that were there. The saw found in the cottage matches the cuts.'

She pointed to a photo on the board showing a long silver saw with a green handle made of moulded plastic, and a blade still stained with blood.

'It's possible they had an anatomy book to work from, she thinks, given the placement of the cuts,' Sinead continued. 'But she doesn't think whoever did it had any experience of cutting people up.'

Logan almost smiled at that. 'You asked her about Dr Singh, then?'

'I did, sir, aye. She says he's not particularly well-liked, but she doesn't think this was him. Reckons his professional pride wouldn't let him be so sloppy. But, and this might be significant, he was the one who removed Nan Hilton's finger last year.'

She was right. That did feel significant. Two of the ten digits found in that freezer had passed through the hands of the same surgeon. What were the chances?

'We heard back from the company that handles the hospital waste yet?' he asked.

'Not yet, Jack,' Ben said. 'But Dave and I did a bit of searching, and they don't have the best reputation. They've been fined a few times for bags of waste left in unlocked bins overnight. Not in Inverness, but at a few other places across the country. Last time was a couple of months back in Edinburgh. A dog got into the bags and set about them. The owner got quite the fright when it turned up back home with a foot in its mouth.'

'Aye, that'd catch you off guard, right enough,' Logan muttered. He shook his head, whispered a, 'Jesus Christ,' then urged the DI to chase the company up as soon as the meeting was over. If there was even a possibility that the Raigmore waste wasn't being stored correctly, then it might stop the finger of suspicion from pointing in Dr Singh's direction.

Which was probably just as well, given what he tended to do with them.

'Tell me again about this missing couple,' Logan said, after taking a quick glug of his tea.

Hamza still seemed distracted by his computer, so Tyler took up the tale. He told the others about how they'd swung by the house to have a chat with the parents of Charlotte Wilson, about the conversation with the nosy neighbour, the signs of forced entry, and the silent, empty house.

'And Hoon was there!' he blurted, forcing the words out before he could have second thoughts about it.

'Jesus. Why am I no' surprised?' Logan muttered.

'He just popped up. He'd been tailing us, boss. He spoke to the neighbour, then came in while we searched the house.'

The confession was enough to pull Hamza away from his screen. 'We told him to leave, sir. Short of arresting him, I didn't know what else to do.'

Logan held up a hand. 'I don't care. I'll deal with him later myself. We've got enough problems right now without worrying about the comings and goings of Bob bloody Hoon.'

'What's happening at the house now?' Ben asked.

'We've got Uniform there, and Palmer's team should've arrived by now,' Tyler replied. 'We haven't contacted Charlotte yet, though, boss. Hamza reckoned we should wait until we've spoken to you.'

'So, she doesn't know they're missing?' Sinead asked.

Tyler shrugged. 'I mean, they've been gone a few days, by the sounds of things, and they live just a couple of miles apart. You'd think she'd have noticed they were gone by now.'

'You'd think,' Logan agreed. He studied the board again. The word 'shed' jumped out at him. 'Did we ever find out anything about her bike?'

'She hired it,' Sinead said. 'From a place in town. It got a bit damaged in the fall, and one of the spokes was bent, so the story checks out.'

'Right.'

Logan ran a hand down his face, giving this some more thought.

'Has she done it before? Hired from them?'

Sinead visibly paled as she realised her error. 'Not sure, sir. Forgot to ask. We'll get on it.'

'We did find a chequebook in the parents' house,' Tyler said, coming to his wife's rescue. 'So, we're getting onto the bank to see when their accounts were last accessed. And we—well, Hoon, if I'm being honest—found a list of numbers on a board in the kitchen. Their own numbers were on there.'

'You try calling them?' Logan asked.

'Straight to voicemail, boss. We're chasing up the network to check on recent calls and when they last pinged the masts.'

'Right. Good. If you need me to shout at anyone, let me know. I'm in a shouty mood.' Logan stared at a blank space on the board for a moment, like he was imagining what might eventually fill the gap. 'We'll go talk to Charlotte Wilson shortly. Tyler, I want you with me. Hand that other stuff over to Dave.'

'No bother, boss.'

'Uh, you might want to do more than talk to her, sir,' Hamza said.

Everyone turned his way. 'Why? What have you got?'

Hamza wheeled his chair back from his desk a little. 'Spokey-Dokey2023.'

'You found a name?' Logan asked.

'Not quite. I mean, not exactly, but... Well, when Dave told me about it, I had an idea. The account was created at the tail end of last year. Twenty-twenty-three. Hence the date in the username. Dave searched, and that name doesn't show up anywhere else, but I got him to work backwards. SpokeyDokey2022, SpokeyDokey2021.'

Logan raised an eyebrow. 'And?'

'Nothing,' Dave replied. A grin crept across his face. 'Until Twenty-twenty.'

'What happened in Twenty-twenty?' the DCI asked.

'There's a couple of comments on a post on an old web forum called The Gathering Place,' Hamza explained. 'About teenagers being out of control. How they don't respect their elders, and all that sort of stuff.'

Ben harrumphed. 'Did they ever?'

'The forum's got a "safety" feature built in, and I use that term loosely,' Hamza said. 'The IP addresses of the posters are visible as long as you're registered and logged in.'

Ben crossed his arms and leaned back in his chair, already checking out of the conversation. He'd started to have doubts at the mention of a 'web forum', but 'IP addresses' was a step too far. He'd check back in once they switched back to plain English.

'Meaning?' prompted Logan, who wasn't exactly the most technically competent of people, either.

'Meaning, by running a reverse lookup, I can get ISP details. And, by running it all through a bit of software that I technically shouldn't really have access to, but don't tell anyone, I was able to get an address.'

'A proper address?' Logan asked, leaning forward. 'Like, of a house.'

'Like, of a house, sir,' Hamza confirmed.

Ben chose that point to re-engage. Physical addresses, he understood just fine.

'And?' he prompted.

'And it's Charlotte Wilson's place, sir,' Hamza announced with the triumph of a man who'd just redeemed himself for all previous errors of judgement. 'The abuse was sent using Charlotte Wilson's internet connection.'

With that, Logan was fully on his feet. Down on the floor, Taggart leaped up onto all fours, his tail wagging excitedly.

'Right. Now we're talking,' the DCI declared. 'Tyler, get your coat. We're heading straight there. Hamza, you and Ben go finish up with Richard Mathers. Get his statement, make sure he knows not to leave the country, then get him tae fuck. I want the interview room ready for Charlotte Wilson.'

'Will do, sir.'

'Oh, and good work, Sergeant,' Logan said.

'Aye. Well done, son,' Ben said, raising his mug in a toast to the detective sergeant's technical prowess.

'Cheers, sir. Couldn't have done it without Dave, though.'

'Speaking of which,' Logan turned to the constable. 'Dave, I want you to follow up on all the other stuff we mentioned. Banks, phone networks, waste management company. All of it.'

Sinead half-raised a hand to volunteer her services. 'I can take some of that.'

'Not yet, you can't,' Logan told her. 'There's something else I need you to deal with first.'

'Oh? What's that, sir?'

Logan scratched at the back of his head. It was rare to see him looking so uncomfortable, and the Incident Room descended into an intrigued silence while everyone waited for his response.

'I, eh, I thought it would be best if Taggart went home. So, I told Olivia to come and pick him up after school. Which, by my reckoning, means she should be here any minute—'

His phone gave a sharp, sudden *bleep*. Something about the tone made it sound like the sender was royally pissed off.

Logan flinched.

'Now.'

Chapter Thirty-Four

The operation hadn't gone as well as he would have liked. It had been a pretty mundane op—an incision in the palm, then a simple cut to the transverse carpal ligament in order to relieve pressure on the median nerve. He'd done it for dozens of carpal tunnel syndrome sufferers over the years, and the success rate was high.

Today's had been touch and go, though. He'd almost clipped the median nerve with the edge of the scalpel, which could've potentially condemned the patient to a lifetime of tingling, numbness and weakness in her right hand.

He'd managed to avoid it, though. When all was said and done, the patient shouldn't have much to complain about beyond a slightly larger scar than might usually be expected.

He hoped.

Still, he could feel a tremble in his legs as he made his way back to his office. Once there, he'd grab his jacket and briefcase, and head for home. Rita would make dinner. He'd have a glass of wine, maybe two. Tomorrow would be a whole new day.

The pathologist had other ideas, though. She almost bumped into him as they both rounded a corner at the same time, and he heard a little squeal of shock escaping him as he leaped back in fright.

'Sorry! Dr Singh! I was just looking for you,' she said, with the good grace to pretend that she hadn't heard his panicky cry. 'I went to your office, but you weren't there.'

'I was in theatre,' Dr Singh replied. He sniffed, then rubbed at his forehead with a finger and thumb. He didn't actually have a headache, but acting like he did might hurry the conversation along. 'Was there something you needed, Dr Maguire?'

'It's just a quick question,' Shona told him. 'About a patient of yours. Nan Hilton. Do you remember her?'

Dr Singh stared blankly off along the corridor for a moment, then sniffed and shook his head. 'No. Should I?'

The pathologist smiled. 'Probably not. You operated on her in August of last year. She had a finger removed. Ring finger of the right hand.'

The surgeon checked his watch, making his impatience clear. 'And?'

'And I just wondered if you could give a bit more clarification as to what actually happened to her?'

Singh started walking towards his office, partly hoping the pathologist would simply hang back and leave him alone.

She didn't. When she fell into step beside him, he had no option but to answer.

'I don't know. I can't be expected to remember all the details. Do you remember the details of everyone you've'—he waved a hand as he searched for the word—'dissected?'

I try to, Shona thought.

'No,' she said.

'No. There we go. I'm sure it's in the notes.'

He picked up the pace, but Shona walked faster, keeping up. 'Yeah, that's the thing. It isn't. Not in any detail, anyway. It just says she had a "power tool accident".'

'Well, there we go, then. What more do you need to know?'

Shona held her hand out, fingers splayed. 'I suppose I'm just having trouble figuring out how you partially amputate the ring finger of your right hand with a power tool, without damaging any of the other fingers. I can't picture it.'

The surgeon sniffed noisily. 'Why are you even trying?'

'She's right-handed, too,' Shona continued. 'So that's weird, isn't it?'

Singh stopped outside his office door and sighed. 'Why is that weird?'

'Well, if she's right-handed, and she cut one of the fingers off that hand, she must've been holding the tool in the other hand. Her left. They're generally designed for right-handed people. It would've been awkward to hold.'

'Well, maybe that's why she ended up cutting her own finger off,' the surgeon suggested, after a pause.

'She didn't cut it off, though. She just *mostly* cut it off, and mangled it,' Shona reminded him. 'You cut it off.'

Singh pressed the tips of his index fingers to his temples and massaged them, really pushing the headache angle. 'What's your point, Dr Maguire? Why are we talking about this?'

'Well, because the finger turned up earlier,' Shona told him. 'Along with nine others. Well, seven other fingers and two thumbs.'

'What? God. Not another one,' Singh muttered. 'There was some big bloody oaf of a detective in here earlier asking about a different finger. I told him it was likely a failing by the waste management company. Suggested he talk to someone in admin. What are you smiling at?'

'What? Oh. Sorry. Just the description. "Big bloody oaf".'

'Well, he was. Big lumbering ox. Quite unpleasant. Rude, in fact.'

Shona nodded solemnly while trying not to laugh. 'I can imagine. But, anyway, I was thinking, if you've got time, we could go over the X-rays and the notes from both procedures, because they both seem a little bit odd to me.'

'Odd?' Dr Singh sniffed. 'How are they odd? What's odd about them?'

Shona smiled apologetically. 'Sorry, have I offended you? I didn't mean the actual operation, as such. Just the… I suppose the need for them.'

The surgeon stepped back, his thick dark eyebrows bunching together into a scowl.

'Are you questioning my professional judgement, Dr Maguire?'

'What? No. No, that's not—'

'Maybe you and your patients have the luxury of time, but in my department, snap decisions have to be made. I don't get to shove my patients in the fridge while I mull over next steps, I need to make my calls there and then.'

Shona ramped up her smile in an attempt to defuse the situation. 'Of course. Yes, I understand that, I just—'

'Do you, though? Do you really?' Singh asked, the harshness of his tone shutting the pathologist down. 'What you do down there, it's important of course, I'm not saying that, but it's not life or death, is it? You don't have to make those calls. You don't make those life-changing decisions on a daily basis. I do. I have that pressure. I make those calls. And if you're implying that my judgements are flawed, then I suggest you take that up with the board.'

'Sorry, that wasn't—'

'We are *done here*, Dr Maguire!'

His voice rose. His face contorted momentarily into a mask of rage.

'Is that clear? This conversation is over!'

Shona took a step back. Her smile had fallen away during the surgeon's outburst, and though she tried to find it again, it proved too elusive.

'I'm sorry if I've offended you, Dr Singh,' she told him, as he turned away and opened his office door. 'Thank you for your—'

The door slammed closed in her face. She heard a *clang* from the other side, like he'd just booted a metal waste paper basket across the room.

'Time,' she concluded.

Then, she looked both ways along the corridor to make sure that nobody was watching, and raised both middle fingers towards the surgeon's door.

–

'Uh, hi. Olivia? I'm Sinead. Not sure if you remember me?'

Olivia's initial response to the question was to sigh and roll her eyes, but she at least had the decency to follow that up with a, 'Nope.'

Sinead smiled. 'Right. No, that's fair enough!'

'I'm supposed to pick up the dog,' Olivia said. She had her phone out and was idly flicking through photos of girls in the same school uniform as she was wearing now. 'Is he ready?'

'Uh, yeah. In a sec. Can I have a quick word first?' Sinead asked. She looked around, then pointed to a door a few yards along the corridor. 'In here. It'll just take a minute.'

Olivia grimaced, like this was the greatest imposition that anyone had ever had inflicted upon them in the history of the world.

Conveying her annoyance with her slow, plodding footsteps, she followed the detective constable into the room, and started moaning even before the door was closed.

'This had better not take long. This whole building stinks.'

'Cut the shit, Olivia.'

The girl's eyes widened in surprise, but then her scowl returned. 'What did you just say to me?'

Sinead closed the door.

Then, with the twist of a latch, she locked it.

'I think you heard me,' she said, turning to the teenager. 'But, just in case you didn't, I warned you to cut the shit.'

'You can't say that,' Olivia bit back. She tried to puff herself up, make herself look more threatening. Sinead, however, was unfazed.

'Well, I just did, so what are you going to do about it? Call the police? Set your dad on me? Not a lot he can do, is there?' Sinead folded her arms and leaned against the door, ensuring the girl had nowhere to go. 'You could go and tell Shona and Jack, of course, but then why should they listen? You've made it clear you don't give a shit what they think. Be a bit shallow if you went running to them now, wouldn't it? They'd see right through that.'

Olivia's tongue flitted across her lips. Her eyes narrowed, like she was sizing up her chances if she just flew at the detective with her fists and feet flailing.

Sensibly, she decided against the idea.

'What is this meant to be? What am I even doing here?'

Sinead gestured to the back of the room, where a table and five or six haphazardly arranged chairs stood. Technically, this was a meeting room, though it was generally only used if every other available space was already occupied.

There was a small folding bed in the corner so detectives could get an hour or two of sleep during extended late-night investigations. Sinead knew from personal experience that it was no more or less comfortable than the wooden chairs.

'Sit down,' she instructed.

Olivia crossed her arms and slunk her weight onto one hip, her eyebrows lowering to become a single straight line that cast her eyes into deep pools of shadow.

'Why would I sit down?'

'Because I want to talk to you,' Sinead said.

'So? I don't want to talk to you.'

The detective constable shrugged. 'I don't care what you want, Olivia.' She raised a finger to stop the girl before she could reply. 'But, I'll tell you what. I'll sweeten the deal. If you sit down, I'll tell you a secret.'

'Why would I give a shit about your secrets?'

'It's something I've never told anyone before. Not my husband. Not my brother. Nobody. Only two people have ever known it, and one of them's dead. But, if you sit down and talk to me, I'll tell you.'

She moved away from the door, and didn't look behind her as she headed to the back of the room and pulled out a chair.

Olivia hadn't moved. The coast was clear—she could unlock the door and get out anytime she wanted—but she hadn't moved an inch.

'So?' Sinead said, indicating the seat with a nod. 'You in?'

Chapter Thirty-Five

Tyler watched as DCI Logan shot another wary look up at the front of the Burnett Road Police Station. It was the third or fourth time he'd done it since leaving the building, and that, combined with his silence, was becoming unnerving.

'Something wrong, boss?' Tyler asked, when they reached the DCI's car.

'What? No.'

'Eh, not calling you a liar or anything, but aye there is, boss. Something's up.'

Logan unlocked the doors, and they climbed into the front seats, Logan behind the wheel, Tyler in the passenger seat—or 'riding shotgun' as he annoyingly insisted on calling it.

'Your wife has very kindly offered to help me with something,' Logan explained, though neither his words nor his fifth worried look up at the building did anything to put Tyler at ease.

Quite the opposite, in fact.

'Sinead? What's she up to? Why are you looking so nervous? What have you got her doing?'

Logan chewed momentarily on his bottom lip. 'She's talking to Olivia.'

'Oh. Wow. Right. I see.' Tyler stared ahead at the building, then a whole body shudder rippled through him. 'Well, good luck to her. Rather her than me. No offence, boss. I gave it a shot, but—and I hope you don't mind me saying this—she's quite mean. I felt like I was back in high school being bullied by one of the bigger kids. I half expected her to give me a wedgie and demand I hand over my dinner money. And I probably would've done!'

'Aye, she's hard work,' Logan confirmed. He'd just clipped on his seatbelt, but pressed the button to release it again. 'I should go put a stop to it. It wasn't fair to ask her.'

'Do you know what I love about Sinead, boss?' Tyler asked, and the bluntness of the question stopped the DCI before he could open the door. 'She's full of surprises. Like, when I met her, I thought she was just this really fit lassie, and then I found out that she was a good laugh. And then I found out that she was all these other things. Clever. Weird. Kind. Wise. Bizarrely wise, actually, like she's ten times as old as she actually is. Like she's some old man living in the mountains.'

'Maybe don't tell her that part, eh?' Logan suggested.

Tyler smiled. 'No, maybe best not. But, see, the thing is, boss, she's all these things, and I honestly think I've just scratched the surface. Every day, she does something that blows me away. The way she is with the kids. The way she is with everyone. To be honest, I'm just waiting for the day when she realises she's way out of my league and divorces me, but I'm making the most of it until then.'

Logan shot another look up at the front of the building, though this one seemed a little less worried than the previous few.

'The point is, boss, she's full of surprises. If anyone can find a way to get through to Olivia, it's Sinead. Or, failing that, some sort of lion tamer, maybe. You know, with the chair and the whip? But, I reckon Sinead'll have a good go first.'

A suggestion of a laugh wheezed through one of Logan's nostrils. His seatbelt's metal tongue gave a *ca-clunk* as he inserted it into the buckle.

'Good points, well made, son. But what you said there, about how she's out of your league?'

Tyler's eyebrows crept up his forehead. 'Aye, boss?'

'You're bang on the money. Don't know what the lassie was thinking.' Logan smirked and tapped the side of his nose. 'But I won't tell her if you don't.'

–

It had taken almost a minute of standing there in silence, but Olivia had finally given in and taken the seat Sinead had directed her to. The detective constable sat beside her on the same side of the table, the two of them separated by a foot and a half that might as well have been an abyss.

'Well?' Olivia demanded. 'What's the big secret, then?'

Sinead smiled. 'Give me a minute. I need to build up to it. First, I want you to know that I know how you feel.'

Olivia scoffed. 'Feel about what?'

'About everything. About the world. About how unfair it is. How cruel it can be.'

The teenager faked a yawn and patted her mouth. 'You're boring me. What's the secret?'

'You've got every right to be angry,' Sinead told her. 'The things you've been through, everything that's happened, you *should* be raging.'

'Well, I'm not. I don't care, so… Sorry. You're wrong.'

Sinead shrugged. 'Maybe I am. We're all different. Maybe you deal with pain differently than I do.'

Olivia tutted. 'Pain? What, you with your two kids and hot husband? Well, hot-ish, he's starting to show his age. But you've got no idea what I've been through. You've got no idea what it's like.'

Sinead tapped a finger on the table, then nodded. 'You're right. I don't. Nobody does, because you won't tell them. But that's not just a you problem, that's all of us. We all hold on to so much shite. We keep our pain private, like it's embarrassing. Like exposing the wound'll just make it worse.'

Olivia rolled her eyes and stood up. 'Spare me your shit. I don't care. Just give me the dog, so I can go.'

'My parents died in a car accident when I was nineteen,' Sinead said. 'I was on duty. I got the call about the crash. I was first on the scene. I was the one who found them.'

This time, Olivia said nothing. She just stared down at the detective constable sitting on the uncomfortable chair.

'I had to wait there until the ambulance arrived. Not that there was any saving them. It took another twenty minutes for someone to come and relieve me.' Sinead pushed her hair back, then scratched at her neck. 'After that, I had to go tell my wee brother. He was still in primary school. Just a kid. I had to go and get him out of school, and tell him what had happened.'

'What did he say?' Olivia asked, interested despite herself.

'He cried. He shouted.' She smiled, but it was forced. A defence mechanism. 'He used language I didn't even know he'd even heard before! He hit me, called me a liar, told me he hated me and that he was going to tell Mum and Dad what I'd said. And then, he just sort of… stopped. Like he'd just shut down. He realised I was telling the truth, and the shock of it just shut him down.'

'But he's all right now?'

'Yeah. Mostly.' Sinead shrugged. 'I mean, are any of us really all right, deep down? But he's no better or worse than the rest of us. It was good that he cried, I think. I think that helped. I didn't. I couldn't. Because I had a job to do.'

'Police,' Olivia said.

'No. Big sister. Mum. Dad. Everything. Aye, police, too, but Harris was the main thing. Making sure he was OK. Because I'd promised that I'd look after him. I swore.'

She leaned back and looked very deliberately at the empty seat across from her, then turned her attention back to the girl.

'I think I'm ready to tell you my secret now,' she said in a low, unsteady voice.

The old wooden chair made no sound as Olivia lowered herself onto it, like even it was holding its breath, waiting for the truth to come out.

'What is it?' the girl asked, and there was no attitude this time, just a genuine curiosity.

Sinead placed her hands on her thighs and rubbed them, building herself up. She looked around the room—at the folding bed, at the door, at the window with its shuttered blinds—then forced herself to look into the eyes of the girl sitting across from her.

'When I was asked afterwards about finding them. My parents. When I was asked about what happened, I lied.' The words were a whisper of confession. 'When I got there, my mum was already dead. Like… there was no… She was just dead.'

The pitch of her voice changed as the chords of her voice box drew tighter.

'But my dad…?' Sinead swallowed, but couldn't shift the ball of lead that was sitting in the centre of her chest. 'My dad was still alive. He was alive, and he was awake. And he—' She dabbed at an eye with the back of a hand. 'He knew what was happening. He could see my mum. He knew she was gone. And he knew that he was going, too. We both did. There was so much blood. There was just so much—'

The words choked her. She clasped her hands and lowered her head as if in prayer, hiding her tears and her shame.

A hand reached over and rested on hers. Only briefly. Only for a second.

It was enough.

She wiped her eyes and sat up straight, forcing herself to carry on.

'I held his hand. He couldn't speak, but I could see it all in his eyes. All his fear, and pain, and worry. But love, too. So much love. He wasn't scared for him, I don't think. He was scared for me. For us. Me and Harris. So, I promised him. I promised him we'd be OK. That I'd look after my brother, be everything he needed me to be. And that moment. That promise. That's what saved me.'

Olivia's face was rigid and fixed, like she was willing every muscle to stay in place. 'From what?'

'From myself, I suppose,' Sinead explained. 'From losing my mind. From lashing out at everyone who was just doing their best to help. I mean, don't get me wrong, I wasn't exactly a barrel of laughs for a while, but I also knew I couldn't give in to it. All the grief, and the pain. I couldn't lie down to it. I knew that I had to be strong, and at first, I thought that meant doing everything myself. If I did it myself, if I pretended to be fine, nobody could see what was really going on with me. How I was struggling. How scared I was.'

'I'm not scared,' Olivia insisted, though she didn't really sell it.

'I was. I was bloody terrified all the time,' Sinead admitted. 'Thought I was messing everything up, that I couldn't do anything right. But I kept going. Slapped on a brave face, and got on with it. And you know what I realise now?'

Olivia shook her head.

'I did mess up. I got through it all, aye, but I didn't need to do it on my own. I had people who cared about me. People who wanted to help—who *could* help, if I'd just let them. And they did. When I let them in, they did help. Don't get me wrong, I still have bad days. I still have days when it all seems so cruel and unfair. And, you know what? The people who helped me then still help me now. Even the ones who aren't in my life any more. By letting them in, by letting them know how I was really feeling, and accepting that, like it or not, they actually cared about me, that stuck with me. Those people are still helping me now, and they don't even know it.'

She slapped her hands on her thighs, and the *thwack* was like the breaking of the spell. She got to her feet and shrugged, the conversation apparently over.

'You're right, though, Olivia. I don't know what you're going through. No one does. But there is a way to change that, if you'll just give it a go.'

She gave that a few moments to sink in, then shrugged. 'Now, c'mon,' she said, heading for the door. 'Let's go get that dog.'

Chapter Thirty-Six

Dr Singh was up to something. That much was obvious.

Yes, he had always been curt, often to the point of appearing rude, but Shona had never seen him that angry before.

Add to that the fact that the files on the two finger operations didn't quite make sense, and it was clear that something was afoot with the man.

She should call Jack, she knew. She should pick up the phone and call him, and let him know what she'd found out.

Except what had she found out? Not a lot. Right now, it was little more than a hunch. She had no evidence that the surgeon had actually done anything wrong, and if Jack went blundering back in there, Singh might get spooked and destroy any proof of his crimes—whatever those might be—before it could be discovered.

No. It was too soon to get the police involved. She needed to be able to give them more than a gut feeling and some half-assed and partially completed medical reports.

She needed to find a smoking gun.

'Neville. The very man,' she said, when her assistant emerged from the mortuary. 'I need you.'

Neville pulled off his rubber gloves and placed them in the medical waste bin. He looked the pathologist up and down, and there was something a bit wary about it. 'In what sense?'

'You know Dr Singh?'

Her assistant shook his head. 'No.'

'Right. Well, lucky you. He's a right prick. But I think he's up to something. Or has been up to something. In the past. But maybe now, too.'

'Up to something like what?'

'I don't know. Crime. Or, you know, morally questionable things, maybe. Let's not get ourselves bogged down in the details.'

'I see.' Neville unhooked his bloodied apron and placed that in the bin alongside the gloves. 'So are you going to report him?'

'Yes. No. Not yet. Sort of,' Shona said, rattling off more or less all possible options. 'I will. I absolutely will, but I need to get an idea of what he's up to first. I can't very well just call HR and say he's a shady bastard. That's not how it works, Neville.'

Neville shook his head vaguely. 'No. So…?'

'So, I need evidence. And I reckon the best place to look is in his office.'

Her assistant looked confused by this idea. 'Why would he let you look in his office?'

'He wouldn't. Not in a million years. Which is why I'm going to sneak in and nose around.'

'What?!' The idea almost knocked Neville backwards off his feet. 'You can't do that! You'll get into trouble!'

'Only if I get caught. Which I won't.'

'How do you know?'

'Because you'll be standing watch.'

The colour drained from Neville's face. He wrung his hands together, his head twitching from side to side, not so much like he was refusing the mission, but refusing to acknowledge it was even being discussed.

'That's… We can't! We'll lose our jobs!'

'Or, we'll help bring a criminal to justice!'

'N-no.'

'But—'

'No!' Neville squeaked, and his eyes glistened with raw emotion. 'I can't. I can't lose my job. My mum'll kill me.'

'What?'

Neville sniffed hard, drawing a trickle of snot back up the nostril it was trying to escape from. He paced back and forth, one hand flapping on his chest like he was trying to counteract his racing heartbeat.

'If we go up, we'll get caught! We can't do that. We'll get into huge trouble!'

Shona's shoulders sagged and she let out a big, rolling sigh. It wasn't through disappointment, though, but relief.

'Oh, God! You're a coward!'

Neville tried to argue, but the crack in his voice and the tears in his eyes said otherwise. 'No, I'm not. I'm not a coward!'

'No, it's not a bad thing, Neville! It's great!' Shona assured him. 'It's brilliant. Because, you know, I had this idea of you being, like, a fecking superhero or something. Just, like, this perfect man who could do no wrong. So this? God Almighty, it's great. It's a relief, is what it is. It's going to make this whole working relationship *much* easier from now on!'

Neville seemed completely lost. He stumbled over a few words, then sniffed and pulled himself together. 'I'm not *scared*,' he insisted, though even he didn't look like he believed it. 'I just don't think it's sensible.'

'Of course. No. Fine. You're absolutely right, Neville. Sorry I asked. I shouldn't have put you on the spot like that. You go home. I'll be fine.'

The assistant almost leaped for his coat. 'I'll bring you something nice for breakfast,' he promised.

Shona beamed at him. 'I'm going to try and grab something at home with Jack, I think, so don't you go stressing yourself. I'll see you tomorrow, Neville, all right?'

Neville glanced back over his shoulder at the mortuary doors. 'I'll just do a final quick check of the place and then I'll shoot. But, eh, you're not going to do anything stupid, are you?'

The pathologist frowned and shook her head. 'Nah. Course not. You're right. Mad idea. Don't know what I was thinking.'

Satisfied with this answer, Neville smiled and scurried through to the mortuary.

Shona waited for the doors to swing closed, then pulled open a drawer and took out a pair of surgical gloves. The last thing she wanted to do, after all, was to leave fingerprints.

'Right then, Maguire,' she whispered. 'Let's go and channel your inner Jack Logan.'

–

'How come you decided to bring me along, boss?' asked Tyler, as Logan pulled the BMW into the kerb along the street from Charlotte Hilton's front door.

Ideally, he'd have been able to stop right out front, but other cars had got there first, including the suspect's own bright green Volkswagen Beetle with the flowers painted on the side and the ridiculous plastic eyelashes.

The detective constable winked and grinned. 'Is it so I can use my masculine wiles to charm her?'

Logan shut off the engine. 'Right. First of all, son, if I ever hear you say the phrase "masculine wiles" again, I'll cut you in half. And no' horizontally, either. Vertically. Down the middle.'

Tyler nodded. 'That sounds more than fair, boss.'

'And secondly, no, I didn't bring you for your charm.' He unclipped his seatbelt and opened the door. 'I brought you because you can run faster than I can.'

'You think she might leg it?'

'Don't know. Hopefully not. But I want you to hang back here just in case. I'll go to the door. If she bolts, this is the most likely direction she'll run. Other way's a dead end. So, if you see a woman in fucking awful dungarees coming racing in your direction, you grab her. Think you can handle that?'

Tyler raised both thumbs. 'No bother, boss. She won't get past me.'

'She'd better not. Stand by the car. Be ready.'

They both got out of the Beamer, and Tyler hung back by the passenger side door while Logan went marching along the pavement, his hands in his pockets, his head lowered against a mist of fine drizzle.

'Don't see why I couldn't just wait in the car,' Tyler grumbled, zipping up his jacket and bringing his shoulders up around his ears. The car had been lovely and warm. Out here, the rain had a chill to it, and the wind packed a bitter punch.

He almost hoped that she did make a break for it. Running after her would at least warm him up a bit.

Tyler limbered himself up by bouncing from left to right, his weight seesawing from one foot to the other as he stretched his tendons and ligaments.

He had just started to jog lightly on the spot when he heard the roaring of an engine. Although, 'roaring' wasn't quite the right word. It was less of a throaty growl and more of a nasal whine. It reminded Tyler of a wasp trapped behind a pane of glass.

Along the street, Logan lunged, but he was too slow. Belching smoke, Charlotte Hilton's Volkswagen Beetle swung out of its roadside parking space. Her foot went to the floor. The wasp lost its shit.

Tyler blinked in surprise as he realised in a moment of sudden clarity, that he was once again directly in the path of a fast-approaching vehicle.

'Tyler!' Logan roared.

The whole world went into slow motion. The sound of the engine. The movement of the car. The panic on the DCI's face as he broke into a frantic, desperate run.

Unfortunately, Tyler's reaction went into slow motion, too. He stumbled away from the BMW, his legs warning him that he should be running, but his brain not willing or able to settle on a direction.

He saw the look of horror on the face of the woman behind the steering wheel. He watched, frozen, as she locked her arms, screwed her eyes tightly shut, and pushed the accelerator all the way to the floor.

Like a switch had been flicked, the world came crashing back into full speed. Tyler heard Logan's roaring at him to move, felt his body come fully back under his control.

But too late, too late, *too late*!

The car was right there.

There was nowhere for him to go.

The impact, to his surprise, came not from the car's bonnet, but from somewhere on his left. He heard a grunt, felt the air leaving his body, then he slammed against the side door of Logan's car just as the Beetle howled past.

There was a sickening crunch of man meeting metal. Tyler turned in time to see a flailing figure shattering Charlotte Hilton's windscreen into a spiderweb of fractured glass, before it went rolling over the rounded roof and landed with a clatter on the road behind it.

Blinded, Charlotte lost control of the car. Her tyres and brakes screeched. Her scream rang out, and then was silenced when she ploughed into a lamppost and came to a sharp, sudden stop.

The Volkswagen's horn blared a long, steady note.

The car was old—pre-airbag old—and Tyler wasted a second making sure the woman was still moving before turning back to the man lying sprawled on his back on the tarmac.

'Shite. Bob! Bob, you all right?' the detective constable cried, rushing to his side.

A low groan of pain rose from between bloodied lips. Closed eyes twitched open, the pupils swimming as they searched for focus.

'It's Mr fucking Hoon,' came the reply. 'And fuck me, son, did no bastard ever teach you the Green Cross fucking Code?'

'Is he all right?' Logan asked, arriving slightly breathlessly on the scene.

'The fuck kind of question's that?' Hoon demanded. 'Do I fucking look all right? I'm lying spangled on the fucking ground. I just got hit by a… What kind of fucking car was that, by the way? And was it just me, or did it have fucking eyelashes?'

Tyler glanced back at the crashed vehicle. Charlotte Wilson was attempting to get out through the passenger door, since the driver's side was tightly wedged against the front of a parked van.

Given that the passenger door was just a few inches from the back of another car, though, she wouldn't be going anywhere anytime soon.

'Volkswagen Beetle,' the DC said.

Hoon tutted. 'Fuck's sake. I'm no' lying down to one of them tubs of shite.'

He held out both hands for the detectives to pull him up, but neither man reached down to help.

'You need to stay there, Bob,' Logan told him. 'We'll get an ambulance.'

'Aye, well, you might want to go ahead and order a couple, because you'll both fucking need one if you don't give me a hand up.'

'You're hurt, Mr Hoon,' Tyler said.

'Am I fuck. By that thing? I've had more damaging bowel movements. I'm right as fucking rain. Help me up.'

'Bob.' Logan waited until Hoon had raised his head to look at him, then pointed to the fallen man's left foot.

'What are you fucking whinging about now, you…?' Hoon frowned when he saw what Logan was directing his attention to. 'The fuck's that pointing that way for?'

He stared at the foot for a while, his frown slowly deepening. Darkening. The black pools of his eyes widened, jolted open by a surge of adrenaline.

His lower leg, from what he could gather, was facing almost completely the wrong direction. It hadn't quite been twisted all the way into a one-eighty, but it wasn't far off.

Right now, though, that didn't matter.

A broken leg was the least of his worries.

'How can I no' feel that?' he muttered.

His gaze shifted from the twisted foot to the other one. He fixated on it. Scowled at it. Gritted his teeth against a rising sense of horror.

He looked up at the detectives. Logan was already on the phone, talking in hushed, urgent tones. Tyler knelt beside him, and the boy looked so scared that Hoon almost told him to get a fucking grip of himself.

'How the fuck can I no' feel anything?' he whispered.

He let his head sink back down onto the road.

'Ambulance is on its way, Bob,' Logan assured him. 'You're going to be fine.'

But Hoon couldn't hear him over the booming of the heartbeat inside his head.

'Stay with him,' the DCI instructed, leaving Tyler at Hoon's side.

A car had pulled to a stop just beyond where Charlotte Wilson had wedged her Beetle between the other vehicles. The driver was just getting out to find out what was going on when Logan pointed to him.

'You. Arse back in the car and stay where you are. You're my roadblock. Anyone without a flashy blue light gets past and I'm holding you personally responsible.'

Message delivered, Logan strode over to the crashed Volkswagen. Charlotte, having finally realised that she wasn't going to get either door open enough for her to get out, had wound down the passenger window and was attempting to climb out. The sight of Logan approaching only made her try harder.

'N-no, please! Please, I can't! I have to go!' she begged, her face a wet slick of tears, blood and snot. 'You have to let me go. I have to get to them!'

'You're not going anywhere, Miss Wilson. Except to the station with me.'

She let out a sound like a wounded animal. Something between a scream and a sob that rose from somewhere deep and primal.

'N-n-no, please, please,' she begged, her body half-wedged into the gap between her car and the one beside it, her hands clawing at the roof as they tried to find purchase, all nine digits leaving streaks on the metal. 'You don't understand! You don't get it! I have to go. I have to go now, or they're dead.'

Her face crumpled. The words wedged themselves in her throat. Her whole body was shaking as shock dug its hooks into her.

'If I don't go, he's going to kill them. If I'm not there, then he's going to kill them both!'

Chapter Thirty-Seven

The door to Dr Singh's office was locked. But then, she'd been expecting that. Fortunately, she had a trick up her sleeve, in the form of a fully grown adult man named Dougie, who had a master key that opened most of the doors in the building.

Dougie had been part of the fabric of Raigmore since before Shona had first left Ireland, and he had been one of the first people to make her feel at home in the hospital. Despite the age difference, they shared a similar sense of humour and taste in music, though for the life of her, she couldn't get him to even entertain the notion of a Pot Noodle.

What she *could* convince him to do, though, was to let her borrow his magic key.

He'd asked questions, of course, and she'd supplied him with answers that he didn't believe, but which afforded him a degree of deniability. There was no chance of Dougie giving the game away directly to Dr Singh, either, because the surgeon rarely even spoke to junior doctors unless he absolutely had to, and drew the line at talking to anyone lower down the pay scale than that.

It would be a cold day in hell before Dr Singh made conversation with anyone from cleaning or maintenance.

After a quick check to make sure that Valerie wasn't hanging about somewhere, Shona sidled up to Singh's office door, unlocked it with the magic key, and slipped inside.

She realised, once she was in the office, that anyone watching her would've immediately been suspicious. She should've just entered the room confidently and like she was supposed to be there, rather than inching the door ajar and hurriedly squeezing through the narrowest possible gap.

Still, she could hardly be blamed for that. This was her first time doing this sort of thing. Breaking and entering was not something she made a habit of.

She spent a few panicky moments wondering what the hell she thought she was doing. Neville was right. This was madness. She could lose her job over this. What was she thinking?

Shona turned back to the door, already writing this whole thing off as one of the worst ideas she'd ever had. And, considering she'd almost died while hiding in a fridge a few months back, that was saying something.

Her hand rested on the handle. Meanwhile, her mind replayed what she'd seen of the drab, grey office.

His desk, with their big drawers.

His filing cabinet, full of his records.

His notepad on the desk, where he jotted down his thoughts.

So much potential. So many places where she might find the truth.

She adjusted her grip on the door handle.

Just a quick peek. That was all. Just a quick scan around to see if anything obvious jumped out at her.

Then, she'd bring whatever it was to Jack and let him deal with it.

It'd be quick. She'd be in and out. She was already halfway through that process, in fact. The 'in' part had already been accomplished. She was more or less home and dry.

All she had to do was find something. All she had to do was look.

She let go of the handle. She turned from the door.

And, oblivious to the footsteps padding along the corridor towards her, Shona Maguire set to work.

Chapter Thirty-Eight

DI Forde took off his glasses, pinched the bridge of his nose, then let out a low groan as if something was painful. Something was, of course—he was of an age where at least two or three different parts of him were aching at any given time—but that wasn't the reason for the groaning.

'How bad is he?' he asked.

Logan may only have been thirty-odd miles away, but his reply sounded distant and tinny. 'He's pretty bad. He had no idea his foot was fucked. Pointing completely the wrong way, and he didn't have a clue.'

'Shite.' Ben grimaced. 'What are the paramedics saying?'

'Not a lot,' Logan replied. 'Which in itself is saying plenty.'

'What's his mood like? He'll be bollocking everyone in sight, I'm guessing.'

He heard Logan mutter an order of some kind to someone nearby before turning his attention back to the call.

'No, actually. Weirdly subdued. I think he knows something's wrong. Something major.' Even down the phone line, Ben heard the DCI scratching at his stubble. 'He saved Tyler. Stupid bugger wasn't shifting, so Hoon pushed him clear. Came out of nowhere. The car hit him at full tilt.'

'Christ. Tyler's OK, though?'

'He's fine. He's away to the hospital with Hoon.'

'Blimey. And Hoon was all right with that?'

'Honestly? I think he was pleased. Bob'll never admit it, of course, but I think he's scared.'

Ben narrowed his eyes and shook his head, like he couldn't imagine what that might look like. 'Don't blame him,' he said. 'I'd be shiteing myself. What if he never walks again?'

'Then, we'll never hear the bloody end of it,' Logan reasoned. 'But we'll cross that bridge when we come to it.'

'And the driver? The suspect? Charlotte Wilson. You got her?'

'Oh, aye,' Logan said, and there was a heavy, foreboding edge to his voice. 'We've got her. That's the main reason for phoning, actually. Soon as the paramedics have checked her over, I'm going to talk to her again, but there's something she said that I need you to check out.

'You might want to go grab a pen, if you haven't got one handy, because this is going to get a wee bit complicated...'

-

The man on Logan's left smelled strongly of soap and medicated shampoo.

He was a red-faced and rugged-looking lad, not much shorter and narrower than the DCI himself, but with a demeanour that skewed more towards the positive. At first glance, they could've been mistaken for a happy-go-lucky son and his miserable bastard of a father.

He was, Logan reckoned, one of the jolliest police officers he'd ever met. This instantly made him distrust the man, but his name had come up in conversation with the other Uniforms while they were checking Charlotte Wilson into the station in Aviemore, and Logan had specifically requested his presence.

'How you feeling now, Charlotte?' Logan asked.

It was a daft question, really. She had her arms wrapped around herself, and was rocking back and forth on the other side of the table, still a mess of throaty sobs and hot, bitter tears.

'I can't be here,' she insisted. Logan had lost count of how many times she'd told him that. 'He's going to kill them. He'll kill them if I'm not there.'

Logan held up a hand, partly to offer some reassurance, but mostly just to shut her up.

'We've got some of our best men going to the location you gave us, Charlotte.'

She leaned forward in panic, shaking her head so violently that her tears arced through the air. 'No, no, n-no, no, if he sees police, he'll kill them. He can't see police. He told me. He warned me!'

'They'll be in plain clothes,' Logan assured her. 'They'll keep their distance. They know what they're doing.'

She broke down at that, burying her face in her hands, her whole body shaking.

Logan indulged it for a few seconds, then raised his voice to make sure she heard him over the sound of her own sobbing.

'I'm told you know Constable Donaldson here.' He turned to the uniformed man. 'Iain, wasn't it? Can we call you that?'

'Course you can, sir,' Iain replied, and he looked genuinely honoured to be on first-name terms with the DCI, one-sided as it currently was.

'Do you recognise Iain, Charlotte?'

She didn't look at either man, just kept her head down and her hands over her face.

'Take a look at him,' Logan instructed. 'But take your time. We've got all day.'

When she once again failed to reply, Iain caught Logan's eye, then nodded inquisitively in the woman's direction.

'By all means,' Logan said, folding his arms.

Iain smiled, then gently cleared his throat. 'Miss Wilson? Miss Wilson, it's me. Iain Donaldson. You probably don't remember me, but you had me for science in First Year. Big spotty kid. Sat down the front. Peein' Iain, they called me, because they said I stunk of pee. I didn't, though,' he assured the DCI. 'It just rhymed.'

The constable seemed genuinely worried that Logan might think that he had once stunk of piss, so the detective acknowledged the explanation with a vague wave that made clear the explanation wasn't necessary.

He was well aware that rhyming nicknames were nothing new, and rarely had any basis in truth. For a couple of years in high school, half the kids in Logan's year had exclusively referred to him as, 'Wogan'; despite the fact that he had almost nothing in common with the much-loved Irish broadcaster of that name, beyond a shared disdain for the Eurovision Song Contest.

Even then, they'd demonstrated their contempt in very different ways—Terry Wogan by providing a sarcastic running commentary for the BBC's live coverage of the event, and Logan by just refusing point-blank to ever watch the fucking thing.

'Here's the thing, Charlotte, Iain here was in your class. But he went to the same high school as Eleanor Howard. They were in the same year, in fact. But you told me that you didn't know Eleanor. That you taught in a different school.'

'I didn't know her. I do teach in a different school. I'm not… Please, I can't do this!'

'We checked with the head teacher at the school in Kingussie. Turns out you left under a bit of a cloud, Charlotte. You had a run-in with a couple of pupils, didn't you? A couple of girls. One of which was Eleanor Howard.'

Charlotte shook her head, her voice barely squeaking through the gaps in her sobs. 'I don't remember!'

'No? Do you remember stalking Eleanor's OnlyFans page? Do you remember the stuff you wrote?' Logan opened a folder. 'Because I can read it out if you need reminding? I'd rather not, it's pretty foul stuff. Quite graphic.'

The woman across the table said nothing, just trembled, and shook, and cried like she was facing her end.

'You told her to kill herself, didn't you, Charlotte?'

'N-no, I… Please!'

'You did. You told her she should go and kill herself. It's right here in black and white. You want me to read it?'

'No. Please. Don't. I'll tell you. I will. I'll tell you everything, but I can't. Not yet. I can't say anything.' Charlotte's words were a shrill, scratchy whisper that made Constable Donaldson squirm in his seat. 'I can't say anything until I know they're OK. I can't say anything. He told me. He made me swear.'

'Who did?' Logan asked. 'Who made you swear, Charlotte?'

She seemed to explode, her body jerking violently towards them, the flats of her hands slapping against the desk so the sound rang out like a gunshot. To his credit, Iain barely even flinched. Logan didn't so much as blink.

'You're not listening to me! I can't tell you!' Charlotte screamed, and her voice rang like a siren around the room. 'You have to let me go get them! You have to let me go get my mum and dad before it's too late!'

–

Hamza squinted through a pair of binoculars at the car that sat parked in a lay-by on a narrow, unnamed road that ran alongside Loch Morlich, five or six miles to the east of Aviemore.

The loch and its beach were a popular spot for water sports enthusiasts, but several days of grim, wet weather meant the car park had been empty when Hamza had pulled up in his car with a couple of unmarked police vehicles in tow.

Over on his right, above the loch, a helicopter was trying to make itself inconspicuous. While this wasn't an easy thing for a helicopter to do, the proximity to the Cairngorms mountain range helped. Choppers were often buzzing around the place, searching for climbers lost on the snowy peaks.

Rather than scouring the mountains, though, this one was searching the woodlands around where the car was parked, its thermal cameras scanning the trees and foliage below for any signs of life. So far, it had spotted nothing larger than a rabbit.

The car, too—a twelve-year-old silver Ford Mondeo—was reading cold. No heat from the engine. No body warmth registering inside.

Hamza lowered the binoculars just as one of the constables from CID returned from his car. 'I ran the plate like you asked, Sarge. Car is showing as having been nicked from just outside Aberlour three weeks ago. Not really worth anything, and the owner was happy to take the insurance, so it wasn't followed up on.'

Three weeks. Potentially, it could've been sitting here since then, tucked away on this back road, out of sight.

'This has to be it,' Hamza said.

The location fit the instructions that Logan had relayed to DI Forde—a right turn off the B970 just after the Rothiemurchus Caravan Park, then twelve lay-bys along on the left. If Charlotte Wilson was to be believed, here, with the looming Scots pines turning the road into a narrow canyon, was where the handover of her parents was supposed to take place.

But there was nobody around. Nobody but the bunnies.

'What do you reckon?' the constable asked.

Hamza took another look through the binoculars, chewing anxiously on his bottom lip. There was nothing obviously wrong with the scene—it was just a car parked at the side of the road—but something about the whole thing was making him uneasy. Something was wrong here, he could feel it.

'Get the helicopter to do another sweep,' he instructed, and the constable left to relay the order.

Hamza lowered the binoculars again. Behind him, he heard the constable radioing up to the pilot, and the low muttering of the other plainclothes officers who had started to grow impatient.

He couldn't hear the words, but he got the general gist.

What was he hoping the chopper would see? It had already covered the area three times. There was nobody around. Ordering yet another sweep was just the DS stalling for time until he grew a pair and made a decision. Meanwhile, they were all standing around getting drenched.

A prickle of embarrassment crept up the back of Hamza's neck. They were right, of course. If DCI Logan had been leading the team, the car would've been searched already. There'd have been no messing around, no abundance of caution. He'd have come in, got the job done, and been on his way.

The rush of self-doubt made him think back to the night before, to the man at his breakfast bar, to the way his wife had been acting. Embarrassment gave way to anger. He wheeled around to face the gaggle of constables.

'You lot got a fucking problem with how I'm running this?' he demanded.

Glances were exchanged. Feet were shuffled. Nobody answered. Nobody dared.

'Well? Do you?'

'No, Sarge,' one of them mumbled. 'No problem.'

'Good. Keep it that way,' Hamza warned.

He turned back in the direction of the stolen car, but his blood was surging through his veins now, twitching his fingers and making him itch. He thought of them standing there talking about him, laughing away behind his back, thinking he couldn't hear them, that he didn't know what they were up to.

Doubting his judgements.

Drinking his coffee.

His heart was a hummingbird in his chest, and he couldn't just stand around any longer. A burning need in his gut drove him to toss the binoculars into the boot of his car, grab his torch, and set off at a march towards the Mondeo.

'Sarge?' one of the constables called after him. 'Are we moving in?'

'Stay where you are,' Hamza barked, not looking back. 'I've got this.'

The road was deserted. The only sounds were the soft crunch of his footsteps on the carpet of pine needles, and the *whum-whum-whum* of the helicopter as it banked above him.

Soon, even those seemed to fade away into silence.

'I've got this,' he repeated, more quietly.

The rain fell around him, dotting the puddles at the side of the road. He could see it striking the rear windscreen of the Mondeo now, hundreds of tiny explosions every second as the drops detonated against the glass.

He bounced the torch against the side of his leg as he drew closer, feeling the weight of it, letting it reassure him. Not far now. Just a few more seconds.

The other officers would be watching him from behind through the binoculars. Peering down on him from above.

Had it not been for their eyes on him, he might've slowed. Might have hesitated. Might have played it safer.

But, though the thought had never even occurred to him before, suddenly, he didn't want to look weak. Suddenly, he didn't want them to think of him as ineffectual, as the sort of man who couldn't do his job properly, couldn't handle pressure, couldn't even keep his own family together.

He shook his head and wiped the rain from his face.

He clicked on his torch, checked beneath the car, then shone the light in through the driver's side window.

The front seats were empty.

The back seats were not.

No heat signatures.

No wonder.

'Oh, shit. Oh, shit,' he whispered.

Despite all the eyes on him from above and behind, Hamza stumbled backwards in fright, his torch bulb smashing as he tripped and fell hard onto the cold, wet ground.

Chapter Thirty-Nine

This was not going as well as Shona had hoped.

Inconsiderately, Dr Singh had locked both his filing cabinet and his desk drawers, and though Shona had Dougie's magic key, it wasn't mystical enough to shrink down and fit either of those locks.

Technically, not all the desk drawers were locked. There was a shallow one on the left-hand side that contained an assortment of pens, paperclips and Post-it notes, but none of these suggested a crime worse than some overly enthusiastic visits to the stationery cupboard.

Still, there was something about it that made her hesitate. Jack had spoken before about an itch in his brain when there was something he should be seeing, but wasn't. He took it as a signal from his subconscious to slow down, focus, and pay attention to what was staring him in the face.

Shona felt a similar itch now, but as she had no idea how long it would be before Dr Singh came back, she couldn't afford to dwell on it.

She turned her attention to the pad on his desk. It sat just to the left of centre, and a quick peek revealed pages and pages of handwritten notes.

Unfortunately, Dr Singh really leaned into the whole stereotype of doctors having terrible handwriting. The steeply sloping words on the page were almost completely illegible, and the few words she could make out seemed to mostly be concerned with the hospital parking situation, and the quality of food in the staff canteen.

Shona couldn't disagree that both were a problem, but when it came to finding out if he was up to something, the surgeon's notes weren't in any way helpful.

And yet…

Like the drawer, there was something about that pad, too. Something about the writing on the page, and the placement of the pen beside it on the desk. Something that kicked the itch in her brain up a gear.

No time for that, though. Not now.

She turned her attention back to the filing cabinet. Maybe there was a way of opening it. Maybe if she just shoogled it enough, the drawers would miraculously unlock, and she could snoop around inside.

She gave the cabinet a shake. The worn old tennis ball that sat on top rolled off and landed on the floor with a *thock*, but other than that, her efforts had no real effect.

Stooping, she retrieved the ball.

When she straightened up again, Dr Singh stood in the doorway, staring at her in surprise.

For a moment, neither of them said anything. The surgeon's expression was rapidly darkening, though, suggesting some sort of angry outburst was on the immediate horizon.

Shona thought fast.

'Thank *Christ* you're here!'

That caught him off guard. The surgeon hadn't seen that coming.

'Wait. What? What do you mean?' he asked, confusion taking over. 'Why are you in here?'

'Smoke,' Shona said. She lifted her nose to the air and inhaled like it was her final breath. 'I smelled smoke. Do you smell smoke? I thought I smelled smoke.'

Dr Singh sniffed. It was unclear if this was just his usual sinus issue, or an attempt to answer the pathologist's question.

'How did you get in here?' he demanded.

He was still halfway into the room, partly in the corridor.

'The, uh, the door was unlocked. I smelled the smoke, and—'

'No, it wasn't.'

'What wasn't what?'

'The door.' He stepped inside and closed it behind him. 'It was locked. I know it was locked.'

Shona pulled an exaggerated frown of confusion. 'Well, someone must have unlocked it then, because…' She swallowed, then sniffed again. 'I think maybe I imagined it. I don't think I can smell smoke, actually.'

The surgeon still stood planted in front of the door, blocking the only way out of the room that didn't involve a fifty-foot drop onto concrete.

'What are you doing here, Dr Maguire?'

'Look, it's nothing. It's silly. I can explain. You don't have to call security or anything.'

'I wasn't planning on calling security,' the surgeon replied, and the coldness of his tone made her wish that he would. 'I just want to know why you're here.'

Shona passed the tennis ball anxiously from one hand to the other.

'I, uh, I just… I wanted to talk to you. The door was unlocked.'

'It wasn't.'

'It, uh, it was. I don't know… Maybe someone else unlocked it when you were out? Anyway, I just wanted to say sorry for earlier. If I annoyed you, or said something to upset you, I didn't mean—'

'What were you doing at my filing cabinet?'

Shona tried very hard to pretend she hadn't spotted the cabinet. Given that she was standing directly in front of it, this wasn't easy.

'What? Oh! I didn't even see that.'

'You're holding my tennis ball,' Singh pointed out. 'It was on top of the filing cabinet. It's *always* on top of the filing cabinet.'

Shona could sense his anger bubbling away inside him, rising towards the surface, contorting his expression and tensing his muscles.

This was a mistake. She should never have come here.

'Uh, I didn't even know I was holding that!' she said, forcing a laugh. She tossed the ball towards him and he caught it in one hand.

The left.

The itch stopped.

Left hand.

Left side drawer.

Notebook to the left of his desk, handwriting sloping in the same direction.

The bloodied saw retrieved from the cottage had been a standard one, the plastic handle moulded for a right-handed user.

Shona had told Jack the killer had been someone familiar with anatomy, but not, she thought, with the act of actually slicing anyone up. The cuts had been too ragged, too clumsy.

But what if they hadn't been made by an amateur?

What if the cuts had been done by a professional with his non-dominant hand?

Dr Singh squeezed the tennis ball between his fingers, like he was massaging it. He sniffed as he looked the pathologist up and down.

'I'm sorry, Dr Maguire. I just don't believe you,' he told her.

Then he turned and locked the door.

Chapter Forty

They'd broken the news to Charlotte Wilson as gently as possible. Although, there was only so gently something like that could be done.

Her parents were dead. And their deaths had not been good ones. Someone had taken real time over them.

They had been blinded, each of their eyes removed. Their ears had been hacked off, not cleanly. Their tongues were missing, too.

See no evil, hear no evil, speak no evil.

But evil had done this. Evil had been there with them, right up close, face to face. Nobody who had seen those bodies could argue with that.

Logan had played it all down, of course. He'd told her the bare facts, and nothing more. Her parents had been murdered. They'd been dead for days.

She broke then. Of course she did.

At first, she refused to believe it, screeching that Logan was lying, demanding to see them for herself.

Her anger had soon been redirected, though. *He'd promised*, she insisted. She'd done everything he'd told her to do. He'd promised, if she did it all, that he'd let them go!

'Did what?' Logan asked. 'What did you do?'

'What he asked. Everything he asked. He promised not to tell people. He promised they'd be safe. He promised me!' She was scratching at herself now, her nails leaving red trails on the back of the opposite hand. 'He promised me he wouldn't hurt them.'

'Slow down, Charlotte,' Logan urged. 'I need you to explain clearly what's happened. Can you do that for me?'

Iain, the constable, smiled kindly at her. 'You're OK, Mrs H. Just tell him what he needs to know, and we can sort all this out.'

'Sort it out?' The teacher's words were like venom. 'How can we possibly *sort it out*, Iain? How can we possibly fix this?! Jesus Christ, you were always a fucking *idiot*. You haven't changed, have you? You're still the same spotty-faced loser you always were!'

She turned to Logan but stabbed a finger in the constable's direction. 'I want him out! I don't want him here! I'll talk to you. Just you.'

'Fine,' Logan said. 'But everything'll continue to be recorded.'

'I don't care. I just… Get him out.'

Iain didn't appear to be the slightest bit put out by any of this, and just nodded and smiled when Logan asked him to leave the room.

'If anyone needs me, I'll be outside,' he said, getting up from his seat. He looked fondly at his old teacher. 'I'm sorry you're having to go through this, Mrs H. I really am.'

She put a hand to her forehead, shielding her down-turned eyes. The moment the door was closed, she let out a sob she'd been fighting back.

'I shouldn't have said that. I shouldn't have said those things. He was a good boy. He was one of the nice ones. Tell him I'm sorry. Please. Will you?'

'Of course,' Logan said. 'And he'll understand. You're going through a lot. And I know it might not seem like it, but I can help. You'll feel better getting it all off your chest. I promise.'

He decided to start things off gently, and indicated the bandage on her hand.

'What happened to your finger? What really happened, I mean?'

Charlotte swallowed. She stared at the bandage, her hand shaking in time with her bottom lip.

'Did it start with a purple postcard?' Logan asked, and the look of surprise on her face told him he was right.

'It… it came with a note. He told me I had to do it.'

The words were a whisper, but their impact rolled like thunder around the room.

'He told you you had to cut your finger off?'

She shook her head.

'What, then?' Logan asked.

'I couldn't cut it. It had to be more… creative, he said. I couldn't just use a knife. That wasn't allowed. That was too easy. And it had to be somewhere public. He told me where to go. Said I should take a bike and just…'

The tears came again then, the memory proving too harrowing for her to describe in further detail. Fortunately, Logan knew enough to be able to take over.

'So, you followed his instructions. You got a bike. You hired it. We checked that. It was a one-off, though, wasn't it? You'd never hired one from them before?'

She managed a little shake of her head.

'So, you hired the bike, took it out on the track, stopped where you were told, then stuck it into the spokes while they were spinning?'

'It hurt. It hurt so much. I knew it would, but it was way more. So much more than I thought. And… and it didn't come off. Not all the way. So, I tried to pull it, but the pain… I thought about sticking it back in, turning the wheel again, but then that woman came along, and I couldn't. I just couldn't.'

'Of course not,' Logan said. He smiled encouragingly. 'You're doing really well, Charlotte. I appreciate how hard this is, so well done. Now, who was it that made you do this?'

Her whole body tensed and she shook her head, like she couldn't go there. Like she wasn't ready. Logan took the hint and changed direction.

'What did he have on you, Charlotte? What did he have that made you cut off your own finger? It wasn't your parents. They were at the hospital. Was it the abuse on Eleanor's OnlyFans account? Did he know about that?'

Her eyes went wide. She stared back at him in surprise.

Question answered.

'And he threatened to tell people? And that would've cost you your job, right? Plus, small town. You'd be the talk of the place. Everyone would know.'

'I didn't mean it to get so out of hand. I just... I found out what she was doing, and she'd made my life hell. For years, even after I left that school, she made my life hell. She tormented me. Accosted me in the street. Threw stones at my windows. Pushed dog shit through my letterbox.'

Her face knotted up in disgust, and for a moment it looked like she was about to throw up on the table. She held it together, though, and with some encouragement from the DCI, she carried on.

'So, when I found her online. When I saw what she was doing. Degrading herself like that. I actually laughed. I actually thought it was hilarious that that's where she'd ended up. Shagging on camera so a load of sad bastard men could crack one off over the pretty young lassie.

'I thought that was enough for me. Just knowing that her life was that shit, I thought that was enough. But then I came back. I kept coming back. I kept *watching*.'

The teacher recoiled, like she was horrified at hearing those words spoken out loud, let alone coming from her own mouth.

'And then, I started to comment. I told her she was a slut. I told her she was dirty and disgusting.'

'Did you tell her she should kill herself?' Logan asked.

Charlotte hesitated, but then nodded. 'I didn't mean it. Not really. I just wanted her to feel how I'd felt. How she'd made me feel. And, he found out. I don't know how, but he found out, and he said he'd tell *everyone* if I didn't do what he said.

'I thought he had to be joking at first, about the finger. I thought he couldn't be serious. But he showed me a big list of names and email addresses. The staff at the school. My mum and dad. My friends. Newspapers, too. He said if I didn't do it, they'd all get the evidence, making it look like I was some sort of internet troll or something. My life wouldn't have been worth living.'

'So, you did what he said.'

Charlotte glanced down at the empty space where her finger should be.

'I did what he said,' she croaked.

'But that wasn't the end of it, was it? He asked you to do more.'

A tremble rippled through Charlotte from head to toe. She scratched at her injured hand again, her head shaking in denial, tears and snot in full flow again.

'I can't. Please, don't make me say it.'

'I have to ask. I'm sorry.' The DCI leaned forward, clasping his hands on the table. 'Did you kill Eleanor Howard, Charlotte?'

'*Please.*'

'I really am sorry, but you have to tell me the truth now. No more lies. Nothing else to hide. The truth. Did you kill Eleanor?'

Her throat and chest were constricting her. No two breaths were the same.

'He told me I h-had to pick someone.'

Not a muscle in Logan's body moved.

'To kill?'

Her head jerked up and down. 'I said no. I said I wouldn't. I said h-h-he could tell everyone, I didn't care, I wasn't doing that.'

She looked down at her lap, pulling herself together, forcing herself to carry on. To say the words that would free her and condemn her at the same time.

'But he took my parents,' she whispered through a cascade of fresh tears. 'He took my mum and dad. He went to their house and he took them. He s-said if I didn't do it, he'd kill them both. Said it was their lives for someone else. 'Two for the price of one,' he kept saying. 'Two for the price of one.' I just had to choose someone. It could be anyone. I just had to choose.'

'And you chose the girl who'd made your life hell.'

Her breathing steadied, becoming more shallow. She met Logan's eye, just for a moment, then nodded.

'Out loud for the tape please, Charlotte.'

'Y-yes.'

'You killed Eleanor Howard?'

Another sob tried to break free, but she choked it back. 'I did. I did it. I killed her. I killed Ellie.'

Logan shifted his weight back. His chair groaned, like it had been hoping the detective's suspicions were wrong.

'But that's all I did,' Charlotte whispered, her eyes pleading with him to believe her. 'I killed her, but I swear, I didn't cut her up. That wasn't me. That was someone else…'

–

Dr Singh was still standing in front of the door, blocking the way. He was quite a slight man, so, if it came to it, Shona reckoned she could get the jump on him. A couple of quick rabbit punches to the throat and a God Almighty kick to the bollocks and he'd no longer pose a problem.

So, with that in mind, she decided it was best to find out what he had to say for himself.

'You knew about the fingers, didn't you?' she asked. 'You knew they hadn't been disposed of properly.'

'What kind of accusation is that?' Dr Singh spat. He was twisting his hands together around the tennis ball, like it was the tiny neck of some imagined enemy. 'First, you break in, then you make… What? Wild accusations about my being involved in… I don't even know what you're accusing me of being involved in.'

'It was you who stopped them going into the waste, wasn't it? You kept them.'

Singh made a series of incredulous noises and hand gestures, but didn't otherwise refute the allegation.

'Did you put them in that house? Where are the rest from? Because I've looked, and you haven't removed any others. Not in the last few years, anyway.'

'Again, Dr Maguire, I really can't…'

He forcibly cleared his throat, like there was something obstructing it that he was struggling to shift. One hand rubbed at his forehead, forefinger and thumb pressing so hard against the skin that tiny rolls of grey dirt formed beneath the fingertips.

'Did you kill that girl?'

'What?! No! No, I… How dare…? No! My God. What a thing to even…' He shook his head with a vaguely disappointed sort of air, like someone had accidentally put one too many sugars in his coffee. 'I mean, of all the things to…'

'Did you?' Shona pressed.

Singh laughed. There was no trace of humour in it, just a home brew of desperation and stalling tactics.

Shona's chest tightened. She'd been hoping she was wrong, that this was all just mad speculation on her part. But right then, there in his eyes, she could see she was right.

'You killed her. Then you cut her up. Didn't you?'

'This is ridiculous. I should be calling security.'

'Please do,' Shona told him. She made for the door. 'In fact, why don't I go get them?'

He didn't move to get out of her way. She didn't try to make him.

'Stay where you are,' he told her.

She stopped, just as instructed, that kick in the balls still firmly in her back pocket, ready to be whipped out at a moment's notice.

The pathologist watched in silence as the surgeon brought the tennis ball up to his mouth and clamped his teeth around it. He bit down hard, grimacing, tears swelling.

His whole body shook with distress, or rage, or some other raw, primal emotion. Then, once whatever it was had passed, he relaxed his jaw, and the ball fell to the floor at his feet with a dull, hollow *thunk*.

'You're wrong. I didn't kill her. I didn't kill anyone. I wouldn't do that.'

This time, his eyes told a different story, and Shona suddenly got the sense that he was telling the truth.

She recalibrated and tried again.

'You cut her up, though,' she ventured.

That was the bit she'd figured out. Maybe he hadn't killed her, but the evidence—entirely circumstantial as it was—pointed to him being the one who'd done the dismembering.

'Didn't you, Dr Singh? You cut up her body?'

'No! No, I didn't do anything of the sort!'

'You went into that room in that house, and you hacked her up.'

'No!'

'Why did you do it?'

A bubble of snot burst from one of the surgeon's nostrils. 'I didn't!'

'Why did you use a right-handed saw?'

'*Because that's what he told me to use!*'

The confession hung there in the silence that followed. Shona swallowed. She still hadn't fully believed that she was right. She'd still been holding out some hope that she wasn't.

So much for that.

'Oh, no. Oh, no. That's not— I didn't—'

Singh sniffed heavily as he gripped his head and stared at her, his eyes like two dark pools of despair.

'That's not real. What I said. It's not true. I didn't do anything!'

Shona managed a smile. It was quite an accomplishment, given the circumstances. 'OK. Good. I'm glad. Sorry I doubted you,' she said, sidling closer to the door. 'We'll just say no more about it and—'

His fist came at her out of nowhere. The first she knew of it was the flash of white and the explosion of pain that sent her staggering back against his desk.

By the time her vision cleared, so had the route to the door. She threw herself towards it, but a hand tangled in her hair, pulling her back, swinging her spiralling to the floor.

His knee pressed on her chest. She tried to struggle, but a glint of light on a scalpel blade made her stop.

'Please, don't!' she wheezed. 'Please.'

The surgeon brought a shaky finger to his lips. Two shiny lines of tears ran down both his cheeks. 'I really don't want to,' he whispered. 'But if you make another sound, I'm going to have to slit your throat.'

Chapter Forty-One

Ben replaced the handset of his desk phone, stared at the screen for a few moments, then prodded at random icons until the display showed the home screen again.

'Stupid bloody thing,' he muttered, before turning to the rest of the room.

Sinead was over by the Big Board, adding all the info that Dave had gathered with his afternoon of phone calls and escalations.

Dave himself, meanwhile, was knocking back a can of Irn Bru and psyching himself up for another call to the bank. Hopefully, he'd get someone more helpful this time. Or, at the very least, someone who could understand his accent.

'Well, that is weird,' the detective inspector announced.

'What's weird, sir?' Sinead asked, looking back over her shoulder as she pinned another card to the corkboard.

'I've been trying to get hold of Shona about those bodies Hamza phoned in. Palmer's already on the way, but I can't get hold of Shona at all. Not in the office, not answering her mobile. Even tried the house to see if she was there, but nope. Not a cheep from her. It's like she's disappeared off the face of the earth.'

'Or she's in a meeting,' Sinead suggested.

Ben nodded. 'Or she's in a meeting, aye. Still, even then, unlike her no' to answer. I even called from the desk phone so it'd show up as official polis business. Nothing.'

He tapped his pen on his desk and regarded the phone as if he could will it to ring through the power of his mind alone.

It remained steadfastly silent, and Ben tutted before spinning around in his chair again.

'Is Tyler still at the hospital, do you know?'

'Eh, as far I know, sir, yeah,' Sinead confirmed.

Ben tapped his pen a few more times, deep in thought.

'Something doesn't feel right,' he announced. 'Do me a favour. Give him a ring and get him to swing by the mortuary, will you?'

Sinead turned away from the board and reached for her phone. 'Why, do you think something's happened?'

'Eh? Oh. No, no. No, I doubt it,' Ben said. He looked back at the phone. Still nothing. 'But better safe than sorry, eh?'

–

'Are you eating my fucking grapes?'

Tyler looked around the room in case there was someone else there that he hadn't previously been aware of, then turned back to Hoon lying strapped to the spinal board on the bed.

'You haven't got grapes,' the detective constable informed him.

'Eh? How the fuck have I no' got grapes? Has no bastard even brought me one measly fucking bunch of grapes?'

'You're not long in,' Tyler reminded him. 'You had the scan and the X-ray, now we're just waiting for the doctor to come back and tell us what's going on.'

'Jesus Christ, son, it's no' fucking dementia I've got,' Hoon spat back. He hit Tyler with the most abrasive side-eyed look he could muster, since he couldn't turn his head to fully glare at him. 'I do remember the events of the past few fucking hours, thanks very much. You don't need to do a fucking "Previously on…" for my benefit.'

Tyler squirmed on the hard plastic chair. He had already established that there was no possible way of getting comfortable, but it didn't stop him trying.

'No. Sorry. I just thought, you know, you're on quite a lot of painkillers and they can make you a bit…'

'A bit fucking what?'

'Doolally.'

'Jesus Christ, son, don't spare my fucking feelings, or anything. Don't fucking hold back on my account, you heartless, plastic-haired wee prick.'

'Sorry,' Tyler said.

Hoon grunted, and went back to looking at the ceiling. It wasn't very interesting, even by ceiling standards.

'Have I got a catheter in?' he asked.

Tyler shifted in his chair again. 'Uh, no. They haven't done anything like that.'

'Aye, well, keep your fucking teeth sharp, in case they do.'

Tyler stared blankly back at him. He had no idea what the former detective superintendent was implying, and he was fairly sure that he didn't want to know, either.

When Hoon had been taken into the A&E department, Tyler had hung back. To his surprise, though, Hoon had asked him to stay. Well, technically he'd ordered him to stay, but Tyler had seen through the bluff and bluster, and the eight different variations on the word 'fuck'.

The detective constable had hovered at the edge of the room while Hoon was checked over. He'd been there for the X-ray when the broken leg had been confirmed, although no one had been in any doubt about that.

The lack of feeling in his legs was the bigger issue. Tyler had watched and tried to listen as three different doctors had gathered at the far end of the room, whispering among themselves, and occasionally glancing back at the man on the bed.

Nobody had told Hoon anything more yet, but things weren't looking good.

'You think I'm fucked, then?' he asked, gaze fixed on the blank, featureless ceiling. 'You think I'm going to be stoatin' around in a fucking wheelchair?'

'What? No. Nah. No way,' Tyler said.

'Too fucking right, I'm not. Too fucking true.'

Tyler nodded, and looked along the bed to where Hoon's feet were still pointing in wildly different directions. 'You feel anything yet?' he asked.

'I do, actually.'

Tyler sat up. 'Aye?'

'Deep fucking regret at no' just letting you get flattened, you reactionless bag of hot pish.' Hoon sighed. 'I mean, fuck's sake, son, if a car's speeding towards you, it doesn't take a fucking rocket scientist to know you should move out of its fucking way. But, oh no, you just fucking stand there like you're willing it on. Is that how shite your life's become? Welcoming death by Volkswagen fucking Beetle?'

His eyes darted in Tyler's direction, his brow furrowing angrily.

'Oh, and if anyone asks, it was a fucking truck, all right? It was a big fucking juggernaut going at full tilt. If I'm being paralysed for life, I'm no' having fucking *Herbie Goes Bananas* be responsible for it. They'll be giving it, "Ye hear Bob Hoon's been fucking crippled?" "Aye, I hear he was mowed down by the fucking Love Bug."' He attempted to shake his head, but the straps wouldn't let him. 'That's no' fucking happening, let me tell you.'

'You won't be paralysed, Mr Hoon.'

'No? Oh, that's fucking magic news! What a relief. Cheers for that, son. Didn't realise you'd popped out to fucking medical school between here and Aviemore. That's a big weight off my mind.'

A melody played from Tyler's pocket.

'That'd better no' be your fucking phone I'm hearing,' Hoon warned him. 'Whatever it is, you fucking tell them you're doing something more important, then hang up. In fact, don't even fucking pick up. Just dinghy the call. You've got more important things to worry about, like the current whereabouts of my fucking grapes.'

'Um, but...'

'I fucking mean it, son. Answer that phone, and I'll stick your foot where your head's meant to be, and your arms up your arse.'

'But you can't move,' Tyler pointed out.

'I can move my eyebrows, which is all I'll fucking need.'

Tyler held up the phone to show the screen. 'It's Sinead.'

Hoon tutted. 'Well, fucking answer it, then! Jesus Christ, son, it's a miracle she's no' dumped your arse already. Her self-loathing and pity are both going to run out sooner or fucking later, so don't keep her hanging on, for fuck's sake.'

Tyler nodded gratefully, then half-turned away and swiped the button to answer.

'Hey, what's up?'

'And tell her to send me in some fucking grapes,' Hoon instructed.

Tyler put a finger in his ear and pressed the phone closer to the other. 'Eh, aye. Yeah, I'm still here. We haven't heard much more yet, so I don't... What? Shona? No. Not seen her. Why?'

'What the fuck's happening? I can't hear what she's saying,' Hoon said. 'Put her on speakerphone.'

Tyler pretended he hadn't heard any of that and carried on the conversation as normal.

'I mean, I can maybe go and take a quick look, but Bob—'

'*Mr Hoon.*'

'But Mr Hoon needs me here.'

'Do I fuck,' Hoon objected.

Tyler turned back to him. 'But, I thought you said...?'

Hoon motioned him into silence using just his eyebrows. 'Just get back here before they put the fucking catheter in,' he instructed. 'And if you turn up empty-handed on the grapes front, on your own fucking head be it.'

–

'Shh. Shut up and stop wriggling around.'

Olivia didn't know what the rules were with regards to bringing dogs into hospitals. You could get away with guide dogs, she reckoned. Guide dogs were allowed everywhere. But daft wee mutts that tripped over their own ears and suffered occasional incontinence issues when over stimulated? She felt that type of dog was probably less welcome.

Fortunately, Taggart was able to fit quite neatly in her schoolbag. Most of him, anyway. His head and front paws stuck out of the top, but she'd covered him with her school jumper.

It would have been the perfect disguise, if it wasn't for the fact he kept barking excitedly and trying to chew through the fabric.

She was supposed to go straight home, but she'd got off the bus at the hospital and headed for Shona's office. There was something she had to say to the pathologist. There was something important she had to tell her.

Admittedly, she hadn't quite figured out what that was yet, but she hoped the words would present themselves when the time was right.

A stern-looking nurse walked along the corridor in the opposite direction, eyes locked on the girl and her curiously carried bag. Once upon a time, Olivia might have been intimidated by her, but that girl was long gone.

Instead, she strode confidently past the woman, disguising Taggart's snuffling noises with a well-timed cough. The nurse slowed for a step or two, but then carried on without looking back.

The rest of the journey to the mortuary was uneventful. When Olivia got there, she found the door to the outer office unlocked, and all the lights in the windowless room still blazing. There was nobody inside it, though, and Olivia's gaze went to the double doors at the back of the office.

This was it, then. Shona must be in the big creepy room through the back, where all the action happened. Olivia closed the door behind her, tipped Taggart carefully out of her bag, then loudly cleared her throat.

'Uh, hello?'

There was no answer from through the back.

'Shona? It's me. It's, uh, it's Olivia. Hello.'

Silence.

Damn.

Olivia approached the double doors that led through to the back. The windows were covered so nobody could peek in and accidentally get an eyeful of someone's lungs being plucked out, or their stomach contents poked around in.

A light from under the door and the movement of a shadow told her someone was in there. She knocked lightly, then brought her face closer to the door. Behind her, Taggart darted around, exploring all the fun new smells.

'Listen, um, I just wanted to say that… I'm sorry. I just… I haven't been very nice to you. To anyone. Since'—she bit her lip—'you know. Everything. But that's not fair. It's not your fault. It's no one's fault but hers.'

She shuffled on the spot and looked the door up and down, like it might give away some indication of what was happening on the other side.

'So, I just… I wanted to say I'm sorry for behaving like such a dick to everyone.'

'Apology accepted.'

Olivia wheeled around to find Tyler standing in the doorway, grinning back at her. She tutted and scowled, reverting to form.

'That wasn't meant for you.'

'Well, you did say "everyone" and that includes me, so…' He put his hand on his chest. 'Thank you. It means a lot.'

The girl rolled her eyes. 'Yeah, yeah. Shut it.'

Tyler decided not to push his luck, and nodded past her to the double doors. 'Is Shona in there?'

'Think so, yeah. But she's not answering.'

Tyler grimaced, then straightened up and set his jaw, like he was squaring up to the doors.

'OK. I'll go in. You look away, though, in case there's anything, you know... Gory.' He winced. 'God, I hope there isn't.'

'Should I hang onto the dog?' Olivia asked.

'Why?'

'Well, in case he runs in and, like, steals a bone or whatever.'

'Oh shite. Aye. Best hang onto him,' Tyler agreed. 'I'd never hear the end of it if that happened.'

He clapped his hands and rubbed them together. He puffed out his cheeks, whispered some words of encouragement below his breath, then he marched over to the doors, knocked once, and pushed them open like a cowboy entering a saloon.

'Oh fuck, fuck! It's not what it looks like! It's not what it looks like!'

Across the room, over by a half-open body drawer, an incredibly attractive young man frantically tried to pull up his pants and trousers, which had been dropped down around his ankles.

Unfortunately for the lad, his erect penis was making this significantly more difficult.

'Holy shit!' Olivia remarked, leaning into the room.

Tyler took an immediate sideways step to his right, blocking the girl's view.

'Eh. OK,' the detective constable said. There was no real emotion in his voice, because he hadn't yet settled on the right one. Shock and horror were in there, obviously. Disgust, too. Confusion? Outrage? Both present and correct.

But by Christ, what a story this was going to make back at the station.

'It's not what it looks like,' Neville insisted again.

'Right. Good. I mean, thank God for that. Because from where I'm standing, it looked quite like you were having a wank over a dead body.'

'This is amazing!' Olivia chirped, and Tyler moved to block her view again.

'They just fell down!' Neville insisted, frantically doing up his buttons. His face was a shiny sheen of sweat, but Tyler couldn't tell if that was through panic or exertion. Probably a little bit of both. 'I was just working here, and they fell down!'

'It's all right. Calm down. Sorry, what was your name?'

'Neville.'

'Neville. Good. OK. Well, two things, Neville. One, do you know where Shona is?'

'Y-yes. She went up to Dr Singh's office.'

Tyler frowned. 'The surgeon? Why?'

Neville swallowed. 'She, uh, she didn't say. Something about fingers or something?'

'OK. Fair enough. Thanks for your help on that. Second thing,' Tyler continued. He reached into his pocket and produced his warrant card. 'You are *so* under arrest right now.'

'Oh my God,' Olivia sniggered, and Tyler realised she'd been filming the last few moments on her phone. 'You were almost pretty cool there,' she told him. 'And this is the funniest single moment of my entire life to date.'

Chapter Forty-Two

Charlotte claimed that she didn't know who had cut up Eleanor's body, and Logan had no reason to doubt her. She had spilled her guts on the other stuff, after all.

She'd been allowed to pick her target, but the man on the other end of the phone had been the first to mention Eleanor. That had made it easier, Charlotte said. If she'd had to actually name someone out loud, she didn't think she'd have been able to, but agreeing to the target being the girl who had made her life such a misery had been relatively simple.

Once that was settled, she was told to go to the car park of some forest high-wire adventure place just outside Aviemore, and to wait for Ellie to arrive.

She'd sat in her car for twenty minutes, huddled over the heater, praying that nobody would show up. But then, Ellie had come strolling out of the woods, talking to someone on the phone.

Charlotte's phone had pinged to tell her it was time. She'd picked up the knife that she'd taken from the wooden block in her kitchen back home, and she'd left the car.

'He was watching. He must've been to know she was there,' Charlotte said. She was no longer crying. Her tear ducts had nothing left to give. 'And I could feel him. I could just sort of sense him, you know? Hanging around and watching us. Me and her. He likes to watch. He said that. He likes to make sure that I'm behaving myself.'

'Did you recognise his voice?' Logan asked.

'Yes. I mean, no. It wasn't real. It was a computer.'

'A computer?'

She sniffed and nodded. 'Like Stephen Hawking. Artificial. Robotic. When I answered him, or said anything, there were pauses while he typed in a reply. I could hear the keys.'

Logan sat back, considering this. 'And you've never heard his actual voice?'

'No.'

'And you've never seen him?'

Charlotte shook her head.

'So, there's no saying it's actually a man, then. If it's a computer, anyone could be typing it in.'

'I mean, yes. Could be.'

Logan opened the folder in front of him, searching for a name. 'Do you know a Sandra Hogg, by any chance?'

Charlotte's brow creased. 'Yes, why?'

'How do you know her?'

'I taught her for a while. Wild girl. Bullied a lot.'

'She was bullied, or she bullied others?'

'Both, I think.'

Logan wrote a quick note on his pad, then set the pen down again. 'What happened after you got out of the car, Charlotte? Did Eleanor see you?'

'Uh, yes. She seemed upset. Quite drunk, I think. Or drugs, maybe. I don't know. Kept asking what the hell was going on. She was very confused, and there was'—she plucked at her hair—'twigs and leaves sticking to her everywhere, like she'd been dragged through the woods.'

The teacher drew in a big, unsteady breath that seemed to give her tear ducts their second wind. She stared at the table as she spoke, frowning like she was struggling to remember something from a previous life.

'She screamed at me. She wouldn't stop. She lashed out, slapping at me, and I kept telling her to stop. I kept warning her, but she wouldn't. She kept going and kept going. And then, she said she was going to call the police. She told me I was a freak, and she was going to have me locked up. She took out her phone, and she… and she turned away, and then…'

Her strength left her, and she fell forwards so her forehead was resting on her clenched fists on the table. Logan gave her a moment to rock back and forth there, pulling herself together, then forced her to continue.

'And then?'

'Don't make me. Please, don't make me.'

'What happened then, Charlotte? What did you do?'

The reply was a whisper, so soft as to be almost inaudible. 'I killed her.'

'Louder for the recording, please.'

She sat up suddenly, like some nightmare creature rising from the grave. Her face was red and once again shiny with tears and snot. 'I killed her! I stabbed her. Over and over, like he'd told me. Like he said I had to. It was the only way. It was the only way he said I could save them, so I did it. I did it, and I shouldn't have. I shouldn't have done it. I'm sorry. I'm so sorry!'

'And then what?' Logan demanded. 'You stabbed her, and then what?'

She pawed at her eyes with the heel of a hand. 'And then… And then I drove away. That's what he told me to do. I just had to do that bit, I just had to kill her, then go. That was my only part in the game, he told me.'

The words made Logan sit forward again. 'The game? What do you mean, "the game"?'

'That's what he called it. That's what he said. He sent me a card. That was how he first contacted me, telling me I was a new player in the game. I ripped it up and binned it, thinking it was some weird joke by one of the kids at school. But then the phone calls started.'

'But what game? How is it a game?'

'I don't know,' Charlotte replied in a hoarse, throaty rasp. 'He just said I was a player in his game, and that we all had special jobs to do. I'd done my bit, someone else was going to handle the rest. I don't know who. I don't know. I swear.'

'You must have some idea.'

'N-no, I don't. That's what he kept telling me. That I didn't know who else was in the game, and who might be watching. Said it could be anyone. Other teachers. Pupils. People at the shops. Even the police. He told me he'd know if I tried to get help. He told me he'd...'

She fell silent, like she was listening to the words that had come tumbling out of her mouth. Like she was processing their meaning for the very first time.

'Oh, no. Oh, no. Is it you?' she asked, her breath catching in her throat. 'Is it you? Are you in the game? Did he send you?'

'No.'

'But how do I know that? How do I know you're not one of them? How do I know you're not *him*?'

'Because pissing about playing games isn't really my scene, Charlotte,' Logan told her. 'Just ask my other half.'

–

The scalpel was the bigger concern, but the knee on Shona's chest was the more pressing problem, in every sense of the word. His weight made it hard for her to catch her breath, and the shallow sips of air weren't enough to push down her rising sense of panic.

Also, the knee was really hurting her left boob.

There was a chance she could twist out from under him and try to make a run for it again, but unless she got lucky, he'd be back on her before she could get to her feet, and there was no saying what he'd do to her then.

'Stop squirming!' he said. He sounded more like he was pleading than ordering her, but the scalpel in his left hand made quite a compelling case for her compliance. The surgeon sniffed so hard his head jerked back. 'You did this, you silly bitch. This was all you. You shouldn't have been in here. You shouldn't have been poking around. What am I meant to do now?'

He pressed down harder, gritting his teeth as he waved the blade in her face.

'Tell me! You seem to think you know everything, so what am I supposed to do now?!'

'Please, just let me go. We can talk. This isn't helping.'

'Talk? About what? What do we possibly have to talk about? Unless…' He searched her face as she lay there, pinned beneath him. 'Are you playing? Are you in the game?'

There was uncertainty in his eyes, and within that, an opportunity.

It was risky, but given her current situation, it was worth a shot.

'Yes. I'm playing the game.'

The surgeon put a hand over his mouth like he was muffling a scream. His eyes bulged, tears pooling in the lower lids.

'Oh, shit. Shit. Shit, shit, shit.'

He jumped off her like she was smothered in dogshit, but kept the knife hand raised, the tip of the blade pointing at her as he backed off a few paces.

Shona coughed a couple of times, then dragged herself up onto her elbows. The knife followed her movements, but he didn't try and stop her as she got all the way to her feet.

'Is this a test?' Singh whispered. His eyes darted around the room, like he was suddenly afraid they were being spied on. 'Is that what this is? Is it a test?'

'What do you think?' Shona asked.

The door was a couple of feet away on her left. He was closer. No way she'd make it.

'Is he watching? Is he seeing this? Is he watching us right now?'

'I don't know,' she said, mirroring his body language and scanning the room. 'I'm as much in the dark as you are.'

The knife hand fell to his side, and for a moment, Shona thought he was going to hug her. Instead, he just covered his mouth with a hand again, smothering an outburst of uncontrollable sobbing.

'What did you do?' he asked, his voice muffled by his fingers. 'What did he make you do? Did you move her? Was that it? Oh, God, did you have to move her?'

'I, uh…'

'Of course you did. That would make sense. He uses your skills. You're used to that stuff. You've seen it all before.'

'Um…' Shona began, but she was saved from answering by a knock at the door. Singh put his finger to his lips again, the scalpel raising, taking aim at Shona's throat.

Voices murmured out in the corridor. Both occupants of the office looked down at the sound of something snuffling at the bottom of the door.

'Shona? You in there?'

The finger pressed more firmly against Singh's mouth, his head trembling, the razor-sharp scalpel blade swinging in a tight figure of eight in the air.

Shona's heart rattled in her chest. She bounced on the balls of her feet. He was still closer to the door than she was. Still blocking the way.

There were more muffled voices outside. Quieter this time, like they were turning away.

They were leaving. This was her only chance.

Salvation came from the unlikeliest of sources. Dr Singh had been ignoring the pull of his sinus problem for too long, and finally succumbed to a sniff so loud it almost had an echo.

There was a knock at the door, sharper this time. 'Hello? Is someone in there?'

Shona knew it was now or never.

'Tyler, help!' she cried, stumbling backwards out of the surgeon's striking distance.

'Shona?' The flimsy internal door shook in its frame. 'Shona!'

'Don't just stand there!' Shona was surprised to hear Olivia's voice. 'Get in there!'

Dr Singh stood frozen, the knife still pointed at the spot that Shona had previously occupied. It meant he caught the full force of the door as an overly enthusiastic shoulder barge brought Tyler barrelling through it into the office.

Off balance, Tyler just had time to let out a quick, 'Ooh, shit,' before he crashed into the surgeon's desk and catapulted himself over the top of it. His splayed legs momentarily formed a perfect letter V in the air, then he landed on the floor on the other side, quite awkwardly and mostly upside-down.

'S-stay back!' Singh warned, swinging the knife in Olivia's direction.

'Don't! Leave her alone!' Shona cried.

Down at floor level, Taggart erupted into a frenzy of high-pitched barking. Singh swung a foot at the dog, but Taggart dodged it, then hung back looking positively indignant about what had just happened.

Olivia retreated a step, her hands held up in surrender. 'I don't even know who you are, mate. If you're going to run, just run.'

And run, he did. With a final spite-filled look at the pathologist, he launched himself into the corridor and set off in the ungainly lumber of a man who'd had no call to move at anything faster than a sedate walking pace in years.

While Shona helped Tyler back to his feet, Olivia bent down and retrieved the tennis ball that lay on the floor just inside the office. She turned it over in her hands a couple of times, then whistled once, and tossed the ball as hard as she could along the corridor.

Instinctively, Taggart launched himself after it, streaking off after the fleeing doctor. Tyler stumbled out of the office just in time to see Taggart race straight between the surgeon's legs.

There was a yelp of annoyance from the dog, and a scream of terror from the human. Taggart continued after the ball, while Singh went sailing headlong through the air, arms flailing frantically as he grabbed handfuls of nothing in an attempt to stop himself falling.

He was unsuccessful.

'Well,' Olivia said, giving the detective constable a shove. 'Go get him, then!'

For once, Tyler didn't need to be told twice. He set off at a sprint, and Singh cried out in dismay when the detective kicked the scalpel far beyond his reach, and pinned him to the floor.

'What are you doing here? You shouldn't be here!' Shona said, hurrying to the office door. 'Are you OK? Did he hurt you? Are you—'

She stopped talking when Olivia threw her arms around her and hugged her like there was no tomorrow. She could feel the girl crying on her shoulder, her face hot, her breathing unsteady.

'You're all right. You're fine. We've got him. Tyler's got him.'

Olivia released her grip and stepped back. She worked hard to wipe away her tears, but new ones quickly arrived to replace them.

'Can we go home and watch a film?' Olivia asked.

This time, it was Shona's turn to initiate the hug. Olivia made no attempt to resist it.

'I'd really like that,' she whispered as, along the corridor, Tyler hauled the restrained Dr Singh to his feet. 'I'd like that very much. But—and don't take this the wrong way, because I'm glad you are—what are you doing here? How did you know where to find me?'

'Your assistant told us.'

'Neville! Ah, bless him!' Shona laughed. She pulled away so she could see the reaction on the girl's face. 'What do you think? He's great, isn't he?'

Olivia, to Shona's surprise, did not look as impressed as the pathologist had been expecting.

'Well,' the girl said, fighting back a smirk, 'he's got some very interesting hobbies…'

Chapter Forty-Three

Forty minutes and one frantic drive up the A9 later, Logan stood in Shona's office, with Olivia, Tyler and the pathologist herself either perched on stools or leaning against the desk. Taggart was sniffing around at the bottom of the mortuary doors, but lacked the weight or cranial strength to push them open and explore inside.

'So, where is he now?' the DCI asked.

'Uniform came and took him in, boss,' Tyler said. 'He cut his head when he face-planted onto the floor, but one of the nurses bandaged him up and gave him the all-clear. He's being processed now, so we can interview him tonight.'

Logan nodded slowly, then he caught the detective constable completely off guard. 'Well done, son. Sounds like you saved the day.'

Tyler looked over to Olivia. 'Well, actually, boss—'

'You should've seen him,' Olivia said, jumping in. 'Battered the door down, chased the guy out into the corridor, and tackled him to the ground. He didn't even care about the knife. It was—and I hate to say this—pretty fucking amazing.'

'Language,' Shona warned.

Olivia rolled her eyes, but it was more 'good-natured humour' than her usual scathing indictment.

Logan stared at the girl in confusion, then turned to the pathologist. 'Who the hell's she, and what have you done with the real one?'

'I don't know, but I'm making the most of it,' Shona said. 'We're going home to watch a movie. Popcorn, hot chocolate, the works.'

'I'm picking the film, though,' Olivia said.

'Deal,' Shona agreed. 'Unless it's shite, in which case, no deal.'

Logan scratched at the back of his head, visibly uncomfortable. 'You, eh, you haven't heard, then?'

Shona groaned internally. Only Logan was tuned to the right frequency to hear it. 'Heard what?'

'We found two bodies. Palmer's team's waiting for you at the scene.' Logan shuffled his weight from one foot to the other. 'I'm sorry.'

Olivia hid her disappointment far better than Shona did. 'It's fine,' she said. 'We can do it at the weekend.'

'No, it's not fine. You don't ask for much, and I said we could. One film. It's not a lot to ask.'

'Could we no' get someone flown up, boss?' Tyler suggested. 'There's a fella in Glasgow, isn't there?'

Shona shook her head and sighed. 'Ozzy's on holiday. Again. Cover's already stretched.'

Logan cleared his throat. There was something deeply self-conscious about the sound it made. 'I could do it.'

Shona and Olivia both turned to look at him. 'What, go to the scene?' the pathologist asked. 'I'm not sure you're qualified, Jack.'

Logan tutted. 'No. I could watch the movie, I mean.' His glance at Olivia was a brief one, but enough to bring a blush of red to his cheeks. 'I mean, just if you want.'

'Uh, sorry, boss, what about the interview?' Tyler interjected.

'It can wait until the morning,' Logan replied. 'We've got Charlotte Wilson in custody, too. They're going nowhere. It can all wait.' He shoved his hands in his pockets to stop himself fiddling with them and turned his attention back to Olivia. 'What do you reckon?'

Olivia drew in a deep, thoughtful breath. 'Well, you're a pretty poor substitute,' she began, hopping down from the stool. 'But you'll do, I suppose.'

Logan's eyebrows rose in surprise. 'Aye? I mean, aye. OK. Good.'

'But I get the big couch,' Olivia told him. 'And if you fall asleep with your mouth open, I'm going to throw popcorn in it, and if you choke to death, it's not my fault.'

'Eh… OK,' Logan said with a little less certainty.

'Everyone heard that, right?' Olivia said, as she clipped Taggart's lead to his collar. 'If he chokes on popcorn, I'm in the clear.'

'I'll vouch for it,' Tyler said.

Shona got down off the stool and reached for her jacket. 'Right, well, I'll be there as soon as I can. I'll just do the stuff at the scene, then we can fridge them until the morning. Neville will be in then to give me a hand.'

Tyler, who had been leaning against the pathologist's desk, straightened up. 'Oh. Aye. Neville. About him…' he began, but Olivia shouldered him out of the way, her face positively glowing with excitement.

She opened her phone, tapped on a video, and thrust it in Shona's direction.

'Oh my God!' the girl cheeped. 'You have *got* to see this!'

A moment later, just outside the room, the pealing of Logan's laughter rang along the corridor.

–

'Oh, here he comes. Tweedle-fucking-dumb-dumb himself.'

Tyler paused just inside the door of Hoon's hospital room. 'Um, all right, Berta?' He glanced around, noting the distinct absence of either of his children. 'Where are the kids?'

'Never you mind where they are,' Berta told him.

'Uh, well, I do mind, actually,' Tyler said, standing up to the woman once described by her own brother as 'sourer than the milk from a demon's tit'. 'Where are they?'

Sitting in the chair by the bed, Berta tutted sharply. 'Your other half's got them.'

'His better fucking half,' her brother added.

'Much fucking better. Infinitely better,' Berta concluded. She gave the detective constable a quick look up and down. 'Mind you, that's not exactly a fucking challenge, is it?'

'All right, steady on!' Tyler protested.

'Where's my fucking grapes?' Hoon demanded.

Tyler shook his head. 'Couldn't get any. They don't sell them.'

'What, no one? No one in the fucking world sells grapes?'

'The hospital shop, I mean. I'd have to go to Tesco.'

'Well, go to fucking Tesco then!' Hoon cried. He shimmied himself up the bed. 'Jesus Christ, son, it's five minutes' fucking walk away, and you did fucking paralyse me for life.'

'No, you're right, I should…' Tyler stopped. 'Hang on. You're out of the back brace.'

'What?' Hoon grimaced, like he'd been hoping Tyler wouldn't notice. 'Oh. Shite. Aye. So I am.'

'What do you mean *so you are*? What happened?'

'His scan results came in. Not that you'd give a flying fuck, gallivanting all over the place,' Berta said. She had her big tartan handbag sitting on her knee, and tightened her grip on the straps like she was just daring someone to try and steal it from her.

'And?' Tyler asked, putting his hands on hips. 'What did it say?'

'That there's fuck all wrong with him,' Berta replied.

Hoon scowled at her. 'Is that fuck what it said. Broken leg. I mean, that's a fucking given. Needs an operation. We're waiting on some surgeon coming down.'

Tyler tugged at the collar of his shirt. 'It's, eh, it's not Dr Singh, is it?'

'The fuck should I know?' Hoon spat. 'Why?'

'No reason,' Tyler said, deciding it'd be better if Hoon found out for himself, and preferably when the detective constable wasn't present. 'What about the, you know, your spine? The lack of feeling.'

Berta gave her brother a slap on his broken leg. He yelped in pain and almost folded in half at the middle.

'Aaaah-ya-fucking… Ow! The fuck was that for? Them fucking painkillers haven't kicked in yet!' He slumped back onto the pillow, his teeth gritted. 'You're lucky I'm still fucking numb.'

'Oh, aye, like it'd put me up or fucking down how sore it was,' Berta replied.

'You can feel again?' Tyler gasped. 'You're not paralysed?'

'No fucking thanks to you, but no, I'm no' fucking paralysed,' Hoon said. 'It was some sort of nerve compression, or some shite, they reckon. "Nothing major", they said, which is easy to say when you're no' the one who accidentally pissed himself without fucking noticing.'

Berta tutted. 'Aye, but then that's pretty much just a usual Saturday night for you, isn't it?' She looked up at Tyler. 'Oh, and he doesn't even fucking like grapes. He's just being an awkward bastard.'

Tyler smiled at her like they were sharing an inside joke, but she simply glared back at him like he was the perpetrator of a fart in a lift. Or, perhaps even the fart itself.

'Eh, right. OK. Well, no point me hanging around then,' Tyler said. 'I, uh, I should go help Sinead with the kids.'

'Oh. Right. Aye, just you fuck off and leave me here alone,' Hoon said.

Berta slapped him on the leg again, drawing another hiss of pain. 'Here! Cheeky bastard. You're not alone.'

Hoon groaned. 'Aw, fuck. You're no' staying, are you?'

Berta set her bag on the floor beneath the chair, then stretched out her thick, sturdy legs. 'I'm not going anywhere, Bobby. I'm staying right where I fucking am.'

Tyler sidled towards the door. 'I'll, eh, I'll pop in tomorrow and see how you're doing. I'll bring grapes!'

Before either of the Hoons had a chance to object, he darted out of the room, and closed the door behind him.

'Christ,' Berta muttered. 'What a fucking waste of skin that boy is.'

'Ah, shut it, ye old bastard,' her brother retorted. A smile tugged at the corners of his mouth. 'He might be a hopeless bastard with a cartoon man's hair, but he's one of the fucking good ones.'

He appeared momentarily confused by the words coming out of his own mouth, then he let his head sink down into the pillow, a goofy smile spreading across his face.

'Ah, thank fuck.' He sighed. 'I think that must be the painkillers kicking in.'

–

There were no strange cars parked outside Hamza's house when he arrived home that evening. There was no Kamila waiting to run into his arms, either. All that met him at the door was the smell of something spicy, and a music track that was heavy on the saxophone.

He found Amira sitting at the dining table at the far end of the living room, her satin red dress reflecting the soft glow of candlelight. She smiled at him over the rim of a glass of what he assumed was alcohol-free wine.

But then again, everything about this picture was odd, so there was no saying it wasn't the real stuff.

'Uh, where's Kamila?' he asked, pulling off his tie.

'She's at my mother's.'

Hamza winced. 'Oof. What did she do to deserve that?'

Amira laughed. 'Nothing. I just thought we should talk.'

'You got dressed up pretty fancy for that,' he said. 'What are we talking about?'

'Everything.' Amira shrugged. 'Nothing. Just talking. We never talk. I made us a nice dinner. Stuck on some music. Think of it like a date.'

Hamza unfastened the top button of his shirt. 'Been a while since we had one of them, right enough.'

'Two years and… eight months? Nine?' Amira said. 'We went to the Starbucks next to Smyths Toys.'

'Because the restaurant we were meant to be going to flooded!' Hamza chuckled. 'Aye. Not quite the big night we'd planned. There was Tyler and Sinead's wedding, though.'

'That doesn't count as a date!'

'No. Suppose not.'

He was hanging back, still not quite sure what was going on. Was this guilt making her do this? Was she trying to throw him off the scent?

Sensing his hesitation, Amira got up from the table and met him in the middle of the room. 'You want to know the truth?' she asked. 'About Thomas being here?'

He nodded. Right now, the truth was all he wanted. All he needed.

'I just… it was nice to have an adult to talk to for once,' she said. 'Kamila's amazing, *obviously*, but you're out working all the time, and then you're exhausted when you come home—'

'So, it's my fault?' Hamza asked.

'What? No! It's no one's fault. You're busy. It's the job. I knew that when I married you. I just…' She took a breath and tried to explain herself more clearly. 'My days are filled with either Kamila, or my mum. And they both just want things. All the time. Which is my job, and that's fine. But sometimes I want to just talk about other things, too. The news. Or books. Or how fucking annoying the new head teacher is at the school.'

'And you can't talk to me about that?'

'I can if you're here, and if you're not asleep, or not fixated on whatever case it is you're working on.' She put a hand on his face, then looked saddened by the way he flinched at her touch. 'But when is that? How often does that happen?'

Hamza said nothing. How could he? He had no argument to offer.

'There is nothing—*nothing*—going on between me and Thomas. Between me and anyone. He's the father of Kamila's friend, and he has opinions on the teaching staff, and yesterday, I just really needed to hear something that wasn't Peppa Pig or Pokémon. That was all. I'm hardly likely to have an affair with someone when both our kids are stomping mud up and down the hall right past the open door, am I?'

She smiled and shifted around until he was forced to meet her gaze.

'Am I?'

'Suppose not, no,' Hamza conceded.

He ran a hand down his face like he was wiping something off it. It all made sense. Of course it did. He'd been neglecting her for years. Not deliberately, of course, and it hadn't happened all at once, but bit by bit, day by day, he'd been letting a gulf form between them.

'So, will I go serve up dinner, then?' she asked, letting her hands fall into his.

Hamza looked down at her fingers, and the wedding ring he'd given her all those years ago.

'Or, we could just skip that bit completely,' he suggested, with a twinkle in his eye.

Amira bit her bottom lip and gave his hands a squeeze. 'Now that,' she said, 'is the best idea you've had in a long time.'

Chapter Forty-Four

Hamza whistled his way across the foyer, up the stairs, along the corridor, and into the Incident Room, to be met by a puzzled look from DC Neish.

'What?' the sergeant asked, practically dancing his way out of his jacket. He whistled a short, jolly refrain as he hung the garment over the back of his chair. 'What are you looking at?'

'Someone's in a better mood today,' Tyler observed.

Hamza dropped into his seat, pretending to be deep in thought. 'Do you know?' he said. 'I think I might be.'

'Nice one. Get everything… sorted out?'

'Oh, yes,' Hamza said. 'Nothing going on. Just school stuff. And, I mean, an understandable desire for some adult conversation, which I've been falling down on. But there's nothing, you know, dodgy.'

Sinead, who had been hovering over by the Big Board, pretending not to listen, sidled over to join them.

'Glad to hear it's all OK,' she said.

Tyler winced, biting his bottom lip. 'Sorry, mate. I had to tell her. She worked out I knew something that she didn't, and she got it out of me.'

Hamza very clearly couldn't care less. He smiled and waved away the DC's apology. 'It's fine. I really should have spoken to you first, actually,' he told Sinead. 'You've probably got more insight than this one.'

'I take offence at "probably",' Sinead replied. She smiled. 'But, aye. It's not unusual for a woman to have male friends.'

'Exactly,' Tyler said.

'I've got male friends.'

'See?' It took a moment for the concern to register on Tyler's face. 'Wait, like who?'

Sinead smirked and tapped a finger to the side of her nose, then returned to the board.

'Bosses not around?' Hamza asked, noting the empty desks.

'Not yet. Although, the DCI's coat's in his office, and there's a teacake wrapper in Ben's bin,' Tyler said. 'So they might be around somewhere.'

It was, Hamza told him, a pretty decent bit of detective work.

'Cheers,' Tyler said. 'Also, the dog's sleeping under the desk, so that's pretty definitive.'

Hamza rolled back his chair so he could look under the desks. Sure enough, Taggart lay on his back with all four legs splayed in different directions.

'Any word on Hoon?' he asked, pulling himself in closer to his workstation again.

'Aye, we saw Berta this morning,' Sinead said. 'We weren't going to bring the twins over, but she insisted. Bob's still in hospital, being a "weapons grade pain up the arsehole" apparently.'

'Nice one. Sounds like he's back to his old self,' Hamza said. 'And a broken leg should stop him appearing out of bushes on us for a while, at least.'

'Let's not count on it,' Tyler said.

Hamza nodded thoughtfully, running back over some of his past experiences with the former detective superintendent.

'Aye, fair point,' he eventually concluded.

The doors to the Incident Room were thrown wide. All three detectives turned, all three of them fully expecting to see a stookied Bob Hoon come striding through the doors, demanding to know what the fuck was being said about him.

To their relief, Dave Davidson wheeled himself in, and looked pleased at all the interest in his arrival.

'All right?' he asked. He looked back over his shoulder in case there was someone more interesting there. 'Why are you all staring? Am I the millionth customer or something? Do I win a shopping spree through the evidence room? If so, I'm having all the drugs.'

'Morning,' Tyler said, as the three of them relaxed again. 'We were worried you might be Hoon.'

'Is he not meant to be in the hospital?' Dave asked, heading for his desk.

'Meant to be, aye, but who knows with him?' Tyler asked.

'Very true,' Dave said. He gave the button on his computer a prod, coaxing a reluctant-sounding chime from somewhere deep within it as the hard drive spun to life. 'Anyone fancy a cup of tea?'

Tyler turned in his chair. 'I'd love one.'

'Nice one,' Dave said, rubbing his hands together. 'Make me one while you're at it, will you?'

'I'll have a coffee,' Hamza said.

Sinead placed her half-empty mug on Tyler's desk.

Tyler looked at them all in turn, then tutted and got to his feet. 'Fuck's sake.'

After gathering up four mugs, he headed for the door, only to narrowly avoid being smacked in the face with it by the return of DCI Logan and DI Forde.

'Oh! You making tea?' Ben asked.

'Looks like it now, boss, aye,' Tyler said, shooting a dirty look back at the others.

'Good lad!' the DI chimed.

'Hang on,' Logan said, striding across to his desk. 'I'll get my mug.'

–

By the time Tyler returned with the drinks, everyone was gathered around the Big Board. They all smacked their lips together, implying that he'd taken far too long and they were all parched, but then saluted him with their mugs as they were handed over.

'And is that a wee plate of biscuits, I see?' Ben asked.

Tyler looked down at the empty tray. 'Uh, no, boss.'

'No,' Ben said, peering reproachfully over the top of his glasses. 'I thought not.'

'Sorry, boss.' Tyler shot a warning look around at the others. 'Oh, and we should probably be on best behaviour, I think that—'

'Detective Superintendent Mitchell,' Hamza said, drawing everyone's attention to the woman in the doorway. 'Morning, ma'am.'

'Sergeant,' Mitchell said, giving Hamza a nod. She entered the room and folded her hands behind her back. 'Everyone.'

There was a murmuring of *mornings*, some more enthusiastic than others.

'I hear congratulations are in order,' she said. 'Full confession to the murder.'

'Uh, aye,' Logan said, then he took a swig of his coffee so he was unable to add any more.

'You were in interviewing the surgeon already this morning, I'm told.'

'We were, ma'am, aye,' Ben confirmed.

'And?'

Ben stole a glance at Logan, gauging how far to go in his response. Fortunately, the DCI saved him the trouble.

'He had a lot to say for himself, put it that way.'

'You think he's connected?'

'I know he is,' Logan replied. 'He told us as much. He confessed to being in that house and cutting up the first victim's remains. The description he gave matches what we found, so no reason to believe he's making it up. He claims to have no idea about the two victims DS Khaled discovered in the stolen car.'

'Well, that's disappointing. It would've been nice and neat.' Mitchell rocked her weight onto her heels, thinking this over. 'But with regards the first victim, you think the teacher and the surgeon were working together?'

Logan shook his head. 'Not knowingly, ma'am.'

'Not knowingly? What do you mean?'

'We believe they were being coerced.'

Mitchell's eyebrows arched in surprise. 'You think there's a third party involved?'

'At least, aye.'

'Good grief. Any ideas yet as to who?'

'Well'—Logan raised his mug to his mouth and blew some of the steam away—'that's the big question, isn't it?'

Mitchell opened her mouth to reply, then sighed and closed it again when her mobile rang. She checked the screen, shut her eyes for a second, then gave the occupants of the room a single wave of one hand.

'I need to take this. Apologies.' She gestured to the board, already partway out of the room. 'Keep me informed.'

They waited until the door had swung closed again, then Logan turned to address the room.

'So, as you all now know, we've had full confessions from Charlotte Wilson and the surgeon, Manish Singh. Charlotte has confessed to the murder of Eleanor Howard, but claims to have been doing so under extreme duress in an attempt to save the lives of her parents.'

'Which, as we also all know, didn't end well,' Ben added.

'Similarly, Singh claims he was being blackmailed,' Logan continued.

'With what?' Sinead asked.

'An affair. The blackmailer sent him photographs, and threatened to expose Singh to his family and colleagues.'

'Cutting some poor lassie to bits seems like a long way to go to hide an affair, boss,' Tyler said.

'It was with a member of his wife's family,' Logan said. He left just the right length of pause before adding: 'Her father.'

A lengthy silence descended, until it was finally broken by Dave voicing what everyone in the room was thinking.

'Fucking hell.'

'We need to try and verify the story with the father-in-law, though I can't imagine he'll be too happy to talk about it.'

Ben slurped thoughtfully from his mug. 'It'd be a hell of a cover story if it wasn't true, wouldn't it? I've never heard "I was having it away with my wife's father" used as an excuse before.' He flicked up a thumb. 'Aye, up the arse,' he added, for the benefit of those who might not have worked it out, which was nobody.

'Thanks for that additional detail, Benjamin,' Logan said. 'And aye, it'd be a weird one, so I'm taking it at face value for now. Both Wilson and Singh referred to an electronic male voice on the phone. That, along with an initial note, is how they were given their instructions. They both also received a "new player has entered the game" card.'

'Like Eleanor and Seamus,' Hamza said.

'Identical, by the sounds of it. They also both said they felt the blackmailer was watching them. That he got a kick out of seeing them doing what he'd instructed.'

Sinead, who had been furiously writing notes, raised a pen to draw the DCI's attention. 'Can we jump back a sec, sir? The electronic voice. Do you mean like a computer voice?'

'Like Professor Stephen Hawking, according to Charlotte.'

Sinead slowly lowered her pen again, thinking this over. 'So… why do that? That suggests it was someone they knew. Or someone whose voice they could identify, at least.'

'Maybe, aye,' Logan agreed. 'Or it was someone trying to hide their gender. Male voice, you assume it's a man on the other end of the line. But there's no way of knowing that for sure.'

Tyler perked up in his chair. 'Sandra Hogg!'

Hamza turned to the DC. 'Did we get any update on where she is?'

'Not that I've seen.'

Dave was already reaching for his phone. 'Want me to call through to Aviemore and see if they've heard anything?'

'Please,' Ben confirmed.

While the constable set to work making the call, the others turned back to Logan.

'So, we know who killed Eleanor. Do we know where, boss?'

'Aye. Car park of some treetop high-wire place just outside Aviemore.'

'Right. OK.' Tyler shook his mouse to wake up his computer, then clicked through to Google Maps. 'So… Right. Found it. So, from there to the cottage where the body was cut up is about twenty miles. Did Charlotte take her there?'

'Not according to her,' Logan replied. 'She stabbed her, then she got a message telling her to go home.'

'Straight after?' Sinead asked.

'Straight after. Which suggests she was right about him watching.'

'So, if she didn't move the victim, who did, boss?'

Sinead and Logan both said the name at the same time. 'Seamus Starkey.'

Logan raised an inquisitive eyebrow in the detective constable's direction.

'Palmer's report came in during the night,' Sinead said. 'I had a quick skim this morning. They found blood in the boot of Seamus's mother's car. Looks like a match for Eleanor.' She shot Hamza a slightly apologetic sideways look. 'The tech team was able to recover some information from the laptop, too. Looks like there was a stash of child pornography on there. They think Seamus himself must've rigged it to trash the drive if the machine was compromised.'

'That was clever of him,' Ben remarked.

Hamza shook his head a little sheepishly. 'There's software that'll do it for you. It's not complicated. I shouldn't have poked around in it without checking for that first.'

Ben shook his head. 'What's done is done, son. And sounds like we've got what we need. Also, sounds like whoever we're looking for knows their way around computers.'

Logan frowned. 'What makes you say that?'

'Well, if Hamza couldn't get into it, but your blackmailer fella could...' He looked to the DS for confirmation. 'He'd have to get access to see the porn stuff, wouldn't he?'

'He would,' Hamza confirmed.

Ben's head gave a little wobble. Clearly, he was pleased with himself. 'There we go, then. So, he must be a bit of a boffin.'

It was Logan's turn to look to the detective sergeant for his opinion.

'They certainly seem resourceful,' Hamza reasoned. 'They found out about Charlotte Wilson posting on the victim's OnlyFans, and managed to get photos of the surgeon's affair.'

'And the electricity company can't figure out how there's power to the cottage,' Dave added. He pointed to the phone that was still pressed to his ear when they all looked over at his desk. 'I'm on hold with Aviemore. They're checking on Sandra Hogg.'

Ben took a quick glug from his mug. 'So, they're switched on, whoever they are. No pun intended. They're well organised, very computer savvy, and enjoy watching others suffer. And they may or may not have access to a van or other large vehicle.'

'Aye, well, that last one covers pretty much everyone on the planet,' Logan pointed out. 'But the rest sounds about right.'

Tyler tapped his pen against the edge of his desk, then stuck the end in a corner of his mouth and chewed thoughtfully on it. 'So, Charlotte kills Eleanor to save her parents, Seamus moves the body to stop the child porn stuff getting out, and the surgeon fella cuts her up so his kids don't find out he's shagging their granddad?'

He pointed to the board with his pen, oblivious to the inky blue stain on his bottom lip.

'That still leaves one more.'

'Who moved the pieces from the cottage to the side of the road?'

'And why?' Sinead asked.

They were both good questions, Logan agreed. However, they were just two among many. Who were the owners of the eight unidentified fingers? Why had only some of Eleanor's parts been packed up and shipped out, leaving the rest in the house? Why had Charlotte's parents been mutilated the way they had?

'We got any more info on the stolen car?' Logan asked, going off on a bit of a tangent.

'Nothing really, boss,' Tyler said. 'Nicked from this side of Aberlour. Owners reported it at the time. Old couple, moaned a bit about the state of the world, but didn't seem too bothered about getting it back.'

Logan stood by the board, looking it over. 'Aberlour,' he mumbled. 'Sinead, the school Charlotte Wilson teaches at. What was it?'

'Speyside Academy, sir.'

There was a clacking of keys from Hamza's desk. 'That's in Aberlour.'

Chairs creaked as everyone who was currently sitting down leaned forward. 'You think that's something, boss?' Tyler asked. 'You think she nicked the car?'

Logan gave this some thought, then shook his head. He could buy the woman as a desperate killer, but a calculated car thief? 'Doubt it. Doesn't fit. She nicked a car to do what? Kill her parents in?'

'Good way of pinning it on someone else,' Hamza suggested.

'Aye, but for that to happen, you've first got to confess to stabbing a woman to death,' Logan pointed out. 'Parents can be a pain in the arse, but that's a hell of a convoluted way of getting rid of them.'

'Could just be someone who knew her, then?' said Sinead. 'Someone who works at the school, maybe?'

Tyler slapped a hand down on his desk in triumph. 'The school IT guy!'

Logan's brow furrowed. 'Who's that, like?'

'No idea, boss,' the detective constable admitted. 'But we reckon it's someone who knows about tech stuff, and let's face it, IT guys are all a bit weird and creepy.' He flashed a smile at Hamza. 'No offence.'

'I'm not an IT guy,' Hamza countered.

Tyler pulled a face that expressed his doubts on that. 'You're basically an IT guy,' he insisted. 'You're IT guy *adjacent*.'

'My foot'll be your arse adjacent in a minute,' Hamza warned him.

Ben puffed out his cheeks and shrugged. 'I mean, it's a shot in the dark, but it could be worth a conversation,' he said.

While the DI was talking, Hamza had been typing quickly, clicking his mouse, and studying the screen of his computer. 'There's no IT guy at the school. I checked the public-facing directory. The role's been empty for over a year since the last one retired.'

His fingers flew across the keyboard as a blur of movement.

'He went to live in Portugal with his daughter eight months ago.'

Ben tutted and shot Tyler a disparaging look. 'Well, so much for that idea.'

Tyler met Hamza's eye and smirked. 'See? You're *such* an IT guy.'

Across the room, there was a *clack* as Dave hung up his phone. 'So, bit of news about Sandra Hogg,' he announced.

'She's dead?' Tyler guessed.

Dave did a double-take at his notes. 'How did you know that?'

DC Neish's eyes widened. 'What, seriously?!'

'Nah, not really,' Dave said, grinning. 'It's nearly as shocking, though. She's turned up for community service.'

Logan turned from the board. 'Eh?'

'Aye. She arrived back last night, according to her mother, got dressed this morning and went back to doing her roadside clean-up.'

'So, where is she now?'

Dave shrugged. 'Picking up litter somewhere at the side of the A9 near Aviemore, I suppose.'

'Right, then.' Logan necked the rest of his coffee, slackened off his tie, then pointed to Hamza and Tyler. 'You two, jackets on. Let's go bring this lassie in.'

'Oh, are you coming, boss?' Tyler asked, his face lighting up with hope. 'Good stuff. We could do with the help. Because she's only wee, but she's properly full-on scary.'

'Aye, just coming, you two go ahead.' He took out his keys, contemplated throwing them to Tyler, then tossed them to Hamza instead. 'I'll be right down. Sinead, a word in my office.'

A look of concern flitted across Tyler's face before Hamza ushered him out. Sinead followed Logan to the back of the room, then continued on into his office when he gestured for her to go ahead.

'Everything all right, sir?' she asked, once he'd shut the door behind them.

'God, no. It's all mostly awful, as per usual,' he told her. He looked down for a moment, then met her eye. 'I won't keep you long. I just wanted to say thank you.'

'For what?'

'I don't know what you said to her, but last night, for the first time since she moved in, Olivia wasn't an absolute total arsehole. She was still a bit of an arsehole, don't get me wrong.'

Sinead smiled. 'Aren't we all, sir?'

'Speak for your bloody self, Detective Constable. But, again, thank you. For the first time since agreeing to this whole bloody thing, I can see a light at the end of the tunnel. Aye, it might be the laser sight of Olivia with a bloody sniper rifle, but it's a start. So, aye, thank you. Although, if I never see the movie *Pitch Perfect* again, it'll be too bloody soon.'

'It's a stone-cold classic!' Sinead protested. 'And no bother. Any time, sir.'

'What was it you said to her, anyway?' Logan asked.

Sinead hesitated. 'She didn't say?'

The DCI shook his head. 'No. Not a word.'

'Oh, well then.' Sinead smiled to herself as she turned and reached for the door handle. 'I suppose it'll just have to be our little secret.'

Chapter Forty-Five

The Community Payback van was parked in a long lay-by just south of Aviemore. Logan pulled the BMW in behind it, then all three detectives got out and scanned the treeline for any sign of movement.

'There,' Hamza announced, pointing further south along the embankment to where the mid-morning sun reflected off a hi-vis vest.

'Is that her?' Logan asked.

'Not sure, boss,' Tyler said, squinting and cupping a hand above his eyes. 'They're in silhouette.'

'Do they look about the right size, though?' Logan pressed.

A truck roared past on the road just a few feet away, making Tyler and Hamza stagger in the wind it whipped up.

Once he'd found his footing, Tyler looked at the distant figure again. 'I mean, they're about the size of a glacé cherry from here, boss, so no. She's bigger than that in real life.'

'For fu—' Logan ran a hand down his face. 'Forget it, we'll go and check if it's her.'

He shook his head at the DC to show his irritation, then set off marching along the embankment, the damp grass tangling around his boots and soaking the bottoms of his trouser legs.

'And who the fuck uses glacé cherries as a unit of measurement, anyway?' he demanded.

'It was just the first thing I thought of, boss,' Tyler said, following in the DCI's oversized footsteps.

'Why not a normal cherry?' Hamza asked. 'Why a glacé cherry in particular? I mean, they're the same size.'

'I told you, it was just the first thing I thought of!' Tyler cried.

'Keep your bloody voice down,' Logan growled as, up ahead, the glacé cherry in the hi-vis vest turned in their direction. There was another even smaller figure a little further along the embankment, dressed in the same bright orange tabard.

'I think that is her, boss,' Tyler said, squinting again. 'Now that she's standing up properly, I'm pretty sure that is Sa…*aaaaand* she's running away.'

'Well, don't just bloody stand there!' Logan barked, as Sandra Hogg went crashing clumsily towards the treeline. 'Both of you, get in there and get after her!'

Tyler and Hamza both broke into a sprint, the sergeant diverting straight into the trees to intercept, the constable running along the embankment to follow the fleeing suspect's path.

Logan jogged along for a few feet, then concluded this was achieving nothing, and that there was no point in him tiring himself out for no reason.

Instead, he walked along in the path Tyler had trodden in the grass, and was met by the other person in the hi-vis vest hurrying the other way.

'What the hell's going on?' the man demanded. 'Was that those police officers?'

Logan produced his warrant card. 'Aye. DCI Logan, Major Investigations. You are?'

'Uh, Jonathan. Milburn. Jonathan Milburn. I'm the CP supervisor.' He and the DCI shook hands, then both turned towards the trees.

'Oh, aye. I've heard of you. Was that Sandra Hogg?' Logan asked.

'It was, yes. I'm amazed she can run that fast.'

'Any idea why she ran?'

'I mean…' Jonathan put his hands on his hips. 'No good ones. None that paint her in a good light. Is this about that murder? That poor young woman?'

Logan shoved his hands in his pockets. 'I'm afraid that's not something I can discuss at this stage, Mr Milburn.'

'No. No, of course. Of course not.' He fiddled with the sleeves of his jacket. 'Although, I do have some clearance. You know, through the job?'

Logan didn't answer. Instead, he continued to scour the edge of the woodlands, watching and listening for any signs of movement within.

'I actually considered joining the police a few years ago,' Jonathan continued. 'I really admire what you guys do.'

'Well, that makes a nice change,' Logan muttered.

'Ha! Yes! Believe me, you're preaching to the choir there! My own role doesn't make me particularly popular. And all I'm trying to do is help them.'

Logan looked across at the man. 'Help them?'

'To deal with their issues. To face up to what they've done, and deal with it,' Jonathan explained. 'That's why I didn't go for the police in the end. I didn't want to just be involved in arresting people, I wanted to be on the other side, to help with their rehabilitation.'

'Right,' Logan said, facing front again. 'Aye.'

'It's important. It's so important, don't you think? Making amends. Having that chance to make up for terrible things you've done,' the supervisor continued. 'It's the key to moving on, I think. You hold a mirror up to someone and let them see what they've done—who they truly are—and then you can work on that. Then you can help them get past it.'

Logan lowered his gaze to the ground, the forest momentarily forgotten. 'Aye, that makes sense,' he agreed. 'What was it you did before?'

'Sorry?'

The DCI turned to him. 'You said that you thought about joining the police a few years ago. You must've been, what? In your thirties?'

'Oh. Right. Yes!' Jonathan winced like he wasn't sure how his reply was going to go down. 'I was in the banking sector, believe it or not. In London. But don't worry, I wasn't involved in any of the actual financial stuff. I wasn't a trader, or what have you.'

'No?'

'No,' Jonathan replied. 'I was involved in coding and maintaining the web services for a couple of the big national banks.'

He smiled self-deprecatingly. A car sped by behind him, the roar of the engine making him draw out his silence for a few more moments.

'Which is basically just a fancy way of saying I worked in IT.'

-

Tyler crept through the trees, the foliage crunching softly beneath his polished shoes. By the time he'd reached the edge of the forest, Sandra Hogg had a solid head start. Her short legs and stocky frame meant she wasn't really built for speed, but given her early lead, Tyler reckoned his chances of catching up with her were slim.

But maybe, he reckoned, that's what she wanted him to think. His instincts were telling him to plough on through the trees, keep running, and try to catch up with her.

But what if his instincts were wrong? It wouldn't be the first time, after all.

What if Sandra Hogg hadn't kept on running? What if she was hiding? What if she was counting on him charging straight past her, so she could make her escape by heading in a different direction through the woods?

She couldn't double back—Logan would be waiting for her. If she headed to the left, there was a good chance that she'd run into Hamza. That meant she had either run straight ahead, taken a right, or was lying in wait somewhere nearby.

If she went right, she'd have nothing but forest for miles. If she went straight on, she'd sooner or later reach the B road that ran parallel to the A9. From there, she could feasibly get away, though she'd have to flag down a car, and a squat, surly, tattooed lassie bursting out of the woods likely wouldn't make for the most appealing of hitchhikers.

Hiding made sense, then. She hadn't kept running, she'd ducked for cover. He was sure of it.

A twig snapped behind him and he spun around, hands adopting a karate pose that he had absolutely no hope of following through on.

'All right, steady on, Bruce Lee. It's just me,' Hamza said, emerging from a thicket of trees. His hair was full of bits of foliage, and a branch had scratched a bloody gouge along the right side of his face.

'Oof. Fuck. You all right, mate?' Tyler asked. 'That looks nasty.'

'Aye? Doesn't feel too bad,' Hamza said, gingerly dabbing at the injury.

'You look like an ethnically diverse Action Man,' Tyler told him.

Hamza snorted. 'That's a step up from an IT guy, I suppose.' He looked around. 'Any sign of her?'

Tyler shook his head. He carefully picked his way into a clearing and looked around, paying particular attention to the canopy of trees above.

'She's not going to be up there,' Hamza said, glancing upwards. 'She's not the fucking Predator.'

Tyler put a finger to his lips. 'I reckon she's around here somewhere,' he whispered.

Hamza looked off to the left, in the direction of the B road. 'You don't think she's kept running?'

Tyler shook his head. 'She's here,' he insisted. 'I'll stake my reputation on it.'

'You've not got a reputation,' Hamza pointed out. 'Well, you have, but it's not one you can really use as collateral.'

'She's here, mate,' Tyler said, lowering his voice until the words were barely audible. 'She's here, I can feel it.'

A sharp cry of pain rang out through the woods. It came from a few hundred yards away, off towards the B road.

'Shite. Maybe she's not then, I take it all back,' Tyler conceded, and both detectives broke, once more, into a run.

–

'What was that?' Jonathan asked, peering past Logan into the trees. 'Did you hear someone screaming? It sounded like Sandra.'

'No,' Logan lied. 'If there's a problem, they'll call.'

He tipped his head back, looking up. Despite the earlier promise of sunshine, dark clouds were forming overhead. It would be tipping down within twenty minutes. Just another day in the Highlands.

'Must be quite a change,' the DCI said. 'Going from London to this.'

'Massive,' Jonathan replied. 'Huge change. Rewarding, though. There I was just helping make rich people richer. Up here, I'm making a difference.'

'Helping people face up to their sins,' Logan said. 'That's what you said, wasn't it?'

Jonathan smiled. 'I don't think I put it quite so biblically, but yes. And it was nice to come back. London's fine when you're in your twenties, but the novelty soon starts to wear off as you get longer in the tooth.'

'You from Aviemore originally?' Logan asked, turning to face him.

'Near enough. Little place just up the road,' Jonathan replied. 'Aberlour. Most people haven't heard of it.'

'Aberlour?' Logan studied the man's face. 'I know a teacher from there.'

Jonathan's smile remained fixed in place. Behind him, a lorry laden with logs went thundering past.

'Ha!' he ejected, once the wind had dropped again. 'Small world!'

Chapter Forty-Six

Tyler wished someone had been around to see how he'd vaulted that last tree trunk. Ideally, they'd have filmed it, capturing his run-up, his carefully placed hand plant, and his stylish leap over the fallen obstacle.

In his mind, it looked truly epic. In reality, it had been quite awkward and a bit clumsy, with an accompanying soundtrack of panicky *oh shits* as he tumbled over the top of the trunk.

Fortunately for his ego, there had been no one around to point this out.

He stumbled, stopped, caught his breath, then looked around. He could hear Hamza crashing through the trees somewhere on his right. They'd decided on a pincer movement, each taking a different side as they closed in on the source of the scream they'd heard.

Unfortunately, that had been almost a full minute ago, and Tyler had lost all sense of direction since then.

He scanned the treetops again, just to be on the safe side, then heard a faint grunt from somewhere up ahead, like someone was in pain and trying to hide the fact.

Peering through the foliage, Tyler spotted Sandra. She was standing less than thirty feet away, gripping the lowest limb of a tree like she was about to start climbing.

She'd hear him the moment he started to move again, so there was no point in trying to be subtle.

'Sandra, stay where you are!' he bellowed in his best Jack Logan voice, then added a rallying, 'Hamza, over here!' as he plunged through the trees towards her.

Sandra half-turned, still holding onto the tree, her face fixed in a tearful grimace.

'I've got her!' Tyler cried, closing the gap. 'I've got her, she's right—Oh, Christ!'

He flailed wildly to a stop, grabbing handfuls of thin, sharp branches as he tried to slow his charge. Over on his right, Hamza rushed over to help, forcing Tyler to eject a cry of warning.

'She's put her foot on a big stick!'

The detective sergeant ducked under a low-hanging branch and arrived, slightly breathless, into the small clearing. 'What?' he asked.

Tyler stared fixedly at Hamza, very much refusing to look anywhere else. 'She's put her foot on a big stick,' he reiterated.

Hamza frowned. 'So?' he said, then he looked over at Sandra and saw the pointed spike of blood-soaked wood sticking out of the top of her shoe. He turned back to Tyler, wincing. 'Oh. Shite.'

'I can't look at it, or I'm going to be sick,' Tyler stated, with a matter-of-fact air that made it clear he wasn't exaggerating. 'It's right through, isn't it? It's all the way through from underneath.'

Hamza started to turn, but Tyler hissed at him.

'Well, don't look at it!'

'Why not?'

'Because if I look at it, I'll be sick!' Tyler stressed.

'Aye, but you don't see through my eyes, do you?'

'But if you look at it, then I'll have to look at it!'

'You've seen worse,' Hamza reminded him.

'Aye, but they've mostly been dead. She's not,' Tyler pointed out.

'I fucking might be soon if you don't do something!' Sandra yelped.

Tyler grimaced so hard his neck disappeared, his head retreating into his shoulders like a turtle's into its shell.

'Aw, shit.'

He gagged violently at just the thought of what he was about to see, then he ran a hand down his face, summoning a Zen-like state of calm.

'Right. I'm fine. I'm ready,' he declared.

He and Hamza both exchanged a nod, then turned to examine Sandra's injury.

A moment later, Tyler vomited into a bush.

'Right, no. I'm fine now. That's me fine,' he insisted, wiping his mouth on his sleeve.

He chanced the briefest of glances at the young woman's foot. A sharp, jagged stick had pierced her shoe from below, gone straight through her foot, then erupted out through the top. Around the edge of the hole in her trainer, he could see an equally ragged one in her flesh.

'Does it hurt?' he asked.

'What the fuck do you think?' Sandra said through gritted teeth. 'Someone needs to pull it out.'

'I'm not pulling it out!' Tyler cried.

'You need to pull it out!'

'No one is pulling it out,' Hamza said. 'All right? It'll only do more damage.'

He leaned on the tree and squatted beside her, examining the injury. Blood trickled from the pointed tip of the wood. A small blob of something yellowish and blubbery was impaled on the top of the spike. He tried not to dwell too much on what it was, or where it would normally belong.

'Is it still attached?' he asked, leaning down for a better look.

'What, my foot?'

Hamza tutted. 'The stick. Is it still attached to something?'

Sandra gingerly lifted her leg a few inches and shook her head. 'No. It snapped off when I landed.'

Hamza rubbed at his chin, looked back through the trees, then nodded. 'Right, then. Here's what's going to happen.' He got back to his feet. 'We're going to carry you out.'

'What?!' Tyler ejected. 'But she'll weigh a tonne!'

'Oi!' Sandra barked. 'Watch it.'

'It's not a criticism, it's just fact,' Tyler said.

'We can manage,' Hamza insisted.

Tyler groaned. 'Oh, God. Fine.' He put his hands on his lower back and stretched. 'But you can fuck right off if you think I'm taking the feet end.'

–

'Do you take satisfaction in what you do?'

A few cars sped past while Jonathan considered the question. 'My job?' When Logan didn't reply, he nodded. 'Yes. Very much so. I've always been a big believer in consequences. I think that, if people misbehave, there should be repercussions. But appropriate ones, not necessarily prison.'

Logan turned to face him, an eyebrow rising. 'Misbehave?'

Jonathan smiled at him. It was a big beamer of a thing, and seemed at odds with the conversation they were having. 'If they commit crimes. Break the law. That sort of thing.'

'That *sort* of thing?'

A supermarket delivery lorry went past, billowing Logan's coat.

'Yes,' Jonathan said, once the rumbling had died down again.

'So not *just* crimes, then?'

'Well, I mean, look at it this way, Detective Chief Inspector, we've all done things we're not proud of. You of all people should know that.'

'Meaning?'

'In your job, I mean. You must see people who've done things that, while not technically illegal, are just plain bloody awful. Illicit sexual relationships. Betrayals. That sort of thing. Now, you can't arrest them for that, of course you can't. There's no law against being an arsehole, unfortunately.'

He stepped closer, glanced around, and made a secretive little beckoning motion.

'But, here's the thing. I don't think people are arseholes. Not really. I don't think anyone's inherently bad. I don't believe in the existence of evil. I think it's more complicated. But, for the most part, I reckon we're a pretty decent bunch. And, while we might try and hide our mistakes and indiscretions, I think that deep down, we want them to be out in the open. We want to be punished for them. We need it, on some primal level.'

'That's not the case in my experience,' Logan countered. 'The people I deal with generally don't want to own up to anything.'

'Maybe you just haven't found the right way to motivate them. To help them see the error of their ways.'

A trio of motorbikes went roaring past. Jonathan laughed.

'Or maybe all that's just my Catholic guilt talking!'

'That's not the only bit of what you said that I disagree with,' Logan told him.

Jonathan seemed almost amused by this response. 'Oh? What else?'

'The existence of evil,' Logan said.

'Ah. You believe that there is such a thing?'

'I do,' the DCI confirmed. 'I've seen it. Up close. The problem is, though, that sometimes you don't notice it. Not even when you're staring it right in the face.'

The supervisor's smile lingered.

'Well. We'll have to agree to disagree on that one, I suppose.'

'Just you who drives the van, is it?' Logan asked, forcibly shunting them onto a different subject.

Confused, Jonathan glanced back along the road to where the Community Payback vehicle was parked.

'Sorry?'

'The van. Just you that drives it?'

'Well, we don't let the offenders behind the wheel!'

'No other staff? Just you?'

Jonathan regarded him in silence. 'Just me,' he eventually confirmed. 'Why? Is one of the taillights out? Are you going to arrest me?'

Logan chuckled drily. 'Don't tempt me,' he said, then he looked back into the forest. 'Why do you reckon she ran? Sandra? Why do you think she ran off like that?'

Jonathan shrugged. 'Presumably, she thought she was in some sort of trouble.' He waited for a car to roar past. 'Is she?'

'Don't know yet,' Logan admitted. 'But it'll be interesting to hear what she has to say. She was there when Seamus Starkey found the body parts, wasn't she?'

'She was,' Jonathan confirmed. 'Seemed worryingly unfazed by it all, as I told your colleagues.'

'And Seamus?'

Jonathan's whole face seemed to pinch together. He shook his head. 'Very shocked. Horrified. Just horrified. You could see how upset he was. He was close to tears. I mean, not even just close, he was actually crying. Just with the shock and the awfulness of it all.'

Logan turned back to the supervisor. 'Sounds like you were watching him pretty closely.'

More vehicles passed just a few feet beyond where Jonathan stood.

'Yes,' he admitted, breathing deeply as if inhaling the fumes. 'I suppose I was.'

'What was it he did, exactly? Seamus. To end up on your list?'

'What list?'

'Do you have more than one?'

Jonathan smirked. 'Oh, you mean how he ended up doing community service? I forget. Does it matter?'

Logan shrugged. 'I just thought, if you're so big on people making amends, redemption, all that, you'd know what he was meant to be making amends for. Then again, I don't suppose it really matters now, does it?'

'No. No, I suppose not,' Jonathan said, dipping his head in a fleeting gesture of respect for the dead. 'Do you still think he did it? Do you still think he killed that woman?'

'Eleanor.'

'Was that her name?'

'It was. I thought everyone knew that already. Small town, and all that.'

'Not me. But then, I don't live here.'

'Aberlour,' Logan said. 'Aye, I remember. And no.'

Jonathan frowned. 'No?'

'I don't think he killed her.'

'Sandra, then?'

Logan shook his head. 'Not by your logic.'

The supervisor smiled, his eyes narrowing. 'I'm sorry, I don't follow.'

'By your logic, if she was guilty, she wouldn't have run away. She'd have wanted to be caught. She'd have been crying out for it. She'd have practically been begging us to arrest her. She'd have been standing right where you are. Right on that spot.'

'Not necessarily,' Jonathan countered. He spoke again before Logan could answer back. 'She wouldn't necessarily want to be arrested, I mean. Just punished. Just given the chance to make amends. That's all any of us want, really, isn't it? You must.'

'Not really,' Logan told him.

'No? There's nothing in your past you feel remorse for? Nothing you think you should be atoning for?' He stuck a finger in his hair and twirled it, waiting for another truck to pass. 'Nothing that keeps you awake at night?'

'No,' Logan insisted, but a moment of hesitation brought a knowing grin to the supervisor's face.

'I think you're fibbing!'

'And you? What's your deep, dark secret, Jonathan? What are you desperate to confess?'

Before an answer could be given, a cry of, 'Careful!' rang out from the edge of the forest. Logan turned in time to see Hamza shuffling sideways out of the trees, with a sweating, red-faced Tyler waddling along at the other end of Sandra Hogg. Tyler's hands were hooked under her arms, while Hamza carried her legs in the crook of his elbows.

'We are being careful!' Tyler wheezed. 'Maybe if you stopped being so bloody heavy!'

'Sandra, is it?' Logan asked.

'Ow, watch the foot!' Sandra snapped at Hamza. 'And yes. Why?'

'I just have two questions, Sandra,' Logan told her. 'Who found the bag of body parts?'

Sandra sniffed. 'I'm not a grass.'

'No, but you are bleeding heavily,' Logan pointed out. 'And we're not phoning an ambulance until you answer the questions. So, it's your call.'

She scowled at him, and for a few seconds the only sounds were the rumbling of approaching traffic, and the odd, strained, breathless cheep from DC Neish.

'Seamus,' she said. 'He found it.'

'Right. Well done. Halfway there,' Logan told her. 'Last question. Who told you to work in that area?'

'What?'

'You don't pick your own spot, do you? You're told what to do, and where to work. So, who told you?'

'Well, him.' Sandra gestured to the supervisor. 'He picks. He tells us where to go.'

'Right. Thanks,' Logan said. He nodded to Hamza. 'Call her an ambulance.'

He turned his attention back to Jonathan. The supervisor had a faint, inscrutable smile on his face, like he was mildly entertained by the thought of what came next.

'How did you know?' the DCI asked.

'How did I know what?'

'All the things they'd done. All their secrets?'

'I'm afraid I don't know what you're talking about.'

'Aye,' Logan insisted. 'You do.'

A stream of cars passed. Hamza and Tyler lowered Sandra Hogg unceremoniously to the ground.

'Thank Christ for that,' Tyler muttered, groaning as he stretched his lower back again.

'Well?' Logan urged, still fixated on the man standing before him. 'How did you know?'

The smile that had been dipping in and out faded completely. 'Because none of us can hide our true nature for long. None of us really wants to. Not deep down.' He prodded himself in the centre of the chest. 'Not in here. We want to be seen. We want to be known. The real us, warts and all. Don't we, Jack?'

A breeze made the fine hairs on the back of Logan's neck stand on end. He hadn't told the supervisor his name, had he?

'You're going to accompany us to the station in Inverness, Mr Milburn,' he said. 'I have a number of questions I'd like to ask you. I suggest you bring a solicitor, if you've got one.'

'No.'

'Legal representation can be arranged if you're unable to—'

'I meant no, I'm not coming,' Jonathan told him. 'I still have work to do.'

'Don't worry. We'll call your boss.'

Jonathan's smile widened. 'Good luck with that,' he said.

And then, like a startled animal, he broke into a sprint, launching himself away from the detectives and racing back in the direction of his parked van.

Tyler, still panting heavily, let out a weary groan. 'Oh, come on!'

'Don't worry.' Logan shrugged off his coat. 'Leave this bastard to me!'

His big, heavy boots kicked against the wet ground, propelling him off in pursuit of the fleeing supervisor. Jonathan, mercifully, was not fast. He was a few years younger than Logan, and while he was carrying a lot less weight than the DCI, his gangly frame was awkward and uncoordinated, and no two parts of him seemed to be working together towards any sort of common goal.

He was barely halfway back to the van when the thumping of Logan's fast-approaching feet made him realise the game was up. Spinning, he searched frantically inside his hi-vis jacket, then sliced at the air with a hunting knife, the blade whistling as it swished past Logan's face.

'Don't!' Jonathan warned. 'Stay where you are, I'm warning you!'

'It's over, son,' Logan told him. He kept his distance, but rose onto the balls of his feet, ready to lunge if the opportunity presented itself. 'It's done.'

'Done? You have no idea. Of course it's not done. Not yet.'

'We know about the blackmail. The cards. We've got the teacher and the surgeon in custody. They told us everything.'

'That's funny, because they know nothing. None of you do.' His smile became a snarl, and he thrust the knife out, forcing Logan to retreat a step. 'Back! Back!' He pointed past him with the blade. 'And tell that prick to stay where he is!'

'Tyler, stay back,' Logan warned, taking a bit of a punt on the 'that prick' part.

The sound of running footsteps clumped to a stop. 'You all right, boss?'

'Tell him to back off.'

'Back off,' Logan instructed.

'Tell him it's in hand.'

'It's in hand. Go back and wait for the ambulance.'

'But, boss…'

'Wasn't a suggestion, son. Go.'

He waited until he heard Tyler start to retreat, then let out the breath he'd been holding in.

'There. He's gone. But what now, Jonathan? What happens now? You going to kill me? Is that it?'

The supervisor smiled, and there was a hint of sadness tucked away behind it. 'You're early,' he said.

'Sorry?'

'This was supposed to happen. Me and you. But not now. Not yet. Not like this.' He sighed and shook his head, but kept the knife raised. 'I've only got myself to blame, I know. If I'd kept my mouth shut, you'd have been none the wiser. So, on the one hand, my bad, but on the other hand... How does that make you feel? Knowing that you only worked it out because I let you?'

'If you'd let me, you wouldn't be standing here with a knife in your hand,' Logan replied. 'I worked it out because you did what all you lot eventually do. You messed up. You made a mistake, said the wrong thing to the wrong person. In your case, that just happened to be me. Everyone thinks that detective work is all about pouring over clues, and building a picture, and all that stuff. But the truth of it is, most cases get solved because some fucking idiot can't hold his tongue.'

He looked the other man up and down, and was unimpressed by what he saw.

'You're not special, Jonathan. Don't try and kid yourself. You're just another evil arsehole who likes the sound of his own voice. You're ten a penny. In my line of work, I can't throw a stone without hitting one of you bastards between the eyes.'

'No. You're wrong. You have no idea who I am,' Jonathan hissed.

'Maybe. Maybe you're right.' Logan shrugged like he no longer cared. 'Maybe you're the one that's going to prove me wrong. All that stuff you said earlier, about how everyone wants to confess deep down. How everyone wants to be made to pay for their sins. Now's your chance. I'm all ears. Tell me why you killed Charlotte's parents. Tell me why you made those people do those things?'

'Oh, Jack. You still don't get it,' Jonathan said, and his look of sadness had become one of pity. 'You don't see.'

'Help me, then.'

'None of this—none of the things I did—none of it was about any of them. Not really.' Jonathan passed the knife from one hand to the other. 'It was about you.'

Logan took a half step back. 'Me? What do you mean?'

'It was about preparing you,' Jonathan said.

'What are you talking about, *preparing me*? Preparing me for what?'

Jonathan's cheeks hitched up, pulling his mouth into a mockery of a smile. 'For everything that comes next.'

'What do you mean?' Logan demanded. 'What are you talking about?'

'We all have our sins and our secrets, Jack Logan. You should know that better than most.'

Jonathan's eyes crept upwards, then swept left and right, as if searching the dark recesses of his brain for something.

'Right. I think that's all of it,' he announced. 'I think that's me done.'

Then, he took two big backwards steps onto the road.

A horn blared.

Hydraulic brakes hissed.

And twenty tonnes of articulated lorry careened through the space where the killer had just stood.

Logan stood rooted to the spot, his ears reverberating with a piercingly high-pitched ringing tone that was backed up by the bass drum of his heartbeat.

He didn't hear Tyler until he was right behind him, bent double and trying not to vomit onto the grass.

'Oh, Jesus, boss! Oh, God, that's…' He retched and turned away, his eyes watering.

'Tyler?'

The DC pulled himself together long enough to mumble a response. 'Aye, boss?'

Logan closed his eyes and sighed through his nose. 'Better make that two ambulances.'

Chapter Forty-Seven

Word had reached Ben in the Incident Room long before Logan and the others were back on the road to Inverness. There was an air of wary silence about the place as the DCI stalked in through the doors, with Tyler plodding along behind him.

'You all right, Jack?' Ben asked, peering at him over the top of his glasses.

'Aye. Fine,' Logan grunted. 'Palmer and Shona'll be sending reports up later. I want to know when they arrive.'

'Eh, aye. Will do,' the DI confirmed, watching the senior officer go striding past.

'I'm not OK!' Tyler said. 'That's two people I've seen hit by cars in two days. Though the one today wasn't even a car, it was a big truck. And he wasn't so much hit as'—he shuddered at the memory—'burst.'

Sinead smiled sympathetically at him, then ran a hand across the small of his back. 'Sounds rough.'

'It was,' Tyler confirmed. 'And Sandra Hogg put a stick through her foot.'

'Hardy!' Dave said. 'On purpose?'

'If it was, she's a full-blown psycho!' Tyler said. He shuddered again, inviting another back rub from his wife. 'It was horrible.'

'Aw, poor baby,' Sinead said, a little more sarcastically than Tyler would've ideally liked. 'Where's Hamza?'

'He's in the hospital,' Tyler said.

'What? Why?'

'Oh, no. Nothing major. He just got scratched on the face by a branch. Might need a stitch. Boss made him go get checked out.' The detective constable raised his eyebrows hopefully. 'And, eh, gave him the rest of the day off. Very generous of you, I thought, boss. But, you know, fair, given the trauma that he—that we both—had to go through. It's only right—'

'Fine. Go, but I want everyone back here first thing,' Logan said, barely looking back as he headed for the office at the back of the room. 'Good job, everyone. Another one in the bag.'

'Nice! Cheers, boss!' Tyler said, but the DCI had already disappeared into the office and closed the door behind him.

Ben, who had watched Logan closely since he'd entered the room, removed his glasses and got to his feet.

'Um, did he mean Sinead, too, boss?' Tyler asked. 'Are we both allowed to shoot off?'

'What?' Ben turned to him, frowning. 'Oh. Um, aye. Fine. You, too, Dave. Jack and I'll handle what needs doing. But first thing tomorrow, all right? We're going to have a lot to get through.'

'Thanks, sir,' Sinead said.

'Nice!' Dave declared, wheeling himself back from his desk. He looked hopefully up at Tyler and Sinead. 'Pub?'

Tyler winced. 'Eh… we've got to get the kids later,' he said.

Sinead caught the pained look on her husband's face. 'We could go for lunch, though,' she suggested.

Dave raised an eyebrow. 'A pub lunch?'

Sinead smiled. 'That sounds like a pretty good compromise,' she said, and the three of them left the room together, Tyler already filling them in on his version of the morning's events.

The Incident Room was silent once they'd left. Ben crossed to the doors they'd left through, and listened to their fading voices.

Then, when he could no longer hear them, he stretched up and flicked the lever that secured the doors in place.

With a weary sigh, DI Forde began the long, solemn walk to Logan's office.

There was still a full ninety minutes until the end of the school day. Logan had insisted that Hamza get the cut on his face treated at the hospital, and then had told him he could head home for the rest of the afternoon.

The rest of the week was going to be a nightmare of interviews and paperwork, but getting started on it could wait until the morning, and if Mitchell had anything to say on the matter, Logan had made it clear that he would have no qualms about setting her straight.

That meant that, as soon as Hamza's wound had been treated, he'd swung by the hospital shop for a bunch of flowers, jumped in his car, and headed for home. With a bit of luck, there might even be time for a repeat of the 'adult interaction' from the night before. At the very least, though, they could nip out for a quick coffee on the way to school pick-up.

And maybe that would be better, he thought, as he pulled up outside the house and fetched the flowers from the passenger seat. Enjoyable as the previous night had been, maybe a blether would be better. A quick forty-five minutes in a coffee shop wasn't one of the all-time greats as far as dates went, but it was a start. It would be a step in the right direction.

He unlocked the front door and hummed below his breath as he took off his jacket and hung it on the hook in the hallway.

'Hello? Amira? It's me,' he called.

There was silence.

No, not silence.

Not quite.

'Amira?'

A rustle.

A thump.

The bedroom.

'Just me. I got off early, are you—?'

He stopped in the doorway.

His wife stood by the head of the bed, hurriedly wriggling herself back into her jeans.

Beside her—right beside her—Thomas's fingers trembled as he fought to fasten up the buttons of his shirt.

'Hamza,' Amira gasped. 'It's not what it looks like!'

And the flowers that he'd bought for her went tumbling to the floor.

-

'Well?'

Logan sat in his big office chair with his back to the door, trying his best to ignore the detective inspector now standing there.

That was a waste of time though, he knew. There was no way that Ben would just leave without an answer.

'Well, what?'

'What happened? What's up with you?'

Logan shook his head. 'Nothing.'

'Jesus Christ, Jack,' Ben muttered.

He pulled out a seat and sat across the desk. The big chair still had its back to him, Logan still refusing to turn to face him.

'How long have we known each other now, you and me?'

'Too bloody long.'

The faintest implication of a laugh whistled down one of the DI's nostrils. 'Aye. You can say that again. I can see right through you, Jack. Have done for years. You should be happy. We've done it. We caught the bad buggers, the whole lot of them. But there's something. Something happened out there.'

'A suspect died,' Logan said. 'I should've stopped it, but I didn't.'

'My arse. That's no' it,' Ben said. He crossed his legs and interlocked his fingers on his stomach. 'And I'm going to make myself very comfortable here until you tell me, so you might want to hurry it up a bit.'

Logan sighed with exasperation, then slowly wheeled himself around to face the detective inspector.

'There we are. Now I can see your pretty face,' Ben told him.

He studied the pretty face in question, then rubbed at his chin, trying to decipher the precise arrangement of the DCI's features. Whatever it was that was bothering Logan, though, it was a new one on Ben.

'God, don't tell me. He was our man, wasn't he? Milburn. He was the one behind it?'

Logan closed his eyes like he was trying to tune the DI out, but then he nodded. 'Aye. Think so.'

'You think so?'

'I mean, he confessed. More or less.'

'More or less?'

Logan ran a hand down his face. 'He confessed. He did it. He told me as much. The tread on the van matches the tyre marks found at the cottage, and I'll put my life on Palmer finding blood in the back.'

'Well, there we go, then. All wrapped up nice and neat.'

'Aye,' Logan muttered.

It wasn't, though. Not by a long shot.

Why those targets? Why those victims? Why the fingers, or the jigsaw of body pieces, or any of the half dozen other things that didn't yet make sense?

What was he missing?

What more was still to come?

'"I think that's everything."'

'Eh?' Ben asked.

'That's what he said. Before he stepped onto the road. "I think that's everything."'

'Meaning?'

'I don't know. But it was like he was ticking off a checklist, or reading from a script.' Logan drummed his fingers on his desk. 'And he said it was supposed to happen. Me and him. I was supposed to find out, just not yet.'

'You think it was all staged, or something?' Ben asked. 'Surely not. I've seen the photos from the scene, and he's definitely no' pretending to be deid.'

'No.' Logan shook his head. 'I don't know. I just know I don't like it.'

'There's something else,' Ben prompted. 'Something you're not saying. Come on, Jack. Out with it.'

The DCI sighed. 'You're a pain in the arse, did I ever tell you that?'

'Frequently,' Ben said. He beckoned to him. 'Come on, spit it out.'

Logan looked up at the greying ceiling tiles for a moment, then reached into the pocket of his coat.

'Before Palmer turned up, I had a snoop around in the van.'

'Milburn's van?'

Logan nodded, just once.

'And?'

An evidence bag was placed on the table between them. Ben eyed it warily, like too intense a stare might cause it to explode.

'Is that…?'

'Aye.'

Ben's gaze flicked from the bag to the DCI and back again. 'And it was in the van?'

'In the glove box.'

Inside the evidence bag, its corners crisp and sharp, sat a purple postcard.

'Maybe it's just one he hadn't got around to sending,' Ben suggested. His enthusiasm for the idea quickly waned, and he seemed to shrink down into his seat. 'Unless, of course, someone sent it to him. God. What if he was being coerced, too?'

'I don't know if I want to think about that,' Logan said. 'Of course, there's another possible explanation…'

The sentence fell away into a void of silence. Ben raised his eyebrows encouragingly.

'And what's that?' he prompted.

The DCI thought back to the dead man's final words. This whole thing—this whole case—it wasn't about the victims.

It was about Logan himself.

It was preparation.

He picked up the card and studied the blank back of it through the plastic bag.

'Or, maybe it was put there for somebody else to find.'

'Like who?'

'Well, that's the big question,' Logan muttered.

Steeling himself, he turned the bag over so he could see the front of the postcard within.

New Player Has Entered The Game.

It had all been about preparing him, Milburn had said.

But preparing him for what?

He might have been a murderer, an extortionist, and all-round evil arsehole, but Logan knew that Jonathan Milburn had been right about one thing.

They all had their dirty, shameful secrets.

Him, more than most.

A knot of dread in his gut told him that something was coming.

This wasn't over. Not by a long shot.

He read the message on the card one more time.

'Ah, fuck it,' he muttered, shoving the evidence bag in his desk drawer and locking it away. 'I'll stick to Buckaroo!'

And with that, he got up, ushered a protesting DI Forde out of his office, and got to work.